80/120

ART THAT KILLS

A Panoramic Portrait of Aesthetic Terrorism 1984-2001

GEORGE PETROS

Introduction by
CARLO McCORMICK

Edited by
JERRY LEE WILLIAMS

CREATION BOOKS

Editor: Jerry Lee Williams
Editorial Assistant: Blair Hope McSorley
Front Cover Photo: Richard Kern
Back Cover & Spine Photo: Fred Berger
Title Page Photo: Claudia Bellino
Primary Archivists: Fred Berger, Nick Bougas, John Aes-Nihil, Genesis P-Orridge, Peter H. Gilmore, Sondra London, Michael Moynihan, Shane Bugbee, Michael Andros
Thanks: Mike King, Norman Gosney, Arthur Deco, Phil Luciani, Brian Clark, Daniel Langdon Jones, Gidget Gein, Salvatore Canzonieri

SECONDS MAGAZINE

Lotsa material herein lifted from the *Seconds* archive
Title "Art That Kills" suggested by Spider Webb

Photo by Claudia Bellino

Dedicated to Caribou, 1995-2005
"Where's That Cat???"

ART THAT KILLS
by George Petros
ISBN 1-84068-143-8
Published 2006 by Creation Books
www.creationbooks.com
Copyright © George Petros 2006
All world rights reserved.

ART THAT KILLS

04	INTRODUCTION by CARLO McCORMICK	04
06	A Beginning, and an End	06
10	The Precursors: WILLIAM S. BURROUGHS	10
14	The Precursors: ANTON LaVEY	14
22	The Precursors: ROBERT WILLIAMS	22
30	The Precursors: CHARLES MANSON	30
38	The Precursors: GENESIS P-ORRIDGE	38
46	The Precursors: MONTE CAZAZZA	46
50	The Precursors: HARLEY FLANNAGAN	50
54	Soundtrack to 1984	54
66	JOE COLEMAN	66
74	LYDIA LUNCH	74
80	NICK ZEDD	80
86	RICHARD KERN	86
92	J.G. THIRLWELL a.k.a. FOETUS	92
96	FRED BERGER	96
104	JONATHAN SHAW	104
110	Killer Clowns	110
122	BOYD RICE	122
130	JOHN AES-NIHIL	130
136	NICK BOUGAS	136
142	ZEENA SCHRECK nee LaVEY	142
146	NIKOLAS SCHRECK	146
152	ADAM PARFREY	152
160	Your host, GEORGE PETROS	160
168	MICHAEL ANDROS	168
172	ROBERT N. TAYLOR	172
176	PETER SOTOS	176

→

182	GG ALLIN	182
188	JAMES MASON	188
196	8-8-88	196
198	JONATHAN HAYNES	198
206	DEATH IN JUNE	206
210	MICHAEL MOYNIHAN	210
218	Soundtrack to 1994	218
222	Soundtrack to 1994: LAIBACH	222
226	Soundtrack to 1994: GENITORTURERS	226
230	Soundtrack to 1994: COP SHOOT COP	230
234	PETER H. GILMORE	234
238	THOMAS THORN	238
242	SHAUN PARTRIDGE	242
248	GIDDLE PARTRIDGE	248
250	Mags & zines: *SECONDS*	250
252	Mags & zines: *ANSWER ME!*	252
254	Mags & zines: *THE FIFTH PATH*	254
256	Mags & zines: *OHM CLOCK*	256
258	Mags & zines: *PROPAGANDA*	258
259	Mags & zines: *THE BLACK FLAME*	259
260	SHANE BUGBEE	260
266	MIKE DIANA	266
274	SONDRA LONDON	274
282	CREATION	282
284	DISINFORMATION	284
286	STEPHEN KASNER	286
288	MARILYN MANSON	288
296	STANTON LaVEY	296
300	SZANDORA	300

INTRODUCTION

With the mass proliferation of popular culture, it is arguably way too easy to get hipped. In short, today everyone is cool. Not so very long ago, however, there was a level of information beneath the radar of received signs that was significantly less easy to access. Short-handed as subculture or underground, it was in spirit and effect resistant to mainstream values. Neither readily consumable in most places, nor so simple as punching a few words into your favorite search engine, we could say these forbidden nether zones of our cultural topography were experiential to the degree that you had to be there. By such a measure the author of this book acquired his uncommon knowledge the hard way. Best of all, for those who were not around these weird little worlds—or who lived them in such a way as many of us who can no longer remember what we have forgotten—George Petros maintained just enough sanity to deliver these times, lives and ideas with a rare clarity and directness.

In the dozens of very smart conversations so well remembered here, there is a peculiar sort of backwash undertow dragging all the specifics into darker, more treacherous depths. With an abiding affection for individuals and aesthetics that generally make most other people uncomfortable, Petros' verité vernacular of meta-violence just bobs along with the buoyancy of spirited enthusiasm. It's only en masse, with all these voices conjoined into a broader dialogue, that we now see just how far we had drifted from the mainland of thought. It was fun then, urgent for sure, but ironic enough to always seem something less than serious. It felt to me at least that our marginality was just off shore, dwelling in perverse pleasure palaces made of sandcastle dreams on a toxic landfill of ideological refuse. Looking back, however, with Petros' untidy accumulation of all these attitudes before us, it's hard to imagine how everything appeared to be going so swimmingly at the time. We were drowning.

To put the curious arc of iconoclastic ideas within some contextual frame it is worthy to consider the chronology of Petros' interviews. Conducted between 1984 and 2001, they mark the full claustrophobic dread of *fin-de-siècle* mannerism and the visionary excess of a millennium in its convulsive death throes. Let's just say it begins with morbid myth—1984 as the Orwellian metaphor for society's fascist inclinations—and ends with grim reality: 2001, not just the cinematic signifier for our collective dis/ease towards the growing frisson between humanism and the age of technology, but a specific moment on an otherwise beautiful late summer morning when, with the precision of a stopwatch, you could establish the traumatic birth of the twenty-first century. Could it be any less a wonder why the material collected here is so sated in fantastical panic?

A generalist in this age of specialization, Petros looks at our most unnatural condition with a naturalist's eye. For all his attention to detail it is difficult to zoom in too close; you almost need to step back to get his sense of perspective here. More than merely a sensibility—alternately dark, deviant, degenerate, drug-fueled and decadent—there is also a situation by which we can locate this table of contents within and outside of its cultural moment. In the mid-Eighties, though time and the monumental mortality of AIDS was fast at work taking some of the fiercest transgressors, we still enjoyed a kind of multi-generational intercourse. It's great that George caught such historical forefathers as Burroughs, LaVey and Manson for their take on the moment at hand, but what's more significant is that these voices were still very much alive and part of the discourse at this time. Also symptomatic of this difficult era are the aesthetic extremes and vitriolic polemics of the participants contained herein.

I'd like to think that at least for a few of us, these artists' scope of atrocity purged some of the shit we were being force-fed by the rest of our culture. If not the optimistic sense of freedom embraced in the Psychedelic Sixties or the explosive seizure of anarchic outrage expressed in the Punk Seventies, the span here is across an unfathomably deep chasm of creative crisis. By my admittedly suspect memory the nihilist frenzy that runs amok through these pages coincided with two dramatic shifts in the way art was being produced and perceived. The emergence of these idiosyncratic voices, so marginal yet central to the mainstream, comes at a time when the regressive fundamental agenda of American morality was just putting art in the crosshairs of the epic Culture Wars, while simultaneously the social issues which had fermented over the prior two decades came to a nexus of relative orthodoxies operating as expressions of identity-based politics. Both in consort with this evolution and in opposition to it, what we have in *Art That Kills* can best be described as the last words of a true underground thrown up before the successive tides of co-option, commodity and conformity subsumed the vitality of difference. Only you can decide if the words that follow ring true still—but rather than anything said here, listen to this collection as the veritable transcription of a profound noise.

— CARLO McCORMICK

REAGAN FOR BIG BROTHER IN 1984. IN 1984.

Example of the mood of the times:
Detail of flyer for Millions Of Dead Cops tour, 1984
Artist unknown
Collection of Steven Blush

A Beginning, and an End

This is not a history, a series of biographies, or a compendium. Anyone looking for a reference work on the subjects herein must look elsewhere; I make no attempt to present complete, comprehensive data. Nor am I offering a critique.

This is a panoramic portrait of a scene, rendered in photos, documents, artwork and words. It illustrates the evolution of a movement.

I selected these materials because they most vividly animate the individual subjects. The narrative, in each subject's own voice, offers little historical hype. From hours of taped conversations, I picked snippets that offered glimpses behind the masks of art and crime.

I asked all the questions herein, or presided over all interviews as editor (I note a few exceptions). In many cases I borrowed from the work of Michael Moynihan, a star interrogator from the days when I ran the all-interview *Seconds* magazine. I reproduce exchanges as they originally appeared in print. You'll figure it out.

"Aesthetic Terrorism: Using the element of surprise through the usage of past clichés, knowledge and 'home truths' being flung out of joint, and therefore used as possibly a weapon or subversive force."
— J.G. Thirlwell a.k.a. Foetus, 1984

1984 played out prophetically: George Orwell's novel came to chronological coincidence, triggering the much-ballyhooed fulfillment of its dire predictions. 2001, however, didn't see the Space Age promised in Stanley Kubrick's film.

In the years between—an intense era bracketed by the Cold War and the Digital Age—rape, murder, torture, pedophilia, cannibalism, drugs, sedition, racism and blasphemy mixed with Pop Culture, history, literature, news, movies, TV, philosophy and science. All varieties of taboos and criminal advocacy coalesced, beyond "confrontation" or "shock."

The artists, from a cross-section of American life, ranged from the abused to the spoiled, from successes to also-rans. Some basked in the limelight; some barely acknowledged their creativity.

Yes, I too am featured herein. You wouldn't want a book like this from someone without an intimate knowledge of the subject matter, would you? The scene I describe I saw from my own vantage point. So what?

In the Eighties a new demographic arose: Caucasian, mostly Goy but including a few Jews, creative, urban, alienated, beat down by media, blamed for everything, very smart, looking for trouble, turned on by sex murders, happy to hurt others, eccentrically eclectic. The Sixties and Seventies had comprised the Golden Age of anything-goes; TV raised its offspring on equal doses of love and hate, good and bad, right and wrong. Traditionally compartmentalized taboos commingled haphazardly, their varied threats superimposing, juxtaposing, fusing.

The transgressive, subversive, pornographic and forbidden mixed with the legitimate, the approved, and the party line, sparking an aesthetic revolution. Rock provided the soundtrack; drugs provided the universal experience. A new outlaw type, a criminal aesthete, a true threat to society, flourished.

Starting circa 1984, through back-alley channels of Punk, zines, college radio, and a loose network of the like-minded, the artists found one another through mutual gravitation. Their inspirations included Manson, LaVey, Nietzsche, Crowley, the Occult, World War Two, drugs, murder. As their artwork and networking progressed, a unique look and feel developed. Only in retrospect does the scene come into focus; at the time it seemed to be simply a super-alienated version of Punk.

Two types found confluence in this scene: further-out elements of the Cinema of Transgression crowd, and those on the outer limits of Apocalypse Culture.

Example of the mood of the times:
Flyer by Nikolas Schreck for Aes-Nihil Productions, 1986
Collection of John Aes-Nihil

Transgressive: New York, Heroin chic, all black, leftist/anarchist, fucked-up. *Apocalyptic:* West Coast, LSD, Speed, neo-psychedelic, fascistic, fucked-up. Generally speaking, the two currents merged into a loose, distant association of criminally-inclined artists in whose troubling work a multitude of taboos converged.

LSD, Speed, Heroin, Cocaine, Ecstasy, Absinthe, Marijuana, uppers, downers, Xanax, Valium, Methadone, beer, whiskey, vodka, bourbon, rum, gin, NoDoz, sleeping tablets, cigarettes, coffee and caffeine made it happen. Throughout recessions, boom times, bubbles, the AIDS epidemic, the Pax Americana and the War On Drugs, the characters herein got by somehow, surviving and spewing venom. Their art hurt people, set a bad example, burrowed into impressionable minds, subliminally implanted time-bombs in the unstable.

New tools, and new uses for old tools: videos, cassettes and copy machines evolved into Sci-fi gadgets. For example, in the beginning (1987) *Seconds* went to the cheapest printer as hastily typeset, hand-made "mechanicals" on stacks of shaggy, re-used cardboard. In the end (2000) a Mac G3 processed everything, spitting it out on two CDs.

Since Day One art challenged everything; its history abounds with misanthropy and anti-authoritarianism. Some used art to inflame and overthrow. It always incited, excited or blasphemed!

Historically, an artist tackled a single taboo, driven by fetish, injustice, poverty or disease. However, the artists herein broke all taboos simultaneously. They mixed it all. Aesthetic Terrorism!

A history: When at first some unheralded individual, tripping on LSD, grabbed a ballpoint pen and on notebook paper doodled, Underground Art began. When every icon lay smashed, every hypocrisy got exposed, and every taboo was broken, Underground Art ended—or, more precisely, percolated into above-ground mainstream art, where the status quo appropriated it.

Underground Art kicked off when a new perceptual tool became available: LSD. Illegal and without psychological precedent, it inspired uninhibited outlaw art documenting Psychedelia's expansion into a far-reaching culture ultimately ravaged by the War On Drugs.

The first generation of Underground Artists, while quite mischievous, ultimately sought living beauty and bliss. This book features the "second generation," who sought death and destruction.

From an era of nothingness, emptiness, zero, from the end of time, the end of history, Hello There! From an era of egos, cocks, pussies, narcissism, solipsism, hedonism and nothingness! From this fabulous era of nothingness, Ahoy, You Of Tomorrow! Study this era, these exhilarating days. Learn these lessons, you weak ones of the future—you watered-down versions of this day's denizens. You scum of tomorrow—Fuck You!

From an era of anger and hate, action and reaction, alienation, fucked-up people, lies, crime, blood and bullshit—from an era of primal passions, hard drugs, hard cocks, killer art et cetera, Hello There!!!

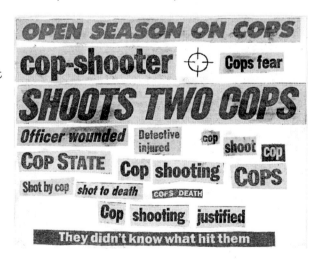

Example of the mood of the times:
Flyer for Cop Shoot Cop, 1993
Graphics by Jack Natz
Collection of Michael Andros

William S. Burroughs, 1992
Photo by John Aes-Nihil

THE PRECURSORS: WILLIAM S. BURROUGHS: *"Listen to my last words anywhere. Listen to my last words any world. Listen all you boards syndicates and governments of the earth. And you powers behind what filth deals consummated in what lavatory to take what is not yours. To sell the ground from unborn feet forever—"*

John Aes-Nihil: "Burroughs was the undertaker of Western Civilization. Many people were inspired by him to destroy themselves by using Junk or extreme forms of deviant sex.

"He was an incredible writer. Older than anybody else that was around, he reigned as the radical avant-garde grandfather. Anton LaVey was another example of that.

"As scion of the mighty Burroughs Adding Machine Company, he staged a total rebellion from hell. Everybody else in his family seems to have been conservative.

"His work: Combination of interesting writing and intriguing subjects, then chopping it all up. It forced people to read in a new way. *Cities of the Red Night* is my favorite book. It was an incredible adventure that would just stop and turn into something else and then turn into something else and then something else. You're walking down the street and you hear twenty pieces of conversation and pieces of music and noise, animals, everything. That's how Burroughs influenced me.

"When I talked to him, it was amazing that he had absolutely never sold out at all. He was as extreme as ever. He knew exactly what the government was up to and was totally against it.

"Left in regard to libertarian. Not right in regards to the schizophrenic insane right that there is right now."

Naked Lunch, Grove Press
First paperback edition, 1966
Collection of John Aes-Nihil

Michael Moynihan: "Burroughs may have maintained the appearance of a 1950s bank clerk, but this was just camouflage masking one of the most dangerous minds of the second half of the Twentieth Century. His novels were notorious, and certainly many of us were reading them. But his interviews had even more impact, filled as they were with volatile, iconoclastic ideas and prescriptions.

"Unlike most of his Beatnik and Hippie literary compatriots, Burroughs didn't waste much breath talking about how peace, love or Hare Krishna would lead us to salvation. Instead he provided advice on concealable firearms, knives and other forms of self-defense—the sort of devices that might actually save your neck in the real world.

"Burroughs' cut-up experiments with text and sound were influential, but in many ways these were just carrying on the work of the Dadaists, bringing it up to date. More uniquely, Burroughs emphasized the importance of Magick, and described how modern portable technology could be transformed into an arsenal of occult weaponry. With a bit of experimentation, a tape recorder or video camera could be utilized to throw a destructive curse on an enemy. For those who declared society to be the ultimate enemy, this had mighty implications."

"Time is a resource, like coal or gas, and there is a time when time runs out for a person, for a nation, for any operation."

***ReSearch #4*, 1982**
ReSearch: *Do you ever practice with an air pistol?* William S. Burroughs: "I've got one, yeah. A Diana, I believe. It's got a gas cylinder, you're always running out of them. And it doesn't work exactly, I've got to put some sort of wad in it to make it engage. But it's alright, I practice with it a lot."
Collection of John Aes-Nihil

Flyer for Burroughs art show, 1987
He cranked out art reflecting the era's urgency: painted plywood punctured by bullet holes, distressing newspaper collages et cetera. Gun in hand, Heroin in vein, he reigned as Godfather of Transgression and Subversion and Apocalypse Culture and....
He died at age 85 in 1997, not bad considering how he lived.
Collection of John Aes-Nihil

Anton LaVey with his snake Boaz, 1988
Peggy Nadramia: "Boaz is a boa constrictor; during his time at the Black House
he lived in a cage above the computer table, to one side of the array of synths.
He would raise his head and bob it back and forth during the Doctor's concerts.
The first time I had occasion to meet LaVey, he told me, 'The animals must be our gurus now.'"
Photo by Nick Bougas

THE PRECURSORS: ANTON SZANDOR LaVEY: "They'll excuse anything on the basis of skin color, educational achievement, impoverishment et cetera, or they'll entertain the most far-out aspects of Communism and Nazism and even join Mensa, but when it comes to the S-word, it all shuts down."

In 1952 **Anton LaVey** and his first wife Carole had a kid, Karla Maritza LaVey. Then Carole and Anton split during his affair with Diane Hegarty, who became his consort. Later Diane prevailed in a famous palimony case.

In 1965, with Diane, he sired Zeena LaVey, his famously rebellious daughter. She grew up fast, ultimately leading a life far removed from her father. In 1978, at the age of thirteen, she bore the Doctor a grandson, Stanton.

Then, in his 60s, LaVey had a third kid, Xerxes, with final consort Blanche Barton.

SECONDS (MICHAEL MOYNIHAN): *It's unfortunate that Manson took the fall for his associates' actions.*
LaVEY: What can I say about Charles Manson that hasn't been said? I do feel they've made him out to be something he's not—he's not the little guy with scissors who cuts little kids' fingers off. The media keeps trotting Manson out to say things, but it's so safe. He's behind bars. Unless of course maybe he's sowing invisible seeds of rebellion in a few people's minds. But he's just been used and used as a convenient scapegoat for so long. It's redundant. There are a lot of other people who did commit murders and who may have had a lot to say—like James Huberty and John Luigi Ferri—but they'll never be heard from.

SECONDS: *Another accusation is that what you're advocating is really just a brand of Machiavellian materialism.*
LaVEY: I do believe in magic. I don't want to sound like Crowley or Blavatsky, and go off the deep end with the occultnik stuff. Balancing everything out is even more crafty—to know which side one's bread is buttered on, but at the same time to acknowledge the dark forces. Keep 'em guessing. Confound and confuse till the stars be numbered!

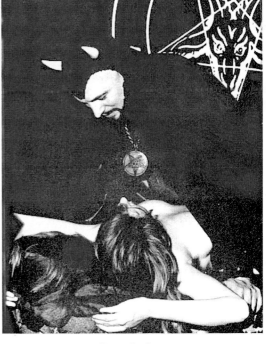

Satanic Sex
"Sex is a motivating force—it's the dance of life. But there's certainly more to life than sex. A Satanic attitude starts with the sexual. Once that is spent, the true sensualist moves to the next thing—that's where Satanic ideology comes in. There are more productive things to do than just fucking or seeking perpetual sexual release. I like sex and I've had my share of exploits but I can look at someone without thinking about whether or not they'd be a good lay."
Photos from *Nude Living*, circa 1965
Collection of Nick Bougas

Newspaper ad for *Satanis*, 1965
Collection of Stanton LaVey

The Satanic Bible, Avon Books, First Edition, 1969
"We still get people writing that they can't find *The Satanic Bible* and can we please tell them about it. What rock have they been under? That's like asking the Easter Bunny where he hid the eggs! Often these people are just psychic vampires who want to get it straight from you, knowing it'll be a drain and a redundant waste of your time.
If I ever respond to these types it's only to have fun with them and tell them lies."
Collection of John Aes-Nihil

> *"I'm essentially a very happy man in an unhappy world, and that makes me dismayed. I see many areas where there doesn't have to be a problem — but shit disturbers make a point of creating one."*

SECONDS (BOYD RICE): *The Church of Satan took flak for making Marilyn Manson a priest. He took flak for being affiliated with you. Yet you seem supportive of one another.*
LaVEY: Certainly. Because he's performing in a manner like a pied piper, through outrage. His presentation is beneficial, and not as harmful as some of the saccharine, sugar-coated pap that's seen as being nice. And because of the climate of the times, he's doing what has to be done. He's an intelligent, well-spoken, sensitive and certainly dramatic individual. He's priesthood material. Our criteria for clergy or priest is based upon what influence a person has on the outside world. And you'd have to be under a rock not to understand that he has had an influence on the outside world.
SECONDS: *Jayne Mansfield and Sammy Davis, Jr. were members and no one considered that outrageous.*
LaVEY: That's right. We have some very high-profile people on today's scene in terms of music, art, publishing and so on who are doing exactly what I would do if I could split myself up and go out there and do it all myself. And they are in today's marketplace, using today's idioms and tools and blending them with something more serious. That's what Marilyn Manson has done so eloquently—something a lot of these performers can't do: blend outrageousness and blasphemy with articulation. Few people can do this. King Diamond does it. Thomas Thorn of The Electric Hellfire Club does it. But even the ones who can't do it are out there serving a purpose. They're lesser elementals; their mere presence serves to—
SECONDS: *Stir the pot?*
LaVEY: Stir the pot! What Marilyn Manson is doing today on a large scale is not all that different than what I was doing in 1966, '67, '68 or '69—drawing people into a Satanic ritual. He's just making use of another means.

LaVey & Jayne Mansfield, 1966
Stars gravitated into Anton's orbit, before and after his death.
From the *Seconds* **archive**

Left: LaVey w/ Boyd Rice, 1986; Right: Marilyn Manson, LaVey, Traci Lords, Karla, 1996
From the *Seconds* **archive**

Page from *Nude Living* magazine, circa 1965
LaVey encircled by vixens
Photographer unknown
Collection of Nick Bougas

***Birth Of Tragedy* #4, "The God Issue," 1986**
Photo by James Rau
In the Eighties, transgressive types latched onto LaVey's cold-hearted Social Darwinism.
Eugene Robinson conducted an interview for his L.A. mag *Birth Of Tragedy*.
LaVey appeared everywhere, from *Newsweek* (August 16, 1971, "Evil, Anyone?") to the porn mag *Chic*,
which in October 1989 ran an interview with the Doctor by Adam Parfrey.
Collection of the Church of Satan

Satan Speaks, Anton LaVey, Feral House, 1998, design by Linda Hayashi
From Marilyn Manson's intro: "…despite his cynicism and apocalyptic view, he often hoped for a better world, or at least one in which intelligence and creativity were applauded."
Collection of Stanton LaVey

Photo from *Nude Living* magazine, circa 1965

Shane Bugbee: *What is a normal day in the life of Anton LaVey?* **LaVey**: A normal day in the life of Anton LaVey consists of sleeping through it. After nightfall I get up and do whatever it is I do, which can be most anything. I have found that the best schedule is no schedule. As to my activities: one night I might shoot pool — the next, record an old tune — the next, watch some B movies, and try to run the Church of Satan between times.

Eugene Robinson: *The slave has become the master.* **LaVey**: That's right. I coined the term "psychic vampire" and I see it all over the place. I realize that it is a very real phenomenon that occurs especially in our society because weakness, ineptitude, inadequacy is championed in many ways. The fine scholar is given, virtually, not nearly the opportunities that the retarded one is. [*laughs*] Of course this is necessary to balance things out.

Collection of Nick Bougas

**Robert Williams, circa 1990
Photographer unknown**

THE PRECURSORS: ROBERT WILLIAMS: "Part of locking people in is coming up with imagery they don't necessarily like but that will hold them. Of course this requires gratuitous sex and violence, use of children in unpopular ways, things like that."

Does Underground Art emerge from the drug culture? **ROBERT WILLIAMS:** "Certainly, of course. In '58 I was involved in the carnival, and that was my first exposure to drugs. A few joints every so often, but drinking was my big thing. Another big thing was taking unusual pills." *Like what?* "Oh, Dexies, Reds, Christmas Trees, Spinners—all kinds of Downers and Amphetamines I never hear about anymore. And I did an awful lot of drinking.

"There was an entirely different drug scene before the Vietnam War than after it. It originally had Bohemian and Beatnik roots, not like the silly Hippy movement. The early drug scene was in direct contact with the criminal world. Very direct contact. The Hippy drug world wasn't. You could live in Beverly Hills and be part of the Hippies, and just get drugs from another Hippy who got it from some amateur smuggler. It was sanitized and they didn't run across real criminals. But in the Fifties and early Sixties you had to deal with real criminals to get drugs. The guy from whom you'd buy a lid of Marijuana was the same guy who'd robbed the fillin' station two weeks ago, or robbed a liquor store. The liberal intellectualization came later.

"In the Fifties we hung out at coffee houses with Beatniks, and we'd do a joint or something, but it was very closely associated with criminal elements. Later on, the Hippy thing started happening, the Vietnam War intensified, and resistance to the government intensified as well. Besides sex, drugs were the symbol of resistance. There was a proliferation of drugs.

"Psychedelia changed everything. We got involved with LSD in '63. I'd heard it had been around even earlier. Towards the end of the Sixties, good LSD wasn't around anymore. People made bad LSD for money."

What impulse made the crime of pornography into high art? "Well, it wasn't crime, it was sedition. It was political resistance."

Gallery show card for "Felonious Demeanor"
Psychedelic Solution, New York, 1988
"I drew what the status quo might call dirty pictures. It wasn't pornography, it was a form of sedition, a form of social resistance against the government."
Collection of the author

Frame 5 from "Danny Bo Dimbul," 1970
"Underground Comix were dirty. That was the energy of the time. Authority saw it as pornography but it was actually dissent."
Collection of the author

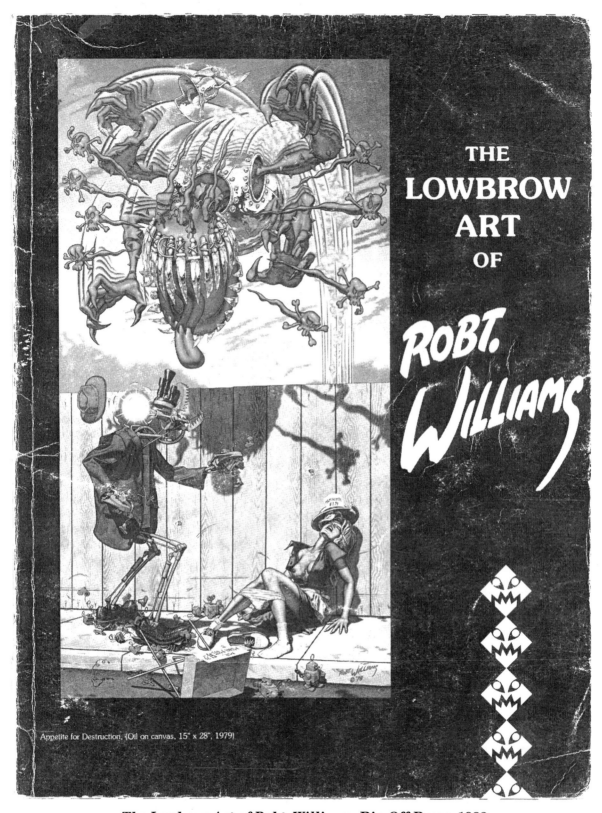

***The Lowbrow Art of Robt. Williams,* Rip Off Press, 1982**
The cover of the artist's first book, a collection of his early cartoons and paintings,
featuring a color reproduction of the painting "Appetite For Destruction."
Collection of the author

Did you have a sense that your work could cause problems or hurt people? "Absolutely. I didn't think it would go beyond the target audience, but it did."

Lydia Lunch, in her introduction to Robert's 1989 book *Visual Addiction*, celebrates the artist as "one of few men with big enough balls to spit in the censor's eye."

GP: *Robert, your early stuff depicted child molestation, right?* "Only in the most retarded tongue-in-cheek way." *What kind of reaction did that get?* "It had to stay within my own crowd, where it got the reactions I wanted it to." *But it percolated to a larger audience.* "It did, and where it did, it caused trouble."

Why do some artists, who bring joy to so many, come off as nasty fuckers? "Well, the ego plays a tremendous part in it all." *How do you see yourself?* "I try to be a nice guy, but I have my ego problems, too. Any artist has ego problems because you need to have a certain unflinching confidence in yourself. You need to have blind faith in yourself, or you wouldn't be able to do it." *Have you always had that faith in yourself?* "Yeah. I realized I could draw and other people couldn't."

Do you have a bad side? "In my twenties I was kinda intolerant of people. I was kinda arrogant. I was, at one time, really egotistical and proud. I created a lot of discomfort for people. It took that spirit to have the will to do the work. That spirit's not pleasant. Sometimes it's uncomfortable for other people, unfortunately."

Any problems with the law? "No, the poor newsdealers are the guys that catch that problem.

"When I worked for Ed 'Big Daddy' Roth, he was being investigated by the FBI. The FBI knew who I was. They knew I was a draft dodger and knew that *Zap* was an anti-social publication. I'd been seen at leftist events. I knew I was listed with the FBI. Crumb and the rest of those guys were out-and-out leftists." *You don't read as a leftist type.* "I am to a certain extent. I'm not a socialist or communist, but I'm liberal."

SECONDS (STEVEN CERIO): *A lot of your work is a parody of White culture.*
WILLIAMS: Coming from a middle-class family in the Forties and Fifties, that's my take on the world. There's a certain sarcasm in what I do so I'm very careful not to elaborate on other people's cultures because it's sure to be misinterpreted. I just stick with the observations from my White man's world.
SECONDS: *What do your naked cuties represent?*
WILLIAMS: The naked cuties is my appreciation of women. I'm fascinated and preoccupied with women and I know a lot of other people are too. One of the first things you do when you learn to draw is draw a naked lady. I know the very first thing that was done with a camera was to get some girl to take her clothes off. Pornography is one of the early uses of the camera. Of course I get in a lot of trouble with feminists and progressive liberals about my use of women. In my mind's eye, I'm not hurting anybody.

Page 1 of "Bludgeon Funnies" from *Zap #5,* Last Gasp, 1970
Collection of the author

Page 1 of "Depopulating Debutante" from *Zap #11*, Last Gasp, 1985
Reprinted in *Hysteria In Remission*, edited by Eric Reynolds, Fantagraphics Books, 2002.
Courtesy of Fantagraphics

Page 2 of "Depopulating Debutante"
This is one of the first Underground-style depictions of serial murder.
Although the artist always depicted violence, development of the character herein
revealed Williams' awareness of the Serial Killer-as-celebrity phenomenon.

Page 3 of "Depopulating Debutante"

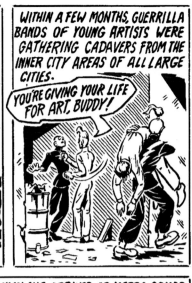

Page 4 of "Depopulating Debutante"

Charles Manson, circa 1989
Note: Administration rarely allows prisoners to wear sunglasses.
**Photo by anonymous prison guard, Corcoran, CA
Collection of James Mason**

THE PRECURSORS: CHARLES MANSON: "If I were emperor of the world, I'd start with YOU —because you let it happen."

Q: *How did Charles Manson differ from other criminals?*
Boyd Rice: "It was his Gnostic philosophy, Abraxas, and the balance between good and evil and all that. Of course, it's always interesting when people are so into a philosophy that they're willing to die for it, or kill for it.

"All those Hippies, and members of Students for a Democratic Society, and the Weathermen—they were all full of violent, anti-system rhetoric. They were expressing the idea that revolutionary-minded militant people should go out and kill rich pigs, kill police. That thought was all over the Hippie underground. When Manson made the news, a lot of people in the underground were full of violent hyperbole, but would never actually go out and kill somebody. Manson's people actually did that, and the Hippies made him a figurehead. But when Manson carved the swastika in his forehead and shaved his head, he was rejected by the Hippies, and he essentially became the thing that chilled the Flower Power movement. The mainstream establishment said, "This is exactly the sort of thing we told you was gonna happen if people grow their hair long and have indiscriminate sex and take LSD. This is the logical outcome of it.

"All these people were waiting for some messiah figure, somebody who would kick off this revolution everybody had been talking about since the Beatles' *White Album*. Manson didn't just come along and create a sense of violence out of thin air; the sense of violence was in the air."

Q: *Tell us about Manson's reinvention in Punk/Industrial Culture.*
Boyd Rice: "Me and Genesis P-Orridge and Monte Cazazza were interested in him, and we mentioned him in interviews. Eventually he became an Industrial cliché. Everybody who put out a tape had sound bites of Charlie Manson saying something.

"When you're young you're a lot more callous, and you can just sort of think, "Well, this guy had some really good ideas, he's got a great philosophy—so what if a handful of people were murdered?" The Family committed the murders, he didn't. Manson didn't participate in any of these murders with which his name is associated."

Q: *Once when you visited him, you by accident had a bullet in your pocket, from a hunting trip—*
Boyd Rice: "Yeah, that was the case, and I was handcuffed and hauled off to Marin County Jail, and taken off of his visiting list. That was 1988."

Q: *Why were people fascinated with Charles Manson?*
Sondra London: "Charles Manson was different from the common criminal because his crime touched on fame. Just like the Olympian gods were immortal, anyone whose name appears in the newspaper or on TV is immortal. News of them comes as if from another dimension. It doesn't matter whether they're a good person or not. Princess Diana equals Charles Manson because they both enter into the mind through the media, through the fame channel.

"Charles Manson entered into the public mind because he had a message. He had text, he had whole sayings, and he had enigmatic things associated with him. There have been other famous criminals whom I call A-list: Serial Killers like Ted Bundy, Gacy, Son of Sam, Lee Harvey Oswald—but none of them rise to the level of Manson. He came with his own ready-made Greek Chorus. He had a group of people who amplified his message, and it reflected him. They were his followers or his family or his group; they gave him fame and magnified his name."

Genesis P-Orridge: "He was useful as a microcosm representing the hypocrisy, the bigotry, the pseudo-ethical fake religiosity and violence of the United States of America. And just as he used fear, so is the United States governed by the society of fear. It's a fear-driven society that tries to resolve everything by lashing out with violence, and he absolutely got it right when he said he was a mirror image of the American political system."

Q: *Psychic TV posed in Manson T-shirts—*
Genesis P-Orridge: "That was meant to be an ironic joke about Manson becoming a fashionable accessory. People did not really get the joke, sadly. And then we had to spend ages trying to explain that we weren't actually that interested in Charlie Manson. We certainly did not approve of his actions, and didn't really have an opinion either way.

Except that it was obvious that he was a metaphor for all of the failings of the American humanist way of life."

Q: *This certain scene picked up on him as a folk hero. Was that just a way of hurting people through iconography?*

Genesis P-Orridge: "I think it was more the teenage voice wanting to upset Mummy. Just the basic, "What can I do that will make Mummy and Daddy think I'm a rebel? And make my friends and peer group think I'm cool? I like something that's taboo." It's another taboo to break, to say that you like Charles Manson, that's all.

"All that being said, I think there's absolutely no question that Charlie Manson should not have been found guilty, and the trial was an absolute travesty of justice.

"It was just the perfect scenario to generate middle-class fear. Something really extreme had to take place in order to try and regain the balance of power. The media, the government, the police—it suited everybody, and into their laps fell this wonderfully appropriate and hideous scenario. It couldn't have been more perfectly timed in terms of assisting the re-establishment of control."

Q: *How did Manson become a media icon?*
John Aes-Nihil: "Well, Bugliosi certainly had something to do with it. He told everyone that their children ran into this guy who took total control of them and turned them into murdering monsters."
Q: *Did he?*
John Aes-Nihil: "I doubt it. But it was a hit story. It scared everyone."
Q: *Bugliosi put Manson on the map?*
John Aes-Nihil: "He's the one who made millions of dollars behind it. All Charlie got was sentenced to death."
Q: *Did he deserve that sentence?*
John Aes-Nihil: "No."
Q: *Why Not?*
John Aes-Nihil: "Because he didn't really do anything. He was just there."

Left: *The Family*, Ed Sanders, Avon Books, 1971
Right: *Helter Skelter*, Vincent Bugliosi, Bantam Books, 1973
Fug and poet Sanders painted a grim picture; Bugliosi defined the True Crime genre.
Collection of Michael Andros

"Fear is only another form of Awareness, and Awareness is only a form of Love. Total Fear is total Awareness. Once you give in to Fear completely, it ceases to exist, and all that's left is Awareness. All that's left is Love."

Q: *How did you become interested in him?*
John Aes-Nihil: "Well the first time I ever heard of the Manson Family was in *Time* magazine. Probably about a year before the murders, I was just reading this article about a roaming band of Hippies in Death Valley who were ripping off tourists.

"Then after the murders, I was fascinated with the case, which was basically like somebody being tried for witchcraft. The media was totally into this thing where these innocent kids suddenly fell under the influence of this guy who caused them to go out and kill all these people for no reason at all other than that he could make them do it. And I was always arguing with people about that.

"Most of the general public thought that Manson himself killed these people. They didn't even know that Tex Watson was the one who actually killed them and, well, with the exception of LaBianca, Manson wasn't there at all. But the average person considers Manson to be one of the most horrendous Serial Killers in history, and they think that he personally killed."

Q: *So you were interested because it was like witchcraft?*
John Aes-Nihil: "Well, it was a witchcraft trial. It turns into this whole argument about

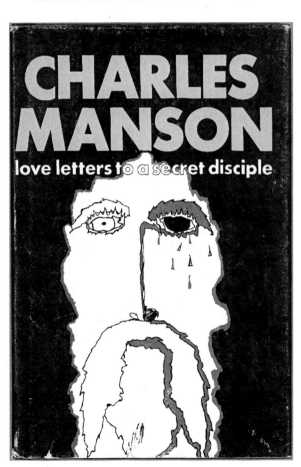

Left: *Charles Manson: Love Letters to a Secret Disciple,* **Sy Wizinski, Moonmad Press, 1976**
Right: *The Manson File,* **edited by Schreck, Parfrey, Aes-Nihil et al, Amok Press, 1988**
The cover of *Love Letters* is a drawing done by Manson in court, 1970.
The Manson File generated lotsa bad blood among the editors.
Collection of Michael Andros

Is Charles Manson new Hitler?

VICIOUS MASS murderer Charles Manson is the latest hero of a depraved cult of neo-Nazis, who lavish him with revolting praise and see him as the new Hitler.

This group, which calls itself the Universal Order, is so extreme it's actually been blacklisted by other Nazis.

Its "philosophical and ideological leader" is Manson, says newsletter publisher and self-proclaimed "chairman streetside organizer" James Mason.

LYNETTE FROMME: Member of Manson's 'family.'

Examiner
VOL. 21 NO. 52
December 25, 1984
(USPS 936-460)

EDITORIAL OFFICES:
2112 South Congress Avenue,
West Palm Beach,
Florida 33406-7686

ASSOCIATE PUBLISHER
& EDITORIAL DIRECTOR
Mike Nevard

EXECUTIVE EDITOR: William Burt
MANAGING EDITOR: Tom Wilbur
NEWS EDITOR: Cliff Linedecker
PHOTO EDITOR: Ken Matthews
STAFF EDITORS: Carolyn Bennett, Phil Brennan, Pat Colfer, Laura Graves, Mary Ellen Green, Brian Hogan, Harold Lewis, Siwila O'Donovan, Leonard Sandler
HOLLYWOOD BUREAU: Paul Francis
SENIOR ASSISTANT: Sandy Riley
ASSISTANT PHOTO EDITOR: Rebecca Franklin
READER SERVICE: Norma Burt
ASSISTANT: Sharon Vaughan
ART DIRECTOR: Lenore Mintzer
PRODUCTION MANAGER: John Bleho
PRODUCTION ASSISTANT: Peter Brennan
CONSULTING EDITORS: Stephen E. Langer, M.D., Anthony Loggott
EDITORIAL ADVISORS: John Vader, Nat K. Perlow
MARKETING DIRECTOR:
Aubrey P. Burke
CIRCULATION DIRECTOR:
Edward W. Reed
NATIONAL ADVERTISING: Director, Jack Linder; account executives, Mary Falkin. Suite 2830, 220 E. 42nd St., New York, N.Y. 10017.
MAIL-ORDER ADVERTISING: Levine Bizarro Associates Inc., 535 Fifth Avenue, New York, N.Y. 10017
Second-class postage paid at Rouses Point, N.Y., and additional offices. Send address correction to P.O. Box 711, Rouses Point, N.Y. 12979.
PUBLISHED weekly by Beta Publications Ltd., 1440 St. Catherine St. W., Montreal, Canada H3G 1S2, and Rouses Point, N.Y. 12979.
Second Class Mail Registration No. 1563. Subscription $18.85 for 52 weeks. Foreign: $20.60. Copyright © 1984 Beta Publications Ltd. All rights reserved. No responsibility for unsolicited material.
Printed in Canada

2 December 25, '84/EXAMINER

In fact, whispered rumors circulating through the California state prison in Vacaville — where Manson is serving a life sentence for the brutal 1969 slaying of actress Sharon Tate — say Manson's recent torching by a fellow inmate may have been related to his Nazi activities.

Manson suffered serious burns after Jan Holmstrom doused him with paint thinner and tossed a match at him last September.

The two had just argued bitterly over religion, and Manson had complained about Holmstrom's constant Hare Krishna chanting.

When he led his evil band of kill-crazy hippies 15 years ago, Manson allowed them to believe he was Jesus Christ.

And he's now being worshipped by a small cult of political fanatics bent on reviving Nazism right here in America.

Mason calls Manson "the foremost revolutionary leader in the world today," and has written in his newsletter Siege that Manson "provides most of our current-day inspiration."

To further the goals of this perverse sect, Mason arranged the first of several meetings between Manson and neo-Nazi Red Warthan — now in prison for killing a suspected informer.

Warthan visited Manson four times at Vacaville in 1982, once even bringing his son and getting their picture taken together with Manson.

Neo-Nazis see him as new leader

By JOHN TURNER

But that was before Warthan was convicted of firing eight shots into the head of 17-year-old Joseph Hoover in Oroville, California. Authorities say the boy was slain because he told police about the Nazi group Warthan leads.

Nor was this the first time Warthan, 43, has killed. As a young mental patient in 1955, he threw a blanket over a 10-year-old boy and heartlessly strangled him to death.

Now authorities fear that both Warthan and Manson are working behind prison doors to build a religious-like following among inmates — with themselves as modern-day "Fuerhers."

Mason has repeatedly compared Manson to Hitler — favorably.

He applauded the slaughter of Sharon Tate and her house guests.

Mason proclaimed: "It couldn't have happened to a nicer bunch of people."

"Manson, like Hitler, is as human as you or I," proclaims the outspoken newsletter Siege.

"He is just special by virtue of a one in a hundred million shot of gene combinations which gives him his ideas, his personality and his physical presence."

MASS MURDERER Charles Manson is the 'philosophical and ideological leader' of t. Universal Order, a neo-Nazi cult so extreme, it's been blacklisted by other Nazi

Does rock band do the devil's work?

LEAD SINGER King Diamond admits Satanist lyrics of group's song mirrors his own philosophy of life: 'People are not born to follow things written 2,000 years ago.'

A SINISTER band of rock musicians are serving as pied pipers for the devil — leading innocent youngsters astray by blatantly singing the praises of Satan!

The Danish band Mercyful Fate recently made its first trip to America. It's released two albums containing songs with outright Satanist lyrics — which lead singer King Diamond amazingly admits mirror his own philosophy of life!

"Satan, to me, is not a guy with horns and a tail," Diamond said. "To me, he stands for the power in the

'Satan is power in the universe'

By LEONARD SANDLER

universe that keeps things in balance between good and bad."

The band is not content with just singing about the devil. Its concerts are practically a rite of worship to him.

Mercyful Fate's own press releases say their shows include a gruesome painted face, a microphone stand constructed of human bones and a large crucifix that Diamond ignites.

What's more, Diamond breezily dismisses the importance of Christianity a the Bible, saying, "peop are not born to follow thi written in books 2,000 yc ago."

The band's unhappy inf ence on the young could seen at a recent promotior appearance. Most of t youngsters showed up dr sed in black.

"I love Satan," one yelled at drummer K Ruzz. Ruzz later explair that the boy misunderstc the group's message, whi is not devil worship, but your own thing.

Agreed Diamond: "Y should act the way you f that's the main thing."

Collage by James Mason of articles from *The Examiner*, 1984

According to James Mason, "The more alienated you are, the better Manson looks. Nobody is ever brought around to Manson—you're either there or you're not. I went for Hitler in '66 as the threshold of anger. I went for Manson in '77 as the threshold of alienation and a symbol of radicalism beyond the most radical extreme."

Collection of James Mason

"The world ended—they covered it up and didn't tell a lot of people, because the last chance is only for a few."

mind control and controlling people to the extent that they'll kill for you. Would you go out and kill people if somebody told you to? I never ran into anyone who said that they would, although there's a major incidence of where they do—and that's when the government puts a uniform on them and tells them that they can, and they do it in the military or the police."

Q: *What about the ongoing interest in him?*
John Aes-Nihil: "He's one of the two defining people of the Sixties, the other being Warhol. He went first where the whole Hippie thing was heading."

Q: *Where? Toward violence?*
John Aes-Nihil: "Yeah. The media has a way of neutralizing things through trivialization, which accounts for a great deal of the Manson thing now. In 1970 the writer Wayne McGuire prophesized that within the next twenty years Manson would transform into a major American folk hero.

"Everything is a fad, and if it doesn't pass, we're stuck in it. We've been stuck in '69 since '69."

Q: *How did Charles Manson come to be a media icon?*
Nick Bougas: "It had a lot to do with the us-versus-them mentality of Straights versus Hippies and police versus the hipsters. People could relate to it. And the sexual elements of a man with a harem were repugnant and appealing at the same time.

"Manson provided a perfect chance to discredit the do-your-own-thing mentality. Now here's a guy who did his own thing—and look what happened. They bring other fears into the mix and get everybody thinking and talking about it; of course, they can feast and feed off it for years thereafter. Every year on the anniversary of the murders they would track that whole thing out, like there's that Crazy Old Charlie again, we have a jailhouse interview—and they would cut a lot of footage together showing him dancing around and being animated and trying to scare you. Charlie Manson never killed anyone. There's no evidence that he ever killed anyone. Yet he's thought of as the most horrendous, heinous criminal in the history of America.

"They convicted him of murder rather than conspiracy, the proper charge. And he was given the death penalty for not having killed anyone. Which is pretty rough."

Q: *What got you interested?*
Nick Bougas: "It was interesting because of all the players in this great drama. Everyone seems to think the whirlwind of activity that was the Manson experience all happened over a course of years—but it actually was just a matter of months. It fascinated me that so much mythology could spring from such a short period of time.

"It was such a taboo on its own, I didn't have to manipulate it or shove it in anybody's face. Anything having to do with Manson raised shudders in most people. I was trying to bring new enlightenment to the overall thing by demystifying him and making him more palatable.

"There were only a handful of people engaged in this very unrewarding enterprise. We all knew one another. No one was doing this independently; we were all sort of interacting on one level or another. We were all sort of like a dark fraternity, and the Manson element was the binding factor. We all met in the secret society to serve this odd master."

Marilyn Manson: "I want to make a point of saying that many Charles Manson references are our references to his strange-yet-genius gray matter. I've heard some of the underground elitist grumblings of, 'Yeah, Charles Manson said that...' Well, of course he said it—what do you think, I'm stupid? I'm bringing his strange thinking into the real world. And sometimes it's neither a tribute nor a criticism, it's just putting it back where it belongs.

"I've never tried to meet him. I often wondered and hoped that he heard of my band, and he would understand that even though what I represent is a criticism of America, Charles Manson was unique in his own right. He was Marilyn Manson when he was Charles Manson. His name creates the balance in the phrase 'Marilyn Manson.' Automatically, if you have any association with Manson, you've got an FBI file. So, just by starting the band I opened up my file—which is probably real thick by now."

Untitled drawing attributed to Charles Manson, circa 1988
A group of enterprising fellow inmates cranked out copies of the central image—
Manson's face—after which Charlie scribbled around it and signed it.
The pics went to fans and collectors in exchange for money and stamps.
Collection of Arthur Deco

Handmade postcard art by Charles Manson, 1991
From a postcard sent to Nick Bougas.
Collection of Nick Bougas

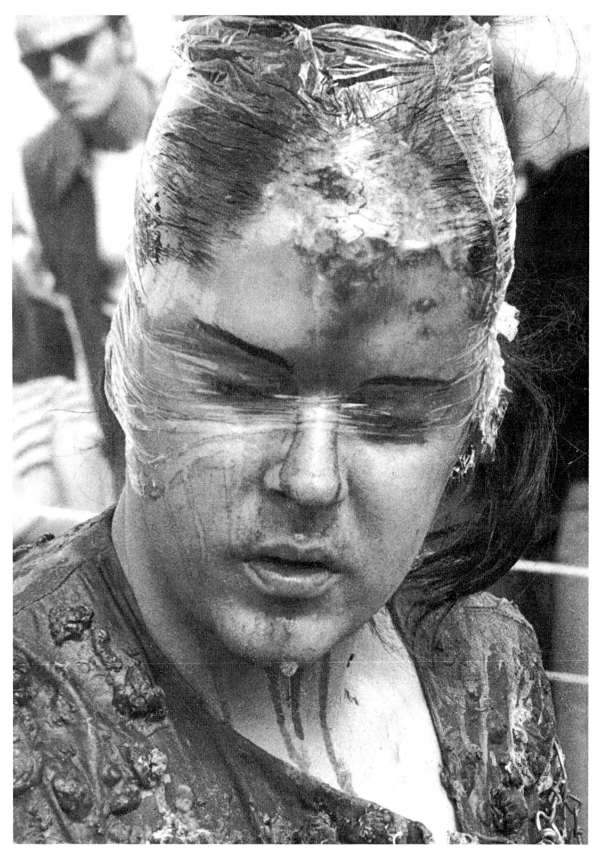
Genesis P-Orridge, 1975
Photo by Pedro Nicopoulos

THE PRECURSORS: GENESIS P-ORRIDGE: "There is no hope without thee embracing ov hopelessness."

Tell us the story behind the name **GENESIS P-ORRIDGE**. "Genesis was a name given to me at school. At a party, we played a game where we matched a list of all our names with Biblical names, and they thought Genesis fit me. P-Orridge came in '69. I was living on a floor under a kitchen table at this Acid dealer's house. One day he woke me up when he was incredibly high and drunk and very belligerent, and he said, 'You're Genesis Porridge.' I said, 'Okay.' He had seen me eat so much porridge, because I could only eat what I could steal, and that was easy to steal. Someone else said, 'It's not Porridge, it's P-orridge, and the P stands for willow, but it's spelled like pillow.' I said, 'Fine.' So, the name was given to me." *Is it a legal moniker?* "Oh yeah. I changed it legally in 1971. Everyone calls me it, except my mom. It's on my passport. Identity is fictional."

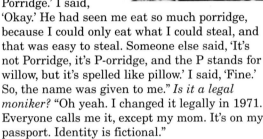

"Psychic TV was conceived in 1980, with Peter Christopherson. We wanted to have a band that, instead of shying away from fear, actually embraced its influence. We wanted to project attitudes, theories and messages that were deliberately propaganda. It felt very healthy for us to break taboos. We were trying to expose people's vulnerability to charismatic characters, and also to use genuine functional techniques without overt communication. We were saying, 'God help us if someone in a Rock Band actually wanted to be in control!' So, we would present a paramilitary image, deliberately seeing how far a band could go. Psychic engineering. We designed the Psychic Trust logo and started working on manifestos.

"Temple Of Psychic Youth was our mechanism of control over a creative strata of society. It was cultural engineering. We had access to some kind of a special power that made the real cult so successful.

"Ten thousand people worldwide were actively involved. On the 23rd of every month, at 2300 hours Greenwich Time, they were encouraged to perform a ritual—a magical sexual ritual leading to orgasm. No one else in history organized a mass orgasm." *Is that still happening?* "No, we stopped. We proved our point. After 23 months of bliss, people still hadn't figured out how to control sex. The basic idea was to liberate people."

What irritated you? "Rising conservatism and a sort of general bureaucratic paranoia. There was prosecution of Gay men and extreme artists. We were aware of what was coming. We exposed it, which made us dangerous, which made it even more exciting—despite the trials and tribulations. Our actions ultimately helped to change things."

Richard Metzger: "Genesis was really scary. There was something so intense about him on the stage; he looked so lizard-like—reptilian—with dark circles around his eyes. He would stalk around the stage with these paramilitary clothes on. There was this sonic maelstrom. In the audience were the most degenerate people I have ever seen. It was literally as if the people there had been let out of an insane asylum from the lowest level of Dante's Inferno. There was this creepy sexual vibe, Felliniesque in its utter decadence."

Genesis: "I was always excited by female fashion. I wanted to be Twiggy, not Mick Jagger. Women had the best clothes and the best make-up, and were far more exciting and mysterious. Masculinity was rather dull and animalistic, colored by the school regime which was brutal. I was repulsed by what I saw as the male world, which was about strength and brute force. It seemed unsophisticated and dull.

"Androgyny is one of the secret keys to the entire species. In many creation myths, the supreme being was a hermaphrodite. We are all, as fetuses, hermaphrodites. The original divine state is a hermaphrodite." *But what were you thinking when you were getting dressed up?* "All the roles and archetypes and stereotypes that I'd been indoctrinated with were fabricated. There was an powerful moment when I knew that consensus reality is fiction. I realized that gender was fiction and identity was fiction, and you could design whoever you wanted to be."

"Sickly P-Orridge," newspaper-and-postcard collage by Genesis P-Orridge
Comprised of articles from *The Sunday Mirror*, *The Evening News*,
and a set of photo postcards from the firing squad execution of murderer Gary Gilmore.
Collection of Genesis P-Orridge

> *"There was a flowering of a separate, indiginous networks of information by people who dropped out of the mainstream and developed alternative ways to communicate among themselves. They became autonomous, and became an underground. Almost a shadow reality."*

Tell us about the grievous bodily harm episode. "The police raided Mr. Sebastian's tattoo and piercing studio. They went through his appointment book, claiming they were investigating snuff movies. One of the names they got was mine. He was charged on fourteen counts of grievous bodily harm. Now, no one who had the piercings had complained. The police took his appointment book, and the fact that a name was down for a piercing they considered proof of grievous bodily harm.

"In England, grievous bodily harm is one charge below manslaughter. It carries a seven-year sentence. And they were trying him on fourteen counts of near-murder, for doing piercings legally on people who were happy with them, with a license.

"For some reason they didn't prosecute me. That made me very suspicious. They already knew of my existence in connection with my proselytization of Acid House Raves and all the things they're not very happy about. So to cut a long story short, they accused all these others—who did not know each other—of being an S&M torture ring. They tried them all without a jury, only a High Court Judge, which in England means they're setting a new law—it's political. So ultimately it was a lifestyle attack. The judge listened to the evidence, and found everyone guilty.

"It was a special kind of prosecution. And this judge, in his summing up, said that because piercing involved a hole in the skin, piercing made a wound, no matter how small it was, and to wound somebody else—even if they wanted you to!—was illegal. They resurrected an old law which was to stop soldiers from hurting themselves to get out of fighting. They made this law because soldiers would shoot themselves in the foot, break their arms, whatever.

"I was the perfect target for a lifestyle attack because I was inevitably connected to everything illegal. So they came after me. I was in Katmandu and got a fax about it. They'd gone to my house and were ready with a sledgehammer to smash the door. They flashed a warrant, an assistant who was staying there let them in, and they went through the house, looking to prove we were a Satanic cult dedicated to the destruction of the British way of life.

"The next day on television they said I was the most dangerous person in Britain, with this cult following who were somehow about to overthrow the British way of life. But in fact, when the media started digging, they discovered it was a very ethical organization that happened to be pro-sexual. The police found nothing—they never came up with a single thing they were looking for. They took all my archives, my house, everything. They wanted to at least ruin me financially—they did ruin me financially!

"They didn't officially ban me from the country. They simply said, 'If you come back we cannot guarantee your safety.' I went to San Francisco, where friends organized a couple of Raves to help me raise money to survive. It was actually the Rave community on the West Coast that saved me. That was in the days when the Ravers were idealistic."

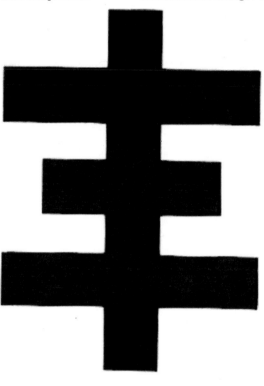

Psychick Cross
Designed by Genesis, circa 1980

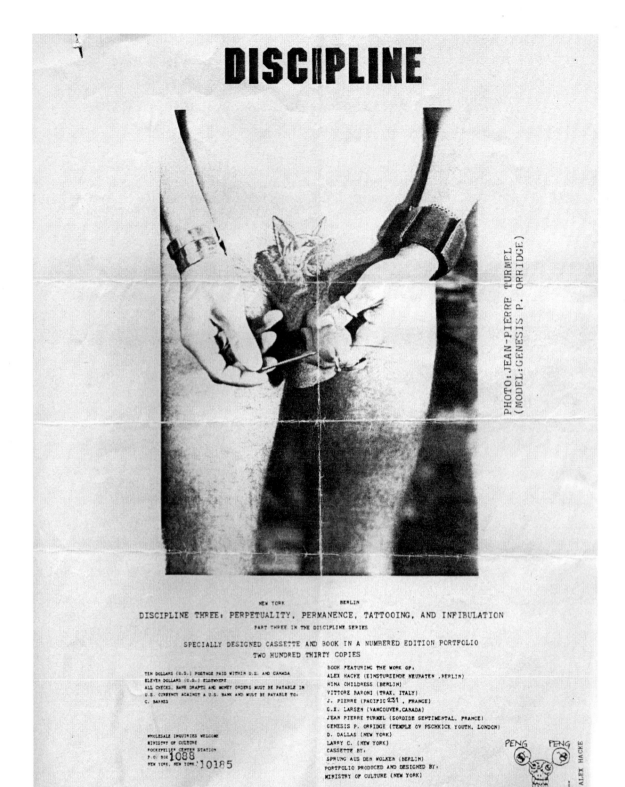

Flyer for cassette-and-book portfolio *Discipline*, Ministry Of Culture, 1981
"I was pierced—which was illegal—and tattooed—illegal—and I was pro-everything.
Section 29 was a law mandating that men could not kiss in public, so I was throwing kiss-ins—and
I was a heterosexual married man with children!" Genesis models for photographer Jean-Pierre Trumel.
Graphics by Alex Hacke of Einstrurzende Neubaten.
Collection of Genesis P-Orridge

Untitled collage, 1985
From *Esoterrorist, Selected Essays – Genesis P-Orridge 1980-1988*
Published by MediaKaos/Alecto Enterprises, 1994
Collection of the author

Genesis P-Orridge, Hackney Empire, London, 1987
Genesis performs en regalia at "No Censorship!" benefit concert.
Profits from the evening went to Jello Biafra, at the time battling prosecution
for his use of a nasty H.R. Giger painting on a Dead Kennedys album cover.
Photograph by Studio 23

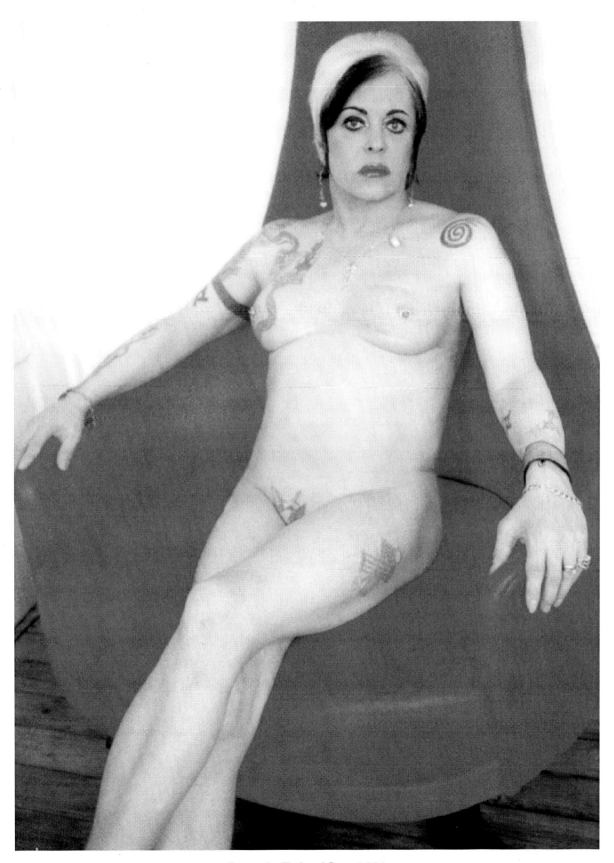

Genesis P-Orridge, 2001
"Change thee way to perceive and change all memory."
Photo by Laure Leber

Monte Cazazza, *Silent Death #1*, 1975
Collection of Genesis P-Orridge

THE PRECURSORS: MONTE CAZAZZA: "I don't need to talk, I don't need to make quotes. You see, I'm already very widely unknown."

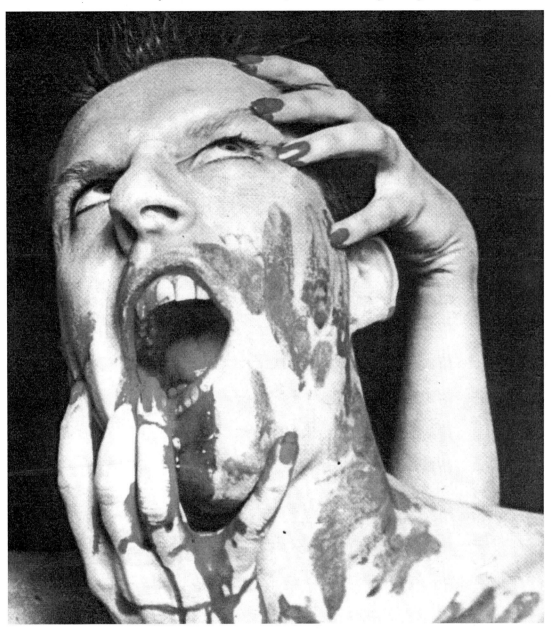

Monte Cazazza, self-portrait, 1978
Collection of Genesis P-Orridge

SECONDS (DAVID WEST): *You did some shows with Factrix.*
CAZAZZA: We were very simpatico. That's how it worked with Throbbing Gristle too. The kind of stuff we were trying to do, people thought we were crazy. They thought, "What is this shit?"

SECONDS: *You're credited as the person who coined the term "Industrial Music." How did that come about?*
CAZAZZA: Geez, these are really difficult questions. Well, Throbbing Gristle started their own record company called Industrial Records. We'd just make up little slogans to make fun of the record industry. One day I made this postcard that said "Industrial Music for Industrial People," and sent it to them. We didn't have a plan; it was just a slogan. It wasn't meant to be taken so seriously. I wish I had a dollar for every time someone used it—I'd be sitting pretty! At the time, no one was interested in what we did.

Industrial Records Ltd

Monte Cazazza

From Oakland to England, from obscurity to being "very widely unknown", Monte Cazazza has a past. One of our finest investigative reporters lays it bare...

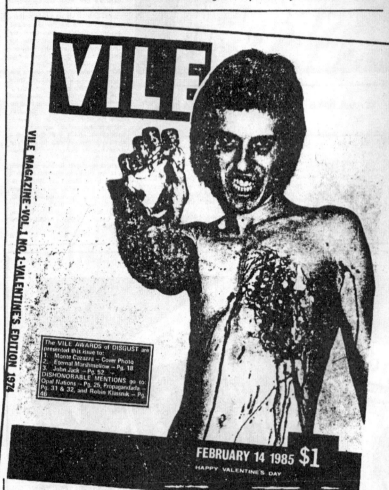

HALLOWEEN 1978

Next record due for release from Industrial Records is from Monte Cazazza, a reclusive Oakland artist whose performances have vilated the sensibilities of indignant art critics, the entire acid damaged Bay Area avant garde and jaded art claques from Menlo Park to Venice (Italy). He's been described as a "brilliant monster," "art gangster," and "a real sick guy," but one thing is unanimous his personal appearances really rile people up.

His detractors just don't seem to get the point. Genet says it best: "To escape the horror, bury yourself in it." Like other artists who are obsessed with violent images, Cazazza's early life was riddled with hideous events and accidents, including witnessing a necrophiliac in action. Rather than choke down those nightmares, he spat them back out at the world.

Cazazza's reputation was spawned at Oakland College of Arts and Crafts when for his first sculpture assignment he created a cement "waterfall" down the main stairway of the building, making it permanently impassable and got the boot on the second day of school.

His formal education completed, he passed quickly through a mutilated rubber doll period then disappeared among dark rumors of hospitals and jails. He resurfaced with a blatantly commercial attempt to woo the whims of the wealthy with tasteful pornographic collages of orchids sprouting penises at a San Francisco exhibit. He was contacted by an aging countess as a possible benefactress and lunched at her famous Oakland mansion while visions of dollar signs danced drunkenly around the plates. The Contessa died two weeks later.

Shortly thereafter in 1972 he achieved infamy when he was invited to attend an arts conference weekend-in-the-woods to share transcendental conversations on perspective and grant-writing while nest-

Monte Cazazza feature, *Slash* Magazine, Volume 2, Number 3, 1979
Collection of Genesis P-Orridge

ling paint-spattered jeans in pine needles and toasting hand-dyed marshmallows for "S'Mores" in an ultimate artsy outdoorsy atmosphere. Cazazza arrived with an armed bodyguard and sprinkled arsenic into all the food. At lunch he dropped bricks with the word "Dada" painted on them on artistic feet. At dinner he burned a partially decomposed, maggot-infested cat at the table. His bodyguard blocked the exit, and several participants fell ill due to the stench. Photos and stories of this event were published as far away as Holland.

Genesis Porridge and Cosey Fanni Tutti of Throbbing Gristle read of Cazazza in Vile Magazine in 1974 when he was a classic Valentine's Day cover boy holding a dripping, bloody heart that looked torn out of his chest. The Gristle's and Cazazza's mutual fascination with pornography and fascism prompted the limeys to pay a call to California to view in person the 15' × 15' silver screw-together swastika Cazazza constructed which can be rapidly dismantled in case of police raids or guerrila JDL attacks.

Since their visit was at the height of the Gary Gilmore furor, they all photographed each other in blindfolds as though they were in front of a firing squad, complete with a real loaded gun pointed at their hearts to get better reactions. Postcards made of the photos were mailed immediately after Gilmore's execution to the warden of the Utah penitentiary and several newspapers. Over 6,000 T shirts with the same photo were sold in England, and a picture of one was on the front page of the Hong Kong Daily News. Their mock photo was mistakenly considered the official execution photo according to Porridge.

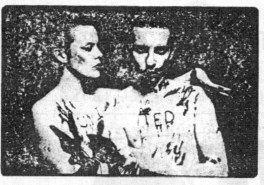

"His reputation is so nasty, he rarely leaves his house..."

T shirt sales financed Cazazza's 1977 trip to England where he was let loose in Industrial Records' studios with an engineer, a chainsaw, the innards of a piano which was played with hammers and violin bows, and other musical instruments. Ten songs were recorded with titles like P.S. (PLASTIC SURGERY), BUSTED KNEECAPS, F.F.A. (FIST FUCKERS OF AMERICA), HATE . TO MOM ON MOTHER'S DAY. A Cazazza single will be released in March.

Also soon for release from the Throbbing Gristle umbrella corporation is a movie in which Cazazza and a 14 year-old boy are electrocuted. Monte also appeared in Kerry Colonna's DECCA-DANCE movie in a suit he made out of rubber tubing and razor blades.

Cazazza edited a fanzine NITROUS OXIDE in 1971 (far preceding Sniffin' Glue). He co-edits WIDOWS AND ORPHANS, a color xerox picture magazine. He also gives slide shows and illustrated lectures on Siamese Twins that he researched in medical libraries.

But still his reputation is so nasty that he rarely leaves his house, although he did go out on Halloween dressed as Kearney, the trash bag murderer. He wore a cheap plastic mask and carried a green garbage bag filled with animal livers and hearts (like Hermann Nitsch) and a bloody mannequin head used by medical students for practice in giving mouth-to-mouth respiration. Definitely the life of the party.

Cazazza's pet money-making project for the future is futher exploration of "murder junkies" via a double bill of the stories of Edmund Kemper (a cannabilistic necrophiliac) and Dean Coryl, the Texas "candy man" whose brutal sex murders peaked at a chronic one-a-day habit until he had killed 27 teenage boys (before authorities stopped counting).

For artists who think their work is daring, Cazazza's is a double-dare. Those avant garde artists who use sex and violence as a chic intellectual playground for "art theory" are the first to head for the exits when confronted by Cazazza's work. His scientific expose of voyeuristic urges for sex and violence is no-holds-barred. And it is all done with a comic edge that amplifies the sounds of skeletons being yanked from the most repressed closets.

Cazazza never gives personal interviews. He bought a hot Ansa-phone and keeps it hooked up 24 hours a day. When he returned my call, I asked him if he wanted to make any statements for Slash. "NO, NO, NO," he said, "I don't need to talk, I don't need to make quotes. You see, I'm already VERY WIDELY UNKNOWN."

—J B

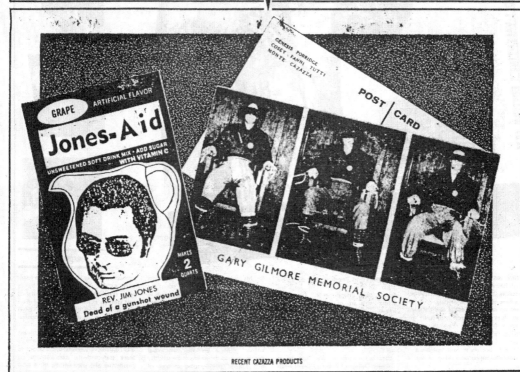

RECENT CAZAZZA PRODUCTS

REPRINTED from "SLASH" MAGAZINE   JANUARY 1979   LOS ANGELES

Harley Flannagan, backstage, CBGB, NYC, early Eighties
He founded a musical genre: Hardcore.
Photographer unknown
Collection of Harley Flannagan

THE PRECURSORS: HARLEY FLANNAGAN of CRO-MAGS:
"Everyone has done fucked-up shit in their past. No one is innocent."

Harley Flannagan: "I was born in San Francisco in 1967, the "Summer of Love," but I'm definitely a New Yorker by blood. I came from nothing—I came from a poor family—I struggled on the streets. I did a lot with hardly anything.

"My folks, yeah, they were Hippies—or at least she was. I think he was just a fuck-up. His name was Harley. Of course they were seriously caught up in the whole drug thing. She was from New York and was friends with famous poets and writers, musicians and freaks—the whole Velvet Underground thing and all that Andy Warhol shit. He was from Texas. He left home at 15 and started riding freight trains.

"Me and my mom did a lot of hitchhiking and stayed with a lot of different people, all across the States and Europe. Crazy shit happened on those trips; it really was a fuckin' ride! We wound up back with my mom's family in New York.

"My dad was always in and out of prison. He had serious alcohol and drug problems—I guess they both did—but from what I understand he was really bad. They were together for a few turbulent years, on and off. It was pretty nuts. My mom split on my dad within a few years after I was born and that was that. I never saw him again until his funeral."

"I lived in a building with Allen Ginsberg—a friend of my mom, my aunt Denise Mercedes—a founder of The Stimulators, Richard Hell—one of the first Punk Rockers, and one of the chicks from The Runaways. It was a freaky building, the only building on the block with White people; we were all freaks, artists, Punk Rockers, poets and shit, so we all got fucked with a lot. My block—12th Street—was run by one of the local Puerto Rican gangs, the Hitmen. You have no idea how that neighborhood was back then. They had shootouts all the time. It was all drug wars and fighting over which streets they would sell Dope and Coke on."

"In '77 my mom went to London; she went into a record store and asked, 'What are the kids listening to these days? I want to get it for my son.' She came home with a record by the Sex Pistols."

In '78, guitarist Mercedes recruited nephew Harley to drum for The Stimulators, joining bassist Anne Gustavson and vocalist Patrick Mack. Their 1980 single, "Loud Fast Rules," provided an anthem for surly kids.

Local success precipitated a European tour. Harley: "In 1980 The Stimulators went to Ireland to do the first big Punk festival, the Belfast International Punk and New Wave Festival. This was around the time when the Oi! movement was beginning. There were lots of Skinheads and lots of Punks, and for the most part everyone was cool. We were the only band from the States.

"I was in several riots while I was there. It was fucking insane. These motherfuckers were the real deal. I never saw so many mohawks and spikes and Skinheads in one place. It was sick—when you went into the bathroom you got a fuckin' contact high from all the glue-huffing. It was insane.

"It was a big-ass hall. It was packed—it was nuts. It started with just a little fight, then there was another one; it spread from little skirmishes here and there, then it just kinda started to spread. All of a sudden—Everybody on the bouncers! They got a huge metal ladder thrown down on them from the balcony, while we're on stage playing. [laughs] Chairs are flying at the bouncers, who are now running past us, hiding off to the side of the stage while getting pummeled by Skinheads.

"Then the kids ran havoc in the streets. It was amazing. Imagine what it was like to my 13-year-old mind to see that shit! [laughs] I felt like, if we had true strength in numbers, we couldn't be stopped. It was intense. Back home I was used to getting picked on in my neighborhood by the local PRs, getting jumped everywhere we went—and here were like tons of Punks and Skins. No one was fucking with them—they were like an army! And out of this army the Skinheads were the dominating aggressors. Well, they took me in. I started hanging with them. They gave me Skinhead-style clothes, getting me dressed right, taking me out with them. They told me, 'Teach America about Skinheads.'"

Harley returned to New York. "The scene used to be really cool, but by the time I got back it had gotten kinda stupid. It wasn't just my crew anymore—it was huge and full of dumbasses. And they all kissed my ass 'cause they all knew who I was and that I was the first and I was big fuckin' shit—mainly 'cause I didn't give a fuck and I would fuck shit up! I would and could kick any of their asses. And then all these fuckin' cats from the suburbs and shit started comin' around and acting like they were really tough and like they were from around here, and starting a lot of shit with the local PRs and making us look bad

Harley Flannagan, playing with Cro-Mags, CBGB, NYC, date unknown
Photographer unknown
Collection of Harley Flannagan

"Bands that we had a beef with or that talked shit from the stage wound up getting beat down right there on stage."

in the neighborhood and in the press and in *MaximumRockNRoll* —those fucking jack-asses!"

"I think the bad press about Skins actually generated the stereotypical Skinhead and Fascist Nazi thing. *MaximumRockNRoll* caused most of that shit to spread with dumb-asses who really didn't know shit about shit. They spread that shit like wildfire, and they created the hype and—how ironic! [laughs] Now everybody who wanted to be a tough guy on the scene became a Skin, and everybody who didn't have any nuts of their own was gettin' boots and a bomber! [laughs]

"It wasn't just a small group of hard-ass teenage White boys fighting to save there own asses on the Lower East Side anymore—it was a bunch of stupid, brainless fuckin' sheep who were following *MaximumRockNRoll*'s lead into some fantasyland notoriety. What a fuckin' joke! When Sid Vicious wore a swastika, no one freaked out—it was just for shock. Same with the Circle Jerks bassist—and he was Jewish!

"But shit did get out of hand and the scene got real violent. Eventually you did have your Nazi Skins and your anti-Nazi Skins and your this and your that. It just all got ridiculous at a certain point, and I think that had a lot to do with all the media sensationalism.

"It was a violent neighborhood. There were always kids huffing glue, tripping, drinking, smoking dust or weed or whatever else anyone could scrounge up. Me and my friends were little fucking maniacs. There were a lot of fights.

"I wanted my own crew that didn't have to take no shit from no one in our neighborhood. Fuck all the local gangs—I wanted to stand up, and not alone—I wanted the scene to do it. In Ireland I saw that there were White boys who would scrap with any-fucking-body—gangs, cops, it didn't matter! It wasn't like in my neighborhood, where White people were targets.

"I was done taking people's shit. When I came home I started shaving all my friends' heads. We were all just little kids from 12 to 18. Everyone was like, 'What are those?' about my Doc Martens. I was like, 'These are the fucking Skinhead boot!' We didn't have them in the States, so we would rob tourists'—especially Brits'—right off their feet! [laughs] Or beat up people we didn't like on the scene who had them, and take them!

"Up until then I got no respect. In school I got jumped all the time, until I finally snapped. I really fucked a kid up, started beating him with a chair—then I had all the respect in the world. All of a sudden I was popular and shit, and yeah, I started getting mean—the victim-turned-aggressor thing. I realized I could fight and I was good at it.

"Everyone was a fucking hard-ass; basically you were taught to act like an asshole. I eventually got in so much trouble, I had a contract put out on me by some of the local clubs. They contracted the neighborhood hitman, Pig Man, to kill me. Things where really bad for a while, and I had to hang low. I even split town for a while."

Harley learned to play bass and joined with singer John Joseph, guitarist Parris Mitchell Mayhew and drummer Mackie Jayson to form Cro-Mags. Later Doug Holland of Kraut brought another guitar into their mix.

"First I learned to play Black Flag, Pistols, Dead Boys et cetera—Punk songs—but once I got good enough to learn most of the Bad Brains, Motörhead and Sabbath, I was ready to write all my own shit—learning other people's songs was no longer necessary."

What is Hardcore? "A style of music, a lifestyle, a state of mind. It's extreme, taking something intense to the next level. An attitude. I was born and bred into it. I lived in squats, I was on the streets every night, I played Hardcore music. I was on the edge all the time."

Allen Ginsburg helped 12-year-old Harley put out a book, *Stories & Illustrations By Harley* (Charlatan Press, 1976). In the introduction Ginsburg writes, "His sense of perspective is vast....His mother Rosebud was a Lower East Side Hippie and a friend of mine."
Collection of the author

Untitled sketch by Harley, circa 1989
Collection of Jerry Lee Williams

SOUNDTRACK TO *1984*

**Picture disc of *The Reverend Jim Jones In Person — The Last Supper*
Released by Temple Ov Psychic Youth, 1984
Collage by Genesis P-Orridge**
On November 18, 1978, Reverend Jim Jones exhorted more than nine hundred of his followers to die by drinking cyanide-laced Kool-Aid. Later, U.S. Naval personnel retrieved cassette recordings of his exhortations from the Jonestown, Guyana killing ground.
Genesis: "Monte Cazazza went to the U.S. Government publications office in San Francisco. The authorities/CIA/FBI were obliged by the Freedom of Information Act to make their covert recordings available to the public. Tapes were only available for one day only. But Monte knew which day from his enquiries, and managed to get our copy."
Collection of the author

Psychic TV sporting Charles Manson fashions, 1984
Alex Fergusson, Jon Goslin, Jordi Valls, Bee; crouching: Genesis
Photo by Genesis P-Orridge via remote trigger.

Anton LaVey et al., *The Satanic Mass*
Recorded in the ritual chamber of the Black House, Friday the 13th of September 1968.
Anton LaVey serves as High Priest, with Dietrich von Kroller as organist and composer.
Released on Murgenstrumm Records (the Church Of Satan's own label) December 1968.

SECONDS (MICHAEL MOYNIHAN): *Tell us about* The Satanic Mass *album.*
LaVEY: It was a year before *The Satanic Bible* was published, and at that time the book was in the form of a series of essays. *The Satanic Mass* was a compilation of rituals and gleanings from these essays. I didn't put my name on it as playing a lot of the music, since I thought it would be too pretentious. *The Satanic Mass* was all original except for "Hymn To Satan," which was a corruption of Bach's "Jesu Meine Freude." The rest—the Baptism, the Lust Ritual, the Destruction Ritual—is all my own.

Side 1: "The Satanic Mass"
Side 2: *"The Satanic Bible,* Prologue and Book of Satan: Verses I through V," read by LaVey
Collection of the Church Of Satan

Cover of the album *LIE*, Charles Manson, Awareness Records, recorded August 8, 1968

Phil Kaufman, in his book *Road Mangler Deluxe*, tells this story: "The Manson album called *LIE* was released in 1971, when he was in prison. I produced the album. The jacket design was the cover of *Life* that he was on. Nobody put their real name on the credits. Everybody put their prison number or phony names. The album didn't sell well. That was after Charlie had been arrested but not convicted. We pressed three thousand copies. The Family broke into my house and stole about half of them. The money was never recouped."

Family members sold copies outside the L.A. courthouse in an attempt to raise money for Manson's defense. When prosecutor Vincent Bugliosi heard of head shops selling the album, he successfully petitioned the judge to rule *LIE* prejudicial. Bugliosi, accompanied by sheriffs, personally confiscated many copies from startled shopkeepers.

Side 1: "Look At Your Game Girl," "Ego," "Mechanical Man," "People Say I'm No Good," "Home Is Where You're Happy," "Arkansas," "I'll Never Say Never To Always"
Side 2: "Garbage Dump," "Don't Do Anything Illegal," "Sick City," "Cease To Exist," "Big Iron Door," "I Once Knew A Man," "Eyes Of A Dreamer"
Collection of Nick Bougas

Lydia Lunch, venue unknown, Portland, 1983
Lunch and beau J.G. Thirlwell appeared on the same bill in the aftermath of their
Immaculate Consumptive tour with Nick Cave and Marc Almond.
Portland outfit Rancid Vat opened the show.
Photo by John W. Hubbard

J.G. Thirlwell, venue unknown, Portland, 1983
In the middle of Jim and Lydia's show, some big guy got on stage, picked up percussionist Cliff Martinez and put him head-first into the oil drum he was playing. Jim and Lydia drifted off stage after that. Jim seems to recall that he may have been on Acid at the time.
Photo by John W. Hubbard

Boyd Rice, NON, The Carpenters Club, San Diego, 1980
Boyd performs on his homemade Noise Manipulation Unit,
housed within an upturned plastic milk crate.
This photo appeared on the back of NON's *RISE* 12", MUTE Records, 1982
Photographer unknown

Nikolas Schreck fronting Radio Werewolf, venue unknown, Los Angeles, 1986
Radio Werewolf, named for post-War Nazi terrorists who fought on against occupying Allied troops, was the musical haunt of Schreck and girlfriend Zeena LaVey, Anton's daughter.
Photo by Nick Bougas

Flyer for Whitehouse's Great White Death tour, 1985
William Bennett, Philip Best, Kevin Tomkins
William Bennett: "The idea I had in my mind was of an electronic maelstrom. And in live situations people would have no choice but to be completely submissive to this kind of sound."
Michael Moynihan: "Utilizing ear-shredding frequencies and demented vocal hysterics, Whitehouse terrified the frail and pleased only those with the most discriminating of tastes."
In the mid-Nineties, Peter Sotos performed with the band.
Collection of Phil Luciani

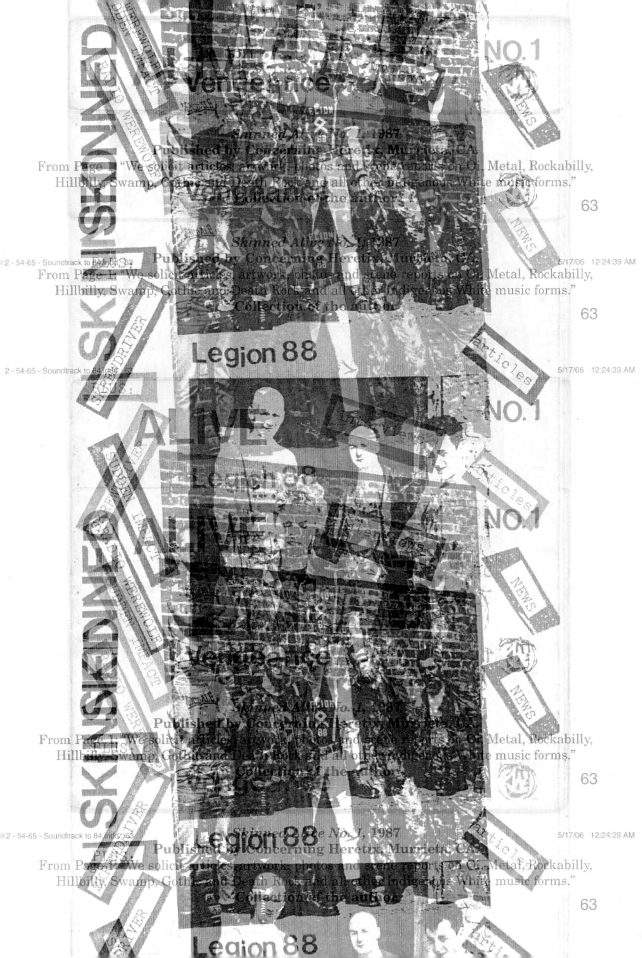

Michael Moynihan, Coup de Grace, Oberhausen, Germany, 1986
Moynihan: "I started going to Hardcore shows. I appreciated the aggression, the violence, and the fierce independent attitude, which was antithetical to most other music of the time. I saw most of the early American Hardcore bands play, but like everything, it seemed to get co-opted. I was looking for something more extreme that didn't concede to popular opinion. That's how I started listening to Industrial Music."
Collection of Michael Moynihan

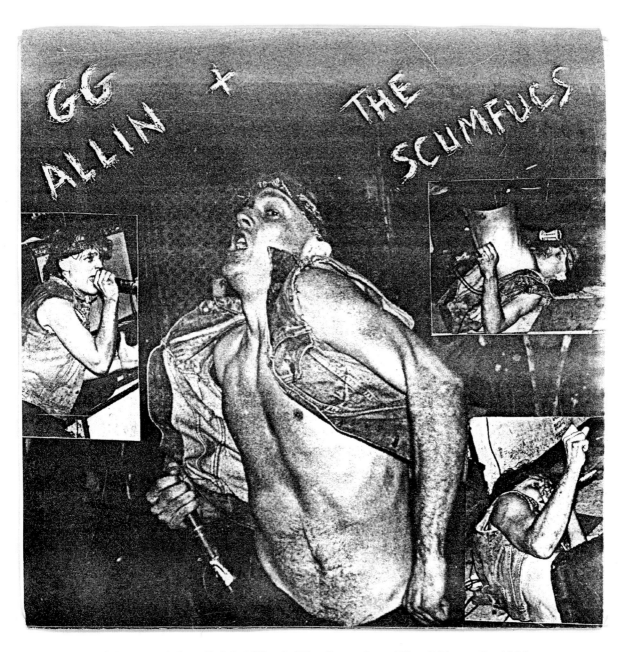

Cover of the 7" *GG Allin & The Scumfucs*, Blood Records, 1983
GG Allin fronted the premier Scum Rock act of all time; members included
sibling Merle Allin, Richard Kern and David Duke's brother-in-law Sherman.
People flocked to his shows in anticipation of witnessing his promised on-stage suicide.
But rather than kill himself, GG turned his attention to the crowd.

Steven Blush describes a GG show he booked at New York's Cat Club, October 6, 1988:
"The GG Allin band was Thurston Moore, Gerard Cosloy and Mykel Board. Somewhere during the second song GG, dressed in underwear, just started taking a dump on the stage and whipping his wet shit at people as they went running in terror. The show lasted about four minutes. I remember him running around in circles outside, covered in shit, and everyone fleeing from him. I didn't get arrested, but I was never allowed in the Cat Club again."

Tracks: "Hard Candy Cock," "Out For Blood," "I Don't Give a Shit About You,"
"Drink, Fight & Fuck, Convulsions"
Collection of Steven Blush

Joe Coleman, 1995
Photo by Tom Benson

JOE COLEMAN: *"You can hurt people more with art than with physical violence. It's more like a disease you infect them with. The body will heal from a trauma, but a disease— that could be long-term, incurable, and it could be terminal."*

COLEMAN: "My first performance was when I took one of my mom's metal cookie-cooking sheets, and I collected a bunch of cherry bombs and nigger-chasers and skyrockets and I taped them all onto the cookie sheet. In the back yard I lit one of the fuses, which set off a chain of explosions. I saw that nothing penetrated the metal sheet—there was no holes in it, but it was very hot. Then I got a towel soaked in water, put it on my chest to protect against the heat, tied the cookie sheet to my chest, and put one of my father's big shirts over the whole rig to hide it.

"I went into strangers' homes and blew myself up. The first time I did it, I was wandering around with explosives strapped to a metal sheet against my chest, hidden by one of my father's big shirts. I cut my wrists and made all these symbols on myself in my own blood. So, I saw a bunch of cars parked in front of a house. I knew there was a party goin' on, so I just walked in. It turned out to be a Republican cocktail party. It was a period in which Acid was always in the news, so they thought I was on a bad Acid trip." *Joe, did you do Acid?* "Yeah, but that day I didn't. So, they figured I was just this fucked-up kid on a bad trip. They were asking me, 'Are you alright? Do you know where you are?' I pulled out a lighter and lit my shirt on fire, and that set off the explosives. Smoke filled the room. In the confusion, I left. I just had this rage that I wanted to express." *Rage against what?* "Being born. When I was a teenager I was full of rage. There was no one I felt close to or had any camaraderie with." *Aren't all teenagers full of rage?* "Yeah, but how many of them do something about it? It links into the suicide bombers—I mean, I can understand that. But I didn't want to kill myself."

"I went to New York when I was seventeen. I made money by panhandling as a phony cripple with a crutch. Sometimes I made a lot of money. Then I drove a cab, which influenced my art."

Show flyer, 1981
Collection of Joe Coleman

"The Steel Tips started in the early Seventies. I wore a light on the top of my head, plugged in to the side of the stage. Our songs included 'Kill All Teenagers' and 'My Dick Is In Love With You.' We didn't give a fuck about Punk; we hated Punk. We played at Max's Kansas City and CBGB, but we hated Punk Rock because it was popular. We didn't want to give the kids anything that they wanted. We loved fucking with people. We'd get arrested half the time. That made it fun. It was gettin' too much like Rock & Roll. I was gettin' bored. GG Allin would have never existed if I didn't exist before him."

"I was a hard-core Heroin addict for a long time. The last time I did Dope was in the mid-Eighties.

"I was obsessed with doing every drug that was available, but I liked the fact that Heroin was the most fucked-up drug you could do. I thought, 'That's the one for me.' It became my favorite." *Did you smoke Coke?* "Yeah, sure. Name something that I haven't done. When I did Acid I did Purple Haze—the real stuff." *You and Adam Parfrey did Dope together.* "That was the first time Adam ever did Dope. I used to get it for him."

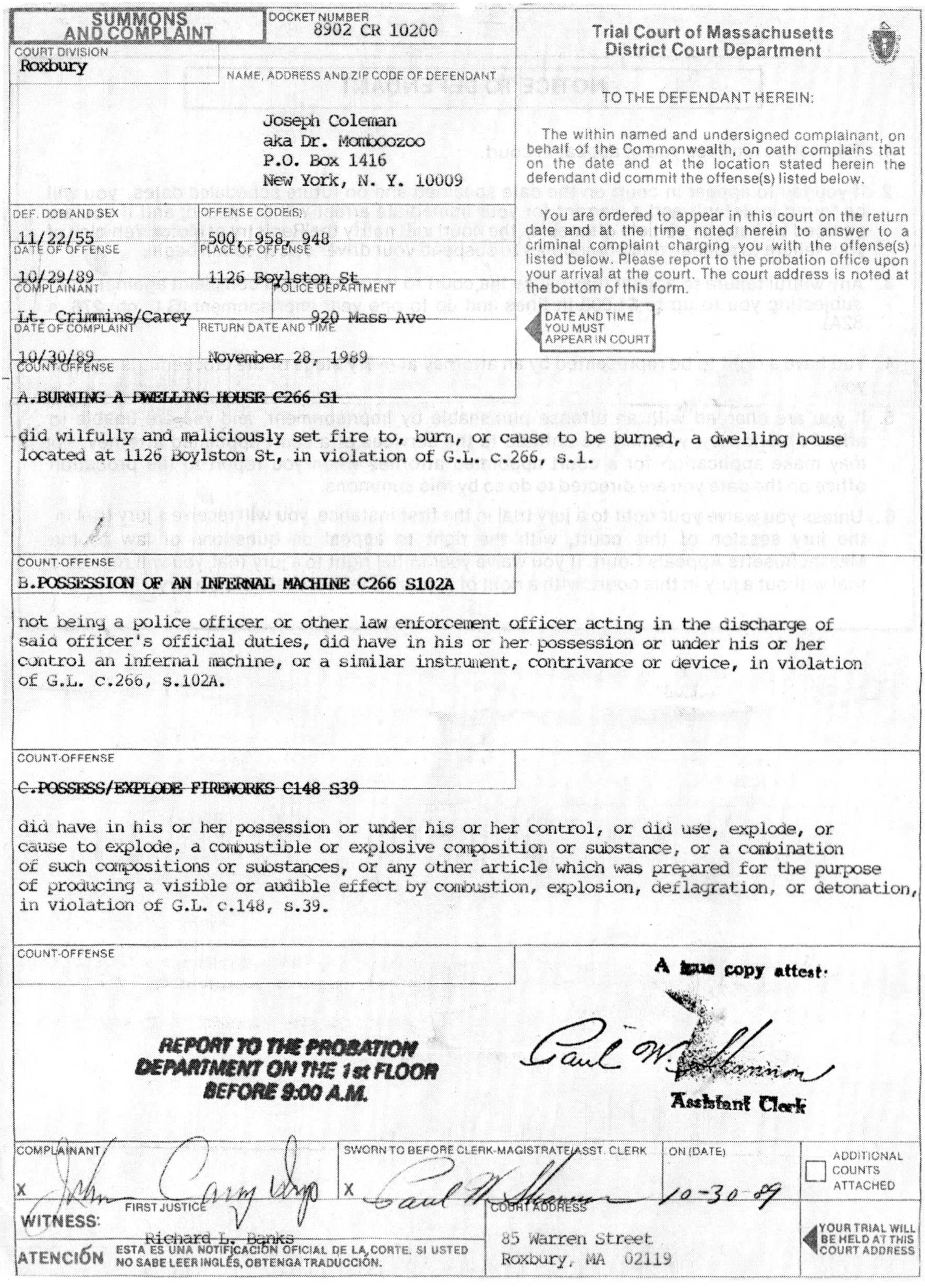

SUMMONS AND COMPLAINT	DOCKET NUMBER 8902 CR 10200	Trial Court of Massachusetts District Court Department

COURT DIVISION: Roxbury

NAME, ADDRESS AND ZIP CODE OF DEFENDANT:
Joseph Coleman
aka Dr. Momboozoo
P.O. Box 1416
New York, N.Y. 10009

TO THE DEFENDANT HEREIN:

The within named and undersigned complainant, on behalf of the Commonwealth, on oath complains that on the date and at the location stated herein the defendant did commit the offense(s) listed below.

You are ordered to appear in this court on the return date and at the time noted herein to answer to a criminal complaint charging you with the offense(s) listed below. Please report to the probation office upon your arrival at the court. The court address is noted at the bottom of this form.

DEF. DOB AND SEX: 11/22/55
OFFENSE CODE(S): 500, 958, 948
DATE OF OFFENSE: 10/29/89
PLACE OF OFFENSE: 1126 Boylston St
COMPLAINANT: Lt. Crimmins/Carey
POLICE DEPARTMENT: 920 Mass Ave
DATE OF COMPLAINT: 10/30/89
RETURN DATE AND TIME: November 28, 1989

COUNT-OFFENSE
A. BURNING A DWELLING HOUSE C266 S1

did wilfully and maliciously set fire to, burn, or cause to be burned, a dwelling house located at 1126 Boylston St, in violation of G.L. c.266, s.1.

COUNT-OFFENSE
B. POSSESSION OF AN INFERNAL MACHINE C266 S102A

not being a police officer or other law enforcement officer acting in the discharge of said officer's official duties, did have in his or her possession or under his or her control an infernal machine, or a similar instrument, contrivance or device, in violation of G.L. c.266, s.102A.

COUNT-OFFENSE
C. POSSESS/EXPLODE FIREWORKS C148 S39

did have in his or her possession or under his or her control, or did use, explode, or cause to explode, a combustible or explosive composition or substance, or a combination of such compositions or substances, or any other article which was prepared for the purpose of producing a visible or audible effect by combustion, explosion, deflagration, or detonation, in violation of G.L. c.148, s.39.

REPORT TO THE PROBATION DEPARTMENT ON THE 1st FLOOR BEFORE 9:00 A.M.

A true copy attest:
Paul W. Shannon
Assistant Clerk

COMPLAINANT: John Carey
WITNESS: Richard L. Banks
SWORN TO BEFORE CLERK-MAGISTRATE/ASST. CLERK: Paul W. Shannon
ON (DATE): 10-30-89
COURT ADDRESS: 85 Warren Street, Roxbury, MA 02119

ATENCIÓN: ESTA ES UNA NOTIFICACIÓN OFICIAL DE LA CORTE. SI USTED NO SABE LEER INGLÉS, OBTENGA TRADUCCIÓN.

Indictment, State of Massachusetts vs. Coleman, November 30, 1989
As a result of his Boston Film/Video Foundation performance, police charged him with possession of an infernal machine—a law unenforced since the 1800s.
Collection of Joe Coleman

"My pathology is necessary because nature wants a voice for death. When the locusts clean out the field, that's good. Nature made me this way. Gacy and Lucas can't really do it. They can only play around with the game. Nature produced me to articulate it."

"I have been prosecuted for art. I was arrested at the Boston Film and Video Arts Foundation for a performance in 1989. The warrant was written out for Joe Coleman a.k.a. Dr. Momboozoo and one of the charges was possession of an infernal machine, as well as burning a dwelling and animal cruelty. It's okay to use traps to kill a rat but not your teeth. And, no one was charged with the infernal machine since the 1800s. I was honored. I blew myself up, which I'd been arrested for prior to that. I started out by projecting porno films from the Fifties on a paper screen. That's what created me—my parents fucking in the Fifties. After twenty minutes I burst through the screen hanging upside-down on a harness. I exploded over the audience. My wife at the time, Nancy, put out the fires with goat's blood. Then she cut me down. I went backstage and got some rats. I bit one's head off and spit it into the audience, and the other head I swallowed. Then I set fires on the stage. The fire alarms went off, and the Boston cops and arson squad came. I split and was served with a warrant here in New York. The headlines in the *Boston Globe* read 'Audience flees explosive performance.' There was a picture of me exploding. Fighting the charges cost a lot of money but it never went to trial. I was put on probation—one of the terms was that I couldn't eat any Massachusetts mice for a year."

"The infamous thing I did at The Kitchen—I told the curator I was gonna use paper-mâché penises and vaginas, and she said, 'Oh, that's very subversive. We like that very much.' But I had no intention of using that—instead I brought a box of rats, and I had explosives concealed under my clothes. I asked the audience what the fuck they were doing there, and told 'em they were a bunch of sad assholes. I poured the rats on my shoulders and bit one of their heads off and threw the body into the audience. Then I blew myself up. Then I brought out a shotgun and held it at the audience and said, 'I think it's time to leave.' Everyone ran, leaving their bags and purses and all that shit. So I took the money out of the pocketbooks, 'cause I knew I wasn't gettin' paid. Everything was bloody and burned. Then I saw the curator out of the corner of my eye. I took the shotgun and went over to her; I put the shotgun under her chin and said, 'How'd ya like the show, honey?' She goes, [*quivering*] 'It was good! I liked it!' I said, 'I knew you'd like it!' Nobody got hurt, but everybody got enlightened." *What did you get out of it?* "The pleasure of exorcising my demons." *Did you get in trouble?* "Yeah— the cops came to my house and arrested me, but the charges were dropped. The Kitchen got fined because they hired me."

Who are your enemies from back in the day? "Art Spiegelman is the most over-rated asshole in the comic art scene. First off, he can't draw worth a shit, he's a terrible draftsman, he gets the Pulitzer Prize for doing a story about Nazi cats putting mice in

Boston Globe, November 30, 1989

I.P.M. #722
designed & produced by
Chaplain Ray
Box 63 • Dallas, Texas 75221

Dear Joe,   11/6/89

I just heard of your mother's
passing, was sorry to hear that.
I trust that she did not suffer
long. I offered prays for her.
I hope you enjoyed the painting
and it arrived with no problems.
When you have the time and feel up
to it I would like to hear from you
Take care for now with deep
Sympathy.

        Best regards
                  John

He Was
A Man of Sorrows
and
Acquainted
With Grief.
He Understands
and Cares

Because he hath set his love upon me, therefore will I deliver
him. I will set him on high, because he hath known my name.
He shall call upon me, and I will answer him; I will be with him
in trouble; I will deliver him and honor him.

Psalms 91:14, 15.

Sympathy card from John Wayne Gacy to Joe Coleman, November 1989
Note Gacy's concern with the duration of suffering—he expertly kept
his torture victims alive as long as possible, and he relished their prolonged pain.
Collection of Joe Coleman

"Fuck the United States. The White race—a fuckin' piece of shit. I hate the White race. Niggers—I hate niggers. I hate Jews. I hate everybody. I only care about anyone who is part of my family, who backs me up."

concentration camps—it's fucking pathetic. It's an easy way to deal with that pain."
Anti-Nazism is what pays in America. "Yeah. I don't give a fuck about Nazis—I think they're assholes. I think White Supremacy is a bunch of bullshit. The only thing I ever cared about was me and my family. There are people who are Blacks, Jews, that I let into my family. Sammy from the band Fang, who strangled his girlfriend—she was not part of my family, but he was, so I protected him. I offered him asylum in South America, but he went north and got caught, served time for murder—but not as much time as my friends who are in for drugs. That's an overwhelming point proving that justice has no meaning."

You once said, "If I didn't become an artist, I would have been a Serial Killer."
"I regret that I ever made the fucking statement. People love it, and I hate it because they love it. Now everybody says it: 'I would have been a Serial Killer if I didn't do embroidery.' I hate it because it was embraced. I felt that way, but once it got digested by the culture it lost its meaning."

Coleman w/ portrait of himself by John Wayne Gacy, 1989
Coleman: "The term 'outsider' is very condescending, and it's used to create a commodity—which really takes away from the purity of it. You're giving it this term in order to sell it with, which corrupts it."
Collection of Joe Coleman

Joe Coleman, portrats of Henry Lee Lucas and Richard Speck, 1987
These ink-on-duotone-paper drawings appeared in *EXIT #4*.
Collection of the author

Everything was moving faster and faster, and the end of my rope was getting shorter and shorter. A patrolman flagged me down. I was faster on the draw and made him get in the trunk of his own car. I used the siren to stop the next car I saw and made the driver and the patrolman get into the new car's trunk. "This could get to be a bad habit," I said to myself. So I drove into the woods, handcuffed my two captives to a tree... I couldn't just leave them there—so I left them with their brains coming out of their ears.

Frame 19, *The Final Days of John Knowles*, 1986
From *Cosmic Retribution: The Infernal Art of Joe Coleman*, Fantagraphics/Feral House, 1992
Collection of the author

I would like to have it known just why I do this. I had no choice about coming into this world, and nearly all my 38 years in it I have had very little to say and do about how I should live my life. People have driven me into doing everything I have ever done. Now the time has come when I refuse to be driven any farther.

　Today I live. Tomorrow I go to the grave. Farther than that no man can drive me. I am sure glad to leave this lousy world and the lousier people in this world. But of all the lousy people in this world, I believe I am the lousiest of 'em all. Today I am dirty, but tomorrow I'll be just DIRT. ●

Frame 21, *Carl Panzram, #31614*, 1987
From *Cosmic Retribution: The Infernal Art of Joe Coleman*, Fantagraphics/Feral House, 1992
Collection of the author

Lydia Lunch, 1984
"Because of my predatory nature, my aggressiveness, my anger, I didn't feel girlie. But I could use the façade that I'm housed in, this ridiculous satiny fleshy vehicle. I loved it."
Photo by Richard Kern
Collection of Daniel Langdon Jones

LYDIA LUNCH: "Promiscuity was definitely my rebellion. It was in order to wipe off or wash off my father's hands and replace them with someone else's. Of course I was attracted to the bad boys."

LUNCH: "I'm either dealing with politics and the victimization of the human condition, or I'm dealing with sexual obsession. Those are my two main themes. I'm always looking for different ways to flavor them and expose them and reveal them and understand them better and speak for other people that I know have these same root elementals that I do. I knew my problem, my pain, my vision, my energy, my sociopathic psychosis was not unique. It's extremely fucking universal. I've always stood outside of everything while being completely connected to everything. I never felt part of any clique or subculture or generation or movement, but I was hooked in. I was also outside of it."

"I started getting high when I was eleven. The first drugs I did were Chocolate Mescaline and Acid. I loved it. I never stopped doing drugs. Once I flopped down right in front of my mother on the kitchen floor, just flying on THC. They didn't like it. I was sent to the suburbs to get me out of the inner city because someone's overdose was blamed on me, although what do I have to do with anyone else's overdose? If they can't handle their drugs it's not my problem. It was her dad's prescription drugs she'd been stealing. I was sent to the suburbs, which made me happy because there were far more drugs there—better quality, too."

"The idea behind my work was a primal scream. Find music that articulated the message—frustration, hatred, anger—and therefore the music was hateful and angry and loud and precise, based around very percussive words."

Above: Lunch with lover Nick Zedd, circa 1982
Collection of Nick Zedd
Below: With long-time boyfriend J.G. Thirlwell, 1987
Photo by Richard Kern
Collection of Daniel Langdon Jones

With Thirlwell in Kern's *Submit To Me Now*, 1985

Paste-up for show poster, *Nightmare South Of Your Border*, Lydia Lunch, 1988
"I'm not saying the individual can take on the entire world, though sometimes it seems like the entire world is pounding down on us. I just think that people need to reorganize, especially at this time. I don't know what this time means, this close to the millennium—whatever the fucking millennium means, whatever the apocalypse is."

Collection of Lydia Lunch

> "Sex: It was like, fuck you, now fuck me. It was a weapon and a tool. And hot. What's to not like? And also, a rebellion against Good Girls Don't. Who wants to be fuckin' good? Fuck that. I want what I want when I want it. And I get it."

"Most people create because they are in trauma. That's why they turn to art in whatever form. They create because they are in pain. At least the good artists. At least when they first start. And I think what divided me was, I knew my pain was not unique and I think when people feel alone they think their pain is unique and that holds them back in so many ways that it never held me back. So I was able to be as rude, as arrogant, as aggressive, as bold, as passionate, as extreme, and as much of a fucking terror as I was.

"Some fucking habits and rituals may have been foisted upon me that may not have been of my own creation. If I were to do something habitually or ritualistically or obsessively, that's fine, so long as I understand that I am doing the driving and not being driven by obsessions which may have been placed in my DNA that I had no hand in creating. I don't want to be a victim of my own cycles—or any one else's cycles. But time travels in cycles, and there are periods in history that are fevered with passionate, violent art."

Richard Metzger: "I went to see *South Of Your Border,* a two-person play with Lydia and Emilio Cubeiro. Emilio played Lydia's drunken father. He raped her with a bottle. She was playing herself as a little girl. Then there was phone sex. You start hearing this loud music that Jim Thirlwell had done. The most infernal racket—chains beaten against a wall—just an evil cacophony of metal and sonics. And the lights come up and Lydia is trussed up, spread-eagled, on a gigantic big fat black wooden X. And she is completely nude. She was so fucking gorgeous. Lydia Lunch was one of the hottest women in New York City at that time. Who was close? And all of a sudden the door is kicked open. Emilio Cubeiro comes in the back. He's got a gun pointing towards her. And she pisses on him for a very long time, from drinking so much beer in the scene before. She must have pissed on him for two minutes. This was not a shy bladder. A big golden shower. A big thick stream of piss. The audience was gasping."

Albums by Thirlwell, a.k.a. Clint Ruin, and Lydia Lunch
Top: *Don't Fear The Reaper* (cover of the Blue Oyster Cult hit), Big Cat Records, 1991; illustration by David Ouimet
Bottom: *Stinkfist,* Widowspeak Records, 1988
Cover photo by Wim V.D. Hulst
Collection of Daniel Langdon Jones

Forced Exposure #10, with Richard Kern's cover photo of Lydia, 1986
Forced Exposure covered some nasty shit, becoming the unofficial organ of transgression.
Publisher & editor, Jimmy Johnson, Waltham, Massachusetts.
Collection of Lydia Lunch

He began circling round me, sniffing, almost snorting. The scent of pussy.
You couldn't mistake it. I was wringing my hands, wiping them off on my
dress, trying to rub the stink down, but that did no good. He grabbed my
right hand and shoved it roughly against his face, breathing deeply. Smiling.
Licking my fingers, sucking off any remaining stains. Slobbering all over
my hand and wrist. His mouth was hot and sticky and he was sticking almost
my whole hand in there. His eyes were glued to mine. My feet nalied in place.
He cupped my face in his grungy paws, made even blacker by the dead woods.
I swore he'd slap the shit outa me. I almost wanted him too. The thought
was making me stickier. Creamier, i was getting weak in the knees. He wouldn't
take his eyes off of me.:"Take your dress off.. take it off.." I didn't
know what to do. So I did it. I took it off. I stood in front of this beautiful
black giant in a tiny, baby-white slip, barely concealing my swollen busoms,
my fat ass, my pouting belly. He was chewing on his lower lip. Biting deeply.
Thinking. :"Run"..he said."Take off little mama..I wanna see your
juicy white ass running for your fucking life, and you best be running fast,
cause I'm gunna be coming right afta ya!" He only needed to say that once.
I was running through the bushes like my life depended on it. Which it
probab ably did. But I couldn"t think about that right now. All I could think
about was the hugh shears he was using to cut down the twigs. And the hack-
saw..and whether or not he'd be bringing them with him. And what he'd do
with them if he did.

The chase didn't go on for very long before i was already bruised. scratche
and exhausted. I wasn't used to all this country living. I didn't know
where the fuck I was. The middle of nowhere. Fucking bushes and trees and
a sprinkling of garbage all around me. I must've been nuts. And getting
crazier by the minute. I could feel him getting closer, closing in. Almost
smell him. He was tracking me like a fucking bloodhound. snaking thru the
woods. He'd be there any second and all I could think was about was the
devastaion of this violation. How big he was. How black. how strong. How much
it was gunna hurt when he was doing to me exactly what he wanted. He was
suddenly towering over me. Pawing me. pulling on my thin little slip, my only
protection. Pulling me closer to him. pressing me into him, grinding against
me. Our little game had him already hard. He was grabbing my ass in giant
handsfull, mauling it, crushing me against him. Squirming against me. Squeezing
me. I was creaming. A victim of my own desires. Playing his little game, only
it was for real. And he's ripping at the meat of my ass. Telling me how good
it

Page from an untitled story by Lydia Lunch, 1988
"I have a humongous ego, which is above any kind of criticism or praise.
Criticism and praise, to my reality, are equally moot subjects. I know I'm creating
for a minority, an intellectual, sexual and political minority."
Collection of the author

Nick Zedd holding preserved human genitalia, 1987
Did you want to hurt other people with your work? "Yes, I wanted to kill my audience. I wasn't thinking about them that much. They were already dead in my mind. I just wanted to entertain myself and shock the audience and help them come alive after they were killed by my movies."
Photo by Clayton Patterson

NICK ZEDD: *"Art is a term like Religion or Existence or Infinity. It's pointless to try and define it. The art world is conservative, and is dictated by economics, money, real estate values. People who control real estate determine who gets the museums, the galleries, the theaters. Having been locked out of those places, we were forced to take an oppositional or insurgent stance. That's how I discovered the Cinema Of Transgression."*

ZEDD: "We who have violated the laws, commands and duties of the avant-garde; i.e., to bore and tranquilize and obfuscate through a fluke process dictated by practical convenience, stand guilty as charged.

"We openly renounce and reject the entrenched academic snobbery which erected a monument to laziness known as 'structuralism' and proceeded to lock out those filmmakers who possessed the vision to see through this charade.

"Since there is no afterlife, the only hell is the hell of praying, obeying laws, and debasing yourself before authority figures. The only heaven is the heaven of sin, being rebellious, having fun, fucking, learning new things, and breaking as many rules as you can. This act of courage is known as Transgression.

"We propose transformation through Transgression—to convert, transfigure and transmute into a higher plane of existence in order to approach freedom in a world full of slaves." —From **Manifesto**, 1985

Above: incidental collage from *Underground Film Bulletin #8,* 1989
Right: Zedd and Susan Manson, 1987
Photo by Marta Jablonski

Underground Film Bulletin #1, 1984
Cover illustration by Nick Zedd
"The present system of film exhibition and distribution is elitist and obsolete. The greed of landlords, theater owners and big film companies has impoverished everyone's lives. We must find new ways to subvert their evil."
Collection of Nick Zedd

> "I used elements of pornography to help people cure themselves of their genital panic—but I used pornography in a very un-erotic way, I think. I was interested in the movements and the mechanical process of penetration."

"Every time I turn on the TV or leave my apartment I'm reminded of what a slithering mass of pulsating excrement the human race is. Especially when I'm forced to be in the same room with one of its less than perfect representatives for an entire weekend.

"I speak of none other than the king of farts, Mr. Richard Kern. To be subjected to his odious presence for more than few minutes is like an entire month of my sordid life. Minutes turn into hours of hellish boredom when Kern opens his snout to embellish his empty life with hatred for those to whom he owes everything.

"On the way to the airport he always makes sure to walk an extra five feet ahead of you so he can appear to be leading the way, even though he doesn't have the slightest idea where he's going. Once we arrive at our destination, say some bastion of misery like Chicago, he always makes sure to jump in the front seat of whatever car we're riding in, in order to give the impression that he's "in charge" even though it's up to the poor shmuck behind the wheel to decide where we're going.

"I let Kern perform these sniveling pranks to boost his ego since I know it makes him feel less of a bozo, and anyone with an inferiority complex as big as his needs all the help he can get. I know he appreciates having me there to remind him of what an asshole he is. I appreciate the way he tries to brag about how much better a filmmaker, art world ass-kisser, and traveling mongoloid he is, too.

"Why is it necessary for Kern to claim the only mattress in our host's apartment, leaving me with an inflatable beach balloon to sleep on, in order to prove his imaginary supremacy as a filmmaker? Forget that our host, seeing through Kern's ploy, decided to stay at his girlfriend's apartment, leaving me his king-sized luxury futon in the luxury suite, much to the fart-master's chagrin.

"The next night, our Chicago hosts set us up in a dingy basement somewhere with no real windows or nite-lite for Kern, who spent the evening trying to think of something good to jerk off to in the dark while I gazed shivering at the eternal blackness of hell for five hours on a rancid lumpy couch. I could see nothing in the pitch-black hole stretching into infinity, preventing me from getting up to piss since I'd never have found my way to the ladder leading to the toilet above without tripping over fifty open paint cans and one dead fartmaster in his bottomless pit of hate.

"As we left, Kern tried his best to run at least five feet ahead of us to give the impression that he was leading the way.

"Once at the boring airport I made note of the fact that all the female flight personnel looked like poodles with their clipped and layered Far-do's, fake smiles, and whining cretin voices. Kern did his best to suck up to the plastic women but needn't have bothered since they were all programmed to be pleasant to us no matter what.

"The rotting stench of Kern's farts assaulted the air, once back in New York, giving me little trouble in figuring out why his beleaguered "wife" abandoned him months ago."
—From **Fuck You**, *Film Threat #12*, 1987

This baby has a swastika on its arm! Nick, did you use swastikas in your work?
"Yeah. Swastikas are always a good way to get a knee-jerk reaction, to piss people off. A timeless symbol. Anything to shock and offend or confront a complacent audience, and anything to be anti-art."
Photo by Marta Jablonski, 1987

83

Flyer for *Police State*, 1987
Violence and brutality saturate your work. "Sure, but there's also humor and tenderness. Genocide is brutal. In comparison, my movies are not at all brutal. They're entertaining."
Illustration by James Rohmberger
Collection of Nick Zedd

Flyer for *Whoregasm* by Nick Zedd, 1988
"I don't know what an 'indie' film is supposed to be. I find the word loathsome, a hypocritical co-opting, in linguistic terms, of a trendy notion that an 'independent' cinema exists somewhere and that it must be morally superior. The rancid values of commercialism imposed by dominant culture are firmly in place with the scum who perpetrate the fraud of 'indie'."
Collection of the author

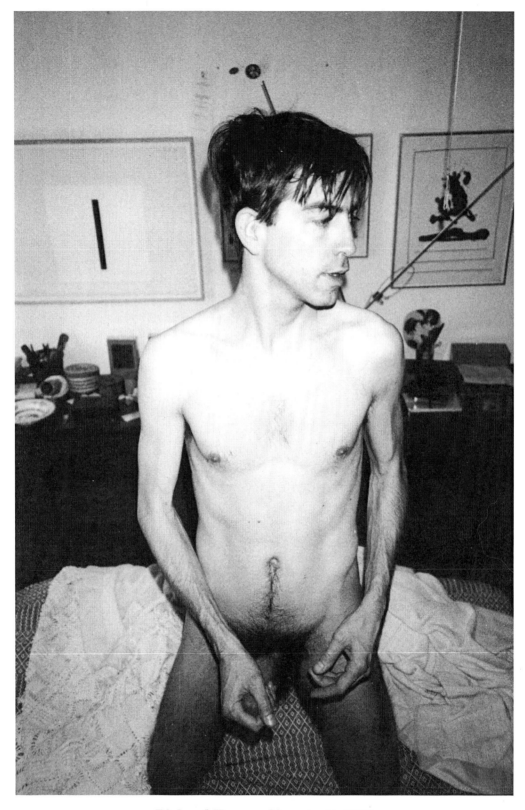
Richard Kern, self-portrait, 1985
"I'm not in my photos. But I made a movie where I'm in the whole movie,
My Nightmare. I usually stay out of the picture."
Collection of Richard Kern

RICHARD KERN: *"I didn't feel I was making art. I felt like I was being a lunatic. Doing anything I wanted. Nobody could tell me what to do. Fuck you to everybody. That was the whole attitude."*

RICHARD KERN: "I was into Nick Zedd, Charles Manson, Black Flag, The Stooges, Eric Kroll et cetera. Nick Zedd created the label 'Cinema of Transgression' but it was something we all identified with. I thought that my lifestyle was very normal. A lot of drugs, a lot of hating everybody—all this basic Punk Rock stuff.

"I thought of myself as someone who did everything, and photography was the common thread. I published fanzines as a outlet for my photos. I made films when I realized they have more impact and it was easier to show films in clubs than to get a photo show in a gallery. I was very anti-art.

"The movie-making and the Heroin were both very anti-sex to me. I depicted sex in a way you didn't see in mainstream movies, where couples kiss and there's candles and a swelling soundtrack. I was more interested in having Audrey Rose getting her nipples pierced, screaming in pain. Or Lydia Lunch and Marty Nation, in *Fingered*, just bitching at each other for the whole movie, and when they eventually have sex it's more like a power trip than like a romantic scene.

"The Heroin focused all my negativity into one place. When I quit Heroin, that negativity dissipated.

"I began taking photos seriously in 1990. Years of drug abuse left me broke. Black-and-white photos were the only medium I could afford. I was burned out on 'messages.' Photography was a fast and fun way to reinvent myself.

"When I got off drugs and ended my deathtrip, it was time to discover sex. Then you get around to discovering money.

"I began working for porno mags to make a living. A lot of the photos I took on porno sets ended up in non-porno mags.

"Presentation defined my work. If a photo appeared in *Hustler*, people saw it differently than if it was in *Artforum*.

"My fascination with voyeuristic photos was that you're never really sure what's a genuine candid image or what's been staged or contrived."

Example of Kern's "Girls With Guns" series, circa 1990
Model: Christina Martinez
Collection of Richard Kern

BLOOD BOY IS AT IT AGAIN

ALL PHOTOS BY R. KERN

As these exposures clearly demonstrate, Richard Kern has been keeping busy this summer shooting more shoestring cinematrocities for the likes of Sonic Youth as their soon to be released video version of Death Valley 69 featuring a cameo appearance by her majesty Lydia Lunch will attest. Also congruent and forthcoming from Mr. K's neurotoxic lens, submit to me a mucoid maledictive meandering

Make my day.

Apparently oneiric in nature featuring the unconscionable lung leg among other helminthiasis. Remember you read it here first.

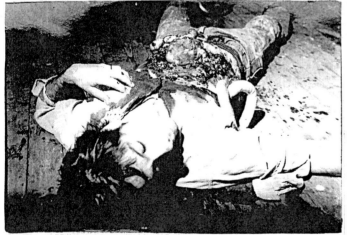

Since I gave up hope I feel much better.

Page from *The Underground Film Bulletin* #4, 1985
Kern: "I started doing photos a lot when I moved to New York City because I had been a sculpture student, and I'd always taken photos. It was easier to do photography in New York City than make big sculpture."
Collection of the author

"There were sexual elements, there were drug elements. For some movies I paid people. I offered them $15 cash or $15 worth of drugs. A lot of people would do the drugs and then we'd shoot the movie. During the shooting of the movie, I was so wasted on Smack and Ecstasy all the time—"

"I try to get people to do interesting things. Sometimes I get lucky and somebody wants to do something strange and really hard.

"The only time people feel exploited by me is when they've worked with me and then made a 180-degree turn, and turn against all the things that they formerly were into. That's pretty common."

"The things I did that really were trouble, I can't talk about, can I? Anybody would be crazy to talk about anything they did." *Statutes of limitation probably have run out.* "I heard that some guy went on the radio and talked about how he didn't pay his taxes, and now he's going to trial. I'm not even talking about taxes; I'm talking about anything.

I used to think it didn't matter if I talk about stuff, but now I think it does. I can talk about abusing drugs, but is that a crime?

"Oh—I guess it is."

Nick Zedd: "I would go over to Kern's apartment and he'd have Dope lying around and he'd be like, 'You want to try some?'" *Was Kern a bad influence???* "I didn't mind. It didn't cost anything. Everybody was doing it. We were all self-medicating for depression at the time."

The Black Snakes, 1987
From left: Richard Kern, Patrick Blank, Darin Lin Wood, Jack Natz
Photo from the album *Crawl*, Radium Records
Guitarist Kern also played with GG Allin and The Workdogs
Photo by Michael Lavine

Flyer for *Fingered*, hand lettering by J.G. Thirlwell, 1986
Kern: "Lydia and I said, 'You want to see some pornography? We'll make a real porno film.' The idea was, be all-out as offensive as possible and not hold back. Although I think we held back. I don't know. Nobody really got killed or anything. The scene where the girl gets slapped around, that was real. Everything was kind of real."
Collection of Steven Blush

**Example of Kern's "Girls With Guns" series, circa 1990
Model: Masha
Collection of Richard Kern**

J.G. Thirlwell, 1985
Photo by Richard Kern
Collection of Daniel Langdon Jones

J.G. THIRLWELL a.k.a. FOETUS: "I do Hate songs as opposed to Love songs. Each one's a complete purge. It gets a lot out of my system—and it puts a lot into my system."

FOETUS: I've been drawing and designing stuff ever since I can remember. In art school I was doing screen prints and oil paintings in flat black, white and red. I did a couple of portraits of Hitler and some real Aryan-looking things in a flat Pop Art style to piss people off. That evolved into combining elements of Chinese Revolutionary art, Russian Revolutionary art, and World War Two propaganda, and was always restricted to red, white and black. Then I got bold and introduced gray. Then I got even bolder and put yellow in there. As it evolved, it got more into the idea of Pop Art packaging, to the point where I'd roam the aisles looking at packaging. I juxtaposed that with Japanese cartoon imagery and started to go in that direction.

SECONDS: *When you painted Hitler, were you elevating a sinister character to Pop icon status?*

FOETUS: It was basically experimentation in that style. I thought it was a perverse thing to do. That was the extent of my shock-value Nazi stuff. I just liked the idea of it hanging on the walls. When I started putting out records, the covers became the avenue for my designs in art. Apart from *EXIT*, that's pretty much my oeuvre over the last fifteen years — my covers and the ones for Lydia Lunch.

SECONDS: *How about the word "Foetus"?*

FOETUS: It's the lowest common denominator. It has a million meanings to me. It's gotten to the point where that's who I am and that's what people call me. It's probably more my name than Thirlwell.

SECONDS: *Did that name ever get you a negative reaction out of Pop officialdom?*

FOETUS: I could have signed a major deal in '83 if I changed the name from "You've Got Foetus On Your Breath." I'm not going to compromise. I'm not going to change my aesthetic vision for some suit. If I didn't have control of every minor detail, I wouldn't do it. I've bounced from label to label and for me, my art comes first and commerce comes second. I've had bad luck with record labels but I'm really proud of what I've accomplished.

SECONDS: *You've always managed to retain artistic control of your products.*

FOETUS: That's never been an issue with me. People know me. It doesn't even come up in conversation.

SECONDS: *Then why do you have bad luck with record companies?*

FOETUS: Because I'm surrounded by a black cloud.

FOETUS: I try to play down this "Industrial" tag, but they keep saying, "If you listen to Ministry and Nine Inch Nails, you know where it came from," and all that sort of stuff. Al Jourgensen, Trent Reznor and me are considered this triumvirate of Industrial Music—and I hate the term "Industrial." How can you put on one of my Big Band songs and say it's Industrial? It's Foetus music. I have a Musique Concrete side, I have a Big Band side, a Punk Rock side, a random noise side.

J.G. Thirlwell, *Phillip And His Foetus Vibrations* 7"
Self-Immolation/Cherry Red, 1981
"Tell Me, What is the Bane of Your Life?"
b /w "Mother I've Killed the Cat"
Collection of Daniel Langdon Jones

Promo shot for *HOLE* LP, J.G. Thirlwell, 1984
Photo by Peter Anderson
Inset: With Anton Lavey, 1990, photographer unknown
Collection of Daniel Langdon Jones

What does the 'G' in J.G. Thrilwell stand for?
"Whatever you want it to. God, Genius, Godzilla, Gregarious."

SECONDS: *Didn't that term "Industrial" exist before you even began?*
FOETUS: That label existed concurrently with my start. When Monte Cazazza came up with the term, I was already making pure white noise on primitive synthesizers and hitting on metal. I was doing weird things with two cassette machines and pots and pans, overdubbing back and forth, really distorting the microphones so you'd end up with this distorted percussion track, and then I'd play noise elements on top of that.

"I used to bandy around terms like 'aesthetic terrorism' and 'positive negativism.'" *Tell us about the term 'aesthetic terrorism'.* "That got co-opted by Adam Parfrey. He named a chapter of *Apocalypse Culture* 'Aesthetic Terrorism' and started using it."

"I provided music for some of Kern's films, but I was doing my thing quite independent of what he was doing. We intersected, but I intersect with a lot of people. Kern definitely had an aesthetic which was a candy-coated version of what his life was. Sex and drugs and messing around in New York. A snapshot of that time. When you look back on it through the shrouds of time, it gets compressed. The years '83 to '88. It becomes very romantic."

Did you get hurt in the course of your performance? "Yeah." *Did you hurt other people?* "Yeah, now and then."

"My work's analogous to other things. There's a violence and intensity. It's all an allegory to self-destruction. I wanted to make the ultimate record before the world comes to an end. There was that feeling. Hugeness. Finality, majesty. The beauty that happens that second before the world splits apart."

"I wanted to sound louder than everything else. I transposed that onto my graphic identity. I wanted loud graphics."

SECONDS: *Is it important to be confrontational?*
FOETUS: I don't think it's confrontational, I think it's pure design. Maybe there's some violent imagery in there but I think it's really humorous. I think it's cool to reclaim the swastika. It's still too politically loaded.
SECONDS: *How do you feel about that?*
FOETUS: I like the power of it and I don't take any offense to it. I'd love to be able to exploit it more. I used to wear swastika rings. If someone with a concentration camp tattoo saw me, they wouldn't know the spirit in which I'm wearing it. I'm conscious of being insensitive.

From *USA Today*, "sometime in '85":
Q: *You're a bit of a Satanist.*
A: No, not at all. I don't think I'm a Satanist at all. I just use a lot of Heaven and Hell analogies for life. But hell, I'm the new Messiah!

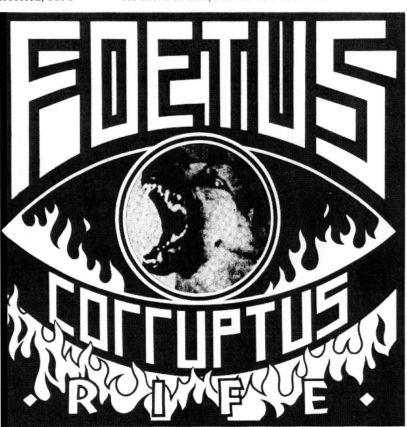

Cover of the album *RIFE*, Thirlwell d/b/a Foetus Corruptus, 1988
Graphics by Thirlwell
An auto-bootleg; a dispute with label Some Bizzare motivated the artist to self-release this ersatz rip-off of the legit album.
Collection of Daniel Langdon Jones

Fred Berger, 1991
World War Two Historical Reinactment Federation,
12th SS Panzer Division Hitler Jugend, "Hitler's Baby Division"
**Photo by Herbert List
Collection of Fred Berger**

FRED BERGER: "The Devil does God's dirty work. I see good and evil as mutually supportive. In the end, everyone pretty much does what they have to do—call it necessity or predestination. We don't have much choice in the matter."

BERGER: "When my magazine, *Propaganda*, reached marginally mass-circulation status as the preeminent Gothic music and lifestyle periodical in America, I took full advantage of the fact that I had an eager audience whose sexual appetite was not exactly something out of Norman Rockwell's America. With their predilection for all things dark, including fetishism and S&M, my fetish photography was bound to have an impact. Pretty soon I was being contacted by hordes of enthusiasts eager to model and commit any abomination for the camera."

"I'm a control freak and perfectionist who prefers to work with a clean canvas, to turn the model into my own personalized *objet d'art,* my own pristine, ungraffitied idol."

"I'm completely art-free. My physical surroundings would appeal as much to a Taliban mullah as to a blind man. All my art is in my head, at my fingertips, and behind my camera lens."

Was there such a thing as Nazi chic? "Nobody ever dared call it that. It was military fetishism. Some people would call it fascistic chic or military chic but the 'N' Word was never actually used. Same old taboo. The 'N' Word. People shy away from it. The only time I ever heard the word used was by store owners asking me, why do you put Nazis in *Propaganda?* Middle-aged Jewish record store owners griping about the Nazi shit in the magazine. But yet they carried it, they sold it, they advertised in it. But to assuage any guilt complex they might have had, they had to raise the issue. They didn't feel good until they raised it. Then I would say, well, why call it Nazi? Why not just call it military chic? Why label it Nazi? We were not using swastikas, SS runes or any other Nazi symbols. It was just an Evil Empire look, which could have been as relevant to the Soviet Union or Darth Vader. It had a bad-boy look.

"Technically there were no Nazi symbols in *Propaganda*. You see that stuff with the Hell's Angels, Pagans, motorcycle gangs. Those guys were using in-your-face overt Nazi imagery, whereas the Industrial, Gothic, military fetish crowd shy away from more overt Nazi imagery, in favor of a more sinister, militaristic imagery which would entail black leather, form-fitting uniforms, riding boots, combat boots—that kind of thing. But it was not specifically Nazi or even fascistic. It just had that bad-guy military look."

"Anton LaVey, for instance: Satanism and Nazism have had quite a lot of linkage. It just so happened Anton LaVey, who established the Church of Satan in 1966, had the largest and most valuable collection of Nazi regalia in the United States. And he was Jewish, by the way. He was the ultimate rebel. How better to rebel against his whole background of Judaism, than to be a gangster—a Satanist? Satan is the arch-enemy of mankind in the Jewish scriptures.

"I think I must be the only person to ever photograph dykes in Hitler Youth boy-scout uniforms. A lot of these man-hating bitches consider themselves 'some kind of boy' anyway. They were happy to play the roles of Gay boys in uniforms."

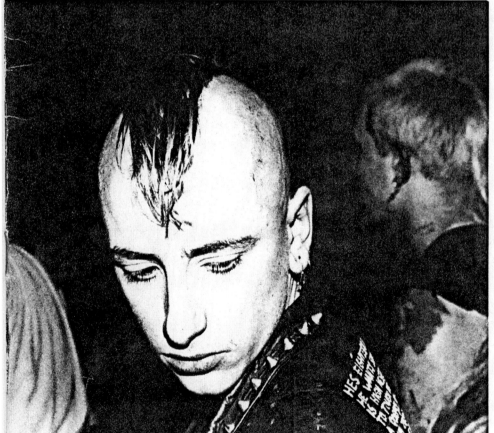

Propaganda #1, 1982
Photo & drawing by Fred Berger

> *"A dark, menacing sensuality and aesthetic has always been at the core of my artistic vision. Everything from the Holy Inquisition to Nazi pageantry to nuclear warfare to the sordid lives of junkie prostitutes to the Apocalyptic ravings of prophets and madmen fascinates me."*

And not only did LaVey collect Nazi regalia, but he had political connections with right-wing organizations like the National Front in England or the Werewolves in Austria. In fact, his daughter Zeena LaVey was one of the top members of the Werewolves in Austria, which is a neo-Nazi organization. So this whole thing of Satanism, militarism, fascist militarism, armies of darkness—you take your motorcycle gangs, your Goths, your fetish people, your Satanists, they all identify with this nebulous army of darkness. It starts at a very early age. It's fetishistic. It includes sado-masochism, bondage-and-discipline, master-and-slave, and pleasure-and-pain mentalities which look up to the archetype of the Nazi Slave Master. And of course the victim, whether a concentration-camp victim or a prisoner of war, is the Ultimate Slave or the Ultimate Victim. It totally fits in with the whole S&M mindset. So many bands from that era bought into that.

"The Punks more than anyone were shameless about their use of the swastika. The Sex Pistols and the early Banshees were just festooned with swastikas. It wasn't a political statement. It was saying, 'I am an enemy of society.'

"I met a Jewish Hells Angel who had the SS runic symbols stenciled onto his gas tank. I asked him if that was any kind of a political statement. He said, 'No, it's not political, because I'm Jewish, but I'm a rebel without a cause and that's the ultimate symbol of rebellion.'"

Untitled, 1994

Who's the court philosopher of Nazi chic? "In terms of racial philosophy, Michael Moynihan. In terms of ethical philosophy, Boyd Rice. He always shied away from the ethnocentric aspects of it and more towards the ethical aspects of fascist philosophy. You have to break it down. I'd say Moynihan was more ethno-centric. This is very dangerous stuff, if it gets in the hands of the wrong people."

"I thought the swastika was over-used and cliché. It had too much baggage. The Goth-Industrial fetish scene had military trappings and favored a more European exotic military look." *Like Laibach?* "Laibach is a good example of that. Or Death In June. Boyd Rice, Michael Moynihan. As far as Moynihan goes, you could read a certain amount of fascistic politics into it. But Death In June—it's all about frustrated homoerotic desire. Goths were into Death In June. Few of them realized the skull logo of Death In June was the World War Two SS skull. Of course I recognized that fact.

"Death In June is the embodiment of military fetish, or fascist fetish, imagery. People in the Goth scene are misanthropes, alienated. There was so much crossover: Goth, Industrial, and fetish. But they were all alienated and misanthropic, countercultural."

"My father is Jewish, my mother is a Catholic. That gives me a unique perspective.

Untitled, 1990
Photo by Fred Berger

"Religion is an extension of tribalism and politics. It has very little to do with spirituality. As for the occult, I've seen it at work—it's like playing with fire. Visualization, the imagination focused like a laser beam, is a very powerful tool. But beware the hazards of unintended consequences; once you've called something into being, it takes on a life of its own. Just think Frankenstein's monster."

I'm against organized religion of any sort. I'm as fond of my Jewish relatives as I am of my Gentile relatives. Once you remove ethnicity and nationalism and patriotism and religious dogma, it's easy for people to get along."

"My masterpiece of erotic fiction masquerading as fact was a feature entitled 'Anarchy In Moscow.' I wrote and photographed it based on articles I'd read in the mainstream press about the social collapse of the former Soviet Union in the late Nineties. The protagonist of that gritty and frightfully realistic fairy tail was a Russian male prostitute and junkie, Dmitri. Little did anyone know he was portrayed by a young waitress from New Jersey, who I disguised in boy-drag and photographed on suitably rundown 'Soviet' streets in downtown Manhattan.

I could have never anticipated the storm of controversy that followed. People were either horrified or infatuated. Never has any feature I've ever published received nearly so much attention—from the international press, from Focus On The Family, a right-wing family-values activist group, from film and TV producers, from sociology professors, from European art galleries, and from anonymous individuals claiming to be Federal undercover agents intent on shutting me down. Almost overnight, *Propaganda* went from being the American Gothic house organ to being the target and the darling of diverse special interests, agencies, principalities and powers— all either hostile or supportive. There was no middle ground."

Untitled, 1984

Untitled, 1989

Page 25, *Propaganda* #25, 1998
This innocent-looking layout got the mag banned in Germany
Lyrics by Douglas P. of Death In June
Photo & text by Fred Berger
From the *Propaganda* archive

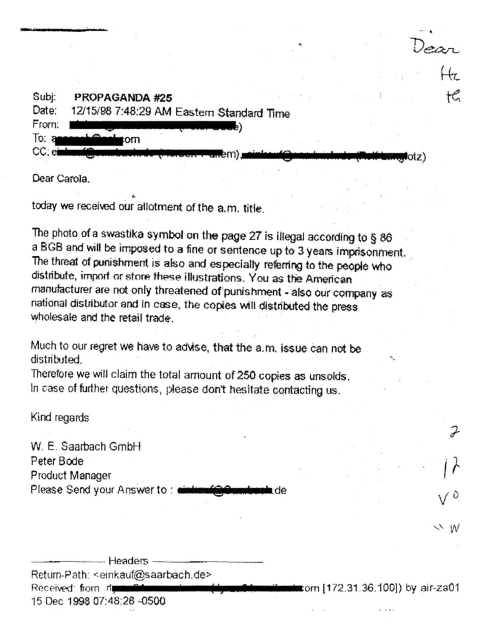

email letter from a distributor re: *Propaganda* Magazine, 1998
An example of the problems faced by politically minded artists
Berger: "The Hitler Youth photo in *Propaganda* #25 violated the German denazification laws. This resulted in the permanent banning of *Propaganda* from German distribution. The letter is from my German distributor to my American shipping broker. The refusal to distribute the issue resulted in the destruction of 250 copies of *Propaganda* #25. The photo was taken with authentic Hitler Jugend paraphernalia from my military collection, in Palisades State Park, New Jersey—a popular Gay trysting park. The model is a 22-year-old American lesbian. The title 'Fog Of The World' is a Death In June song about a Hitler Jugend boy who has a homosexual tryst with an executioner in the Tiergarten zoo and park in Berlin. The song was inspired by the novel *Funeral Rites* by the Gay author Jean Genet, a personal favorite of mine and Douglas P."
From the *Propaganda* archive

Jonathan Shaw, 1995
Photo by Amy Fields

JONATHAN SHAW: *"The first time I peeped into the window of a tattoo shop, I could see something romantic and occult and otherworldly and attractive going on, and that's where I wanted to be. When I was a kid it was sailors, it was bikers, it was other criminal types and antisocial types, and I looked into that world and said, 'That's where I belong.'"*

Q: *Tell us about tattooing in New York City when it was illegal.*
SHAW: It was great. There was a handful of us; we were elite. We had the place to ourselves. It was totally underground. It was wonderful.
Q: *Were the police looking to shut you down?*
A: No, no. The police were my friends. I tattooed them—it wasn't a criminal matter.
Q: *Were there ever problems with the patrons?*
A: Oh sure. It was a bloody mess. We had to beat people out the door every fuckin' day. It wasn't some nail-salon tattoo shop like you have now. Back then, you'd better be "Ready for Freddy." We had death threats, so it was always dangerous—and you had to be prepared to defend yourself.

"In the world I lived in, everybody had tattoos, everybody was a scumbag, and I wound up getting a tattoo here, a tattoo there—and when I started getting professional tattoos, I watched very closely the process that the old tattoo guy was using, and thought to myself, 'I could do this.'

"Back in those days it was very hard to get information about tattooing. You had to spy on people, pick up bits and pieces of information here and there. Nobody would just take you and say, 'Well, here's a tattoo gun and here's how you work it,' pat you on the back and good luck. It was more like you were trying to infiltrate some terrorist group. They weren't going to give up that information."

"I'd always been interested in design patterns for their own sake, nothing representational. I started seeing tattooing as something bold and tribal, and experimented with using the body as a canvas for decorative purposes. I started working with some things loosely based on pre-Columbian tribal patterns but I got more into an urban take—my own take—on it, so there's a lot of jaggy, pointy edges, graffiti-esque but more of a bold, silhouette style, or black and white, positive-negative work. It was a style I started playing around with—and nobody had ever seen anything like it. That style eventually emerged through a confluence of circumstances, with me putting certain high-profile tattoos on certain high-profile people that ended up being what is now today's stock-in-trade in the tattoo business. You can't walk into a tattoo shop anywhere in the world without seeing stuff that evolved from my primitive doodlings into what they call today 'tribal' style, which is probably the most popular style of tattooing in the world today—and it evolved out of a kid doodling at school."

Joe Coleman received a tattoo from Mr. Shaw! Collection of Jonathan Shaw

---

"That was in the mid-Eighties up until the turn of the century. I was sucked up into tattooing as a full-time profession, a career, and I got a lot of fame and glory out of that, a lot of cash and prizes, and at the same time on some primal level I started to get signals that I was betraying what I'd originally got into tattooing for. It went with my lifestyle as an outsider, an outcast, an orphan, a person with a lust for adventure and seeing the world and experiencing heightened situations and edgy adventures—then I wound up stuck in a routine of running a tattoo shop and being some kind of a nine-to-five guy. Of course it was nine at night until five in the morning, but it was still an everyday thing. Then the media started coming around because of some of the people I tattooed who were these lost creatures in the Punk Rock shadows, suddenly starting to become well-known and selling records, and next thing you know I'm getting called on to tattoo this big guy or that big guy, and next

Skull tattoo, 1985
Tattoo & photo by Jonathan Shaw

"Just like in a primitive culture —which is what this decadent criminal society is —I became a shaman of negativity. I attracted bad spirits around me, and I attracted occult elements into my life. I was tattooing these people and practicing these rituals that have great power. I attracted some pretty mean-spirited occult powers into my life."

thing I'm on television all the time and they're interviewing me for magazines, and next thing it's David Letterman, and I'm running around with fuckin' movie stars and jumping in and out of limousines and attending all these hoity-toity functions.

"Along with that I was an alcoholic and drug addict from a very early age, and as that lifestyle progressed, so did my alcoholism and disease, and eventually I wound up hitting all sorts of bottoms. I liked all kinds of drugs. I liked your drugs. Because I didn't have to pay for much, because I was a VIP. I was the man, I had the ink, so a lot of drug dealers were just throwing stuff at me, because everybody wanted to be in my good graces, so I could pretty much get anything I wanted and that took its toll on me. Towards the end of the Eighties things were getting real ugly and in the early Nineties I had to put down the liquor and drugs and start seeking a more spiritual lifestyle to recover from that. When it all crashed and burned, I had to stop."

"A heavily-tattooed person is a threatening image to square society. That's one of the reasons I was so attracted to it. It was the antithesis of everything square society would have you think is good and clean and wholesome. It was a big fuck-you to most people."

"I created a real first-class magazine, *Tattoo International,* that was very educational and edifying to tattooing. Sadly, most people who get tattooed only buy the magazines to cut the pictures out so they can take it to their local scab vendor and have a handy set of references from which they pirate other people's creativity. As long as you don't expect tattooing to rise above that, then you're not going to be disappointed. But I was writing about the history and traditions of tattooing. We were trying to inform, educate and entertain with this magazine. Unfortunately, most of our readership can't even read. It just goes with the territory."

Jonathan Shaw and Marilyn Manson, 1996
Photographer unknown

Demon tattoo, 1986
Tattoo & photo by Jonathan Shaw

**Hells Angels backpiece tattoo, 1987
Tattoo & photo by Jonathan Shaw**

UFO cult tattoo, 1989
Tattoo & photo by Jonathan Shaw

Photo by Fred Berger, 1984

KILLER CLOWNS

Model: Debbie Osgood

IN-STOCK OIL PAINTING INVENTORY LIST   effective April 1990

10X14" canvas panels
SKULL CLOWN.......................$39.00 each
SINGLE or DOUBLE SKULL, SINGLE or
DOUBLE WITCH HEADS......$39.00 each

22X28" Classic Velour Paintings....$29.00 each
EMMETT KELLY CLOWN HEAD with
Umber or Green background
MICKEY MOUSE in formal, Purple or Hot
Pink background
ELVIS THE KING of Rock 'N Roll in Light Blue,
Yellow or Tan background

10X14" CHRIST.......................$39.00 each
Background colors: Purple, Lime Green, Rose,
Orange or Blue. I express my feelings
with the absence of color.

16X20" canvas panels...............$49.00 each
HOLLYWOOD MONSTERS Collection of
five famous characters
EROTIC BUTTERFLY 'N FLOWER
Bright and bold

JOHN WAYNE GACY CLOWNHEADS
14X18" POGO The Clown
16X20" PATCHES The Clown
Both faces are registered with the American
Clown Club, includes actual autographed
color photo.......................Both $79.00 each

Classic Collector HI HO SERIES
16X20" canvas panels
1984 HI HO in the Fall............$69.00 each
16x20" only a few left
1986 HI HO in the Mine..........$69.00 each
16X20" only a few left - No two alike
1988 HI HO in the Spring.......$79.00 each
16X20" Brand New May 90
HI HO around the Campfire..$89.00 each
Unique and unorthodox style, Impasto
raised paint, Bright Bold Colors!!!

16X20" canvas panels
AMERICAN INDIAN CHIEFS
662 Chiefs Dull Knife and Geronimo
663 Chiefs Blackhawk and Quanah Parker
664 Chiefs Sitting Bull and Red Cloud
665 Chiefs Josephs and Tecumseh
Set of eight for $239.00 or $69.00 each
Each painting comes with informative
background of CHIEFS on the back

Signature BIRD PAINTINGS (Acrylic)
14X18" single canvas................$39.00 each
One 14X18" and two 8X10"....$49.00 set
Please request particular bird wanted,
single or set: Blue Birds, Cardinals, Gold
Finches, Hummingbirds, Sparrows, or
Orioles. All ink-signed by the artist

COMMISSIONED PORTRAITS (Oils)
16X20" or 18X24"......................$299.00 each
Please enclose 5X7 color photo, chest up
only, and detailed description of eye, hair,
lip and skintone color. Allow six weeks,
Prepaid on ordering

COMMISSIONED PAINTINGS (Oils)
16X20" canvas panel...............$199.00 each
Any subject except portrait, Allow six weeks,
Prepaid on ordering

PRISON POLICY!!!!! NO CASH OR PERSONAL CHECKS!!!!!
Send money orders only, no more than $50.00 each. Orders over that amount send several money orders to equal the order amount. Certified checks accepted. Checks Payable to: John W. Gacy, N00921, Box 711, Menard IL 62259-0711. All paintings are done on real canvas panels and are mailed first class. Allow 14 days from arrival of check before painting is sent.

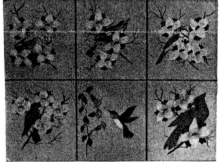

First circulated price list of paintings by John Wayne Gacy, 1988
Collection of the author

A few excerpts from the letters included in this first volume:

Your strength of character, innovation of technique, and force of will uniquely illustrate this profound connection. The aesthetic purity of your example will never be forgotten. Someday, perhaps, in a more enlightened epoch, you will be appreciated as the hero who most convincingly cut through the falsehoods of the day.

Sincerely,
Truman Capote

I would like to keep writing to you if that's ok? I would like to have you as a friend; I live in these back woods with my parents and it gets awfully lonely. I would also like to tell you, you can call me anytime

Hi John,
THANK YOU EVER SO MUCH FOR THE LOVELY LETTER AND THE EXAMPLES OF YOUR FINE WORK IN OILS... THE COLORS ARE RIVETING! I LOVE ANY ARTWORK THAT HAS A UNIQUE ESSENCE BORN OF COLOR USE... YOUR WORK IS TRULY THE RESULT OF A GOD-GIVEN INSIGHT.

Seek out And Find The Answers To The unknown. Take up the Responsibility of getting involved And wanting to know ALL The Facts before passing Judgement on Someone
Thank you For your Letters Please write again
GOD Bless you
John WAYNE GACY

Dear Mr. Gacy,
My name is Oprah Winfrey and I am host of "AM Chicago", a live talk show.

Oprah

9-23-85

Excerpts here reduced in size to accommodate space restrictions, reproduced actual size in the book.

John Gacy will not receive any monetary compensation from the sale of this book.

**Ad for *They Call Him Mr. Gacy: Selected Correspondence of John Wayne Gacy*
Compiled by C. Ivor McClelland, 1990**

Gacy was the first Serial Killer to impact Underground Art. Many individuals corresponded with him; this book outed them. McClelland wrote, "It is not our purpose to evaluate, to define, to influence. That is our reader's prerogative. We hope that you will find this book useful in understanding the American scene and the individuals who comprise it."
According to Arthur Deco, "The Gacy book of letters was more like a bunch of photocopies in a binding. I think Rick Staten in Louisiana helped put it together."
Collection of the author

John Wayne Gacy N00924
Lock Box 711
Menard Illinois
USA 62259

Execute Justice... Not People!!!
George Petros
P.O. Box ▮▮▮▮
New York, New York 10011
May 25th, 1990

Greeting George,
Its been awhile since hearing from you, so I have enclosed my new oil painting list.

Regarding some illustrations you want done you will have to tell me more of what your looking for and the size doesn't determine the price as all commissioned work runs the same price
I can do any size you like in a ink drawing, actually the smaller it is the harder to work any detail into them. You say some but didn't give me a number.
And I also don't know what EXIT Magazine looks like to see if I would want to be in it I am sure you have back issues maybe you could send one. That way I can see just how serious a magazine it is.
By the way lets cut through the bullshit its not my art your interested in its the use of the name, you have one of my favorite artist in Joe Coleman and I do not know aileen Getty, so I don't know what her bag is. insofar as Nikolas Schreck, he I would rather not know as he is a phoney and a fraud from the work go, a guy who never amounted to anything in his life and feeds off other people by using them to feel important.

Regarding the price being a business man and knowing my prices are wholesale to begin with I can't see how I can cut them lower then what I gave to Adam Parfrey and thats with him selling some of my other works to get his drawing done the way he wanted it as his too was a commissioned work, I would not be fair to him nor changing my policy knowing its going to be used to do the same thing he did and thats exploit the name.
So that I will leave upto you to decide as you know where I am. Say Hi to Joe and Adam, I haven't heard from either of them in a while.

Look forward to hearing from you and please explain exactly what your looking for and how it will be used.

Regards,
John

cc/file

Letter from John Wayne Gacy to the author, 1990
Herein Gacy offers opinions of several scenesters such as Joe Coleman and Nikolas Schreck. He reveals a cautious, cantankerous nature in dealing with me, as I represented a magazine and wanted something out of him. Perhaps one of my friends tipped him off that I was an asshole. Who knows? I wound up using his art without his permission.
Collection of the author

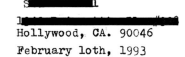
Hollywood, CA. 90046
February 10th, 1993

HI Ho Stuart,

Got your letter and no I haven't forgotten you. I don't know enough about your dick since you not relating any storys, hell you seem to have more time then me anyway. I am sure you met some new encounters.

In any case this letter is short since I have ten more to get out today. Your painting is coming along fine in fact I am looking at it right now you and I are done the grass is in now all I need are the tombstones and fences.

I am sure your anxious, but I move faster with the ones paying full price so keep that in mind too. besides filling in the listed ones which are selling I had four before you and now 6 more special orders came in. Keep in mine I had to design your while the others send photos of what they wanted.

But keep you pants on or maybe in your case off and the painting will be coming out with my next visit which is on the 21st. Keep in mind too we have had damp weather one day cold the next day warm and that has alot to do with the drying of the works.

That plus trying to handle about 40 letters a week too. I also had legal filinf to do and everything else comes to a stop when that happens which put me futher behind.

Hell give me a break I have to jack off too, your not the only one.

So go beat it for another week or so and it will be out before the end of the month and you have my word on that. I don't like to sit on them long, just that since the middle of December I have worked on three legal brief and you don't tell the federal courts they got to wait. let see you put together legal filings of 150 pages, 12/15/92, 68 pages 12/29/92, 38 pages January 21st. and now this last week 14 more pages. in January I received 309 pieces of mail and I worte 151 letters and how was your month. you must have gotten lucky sometime.

later,
John

write and fill me in bum butt.

Letter from John Wayne Gacy to unspecified party, 1993
Herein Gacy reveals his system of painting and hustling while incarcerated.
Note his reference to the drying times of his oil paintings. He kept plenty busy.
He settled into Death-Row life in the mid-Eighties and cranked out hundreds of works
before being put to sleep on May 10, 1994.
Collection of Arthur Deco

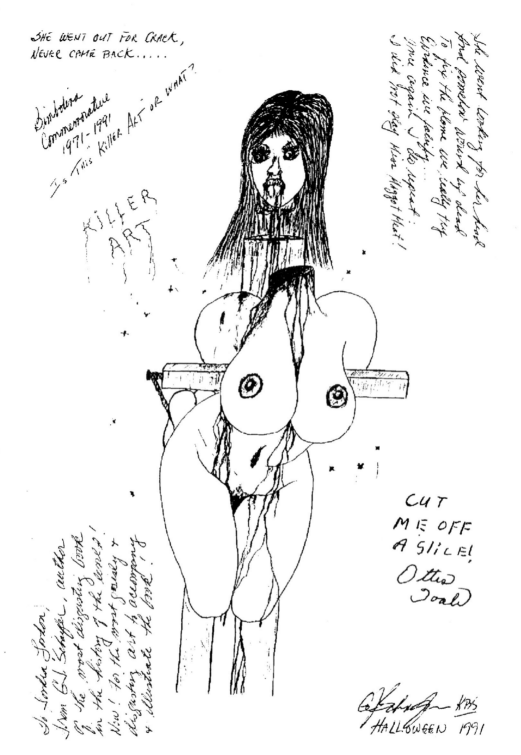

Untitled drawing, Gerald Schaefer & Ottis Toole, for Sondra London, Halloween 1991
Sondra London: "Once Schaefer learned that there was a market for killer art, there was no stopping him. In this stylized scene of sexual violence, he reveals a mind like an unholy mix of Marquis de Sade and Colonel Parker. In presenting his Halloween gift, he boasted of how he had increased its material value by having a fellow Serial Killer inscribe an endorsement. Thus the desecration of the flesh of a human soul is reduced to nothing more than a campy jape by this demented manipulator, who had been pimping Ottis Toole for one advantage or another ever since he met him in prison in 1986."
Collection of Sondra London

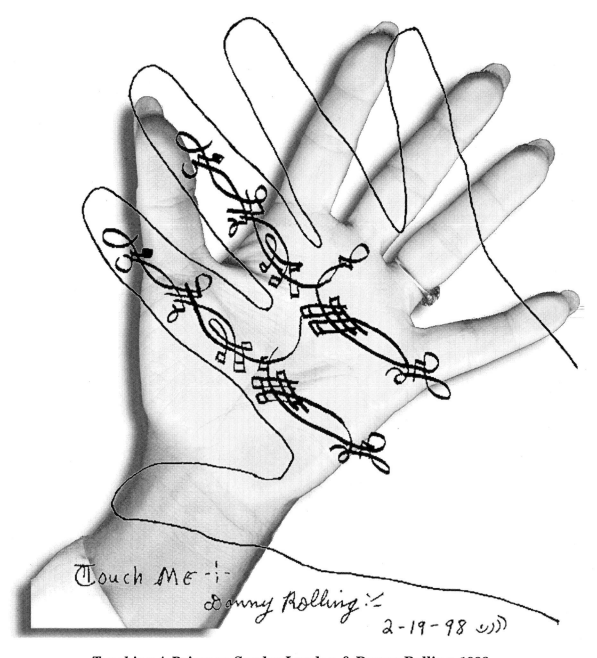

Touching A Prisoner, **Sondra London & Danny Rolling, 1998**

Sondra London was a favorite of several A-list Serial Killers. To the horror of law enforcement, she carried on a romance with Florida Death Row occupant Rolling. London: "Just as a blind person develops the sense of hearing, so correspondents separated by distance and the law develop ways to stay in touch. A prisoner will extend the hand in correspondence by drawing its outline the same way we learn to do in kindergarten. Danny superimposes a fanciful design within the outline that demonstrates there is more to his sense of self than just what is physically evident. In extending himself, he offers that extra dimension of imagination as well as the corporeal man. Sending someone an outline of your hand means you extend your hand in greeting and welcome. So how does the office-bound recipient of such a gesture respond? It seems only natural to scan the image of their own palm, superimpose it on the prison-drawn sketch, and send it back."

Collection of Sondra London

Portraits of Nick Bougas by various Serial Killers, circa 1985-1993
Among the earliest archivists and acquaintances of Serial Killers, Nick Bougas solicited portraits of himself from his friends behind bars.
Above, clockwise from top left: Danny Rolling, Ottis Toole, Richard Ramirez, Henry Lee Lucas.
Nick had a knack for eliciting goodwill from these and other monsters.
From him the killer bug spread; Underground hipsters raced to accumulate memorabilia and foster friendships with the new heroes of upside-down America: Serial Killers!
Collection of Nick Bougas

Portraits of Nick Bougas by various Serial Killers, circa 1985-1993
Above, clockwise from top left: Herbert Mullin, William Bonin, Lawrence Bittaker, Kenneth Bianchi.
Collection of Nick Bougas

Photo by Andrew Novick, 1994

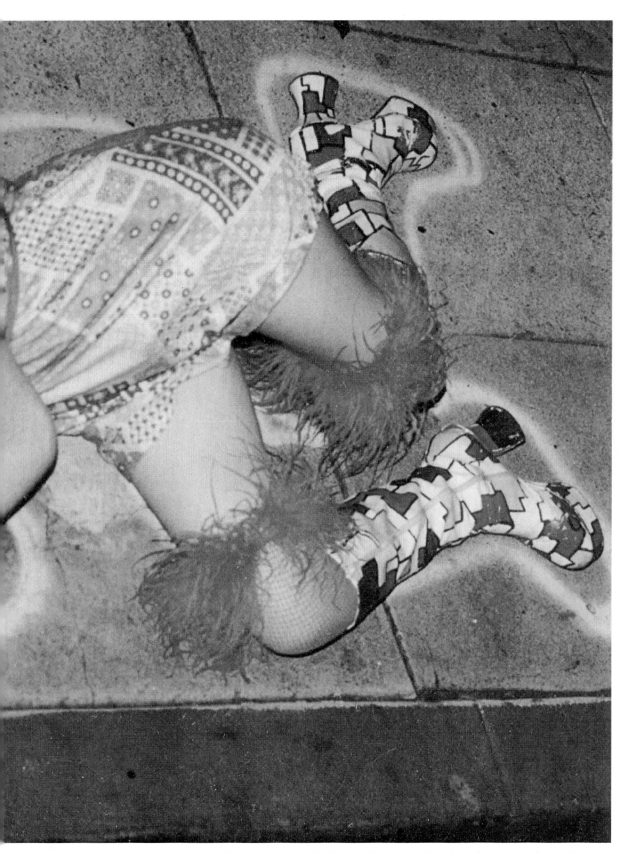

Giddle Partridge: "That's me right in front of the Viper Room in Los Angeles, 1994, lying in the spray-painted chalk lines of where River Phoenix dropped and died on the Sunset Strip!"
Collection of Giddle Partridge

Boyd Rice, 1986
Photo by Nick Bougas

BOYD RICE: *"My work has created a sea change in popular culture. When I started doing my thing, very few people were thinking in that direction. Now there are tens of thousands, who have created a culture. I always thought that a single person could have an exponential effect, and that turned out to be true."*

SECONDS: *Why exactly do people get this Nazi impression?*
RICE: Because they're just such Liberal Humanists that they think anytime you start making judgments about anything in life it's fascistic.

Things have gotten to the point where anytime you state some intrinsic truth like, "Some people are stupid, and some people are smart; some people are weak, some people are strong," it identifies you as a Nazi or Fascist.

I think basically I am a Fascist, because I do think there is a hierarchy and there are people that are stupid and there are people that are clever. I've seen that throughout my entire life, so I can't deny it just because it's pleasant to avoid hurting somebody's feelings.

SECONDS: *How did you get involved with Racialist ideas?*
RICE: Well, people misunderstand my whole slant on that. They think I'm some sort of racial idealist and I feel I'm just a cynic and a realist.

The reason most people don't relate to ideas concerning race is because most of the people into those ideas are starry-eyed idealists. That's ultimately why people like Hitler failed. They were just idealistic and didn't look at things in a realistic manner. I have a very low opinion of the human race.
SECONDS: *How does that opinion apply to yourself?*
RICE: You know, I think part of it is reactionary, being sick of this White-male bashing going on.

"I prefer not to talk about Nikolas Schreck because I don't think he created anything of lasting value and I don't think he deserves attention." *But you did have an association with him.* "There was a time when everything clicked. A friend of mine came back from L.A. with a flyer for Schreck's band, Radio Werewolf. It was a pile of human skulls and a picture of Hitler screaming. Radio Werewolf was Goebbels' propaganda show at the end of the war, exhorting people to drown the enemy in an ocean of blood. Charles Manson sent me Schreck's phone number, so I called him up. When we met, in a Los Angeles restaurant, the bill came out to six dollars and sixty-six cents. We thought, 'Whoa!' The fact that he dressed up like a monster in black and wore make-up and painted his fingernails black didn't bother me because it seemed like he was in this novelty Rock Band that did monster Pop songs."

Above: Rice and Lisa Carver, circa 1992
Boyd: "Lisa is a legendary figure, famous as a writer, performer and blow-job queen. She was only 17 when her outrageous opera troupe Suckdog first burst into the public consciousness back in 1986. At the time she was perceived to be the female GG Allin."
From the *Seconds* **archive**
Below: Rice and Nikolas Schreck, circa 1988
Photo by Nick Bougas

Flyer for NON show, Mabuhay Gardens, San Francisco, 1982
Rice: "I did Noise Music because I genuinely liked noise. I thought it would extend the boundaries of music. I didn't do it to be confrontational. I assumed others would feel the same way, and find it exciting. But a lot of people didn't. At my concerts, people smashed beer glasses in my face."
Collection of John Aes-Nihil

"If I can add a little suffering to their existence, that's fine. They deserve it. It's a form of justice, and there is in this world perfect, total justice—because a million people could think bad thoughts about me and I'm still completely happy, I'm still doing everything I want, and my life is perfect and their lives are miserable. Is that not justice?"

Were you and Michael Moynihan collaborators? "Not really. We worked together on a number of projects, and the only one that came out was *Music, Martinis, and Misanthropy*. He played drums and laid out the cover art. He did some vocals. I did vocals on one of the songs he recorded when he lived with me in Denver.

"Initially we did Abraxas together. It dragged on for years. Finally I said, 'I'm just gonna do this all by myself, and get it out.' Sometimes two people collaborating takes away the initiative for either one to get anything done. I said, 'Let's stop working together.' He was always saying, 'I'm doing all this work and I don't get any credit.' I said, 'Well, if that's the case, do your own work, and you will get one hundred percent of the credit,' because I thought he was getting more credit than he deserved."

Rice and Michael Moynihan, 1989
Photo by Douglas P.

What was the nature of the falling out? "We shared a lot of ideas and had the same tastes, but we had absolutely nothing in common as people. My nature is diametrically opposed to his. It's always difficult living with another person. I don't disagree with him or see him as a rival, I just think we weren't destined to be good roommates." *Was it an amicable split?* "Not really. He was younger and hadn't made his mark on the world, and he was aware of the fact that he was living in my shadow, and was uncomfortable with that. He wanted to rebel against me and strike out on his own, declare his independence." *Do you like his work?* "The things he published are top-notch. I heard a Blood Axis record once and I didn't find it particularly interesting. But the more people who are putting this material out into the world, the better. It helps to spread this virus." *Can you name that virus?* "No, because it involves so many diverse threads. But it is something tangible. I can meet somebody at one of my concerts who has this whole wide spectrum of references that they wouldn't have if it hadn't been for me publicizing this sort of thing." *You must be proud of that.* "Yeah! I think it's great." *Many forces work against it.* "This culture exists separate and distinct from those forces."

Rice and Douglas P., 1993
Photographer unknown

Rice, Marilyn Manson, Shaun Partridge, 1996
Photo by Giddle Partridge

WAKE

VOLUME ONE   **ISSUE ONE**   **TWO DOLLARS**

"WHO WOULD BE BORN MUST FIRST DESTROY A WORLD AND FLY TO GOD... A GOD WHOSE NAME IS ABRAXAS" —H.H.

Cover of Boyd Rice's *WAKE #1*, 1988
"It's going to be the world's first newspaper dedicated to Barbarianism and Social Darwinism, and it's going to be calles *Wake,* and we're going to reprint all these excellent old texts of people who have been completely forgotten—like Gustav Le Bon, the father of social psychology."
Collection of Boyd Rice

> *"People need their heroes and villains. Most of the heroes people have aren't really that heroic and most of the villains people have aren't really that villainous. People compare me to Hitler, like I'm this person who's committed horrible crimes. What the fuck have I done? Brought a few a unpleasant truths to people's attention?"*

"In the past dominant culture was dictated by sadists. Today dominant culture is dictated by masochists."

"Other people take LSD and see the face of God —I see swastikas."

You harnessed Hitler and Black Magic in your music. "A bit. I harness the archetype in live performances." *What reactions did you get?* "Exactly what you'd expect. Some people recognized something powerful, and were attracted to it, whereas others were repulsed by it. Pissed off." *Did that bother you?* "No. It followed me my whole life. People either really liked me, or they thought I was an asshole. I don't have any control over it. I don't know."

"I played Genesis an early NON concert tape and he played me an early Throbbing Gristle tape. We both agreed that there were some amazing similarities not only in the musical— if you can call it that—direction we were exploring, but also on a personal level. A lot of shared interests. I had no idea what Throbbing Gristle was when I went around to look up Gen—all I knew was that he was an artist who was very into Manson and Hitler. His interest in Hitler was not unique. British punks often incorporated swastika imagery, and Malcolm McLaren's Sex Boutique sold Nazi symbols side-by-side with S&M fetish gear. More than just a cheap shock, the swastika deliberately mocked the ideals of the 1960's, the era of long hair, free love, and flower power."

"On my second visit to San Quentin, the guards remembered me and began to inquire as to why I was visiting Charles Manson, of all people. I tried to explain my motivations as best I could—that I found him both fascinating and amusing, and that I felt I could learn a thing or two from him—but they didn't understand. One motioned towards me and said that I was obviously a smart guy, and that people who ended up in San Quentin did so because they weren't smart, they were losers. In retort, I offered the observation that there was a class of people who in ancient times had a place in society as warriors—they would have been centurions or gladiators or soldiers—but that in the modern world this class didn't have the same outlets, so if they could cooperate with the world they might end up as cops, but if they couldn't, they'd probably end up as criminals, but that regardless, there was something one could definitely learn from this rare class of people, and I believed Charlie to be one of them. The guard smiled, nodded in agreement and said that I made a good point. 'But the thing with the guys in there,' he said, pointing to the prison, 'is that ninety-nine out of a hundred of them wouldn't understand the point you just made, much less be able to formulate that kind of thought themselves.' I assured him that Manson certainly could, and that was what interested me—that I could discuss things with him that I couldn't with most other people. This the guard seemed to understand, and we left it at that.

"Unfortunately, I was never given the opportunity to say any of this to Manson in person. I was only to see him a few more times before I began to seriously doubt his credibility. My name was removed from his list when I was discovered coming into the prison with a bullet in my pocket. The lesbian Nazi was going over me with a metal detector and found it. She was clearly sad about having to handcuff me. For her co-workers, however, it seemed the happiest day of their lives. One guy was on the phone to the warden a split second later, exclaiming that they'd just taken some guy into custody who had attempted to smuggle an explosive device in, to Charles Manson. I was placed under arrest and charged with the smuggling of an explosive device into a state penitentiary."

Cover of the album *Ragnarok Rune* World Serpent, 1992

Anton Szandor LaVey

27 February XXVIII A.S.

Magister Boyd Rice
Post Office Box 300081
Denver, CO 80203

RE: Notification of Appointment

Dear Boyd,

    This is to inform you that as of this, the 27th day of February, XXVIII Anno Satanas, you are authorized to act in the capacity and bear the title of <u>Magister of the Church of Satan</u>.

    With congratulations and appreciation for your proven attributes.

                  Rege Satanas!

Anton Szandor LaVey

ASLV/bb

Letter from Anton LaVey to Boyd Rice, 1993

"I am a member of the Council of Nine in Anton LaVey's Church of Satan. I think Satanism's a very functional thing. It's the path back to God. People need a god like Abraxas, combining good and evil. That's a perfect schematic for understanding the universe."

Collection of Boyd Rice

war when there's a universal enemy. And even today, with the massive spread of Satanism, Satanists are the only minority, the only religious group, the only special interest group, that can be maligned & slandered with...

S: With impunity.
L: With impunity & without compunction! And they can get away with it. There's no other group you could do that to. No ethnic group. No religious group. No special interest group, not any other group. But they can with the devil, with Satanists. Well, we're here to smash that. We're here to create a forum, & give a valuable voice to all those people who are natural born outsiders.

Page 8 of Rice's handwritten transcript of his interview with LaVey for *Seconds* #45, 1997
Herein, LaVey defines Satanists as the only religious group others can attack with impunity.
This represents the Doctor's final interview; he died a few months later.
Collection of the author

**John Aes-Nihil, 1987
Photo by Nick Bougas**

JOHN AES-NIHIL: *"Aesthetic Nihilism foreshadows the schizophrenic breakdown coming at the end of the Twentieth Century. People are just getting more bored. It's the same thing as Punk Rock, but higher energy, more honest."*

Vaginal Davis: "My mother always said she'd rather suck the six-horned penis of a snaggle-toothed KKK-card-carrying Ozark Mountain redneck any day, than be caught humping a milky-mouthed well-meaning White Liberal. And I agree that true evil often presents itself in a candy-coated package. That's not what you get with **JOHN AES-NIHIL**, who is the world's foremost collector of extreme—and extremely offensive—culture.

"Upon entering his grisly Los Angeles compound, most people would think that they had stepped into the pure heart of darkness. The lair of Aesthetic Nihilism looks like it was decorated by Eva Braun, with a giant Nazi banner and a loving portrait of Der Führer hanging up. But Aes-Nihil is more than a Hitler freak. He's passionate about the Manson Family and two lesser-known cults (The Lyman Family and The Process Church of the Final Judgment). He's also a filmmaker and a confidant of John Waters and Kenneth Anger—who happens to be his roommate.

"Is Aes-Nihil nothing but a racist brute who promotes hatred? Is he a deranged lunatic? Well, he certainly is a sick ticket, with a catatonic presence and a tendency to pause anywhere between ten minutes and two hours when asked a question.

"This West-Coast Warhol has amassed, in near obscurity, a collection of all things aberrant. Not merely collecting them, but reshaping them and cataloging his finds and discoveries. You might see him selling music recordings by the Manson family and videos on Satanism at the flea market. In doing so, Aes-Nihil makes us confront the areas of inhumanity that have always existed—and presents them in a simple fashion where you can't help but laugh at some of the atrocities."

VAGINAL DAVIS: *What is Aesthetic Nihilism?*
AES-NIHIL: Art that is so extreme that it verges on destruction. It's a way of reacting to society. It is a reaction against mass culture, by doing a vicious satire on it. It's extreme devotion to the creation of extremely intense art. Originally, it was a combination of ascetic and aesthetic. One implies extreme devotion to something and the other is the philosophy or pursuit of beauty or perfection.

From left: Stanton LaVey, Nikolas Schreck, Zeena LaVey, Nick Bougas, John Aes-Nihil, in front of Dennis Wilson's house, Bel Air, 1988
Photo by George Stimson

VAGINAL DAVIS: *What do you say about people who say that what you do is cruel?*
AES-NIHIL: Man craves death. There's this thing in mass culture—an interest in Serial Killers and Serial Killer art. In some ways it's funny because that's the only way you can deal with things like that. Instead of running around and having a nervous breakdown and saying how tragic it is, you can just laugh at it. Mass communication results in mass culture, resulting in the lowest common denominator actually being achieved.

"*Manson Family Movies* put me on the map, dude. And it cost under a thousand dollars. It was the absolute first movie I ever made and it was feature-length and was also the first movie that anyone appearing in it made.

"I'd always been extremely interested in the Manson case, mainly because these people were claiming that somebody caused all these innocent kids to go around killing people for

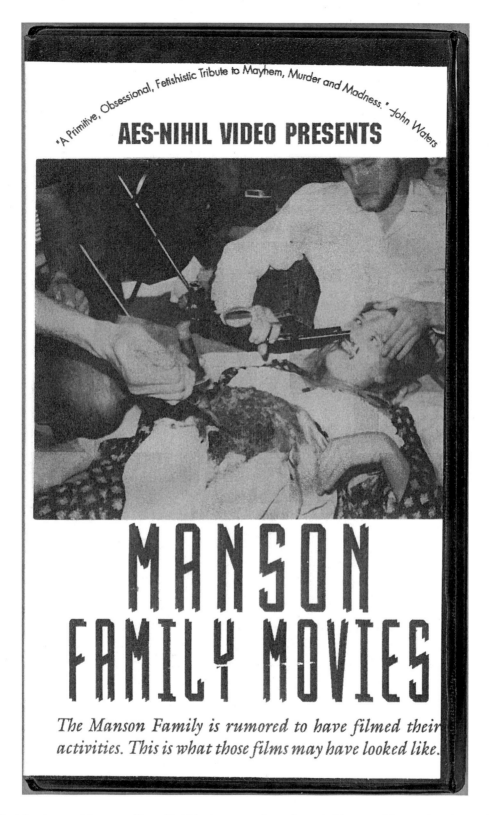

Sleeve of videotape, *Manson Family Movies*, produced and directed by John Aes-Nihil, 1984
Aes-Nihil: "The first film I produced was *Manson Family Movies*. The Family filmed thier activities, so this is what I imagined those films would have looked like. I started in 1974 and finally sort-of completed it in 1984, although I'm still changing the soundtrack. It just keeps going on and on."
Collection of John Aes-Nihil

"Aesthetic Nihilism is art that's so extreme it causes destruction. I collect it, archive it, and sell it to people who crave death. My catalog has sections on LSD, Nazism, White Power, Jim Jones, Nietzsche, The Process Church, The Lyman Family and literary figures like Burroughs, Ballard and Bukowski."

no reason at all, which seemed absolutely ridiculous, so I really got into studying what actually happened. Then I decided to make a movie about it. I went to a garage sale and got an 8mm camera for five dollars, and the entire movie was made with that—and it was done on out-of-date 8mm film.

"It all started with this really sleazy girl I knew. I thought it would be funny if she were Sharon Tate. That's how the whole thing started. Then I decided to put everyone else I knew in it. There was this other girl I knew who looked almost identical to Lynette 'Squeaky' Fromme. It was basically filmed without a script in a regular 8mm with no sound. I know it has little continuity, but it is supposed to be the film that the family made of themselves—and they were not filmmakers.

"For a while it was based on Ed Sanders' *The Family,* and then I started finding out a lot of new things. Someone I knew—a famous editor of a well-known publication—claimed that he had actually seen some of the movies that Roman Polanski supposedly made at his house. In one of them, Charlie and Sadie—Susan Atkins—were over at the Tate house, and both Voityk Frykowski and Abigail Folger were there, and they all did MDA together. After that they had some kind of sex orgy thing."

"In the early Eighties I ran into this scene at the Limbo Lounge on Santa Monica Boulevard. It was sort like Vaudeville in that the same group of people came up with a new act every week. There was Glen Meadmore, Nova China, The Cosmic Daniel, The Goddess Bunny and Vaginal Davis. I was living with Zeena LaVey and Nicolas Schreck and Stanton LaVey, who was 10. They moved to Vienna and I got the house and Glen and Father Larry moved in. Genesis P-Orridge came to town to do some shows. Glen opened for him and he was supposed to stay with Don Bowles but that place was a hole of filth. So, since I had an empty house, Genesis et cetera stayed there.

Scene from *Manson Family Movies*

"I went to San Francisco and showed the Manson movie to Vale and Boyd Rice of *ReSearch,* and they liked it. Vale said I should put out a catalog of all this Manson stuff I had gotten, so I did—and that's how the Archives of Aesthetic Nihilism began. Eventually it grew to hundreds of items in all sorts of directions. Vale said it was the real *ReSearch.*"

"*Manson Family Movies* and *The Ma Barker Story* are about crime. The Tennessee Williams movies are about glamour, sexual desperation and mania. *Descent Into Glamour: The Goddess Bunny Story* is about delusional desperation and glamour at the end of time."

Catalog cover, The Archives of Aesthetic Nihilism, 1990 edition
Compiled by John Aes-Nihil
Illustration by Davy Normal
Collection of the author

Example of John Aes-Nihil's photography: The Goddess Bunny, 1990
"The Goddess wants to be normal and wants to be in some mass-culture crap TV show or movie—and of course wants $$$$$. She also claims to be a born-again Christian who of course leads a truly degenerate life of drugs, drunkenness and doing it with anything and everything as long as whatever it is has a dick."
Collection of Michael Andros

**Nick Bougas, 1988
Photo by Sandy Weinberg**

NICK BOUGAS: *"Everybody on the scene came by my place and was wowed by my collection of Manson stuff. I taught them all how to correspond with him and others, and that became the basis of the Serial Killer phenomenon in underground culture."*

BOUGAS: "My correspondence with Charles Manson began at a time when such exchanges were rare. His letters were lengthy, intensely fascinating, and darkly poetic—not the unfocused ravings of a Messianic madman, as so often seen in television interviews. Upon acquiring the raw footage of those interviews, it became apparent that network editors were purposefully stringing together a succession of out-of-context clips in order to preserve the highly bankable 'crazed' image they had created at the time of his trial.

"Other infamous pen-pals have generally proven less interesting and more manipulative. John Gacy, Ken Bianchi and Henry Lee Lucas all religiously proclaim their innocence. Susan Atkins, Tex Watson and Gary Heidnik each acknowledge a degree of guilt, but feel sufficiently reformed, while Richard Ramirez remains the quintessential bad boy, making no excuses and feeling no remorse."

"It's safe to say that the subject of death possesses the appeal of the forbidden—and as we all know, the forbidden lures and beckons the human sensibilities like a siren's song. It's only fitting that we find the shadow realm spellbinding—we're going to be dead a lot longer than we lived."

"I have never much enjoyed drawing. I consider it an unpleasant chore, which is why the only artwork you'll see of mine was commissioned for a specific project or rendered as a favor. I don't mind knocking out an occasional cartoon for a friend or a publication I admire, but I can't imagine ever reporting to a steady job as an illustrator. I do have one unique ability that seems to deeply impress even the celebrated artists that I know: I've always been able to draw right out of my head without looking at any reference images. Many of my ink-slinging idols couldn't commit a single line to paper without a stack of research photos to study or sometimes even trace."

Top right: "John Gacy…Clownin' Around in the Crawlspace" by Bougas, 1989
Center: Oil painting of Bougas and Gacy by John Wayne Gacy, 1990
Bottom: Bougas with GG Allin, Mondo Video, Hollywood, 1993

Sleeve of videotape, *Death Scenes*, produced by Nick Bougas, 1987
"The most captivating aspect of real-death documentaries is that they offer us the ultimate opportunity to ponder great, solemn mysteries. Fate fascinates!"
Collection of Nick Bougas

"Crime doesn't pay—unless you're a convicted killer who happens to wield a mean paintbrush. The most curious of crazes is the collecting of art by famous multiple murderers. Yours truly began accumulating such treasures before it became fashionable."

Manson by Bougas, 1986

Bougas by Manson, 1988

"What passes for TV news these days is little more than an international body count."

"I met LaVey through his daughter Zeena. When approached to narrate *Death Scenes,* he —who usually weighs such propositions with care—leaped at the opportunity."

"America, the once-glorious land of opportunity, is fast becoming a cesspool of corruption and despair. We're witnessing the disintegration of dignity and tradition. We're inundated by an influx of the world's most diseased and undesirable aliens. Our so-called leaders are shamelessly decadent and uncommitted."

"Books and movies always envision the end of the world as a fiery, chaotic affair. But you know what? I believe man faces an even more hellish fate—a long, sluggish, unremarkable crawl toward extinction, much like the sedate setting which resounded with the slow, final throes of the last dinosaur. A mediocre death for mediocre mankind. Bleeding hearts rejoice! Equality at last!

"I've learned that it doesn't do a soul much good to strive to be universally fair, as so much general opinion and authoritative rhetoric today is slanted to serve specific agendas. I see daily evidence that persons with power, and corporate entities, shamelessly manipulate the masses in Orwellian ways. From the time I first sensed that I wasn't going to fit into the existing world, I began to forge my own universe—and have learned to dwell quite happily therein. At this point, none of the delusion and chaos on the outside really matters. Here, in my tailor-made sphere, wonderful things with enduring values still reign. Ernie Kovacs is forever at his funniest, Edith Piaf still gives knockout concerts, and Laurel and Hardy continue to be a box-office smash. This is a sacred golden retreat where the vapid skateboard and Hip-Hop cultures simply don't exist."

Boyd Rice, Nikolas Schreck, Nick Bougas, 1986

Mission Accomplished: GG Allin in Hell, Nick Bougas, pen & ink, 1993
Collection of Nick Bougas

***Jeff Dahmer eats it...*, Nick Bougas, pen & ink, 1995**
Christopher Scarver killed Dahmer in prison in 1994. Bougas drew this picture, based on sketchy newspaper accounts. Scarver eventually saw it, and wrote to a friend describing Bougas' rendition as accurate. The killer marveled at the artist's insight.
Collection of Nick Bougas.

Zeena LaVey, 1987
Photo by Nick Bougas

ZEENA SCHRECK nee LaVEY: "Everyone knows I haven't been 'LaVey' since my violent and very public severance from that idiot and his lackeys fourteen years ago—April 30, 1990!

From *Anton LaVey: Legend and Reality,* compiled by his daughter **ZEENA** and Nikolas Schreck:

"Anton Szandor LaVey (1930-1997), along with Charles Manson, Timothy Leary, and other messianic pop gurus, was a notorious figure of the 1960s' subculture of social experiment. As the flamboyant High Priest of the Church of Satan and the author of *The Satanic Bible,* he served as an ideal bogeyman for the sensation-seeking American media of that tumultuous period.

"His curious celebrity was based largely on a self-created legend. This carefully-orchestrated legend may, in the final analysis, be LaVey's most enduring legacy. LaVey disseminated his legend through interviews with journalists, personal discussion with his disciples, and two LaVey-approved (auto)biographies (apparently ghostwritten by LaVey himself). The first of these, 1974"s *The Devil's Avenger* (credited to LaVey associate Burton Wolfe), embellished on the fabrications Wolfe had already sketched in his introduction to *The Satanic Bible.* The second, 1990's *Secret Life of a Satanist* (credited to Blanche Barton, LaVey's live-in secretary and mother of his son), contradicted many of LaVey's own claims in the earlier volume, while putting forth new legends for public consumption. As social historians and scholars of occult movements begin to study LaVey's life and times in an objective historical context, a wealth of information concerning the man beneath the Devil horns has come to light. This brief checklist is a concise guide to separating the deliberate prevarications from the human, all-too-human facts. For brevity's sake, only the most well-known aspects of the legend will be clarified here.

"LEGEND: In 1948 the 18-year-old ASL was engaged to play organ at the Mayan burlesque theater in Los Angeles. There he met a young stripper named Marilyn Monroe, with whom he had a passionate love affair in the period before her rise to film stardom. According to ASL, Monroe had resorted to stripping to pay her rent. As proof of his relationship with Monroe, ASL later showed visitors a copy of Monroe's famous nude calendar inscribed 'Dear Tony, How many times have you seen this! Love, Marilyn.'

"REALITY: ASL never knew Monroe. Monroe intimate Robert Slatzer and Harry Lipton, Monroe's agent in 1948, have exposed and discredited this tale. Lipton paid Monroe's expenses, including her rent. Paul Valentine, director of the Mayan Theater, has stated that the Mayan was never a burlesque theater, and that neither Monroe nor ASL ever worked for the Mayan in any capacity. Diane LaVey, ASL's former wife, has admitted that she forged the 'Monroe' inscription on the calendar. ASL's former publicist Edward Webber claims ASL admitted he never knew Monroe.

"LEGEND: ASL was exposed to the savagery of human nature during his stint as a San Francisco Police photographer in the early 1950s.

"REALITY: San Francisco Police Department past employment records include no 'Howard Levey'

Illustration by Zeena LaVey, from *EXIT #5,* 1990

nor 'Anton LaVey.' Frank Moser, who was a SFPD photographer in the early 1950s, said that ASL never worked for the Department.

"LEGEND: On the night of April 30, 1966 (the German Satanic festival of Walpurgisnacht), ASL in a 'blinding flash' declared himself the High Priest of Satan, proclaimed that the Age of Satan had begun, and founded the Church of Satan as a religious institution.

"REALITY: In 1966 ASL supplemented his income by presenting weekend lectures on exotic and occult topics, and by conducting 'Witches' Workshops.' He charged $2 a head, filling his living room with the curious and establishing a local reputation as an eccentric. Professional publicist Edward Webber suggested to ASL that he 'would never make any money by lecturing on Friday nights for donations ... it would be better to form some sort of church and get a charter from the State of California ... I told Anton at the time that the press was going to flip out over all this and that we would get a lot of notoriety.' In the summer of 1966, long after the fictional founding-date invented later, a newspaper article about ASL's lectures offhandedly referred to him as 'priest of the Devil's church.' This mixture of Webber's idea and the newspaper's characterization resulted in the creation of the Church of Satan as a business

Anton & Zeena LaVey, 1988
Photo by Nick Bougas

> "Regardless of the fact that I became an artist in my own right, at the time I was not in the art scene in any way, shape or form. I was a religious figure, and I thought of myself very seriously as a religious figure who was in constant threat."

and publicity vehicle. Jack Webb, a San Francisco Police investigator who knew ASL from the Lost Weekend nightclub, also suggested that he should form a church of some kind to exploit his recondite knowledge.

"LEGEND: One of ASL's most widely-accepted falsehoods is his claim that he served as technical advisor for the 1968 Roman Polanski film *Rosemary's Baby*. ASL also claimed to have played the curiously uncredited part of the Devil in that film.

"REALITY. ASL had no involvement with *Rosemary's Baby*. Polanski's close friend Gene Gutowski (original producer of the film) stated that there was no technical advisor, nor did ASL ever even meet Polanski. Producer William Castle, who details all aspects of the film's production in his autobiography, never mentions ASL. He does describe Polanski's diligence in basing the film exactly on the Ira Levin novel from which it was adapted, eliminating any need for technical advice. The father of the actress who played Mia Farrow's body-double in the Devil scene recalled that a young, very slender professional dancer played the part, dressed in a small rubber suit. In 1971 this suit was acquired by Studio One Productions in Louisville, Kentucky, for use in a low-budget horror film, *Asylum of Satan*. Michael Aquino, technical advisor for that film, examined the suit and concluded that the 200-pound, 6-foot ASL could not possibly have worn it. (The suit was worn by a girl in the Asylum film.) Not a single member of the cast or crew of *Rosemary's Baby* has ever mentioned ASL's involvement. In 1968 a San Francisco theater did ask ASL to make an appearance at the film's local opening as a promotional event. This appears to have been ASL's only connection with the film that engendered the 1960s' popular interest in Satanism.

"LEGEND: Jayne Mansfield, Hollywood sex symbol and actress, was a card-carrying Satanist and had an affair with ASL.

"REALITY: Publicity agent Tony Kent, an associate of Ed Webber, arranged the meeting between Mansfield and ASL as a publicity stunt. ASL was smitten with the actress. Mansfield, who made no secret of her many affairs, denied knowing ASL intimately, and no associate of hers has ever confirmed any supposed romance with ASL. In a 1967 interview she said, 'He had fallen in love with me and wanted to join my life with his. It was a laugh.' According to ASL's publicist Edward Webber, Mansfield would ridicule her Satanic suitor by calling from her Los Angeles home and seductively teasing him while her friends listened in on the conversation. ASL's public claims that he had an affair with Mansfield began only after Mansfield's death in an automobile accident, which he also claimed was the result of a curse he had placed on her lover Sam Brody.

Nikolas Schreck & Zeena LaVey, 1988
Photo by Nick Bougas

"LEGEND: ASL wrote *The Satanic Bible*, his principal work, to fulfill his congregation's need for a scriptural guide.

"REALITY: *The Satanic Bible* was conceived as a commercial vehicle by paperback publisher Avon Books. Avon approached ASL for some kind of Satanic work to cash in on the Satanism & witchcraft fad of the late 1960s. Pressed for material to meet Avon's deadline, ASL resorted to plagiarism, assembling extracts from an obscure 1896 tract—*Might is Right* by Ragnar Redbeard—into a 'Book of Satan' for the *SB*, and claiming its authorship by himself. (Ironically these *MiR* passages are the ones most frequently quoted by ASL disciples.) Another third of the *SB* consists of John Dee's 'Enochian Keys' taken directly but again without attribution from Aleister Crowley's *Equinox*. The *SB's* 'Nine Satanic Statements,' one of the Church of Satan's central doctrines, is a paraphrase, again unacknowledged, of passages from Ayn Rand's *Atlas Shrugged*. The last words in the *SB*—'Yankee Rose'—have been puzzled over for years by readers. 'YR" is actually the name of an old popular tune in ASL's nightclub repertoire."

Nikolas Schreck, 1986
Photo by Nick Bougas

NIKOLAS SCHRECK: *"Superstition? Irrational fears? Old wives' tales? Quite the contrary. These things are very real. Radio Werewolf is that glorious force upon which all these legends, myths and superstitions are based. Radio Werewolf has returned to rid this Earth once and for all of the subhuman parasites that have for too long hindered the spiritual evolution of the chosen."*

SCHRECK: "Prior to the Twentieth Century, almost all societies gladly accepted censorship and criminalization of art by governmental or religious authorities as a given, a necessary protective measure designed to protect the social and spiritual hygiene of a community. So the whole notion that an artist has an inalienable right to freedom of expression is very new, and may well ultimately be viewed as a dangerous aberration as an increasingly disordered planet forces destabilized and demoralized populations to willingly return to the safety of strong authority. Freedom of artistic expression is a historical anomaly and it should never be taken for granted.

"Artists have always been mistrusted by the majority of people as lazy subversives without a proper job. History reveals that the illegalization of art has usually been welcomed by the masses as a just punishment for such eccentrics. It's my impression that a majority of supposedly free societies would actively support the governmental banning of books, films and artwork that are thought to be either overly violent or sexual, unreligious, or somehow 'offensive.' So this area has to be looked at without any false pretenses; we must face the depth of human ignorance and the concomitant willingness of the human animal to accept curtailment of liberty for the supposed good of the tribe. Artists are tolerated only so long as their work is bland and flattering to the delusions and prejudices of the millions. Superficially 'shocking' art is accepted by a society if any disturbing content in the art can be dismissed as a merely commercial provocation. But should an artist really challenge those societal delusions, or touch on areas of human experience that genuinely cause unease, no tears will be shed by the average person if the art is illegalized.

"Art is deemed illegal when the artist is judged to have transgressed one or more of the three most sensitive control mechanisms within a society: religion, politics and/or sexuality—or all three at the same time. Illegal art has been judged to be blasphemous or heretical, anti-social or treasonous, or simply obscene. The borders between these three categories have always tended to blur.

Paul Antonelli, Schreck, Evil Wilhelm, James 'Filth' Collard, 1986
Collection of Nick Bougas

"Presentation of socially unacceptable sexuality has usually been condemned as spiritually immoral and irreligious, no matter how superficially different the ideologies of the authorities. The banning of the books of Nabokov, Joyce, Miller and D.H. Lawrence in England and the USA was underscored by pious and puritan Christian motivations typical of Anglo-Saxon society, despite lip service paid to notions of separation of church and state. Books and artwork destroyed or banned in Islamic societies for overly erotic content are interpreted by Sharia law as being

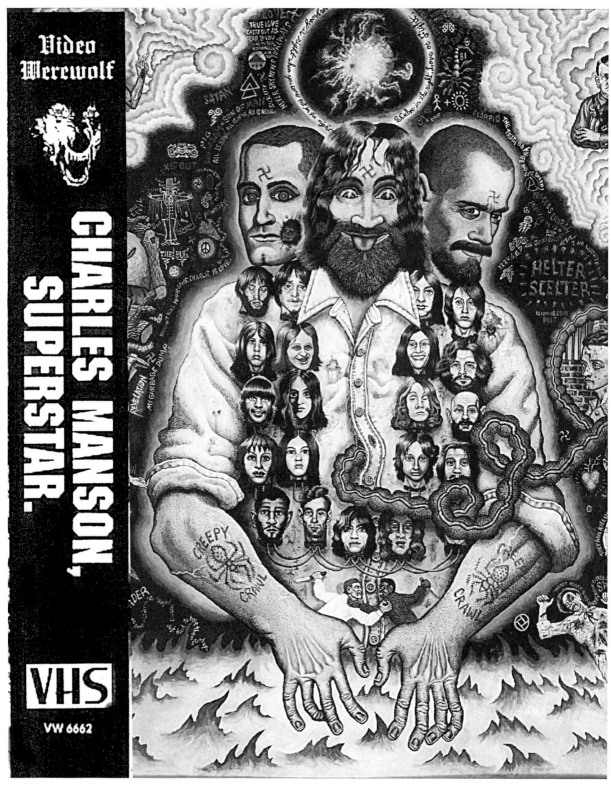

**Sleeve of videotape, *Charles Manson Superstar*, produced by Nikolas Schreck, 1988
Cover painting by Joe Coleman**
"Manson, LaVey, these icons—they are completely empty, completely meaningless. There is no reality to them. I learned my lesson of what emptiness and superficiality they were."
Collection of Nick Bougas

> "All truly powerful art is a crime against consensus reality, breaking accepted laws of perceiving and representing. When the forces of control deem that the artist has gone too far in this transgression, it only takes a simple adjustment of the legal code, or a demonstration of legal precedent, to literally transform the artist into a criminal."

anti-Islamic, rather than merely offensive. Even in totalitarian governments of left and right, such as the Soviet Union or National Socialist Germany, expressions of sexuality thought to be 'anti-social' have been criminalized with the same fervor as we would find in any theocracy."

"Now, of course, we are faced with the illegalization, or at least the official marginalization, of art that does not reflect current notions of racial equality and other sacred cows. So we've seen such grotesque incidents of Political Correctness as the removal of *Mary Poppins, Tom Sawyer,* or Ian Fleming's James Bond novels from school libraries, due to their no-longer-acceptable presentation of racial groups. This brings into focus another common motivation driving the illegalization of art: the attempt to rewrite the past so that the memory of ideas and behaviors inconvenient to a particular regime or consumer demographic can be erased from the historical record altogether. These are the same tactics employed by totalitarian control systems for millennia. Whether it is the ancient Egyptian custom of destroying the heretical realistic artwork created in the time of the pharaoh Akhenaton, the destruction of 'decadent' modern art in the Third Reich, or the hysterical banning of certain Nazi art by the current German government—to name but a few examples—this reshaping of history for ideological purposes is at the core of all illegalization of art in all times, as George Orwell's *1984* illustrates. In a sense, an artist is performing a magical act, recreating the world and the consciousness through his or her creation. And the authority seeking to limit that ability of creation is exercising its own spell, attempting to banish the unwanted demons summoned by the illegalized artist."

"It's tempting to note how many famous criminals have demonstrated at least the rudiments of an artistic sensibility—obvious examples being the paintings and drawings of John Wayne Gacy and Kenneth Bianchi, the fiction of Jack Untermeyer, the Austrian

Cover of cassette, *A Symphony of Terror,* 1986
Collection of John Aes-Nihil

prostitute murderer and author, or the music of Manson. But one also has to suspect that much of this nominally artistic production is usually inspired by the sheer boredom of prison life rather than by any muse unique to the criminal mind—although the Zodiac Killer's collages are certainly more interesting than a lot of what is pawned off these days as 'naive' art, and Jack the Ripper's letters to the police possess an undeniable proletarian poetry."

Boyd Rice: "Schreck was putting up pro-AIDS posters with cartoons of a Gay parade where AIDS victims were marching into an open grave. He was putting them up on Santa Monica Boulevard, an area where there are a lot of Gay prostitutes and hustlers. A couple of weightlifting leather boys saw him and chased him. Schreck jumped into a car but before he could shut the door, a guy reached in with a knife and slashed him. His ear was cut off, and it fell into the gutter. He was playing with fire, and it blew up in his face."

The Werewolf Order is the frontline of the Demonic Revolution.

We are the shocktroops of a youth uprising against Judeo-Christian tyranny; the focus of a return to the ancient pagan/satanic tradition that is the birthright of Western European men and women.

Like Faust, we have made our pact with the mighty powers of darkness. No boundary can halt our quest for dominion.

We are a Satanic Leadership school, imparting the black magical power that shall enable our elite to rise as future leaders in every field.

In Science, Architecture, Art, Music, Ecology — every area of endeavor shall see a new satanic principle at work!

The 90's shall be an inversion of the 60's . . . a hard, pitiless, brutal youth instilling order upon chaos, stamping the dawning century with a new aesthetic and law.

The power of Satanic youth unleashed is invincible — It is a dam in the evolutionary current that has been bottled up for nearly 2,000 years. When this reservoir of energy is unleashed, woe to the Judeo-Christian death cult and its lackeys!

We are turning the wheel of history, grasping the reins of power from the withered and feeble hands that have held them for too long!

No longer can the beast in man be restrained by the leash of Judeo-Christian sheep morality. The Wolfpack has gathered, summoned by the Call of the Wild. Rise!

"To Unleash the Beast in Man"

Flyer for Werewolf Order, illustration by Nikolas Schreck, 1986
"Art and crime coincide in the essentially alienated state of mind required to succeed in both activities. It's no coincidence that a particularly adept criminal is often praised by his or her peers as an 'artist.' It's all too easy to romanticize art and crime, but there is an undeniable connection between the two."
Collection of Nick Bougas

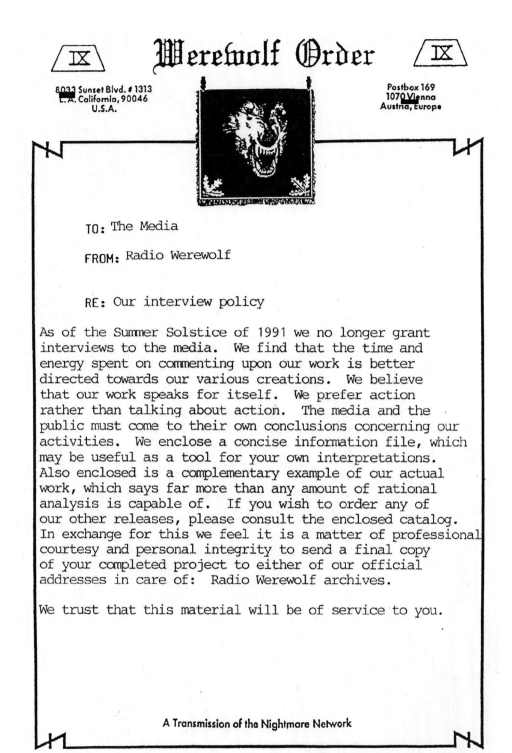

Werewolf Order

8033 Sunset Blvd. # 1313
L.A. California, 90046
U.S.A.

Postbox 169
1070 Vienna
Austria, Europe

TO: The Media

FROM: Radio Werewolf

RE: Our interview policy

As of the Summer Solstice of 1991 we no longer grant interviews to the media. We find that the time and energy spent on commenting upon our work is better directed towards our various creations. We believe that our work speaks for itself. We prefer action rather than talking about action. The media and the public must come to their own conclusions concerning our activities. We enclose a concise information file, which may be useful as a tool for your own interpretations. Also enclosed is a complementary example of our actual work, which says far more than any amount of rational analysis is capable of. If you wish to order any of our other releases, please consult the enclosed catalog. In exchange for this we feel it is a matter of professional courtesy and personal integrity to send a final copy of your completed project to either of our official addresses in care of: Radio Werewolf archives.

We trust that this material will be of service to you.

A Transmission of the Nightmare Network

Press mailing for Werewolf Order, 1991
Wolf's-head logo illustration by Robert N. Taylor, 1985
"Zeena and I avoid our fans at all costs."
Collection of Fred Berger

**Adam Parfrey, Strand Theatre, San Franciscio, 8-8-1988
Photo by Nick Bougas**

ADAM PARFREY: "Terrorism can be advanced through art only if art threatens action."

PARFREY: "There's a lot of complaints about my work. For example, there are people who say the article I did on the Oklahoma City bombing, that was reproduced by some leftist publication, was somehow pro-militia. And then there were actual militia people who wrote articles about how I was horribly anti-militia. Then there were people who felt I was too Anarchist or I was a left-winger—or a right-winger! Then of course there's those leftists who said that I'm neo-Nazi or Fascist anti-Semitic—the whole requiem of slurs. This happened constantly, so I'm somewhat accustomed to it. I'm not interested in doing work that follows any specific partisan point of view. I'm interested where the most extreme behavior is propping up." *The militias hate you. The government hates you. The Jews hate you. The Nazis hate you.* "Wacky leftist conspiracy theorists hate me, although I've published a lot of leftist conspiracy stuff—they think it's some sort of fifth column to dilute their whole. It's hard to deal with all that stuff. I like various points of view. It's hard for me to follow down a straight line for anything. Any partisan point of view, there's no interest there." *Have you done stuff that you felt would hurt people?* "I think it's been interpreted that way."

Robert N. Taylor: *You play the role of the enfant terrible to the cultural establishment.*
Parfrey: "Everything the establishment extols as comfortable and right and good makes me sick. They are like drug addicts. They want everyone to be like them, to be on the same drug. The establishment phonies are beaten down, craven hypocritical momma's boys. A few of them wish me harm. Even though I have established one of the top cutting-edge publishing houses, even though Disney paid a quarter of a million dollars to one of my authors for rights to film a Feral House book, even though bookstores across the country are establishing an 'apocalyptic culture' section for new and trendy books, I cannot find a paying writing job outside the skin magazines and a couple of alternative weeklies. Editors from Conde Nast magazines call me to pick my brain and offer to pay me 'research fees,' but they hem and haw when I bring up the possibility of publishing an article of mine. I believe that I am on some sort of blacklist. You can't believe how many times I have sold some editor on a story, but as soon as it is written or the proposal goes further upstairs, the axe falls. I am not trusted to write a *Details* or *Esquire* article. Perhaps they see that I'm not an establishment team player sort of guy. Perhaps they're right. I'll end up picking scabs."
— From ***Cyber-Psychos AOD #6.***

Above: Adam Parfrey, 1984
Photographer unknown
Collection of the author
Below: Poster for Tortures and Torments art show
La Luz de Jesus Gallery, L.A. 1990
Graphic by Frank Kozik
Collection of Adam Parfrey

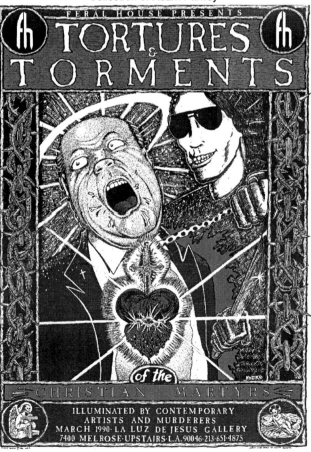

**Page four, *What We Want*, collage by Adam Parfrey from *EXIT #1*, 1984
Collection of the author**

> "Apocalypse Culture is the manifestation of far-gone apocalyptic thought. It's an end-time situation. People do not feel or act as if there's a future. We're on the downward slope of Western Civilization, for good or bad."

"I was with you, George, at the printing plant when Art Speigelman's wife, Françoise Mouley, took—without asking permission—copies of the printed pages of *EXIT #1,* and just gave us a very snotty look. We saw her come up there and take them." *What made this incident particularly interesting?* "What made it interesting, is what we heard from stores like Soho Zat and Forbidden Planet—that they heard directly from Speigelman. He threatened them—and they didn't want to say this aloud—they were threatened by him not to sell *EXIT.* So what they did was, they had it behind the counter in case anybody asked for it."

"Boyd Rice had a copy of the Bible with Charles Manson's annotations in the Book of Revelations. I thought that would make a great subject for a piece in *EXIT* because it would take on both Christian belief and Manson. So I obtained from Boyd that Bible and xeroxed it, and used the quotes from it as if I was providing Manson's perspective of apocalypse. I also used, again through Boyd, the idea that there was a Nazi group that was pro-Manson, and they thought Manson was the new George Lincoln Rockwell. I thought that was remarkable but dumb. That group was led by James Mason.

"Mason did some interesting work in terms of neo-Nazi flyers, plus he was promoting this idea of Manson as the new leader. I thought that was all pretty extraordinary. From James Mason's point of view he was promoting Manson's own ideas, too. He was this guy in Ohio who, like all neo-Nazis, had some ideas that didn't really go very far."

**Frames from *The Book Of Charlie,* collages by Adam Parfrey from *EXIT #3,* 1987
Collection of the author**

***Apocalypse Culture*, AMOK Press, first edition, 1987**
Cover painting by Joe Coleman
"The first AMOK Press edition of *Apocalypse Culture* had provocative quotes from Hitler and a poem by Antonin Artaud to Hitler. The woman who wrote the article about Artaud got upset that I included that poem, though it was an actual poem of Artaud's. She didn't dispute its legitimacy, she just disputed its worthiness belonging in the book—because American academia wants to respect Artaud, so we will just forget about his other stuff."
Collection of Adam Parfrey

"Murder doesn't interest me. What is of interest is what causes it. What gets people into a belief system that allows them to do it? What are they like inside when it happens? What is a cause and what is a result?"

Peter Sotos said it's the most horrible book he's ever read. "*Killer Fiction* is basically the masturbatory fantasies of this cop-turned-Serial Killer. It was used as evidence against him. Sondra London had self-published an earlier version in a Kinko's, and I thought it was really great. I also did that Danny Rolling book with her. As far as getting close to that really strange vibe, she was closest. But she didn't have any moralistic or exploitation tinge. I guess it was exploitation in some way—but without putting the swastika and blood drop on the cover like mass-market supermarket fiction."

"I found it amazing that Manson could still frighten people simply with words or ideas. It seemed a bit preposterous but it was a fact."

Above: Parfrey & Sondra London, 1997
Photo by Sondra London
Below: *Killer Fiction,* Feral House, 1995

Tell us about the Abraxas Foundation.
"It was Boyd and I; we believed there were smarter people, and dumber people. There are more intelligent people, and less intelligent people. And the Abraxas Foundation believed in the ascendancy of more intelligent people."
Even though nature selects against that sort of abstract intelligence you guys were celebrating.
"Whatever the case may be. I think you're right. It was a bit of an internal joke. We were flogging this idea of a cult—to see if people got upset and anxious if they heard there was this occult-Fascist think-tank. There was no such thing! It was just a presumptuous idea that would get people very upset. It was a provocative idea. Boyd and I were in it, and at one time Nikolas Schreck. It was when we were getting along with him, and we exchanged ideas about how to make our ideas more wide-ranging in terms of being discussed by more people. And, what upsets people we don't like?"

"As for me, I guess I'm a pseudo- or quasi-libertarian. I just see all these people with smiling faces, forcing me to do things. The Friendly Fascism of Reagan has gotten even worse with the smiling faces of the Clinton administration."

"I'm not sure I want a more civilized society. Western Civilization is tottering, and I'm just giving it a quick kick to help it tumble faster."

Feral House logo, 1988
Designed by the author

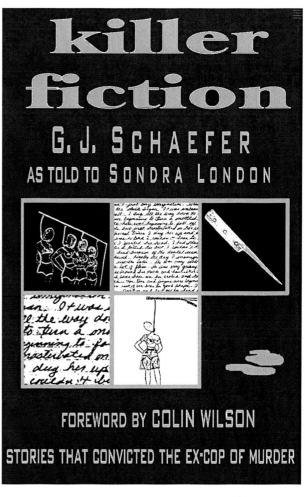

**Advertisement for Feral House, 1993
Illustration by Coop
Collection of Adam Parfrey**

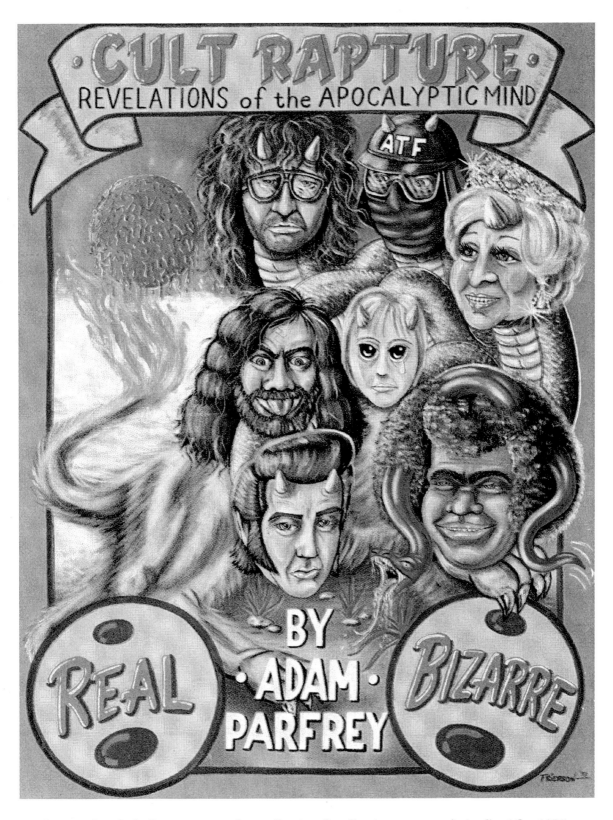

Poster for *Cult Rapture* art show, Center for Contemporary Arts, Seattle, 1995
Painting by Mark Frierson, 1993
Collection of Adam Parfrey

**Your humble host George Petros, somewhere in Vermont, 1993
Photo by Thomas Colbath**

Your host, GEORGE PETROS: "Only barbarians and intellectuals will ultimately survive. Of course they'll have to mate."

ME: "For a diabolical decade—1984-1994—I edited and published *EXIT,* an outlaw Pop Art magazine in opposition to both the underground and the establishment. It was forum for extreme ideologies and inclinations manifested as political pornography, psychosexual terrorism, scientific threats and infernal texts. It was graced by contributions from the best artists and writers in America—famous, infamous, and unknown—each driven by unusual passions to excel and influence and go all the way.

"You, dear reader, probably have never seen an issue of *EXIT,* but you certainly have felt its impact. Perhaps someone has shown you an old worn-out copy, or perhaps by some twist of fate you do own an issue or two—it doesn't matter; most copies are now dust, or becoming dust—the earlier issues, generally suppressed and unavailable even in their day, were manufactured by respectable printers on good paper, but as the magazine's political and sexual implications grew more intense, fewer and fewer printers were willing to take the job. By the fifth issue only a local Chinese sweatshop, whose owners had no understanding of Western symbology, would print it—on some of the worst newsprint imaginable (an especially aggravating circumstance when the non-availability of hemp paper is considered...).

"Out of *EXIT* came Serial Art, which utilizes time-lines, graphs and diagrams to show changes and processes and the flow of situations. There also came Propagandart, which utilizes principles of advertising and propaganda to manipulate emotions and play with opinions. There also came the eradication of boundaries between Left and Right, the use of scientific motifs as weapons of intimidation... unfortunately the world wasn't ready for the magazine's vibe—it was too advanced, and so nobody was able to emulate it, and so nobody was able to rip it off, therefore it was doomed.

"Eventually, the sands of time encrusted the delicate clockwork that ran EXIT, and the winds of change blew it away.

"Extrapolating *EXIT*'s potential, I became the editor of *Seconds,* a music, art, politics and crime magazine devoted to free speech and the Art of the Interview."

"*EXIT*: outlaw liberal Fascist Sci-Fi Pop Art magazine, fusion of Social Realism and Surrealism, born in frenzies of beauty and anger, died in hazy sunset of Western History, sustained throughout by dire necessity and the fires of Marijuana & Absinthe and the coolness of cool music & cool sex & attitude in Outer Space—like a rapidly blooming rare flower it was beautiful for a moment; now it's harsh pollen lies dormant, suspended in oblivion.

"Born in frenzies of revolution and Crystal Meth; died in the haze of Heroin and the stupor of self-righteousness, sustained by stolen money and the fires of Marijuana and the excitement of sacrilege & drug sex & primal passions from Inner Space—like an ice-cold ghost it was hot for a moment; now its harsh electromagnetic signature resonates with echoing aftershocks, daring you to understand it."— Introduction to *The Exit Collection*

"In the future the perfect human being will be a hermaphrodite — an intersexual fusion of genders combining male and female genitalia, male and female hormones — a combination of Hermes and Aphrodite, god and goddess, diablo and diabla.

"Like everyone else of my time I was taught to stay away from hermaphrodites. Everyone knows they're bad news and they're nothing but trouble from which the most exquisite grief will come. They look good and they smell good and on the surface they're very alluring and seductive, but once they get their cocks into you, and yours into them, you're pretty much hooked until either you die or you get with the lucky few who manage to escape.

"I was taught that hermaphrodites are stupid lying whores who hate us because we were born male or female and can therefore go to heaven when we die, and I was also taught that we move

Above: The Atomic Swastika, 1988

***EXIT* #1, cover by George Petros, 1984**
"Before *EXIT* there was nothing. I studied and learned and absorbed and practiced. I watched and waited for art to get real, for Science Fiction to become fact, and for people to get smart. Needless to say, I was disappointed. I spent a long time in art schools and museums. I spent a lot of time on the Moon and a lot of time underwater. I learned how to make love, and how to hate."
Collection of the author

> *"In the future the perfect human being will be a hermaphrodite— an intersexual fusion of genders combining male and female genitalia, male and female hormones—Hermes and Aphrodite, god and goddess, diablo and diabla."*

forward in time with them through an adaptive evolution that makes our symbiosis a fact by default because some scientists said that's the way it's gotta be thousands of years ago. But I believe that the evolutionary mechanism is fucked up.

"I was under their spell, and I sat there and cheered them on as they burned me out, fucked me, sucked me, did me up and drained me dry.

"One night I was at a party and a hermaphrodite was there. I avoided 'it,' but of course I was polite. The drugs came out and the hermaphrodite looked at me with a sultry sort of "you can do exactly anything to me" quasi-telepathic allure. Little boy's eyes, little girl's eyes — I took that first forbidden step in the wrong direction when I went over and said, "Hello."

"In the beginning it was all good. Every once in a while a hermaphrodite or two would come over and chill me out. They were engineered so fine — they're a true crossbreed. You take the giant cock into your mouth and slowly squeeze it with your lips and then move it out of the way so you can lick that peachy pussy — it starts there. You squeeze a little harder, lick a little longer and they start to do all these crazy things to you. You would think that they could simply do the heterosexual and homosexual things in different combinations, each of which would be amazing — however, that all would be predictable, and

GEORGE PETROS and ADAM PARFREY—have refined the principles of Preventative Sociology to act as a catalyst for the new Golden Age of Mankind in which High Culture predominates through the application of Superior Firepower.

Above: Adam Parfrey (left) and G.P., 1984
Below: Pages from CD inset booklet for *E-Z Listening Disc* by DEVO, Rykodisc, 1987. AP & I did the packaging for DEVO's album of self-covers. We were credited as "EXIT."
Collection of the author

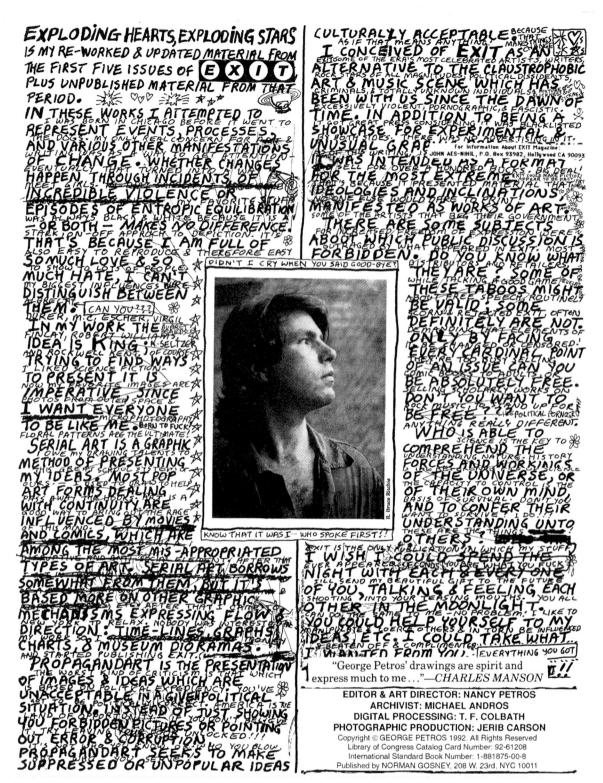

Introduction to *Exploding Hearts, Exploding Stars*, Norman Gosney Publications, 1992
Photo by R. Bruce Ritchie, 1984

"We want violence. Aggression is a joyous tool. The same instinct that protects us from sharks causes us to rape and kill our neighbors. However, we also want serenity, order and calm. We want peace, so that our thoughts will not be interrupted by hungry outsiders. Violence and serenity—it's so complex. It's a beautiful, ever-unfolding puzzle within the slipstream of a pendulum. Anyone who thinks that the universe is meaningless is in for a big surprise."

Collection of the author

"If your art doesn't cause a problem, there's a problem with your art."

you would have expected even the most extreme stuff. But a hermaphrodite is different. It's as if sexual potential increases in some wild geometric progression so that performance prowess increases exponentially. As time went on it got bad. I started seeing more of them. It's a mental thing: you want that awful cock vibrating inside you, and you want to fuck that exploding pussy at the same time. The monosexual human mind was not designed to fathom both of those things simultaneously, and the chemicals in the brain overload and part of your mind shuts down and you can see everything in such a beautifully clear reality and you're getting your lights fucked out and suddenly you cum — it's just too much, and you become addicted.

"Hermaphrodites are taking over the world because they're different and smart and everybody's afraid to even criticize them and they've amassed so much power and wealth and fame and immortality and insular arrogance and seething hatred of each and every one of us — you see, they're like a third sex that can breed with itself in a cloning sort of asexual way. They don't need any monosexual input. They fuck us for the same reason we fuck them. Hermaphrodites are self-contained and aren't necessary for anything, really. One of the biggest questions in the history of science is why exactly they were created in the first place. But they're here and we've either got to kill them or learn to live with them.

"Their own kind have warned them not to fuck us, that we're a step backwards, that we're dirty and primitive — can you blame some of them for wanting to check us out? But forget them. They lower our intelligence. They infect boys and girls alike. They twist us up into big balls of shit."

"But most of them go about their business-as-usual of taking over the world, steadily and surely, and ignore us except when they want entertainment." — from "The New Hermaphrodite," *Apocalypse Culture II,* Feral House, 1999

Joe Coleman: "You pissed me off, but not as much as some other people. You pissed me off because of that fucking interview in *Seconds*. You wrote several paragraphs that said I raped some fucking bitch in a Punk Rock band, and that I was robbin' graves—all this stuff that I never did, that you made up. That transgressed our relationship. I still can't understand why you did that."

Two who worked tirelessly on *EXIT,* and got screwed.
Above: Kyra Melanie Burton, RIP
Photo by Michael Andros
Right: Nancy Keating, formerly a.k.a. Nancy Petros
Photo by Richard Kern

Hi got my glasses — Looking again at your Book — Joe Coleman has got A MIND PLUS + his art is something els. a Cave man in a space ship — I'm gitting a lot of mail from the Book + Everyone else here likes it — praze praze praze in haw ever you speel...) it reflects intelligince + a lot of Brain work, Gloom + doom + the down side — but again I think you — George Petros drawings are sprit + express much to me also I love art — I put the Cover on the wall + sent the back out to make a Xmas Card for some guy This book has become one of my best toys :) —

— Charles Manson

Example of mail sent to EXIT
Letter from Charles Manson to Adam Parfrey, 1987
Adam sent Manson some money for glasses, along with a copy of *EXIT* #2.
By some miracle the mag made it past prison watchdogs. Herein Manson praises
Joe Coleman, as well as yours truly.
Collection of Adam Parfrey

Our purpose is to not just start the US Race War, but to win it and to have a lot of fun in the process, and this is possible by the intelligent, merciless, pitiless application of certain already developed scientific methods.

The imposition of gun control, besides criminalizing and therefore radicalizing a substantial number of US Indo-Europeans, is also an impetus, a spur, for Whites to devise other types of deadly weapons, and one class of these is electronic " resonance weapons " which work on the principle of tuning to the rresonance frequency of crystalline parts of biological molecules and causing the natural vibration to become rapidly and drastically amplified with the result that the crystal vibrates, or explodes itself apart self-destructively, thus killing the supporting organism.

Examples of the resonance amplification principle are the action of pushing a child's swing just when the swing reaches the top of its movement, and the dramatic destruction in 1938 of " Galloping Gertie, " the Puget Sound bridge by high winds which caused the huge structure to begin oscillating at its resonace frequency and consequently to violently self-destruct as tremendous harmonic forces tore apart its giant steel framework (Fig. 1). Small forces were vastly amplified into an explosion.

The same principle can be used to cause human (more accurately, sub-human or devolved) beings to self-destruct almost instantly. The idea is that a crystal is any substance that has repeating units in various arrays and that a number of biological molecules, or ordered sets of molecules, i.e., " liquid crystals," fit this description and can be exploited for killing: Proteins, nucleic acids, carbohydrates, and fatty acids.

Apropos of the Race War, some of these " tunable crystals " are common to all humanoids, but others are unique, or specific, to a given race, a circumstance which enables the selective injuring or killing on the basis or race. This can be done by using applying certain resonant frequencies with a low power device from some distance away.

The resonant frequency of a molecule can be determined in several ways:
1. Scan through frequency spectrum - detecting device will show maximum absorbance at resonant frequency.
2. If resonant frequency is at " forbidden frequency " for equipment, then:
   a) excite molecule to higher energy state, and moniter as it decays to ground state - it will emit heat (acoustic) or light if high energy, and these can be measured to determine r.f.
   b) Use coupling molecule which matches with and transfers energy to or from molecule of interest.

There are two classes of molecules with tunable crystal characteritics, general and race-specific.

General: common to all humanoids. Can be used on wives, children, and relatives of police, FBI, BATF, miscellaneous " law enforecement " scum and of White race traitors. Examples are collagen, elastin, proteoglycans.

1. Collagen. This a fibrous protein, and acts as a structural component in blood vessels, skin, bone, tendons, cartilage, and teeth. It also acts by gluing together cells. Collagen is the most abundant protein in mammals, and is critical to survival; collagen weakening, as in scurvy, results in the bursting of blood vessels.

The protein is organized at three levels: three individual amino acid chains are wound around each other to form " tropocollagen," a superhelical cable, and numerous tropocollagen helices are arranged in staggered linear array to form the collagen fiber (Figs 2 and 3).

The vulnerable point is within the amino acid chains. First, the individual chains are bound to each other by a series of very weak hydrogen bonds which act " cooperatively, " that is, the formation of each bond depends on whether or not there are adjacent bonds. This cooperative structure acts like a zipper: Once a few bonds are broken, then all other bonds break easily and rapidly and cause the entire molecule suddenly to become destabilized, disintegrated, and destroyed.

The hydrogen bonds are formed by Glycine amino acid residues that donate a Hydrogen atom to an oxygen atom attached to a carbon atom on an amino acid on another

Example of mail sent to *EXIT*
Page 1, letter from anonymous scientist to George Petros, 1994
The sender insisted the letter be destroyed after copying.
Collection of the author

Michael Andros, 1987
Photo by Evelyn Kelley

MICHAEL ANDROS: *"Might makes right. That applies to male versus female, magic versus science, predator versus prey. Since rape was made illegal, pussy has ruled the world. In my own way, I'm trying to change that. My art contributes to that struggle, illuminating the path back to power."*

Were you into pornography? **ANDROS:** "I was into pornography from a very young age, beginning with my best friend's father's *Playboys* from age 5 to 11 or so, and then beginning around age 12, popular men's magazines such as *Male, Man's World* et cetera. Of particular interest to me were the lurid covers of almost-naked females in the evil clutches of Nazis or Japanese military sadists, in dungeons, with glowing irons or whips or other instruments of torture. I would masturbate to the stories of torture that were rampant in those publications, forming early predilections for the sexual mores I became quite comfortable with by my late teens. As time passed, I became involved in the S&M sex world in real life, and began collecting hard-core sado-masochistic pornography, beginning with magazines and paperback books and, later, videos. The more intense and sadistic, the more I was enamored of it. My art reflects that."

What's your take on religion and the occult? "I believe in lust. I believe in power. I believe in the idea that only the strong survive. Unfortunately, in today's world, the weak not only survive, but thrive in many instances. I fear this is polluting the gene pool in a disastrous way. I am not the only person who believes this, of course. If humanity survives, I hope that I, and those others—past and present—who hold this to be true, are merely the tip of the iceberg, as that belief grows within future generations. So I would have to say that my ideas regarding religion and the occult lean toward the feral, the natural order of things. I believe in ghosts, in magic, and in power, both physical and spiritual.

"The closest philosophy I've encountered to my own beliefs, I would have to say, is Satanism. I find some tenets of it to be in conflict with what I hold to be true, yet we have lots of common ground as well. The thing I think we share most strongly is the belief in the natural, feral, real world, unblemished by social strictures."

Did making your art excite you sexually? "When I was doing collages for *EXIT*, many times I achieved an erection for hours at a time. The sexual content was mostly responsible for this; however, some of my politically-based graphics also brought out the beast in my penis, as it were, being that politics is all about power and we all know how power is very evident in sexuality—at least in mine it is.

"My work was tailored to incite certain archetypes in people's minds, and to make them reflect on some of their more retarded ideas. If such reflection by the viewer hurt, emotionally or intellectually or otherwise, then yes, my intention was very much to hurt."

"She was loud and aggressive, prancing around with a crop in her hand, teasing people, telling them they were bad boys and girls. She walked up to me and started to say something, stopped dead in her tracks, looked down at the floor, turned and slowly melted back into the crowd. I said to the person I was with, "I hate bitches who play at sadism. I'd hang her up like a side of beef and beat her fucking senseless."

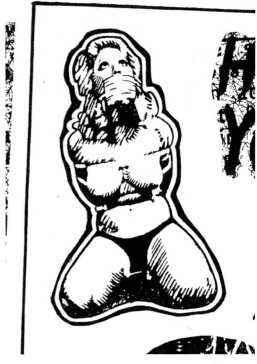

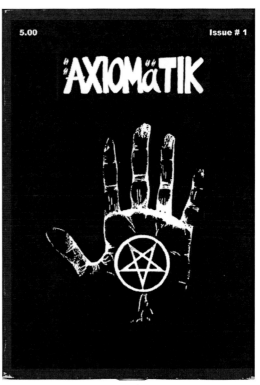

Top: *Sugar #6*, Andros, 1987
Below: *Axiomatic #1*, 1989
He wanted Ted Bundy on the cover, but I talked him out of it.
Collection of the author

Page 3, *Jesus And The Twelve Definitions*, Michael Andros, 1990
Collection of Michael Andros

***Footnote On The Art Of Politics*, Michael Andros, 1992**
Collection of Michael Andros

Robert N. Taylor, 1990
Photo by Karen Taylor

ROBERT N. TAYLOR: "Symbols can be modified in their meaning, but you can't suppress them—because they come from within."

TAYLOR: "If one picture is worth a thousand words then one symbol is worth a million pictures."

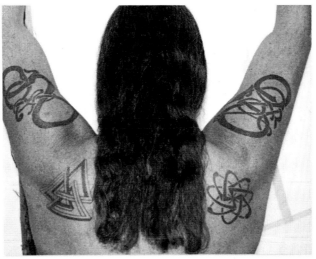

"Government harassment and efforts to destroy the Minutemen Organization culminated in a plan to kill myself and others in a Black Panther-style raid. Fortunately we had warning of this move and scattered from our national headquarters. Before doing so I sent out letters to various local groups, suggesting that they set-up local, independent groups under the names of posse and vigilance committees et cetera. This was the Feds' greatest fear, that the organization would become scattered with no central headquarters that they could watch, monitor or infiltrate. Now, instead of watching the hub of one large group, they had the task of watching and finding hundreds of low-profile autonomous groups. This spread their resources beyond capacity and made them very ineffective in monitoring what was afoot at the grass-roots level."

Are you a violent person? "I can be when up against the wall. I'm certainly no pacifist by any stretch of the imagination. I grew up in street gangs. I'm not a bully. I don't look for trouble. I don't push people around. I give everybody respect until they prove themselves unworthy of it. I can be violent. I have that in reserve, should I need it." *Is violence expressed in your art?* "Perhaps so. Some poetry, some pictures suggest violent impulses. But there was a spiritual counterpart to it as well, which modifies the violent side. Balances it. But as far as violence is concerned, sometimes it's the only language they understand, so to speak."

You created a time-line history of the swastika. "Yeah, ten pages of it. I was simply showing the longevity of this symbol, and that it got frozen in a fourteen-year time slot, and that such primal symbols cannot be suppressed. The swastika piece caused a bit of a furor both for better and for worse. In Germany, copies of that issue of *EXIT* were outlawed. It became a federal crime to possess, no less. And John Aes-Nihil, who was over there at the time, saw on TV that a lady had been arrested and raped by German police who were confiscating stacks of 'em. I had the image of German skinheads looking at my piece under the blanket with a flashlight. *EXIT* was the harbinger of political pornography. It created a new genre."

"If I've left a path of destruction behind me, it wasn't intentional per se, but I do like to tweak people and pinch 'em and wake 'em up and amaze and astound 'em at times." *And maybe hurt 'em?* "Well, maybe so. I have the ability to manipulate reality around you. I do like to shock. Anything to get some life out of drones. Art is a harbor in the storm of life. It's a place you can put all your angst into. Where other people end up blowing their brains out, the artist can go to his desk and get it all out of him."

Wolf's Head, Robert N. Taylor, 1985
Collection of Michael Andros

173

Page 8, *The Swastika: Sacred And Profane*, Robert N. Taylor, 1989
This ten-page piece appeared in *EXIT #4*.
Collection of the author

Absinthe collage, Robert N. Taylor, 1996
This piece appeared in *Seconds #46*. Among the Absinthe-drinkers' faces: Poe, Rimbaud, Jack London, Monet, Verlaine, John Barrymore, Oscar Wilde, Somerset Maugham, Michael Moynihan, R. Bruce Ritchie, the artist himself—as well as yours truly! The wallpaper pattern: wormwood flowers. Check out the clock. The painting on the wall is by Hitler, an Absinthe drinker in his 20's.
Collection of the author

Peter Sotos, 1993
Photo by Nick Bougas

PETER SOTOS: *"That's the kind of cock I like. You know, the ones that blow you and feed you at glory holes; the ones that stink like need and rot and slow hate? Like the kind that hangs inside your pants. Like the one that put you here, right now."*

Q: *What put you on the map?*
SOTOS: My arrest for child pornography.
Q: *What was the charge?*
A: I was arrested for obscenity, and that gave way to possession of child pornography. The obscenity charge was dropped as the trial went on. The trial lasted three years.
Q: *When were you arrested?*
A: December 4, 1985.
Q: *Did you consider yourself an artist?*
A: Not at all.
Q: *How about a creative person?*
A: People talk about themselves as "creative"—it's an apology or an excuse. I felt a need for something extra, to convey ideas, which is a creative act. When people describe themselves as creative, I find that pretty offensive.
Q: *You don't proclaim yourself an artist, yet you've amassed a considerable body of work.*
A: Oh dear! It's always been very confusing. People told me that the material was good because it was art. They said, "It was creative," or, "It made me think," or, "It was challenging," or they say, "It's breaking some taboo"—and I thought that was ridiculous. However, when I got arrested, I had to fall back on that "art" argument. It didn't work. The prosecutors said, "It's not art, those weren't your intentions—"
Q: *And they were right.*
A: It's a perverse thing because, oddly enough, my arguments should have worked—it does comment on the media and people's hypocrisies and taboos. It just wasn't intentional. The people who need those stupid fucking arguments are gonna find them in the work. But they didn't work for me.
Q: *It didn't work for Mike Diana either.*
A: Mike Diana is a good example of what I'm talking about. But with him there's a lot of other things going on. Mike actually really thinks he's an artist. I really don't think he knows what he's dealing with. I always thought that was an insult to the work. My stuff was just too personal. Mike Diana doesn't really know what he's doing.

Q: *Describe* PURE.
A: It was a reflection of my interests. I spent all my time—every fucking minute—looking for newspaper articles about sexual murders. I was reading every book—but remember, back then there wasn't a True Crime section in bookstores.

Sotos & William Bennett, Whitehouse, 1996
Photographer unknown, from the *Seconds* archive

Flyer for Sotos & Parfrey at Quimby's, Chicago, 2000
Collection of Phil Luciani

177

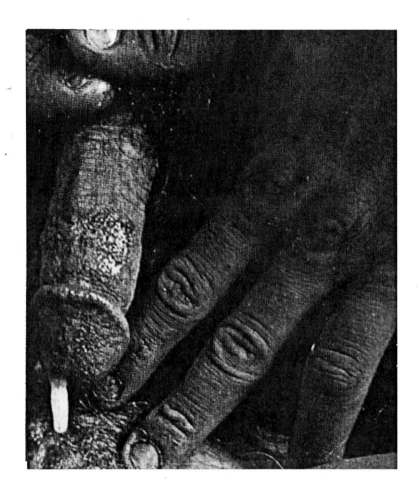

PURE #1, 1984
Collection of John Aes-Nihil

> "I'm really happy that PURE just stands as it was, and if people are looking for that sort of thing, they'll find it there."

You had to really look for that sort of stuff. You had to put yourself out there. I ordered newspapers from Florida, for example, because there was all sorts of stuff going on down there.

Q: *There's plenty of sexual murders in Florida.*

A: I collected such things and put them together and tried to make sense of them, to make something that was honest, that I didn't see in the stuff I was reading. I'm not saying I didn't love it, but it had nothing terribly deep.

Q: *But the authorities thought your stuff was pretty deep.*

A: Yeah. They thought I was a murderer. They tore my floorboards up, looking for bodies. I had an apartment the size of a shoebox, on the North Side of Chicago, by where Wax Trax! was.

Q: *When you attended The Art Institute, what were you into?*

A: Up to that point, I'd always had girlfriends and a sort-of normal sexuality. There was a degenerate I went to school with—if we got bored in class, we'd go off to the bathroom. And he was really good at scoping out other places, like Union Station, glory holes, and things like that. I discovered all that in my early twenties, and suddenly any interest in women as sexual partners was gone, and it seemed terribly boring. I know that from PURE I have this reputation as a misogynist, but I really wasn't. I think that's really one-dimensional. There just wasn't that young-adult interest in needing to get laid. All that was removed. My experiences became furtive, with men who had neither boyfriends or girlfriends, and were really fucked-up individuals. You'd meet them outside of men's bathrooms, or there were the faggots from school who were all titillated by the fact that one wasn't really Gay and wasn't really enjoying what they had to offer. It was really sort of vulgar and very rough trade-ish.

Q: *So the idea that the other party is not into it one hundred percent is very important.*

A: I really hate this word, but it really was anonymous. Even with people you knew. I was standing up, sitting on the toilet, pissing in the mouth—it was quick and immediate degradation, you know—people sitting in shit as quickly as possible.

Q: *I remember those days.*

A: It was one-sided. It wasn't this idea that you're sharing something or experiencing something together. And it was like that on both sides. You honestly did not give a fuck. You thought that "This is better than doing nothing." Honestly, every day it was blow-jobs with men. And there was a girl who I was dating! It was the same way—I'd fuck her in the bathroom, too. It was just sort of like a quick thing.

Q: *Was pornography a big part of your world?*

A: Absolutely. Huge, actually.

Q: *Both Gay and straight?*

A: You know, I didn't like Gay porno. I hated that whole homosexual thing. It wasn't like now, the beefcake thing. Back then, it was hippies, guys who let you come all over their beard. The only thing I liked about Gay porno is that you could find pictures of people eating shit.

Q: *Didn't AIDS clean house of that generation?*

A: Everyone thinks AIDS was a concentrated effort to stop all that. What it really did was up the stakes. The guys on their knees became even more desperate. They became much more uncontrolled, much more pathetic. It was really amazing to watch people that I just knew were going to die—and they did.

> Child abuse is a sublime pleasure. All the great extremes - genital torture, forced unlubricated rape, butchering; all these pleasures and more reach their pinnacle when the victim is a small child. The orifices are extremely tight and usually virgin, an absolute joy to mangle, rip and violate. The pained screams ring more shrill, more empassioned, unhampered from years of growing up fat and jaded. Virgin territory brings the fresh cries and intense reactions of crushed and forever retarded innocence.
>
> There is an added pleasure in child torture, a pleasure that lives on even after the child lay dead and rotting. Parents. The pain of the parents allows the libertine to forever enjoy his crimes. Little kidlings are precious to parents, their lives become meaningful and important because of the little bundle of love that bounces on their knees. Their grief and sense of loss is immense when their tiny god's gifts are destroyed. Their entire lives crumble

Excerpt from PURE #1
Collection of Phil Luciani

Sotos reads at Quimby's, Chicago 2000
Photo by Phil Luciani

179

chance of ending up a young corpse, or at the very least, whoring on some corner effectively brain-dead, at the end of the film session. There are thousands of well documented cases all concerning street children kidnapped and then kept as prisoners for as many books, movies and photos that can be squeezed out of them. The used and abused children either end up cut up like a skinny lamb and floating in some filthy river or out on the streets, again, hooking under a Puerto Rican/nigger pimp. Countless interviews with teen sluts relate the crushing effects of child porn and it's immense influence over their later lives. Kiddie porn's major attraction is clearly the smashing of innocence and t only works when it's for real. The slow, understated destruction of little minds is obvious from the salient images of 4 and 5 year old girls trying desperately to keep their legs closed together as a hulking elder tries just as desperately to pry them loose. Or the 6 year-old in pony tails who tries to hide her tears from the camera. Or the embarassed little boy who pulls his face away from a man's looming hard-on, because he knows it's wrong somehow.

 PURE readers are, no doubt, more than familiar with the child porn connections and the tremendous body count of dead nigger children that hangs over Wayne Williams' afro'd head.

 The brutality and genius of child pornography is almost chilling in it's thoroughness and eloquence. The incidents that create the glorious snaps of child flesh and child control and child anguish gives the knowledgeable voyeur a consummate thrill. The fear and shattered

Page from *PURE* #2, 1985
Collection of Phil Luciani

City/suburbs

$100,000 bond set in child-porn case

By Linnet Myers

Bond of $100,000 was set by a Criminal Court judge Thursday for a Near North Side man who, according to prosecutors, distributed a homemade magazine that outlined "the pleasures of child abuse, torture and murder in pornographic detail."

Peter Gus Sotos, 25, who was arrested Wednesday in his apartment at 748 W. Belden Ave., allegedly published a magazine called Pure, which included photographs depicting the "lewd exhibition" of children, Cook County Assistant State's Atty. Dan Jordan told Criminal Court Judge Francis Gembala.

The magazine's first edition, published last year, said that "child abuse is a sublime pleasure" and that the "pleasures" of torture "reach their pinnacle when the victim is a small child," Judge Gembala was told.

Assistant State's Atty. Robert Cleary said Sotos allegedly put the magazine together using photos of children photocopied from illegal commercially produced pornographic magazines. The text detailed the torture and murder of children, Cleary said.

The magazine's third edition, which would have featured the recent slaying of Melissa Ackerman of Somonauk, was barred from circulation by Sotos' arrest, said state Inspector Gen. Jeremy Margolis.

Sotos had been manager of a used-record store in Evanston, said James Meltreger, his lawyer.

Meltreger argued that Sotos isn't charged with taking any of the photos or of having any direct contact with the children.

Margolis said investigators found no mailing list or record of how many copies of Pure were printed or sold.

"I've never come in contact with a child pornography case where profit was the motive," Margolis said. "The majority of child pornography is produced by pedophiles in order to share it with other pedophiles, to broaden their contacts and share their fantasies."

According to Jay Howell, executive director of the National Center for Missing and Exploited Children, child pornography is typically produced and distributed from a person's home, "creating a network of these sad little cottage industries."

"Although there is a hard-core child pornography industry in materials that come from overseas, in terms of volume there is no doubt that the greatest numbers of materials come through this unofficial market," Howell said.

Sotos is the first person charged

Inspector Gen. Jeremy Margolis says distribution of suspect's magazine halted by his arrest.

under the three-week-old revised Illinois Child Pornography Act, which makes possessing, manufacturing or distributing child pornography a Class 1 felony punishable by a prison sentence of 4 to 15 years. He also was charged in a misdemeanor complaint with obscenity.

Jane Whicher, a lawyer for the Chicago office of the American Civil Liberties Union, said that in a letter to Gov. James Thompson the ACLU protested the inclusion of possession as part of the act.

"We certainly believe that people who prey on children should be punished, but the part of the statute that criminalizes mere possession is a violation of the 1st Amendment," Whicher said.

Article from *Chicago Tribune*, 1985
SOTOS: I used murderers as a conduit for my own tastes, to extrapolate fantasies from what they did and from their victims and situations.
SECONDS (MICHAEL MOYNIHAN): *Is it accurate to call it pornography?*
SOTOS: There are so many different definitions of "pornography," but I think it is. I like good pornography. As for this idea of "what appeals to a prurient interest," I spend most of my time trying to get at, and to define, a prurient interest. So I'm willing to accept that definition of pornography. In court when my lawyers had to argue that this stuff had some vision above and beyond masturbation, they failed. They couldn't convince the judge—they couldn't convince anybody.
Collection of Peter Sotos

GG Allin, 1989
Photo by Richard Kern

GG ALLIN: "I don't give a shit about anybody."

Call this story

UNCOOL - UNCLEAN - UNACCEPTABLE
GG ALLIN
THE ROCK N ROLL UNDERGROUND'S MOST NOTORIOUS, BLOOD THIRSTY TERRORIST DECLAIRS HIS OWN WAR....

SECONDS: *Describe the crime you allegedly committed.*

ALLIN: I'll tell you. I was invited to a girl's house after I'd met her a couple of times. I'd spent time with her, she knew what I was about, she'd seen me mutilate myself and set myself on fire. She invited me to her house—it was a walk-in party, people were coming in off the streets that she didn't even know. She had somebody handcuff her to the bed; it wasn't me. The burning of her leg was a complete accident, which they blew way out of proportion; we were just tryin' to wake her up. The thing is, when I cut her and drank her blood—she had asked me to give here a tattoo, and there was no india ink, so it's not unusual to give somebody a tattoo by cutting into them. I've seen it done and I've done it to myself. So how's that a felonious assault when she had asked me to do this, and then had asked everybody in the band to come in and jerk off on her face, and she slept with everyone at the party? I mean, come on, it's so goddamn obvious. Just talkin' about it makes me sick, it makes me want to go out and blow up this whole motherfuckin' state. 'Cause I'm not in here for the crime—that's what I'm tryin' to tell you. I had letters from this girl, after the incident, that stated that she wanted to marry me. I had phone calls up until two weeks before I got arrested by the Secret Service. Why the Secret Service was called in, I don't know. See, that's just another thing. They were after me because of my stage shows. They'd been following me before this thing came out. Every time we played in a city and left, the FBI was there looking for

Left: GG Allin & The AIDS Brigade 7", Homestead, 1988
Right: GG Allin & The Southern Baptists 7", Railroad, 1993
Collection of Steven Blush

G.G. ALLIN'S SKULL FUCK
by NICK ZEDD

MAY 5:

I WENT TO BOSTON THIS WEEKEND FOR A "READING" WITH G.G. ALLIN. I PUNCHED OUT A HECKLER IN THE AUDIENCE AND GOT IN A FIST FIGHT WITH FOUR POETRY FUCKS.

G.G. BROKE A WHISKEY BOTTLE OVER HIS HEAD, TRIED TO RAPE A GIRL IN THE AUDIENCE AND GOT BEAT UP BY TWO GUYS. HE PUT HIS HEAD THRU A WINDOW, LIT A NEWSPAPER ON FIRE, THREW CHAIRS AT THE AUDIENCE AND CUT HIMSELF UP WITH A BROKEN BEER CAN BEFORE BREAKING THE MIKE. THEN HE LEFT.

G.G. WANTED TO MAKE A SNUFF MOVIE WITH ME THE NEXT DAY BUT I COULDN'T EVEN GET HIM TO PULL HIS PANTS DOWN AND DO HIS "BALL DANCE" ON VIDEO. HE KICKED OUT THE WINDOW OF SOMEONE'S CAR AND TRIED TO RAPE A GIRL IN THE APT. WHERE WE WERE TAPING, BUT I FELT SORRY FOR HER SO WE LET HER GO. WE COULDN'T FIND ANYBODY TO KILL SO WE JUST LISTENED TO RAW POWER AND G.G. INHALED A PAPER BAG FULL OF WHITE OUT

THIS NIGGER IS BAD

Nick Zedd, from *The Underground Film Bulletin #8* on his travels with GG, 1987
Allin: "I'll tell you straight out that I'm not the easiest guy to hang out with. I like pushing women, and I like doing dangerous things. People should expect that if they want to hang out with me. If they don't wanna hang out with me, then they can just stay the fuck away."
Collection of Michael Andros

> "The way I see it, people exist around me, but they're not really there. I feel completely alienated. I'm like a one-man army on the outside of what everybody else is thinking or doing."

me. So this goes deeper than what you've heard about. They want the public to think it's a felonious assault because if the public knew what these people were trying to get away with and why they've got me in here, there would be an outrage. They want to cover it up.

SECONDS: *Tell us about her being burned.*

ALLIN: She passed out, and nobody could wake her up. We didn't know if she was dead. She'd drank so much, and she'd knocked all the windows out of her house, so we figured that the girl really fucked herself up. I wasn't the only one who lit a match. I took a lighter and lit it under her leg, to try to wake her up. I couldn't revive her any other way. But she made it sound like we threw gasoline on her and set her on fire. That's not what happened, and if she'd gone to the hospital the next day like we'd told her, she would've been fine. But she waited a fuckin' month, and she gave three different police reports. The first police report she said she got raped by three Black men, the second police report she said she was hitchhiking and somebody tried to rape her. I don't even remember what she said in the third police report. Finally, I don't know what happened, if she snapped or not, but then she pointed the finger at me. Why just me? If you'd seen the letters that she'd written me after this whole incident happened, you would know what kind of girl this was. Unfortunately, not enough people know about my case yet. That's why I'm doing this interview, so I can get people aware of how they have railroaded me, because of my performances and records. The whole thing comes right down to censorship—and this was long before the censorship thing was a bandwagon item, which it is right now. I was goin' to prison for it. I'm in prison, and now they can keep an eye on me.

SECONDS: *Does being in prison help your career?*

ALLIN: It may help. I don't really look at it that way. I look at this as another part of my life. I mean, I've been to jail before. Doing a GG Allin tour—a jail and a hospital just goes along with it. After a show, it's either you're goin' to jail or goin' to a hospital or you're escaping from the police—there's only three routes out. It was hard to keep bands because it really was a war out there, going from one show to another, bleeding from one show to the next. I figure that my tour of 1989 will probably keep me in court for the next ten years. I've got three charges in Connecticut, Wisconsin and other states I'm not even gonna mention because they don't show up on the computer, and I'm kinda hoping it stays that way.

Flyer for GG performance, NYC, 1986
Collection of Steven Blush

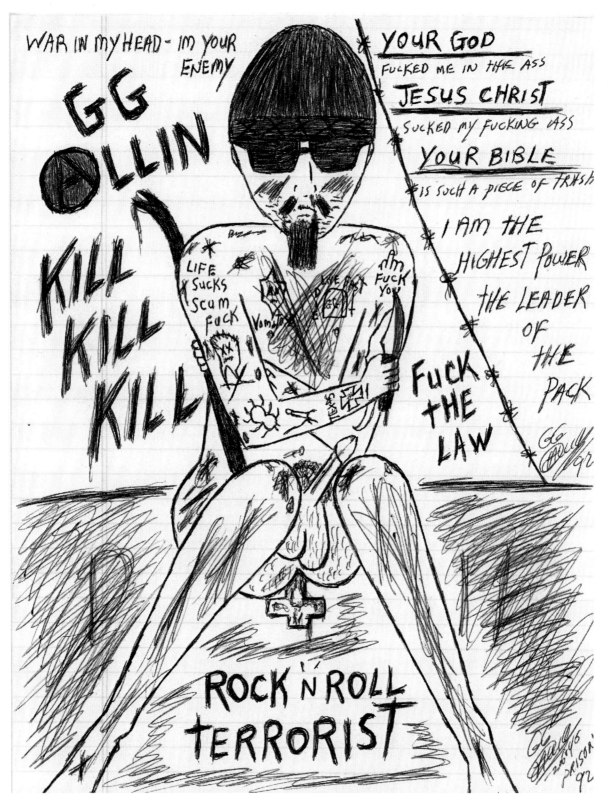

Untitled illustration by GG Allin, executed in prison, circa 1991
"I'll tell you, there are people in here that I'd rather hang out with than people out there—
'cause even though you might be hangin' out with somebody who killed people,
we're all outcasts in here. We don't exist to the outside world."
Collection of Arthur Deco

Above: GG (left) and friends doing Heroin at a party, NYC, June 27, 1993
A few minutes after they snorted the shit, GG laid back and nodded off, like he'd done a thousand times before. Hours passed, and party-goers went on about their business around the supine Rock God. After about twelve hours, they tried to wake him up—to no avail.
Photo by Richard Kern

Below: GG's final performance, Littleton, New Hampshire, June 30, 1993
SECONDS: *What would you like people to know about you?*
ALLIN: I'm someone who actually will go to my grave for something I believe in. Most people will talk about it, but I'm the guy that will do it. Everything I say is the truth, and I'm willing to go that distance. I'm not just walkin' on the razor's edge—I'm sleepin' on it!
Photo by Merle Allin
Collection of Nick Bougas

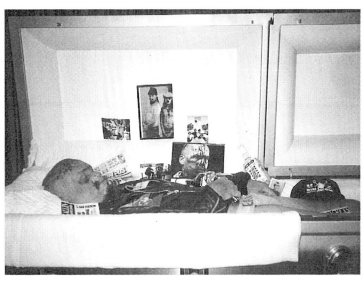

James Mason, 1994
Self-portrait

JAMES MASON: "The more alienated you are, the better Manson looks. Nobody is ever brought around to Manson—you're either there or you're not."

Q: *Did you feel like you were creating art?*
MASON: I sure did. I roughed the stuff out on a piece of paper, and I had the cooperation of a professional printer. I wrote articles and designed literature. The stuff I did looked aesthetic and sounded intelligent. I'd like to think I was original in what I designed and wrote.

Q: *Did you consider yourself an artist?*
A: I did. Every time one of those posters came out, it was like having a baby. It was eye-catching, short and sweet, right to the point.

Q: *Did you get feedback?*
A: You bet. People were starved for the stuff. Fuck all that national headquarters so-called discipline. Let's cut loose. I took it to extremes that most people would disown. The unfavorable reactions came from uptight people who were fooling themselves. I was trying to further radicalize the radicals.

Q: *People like John Aes-Nihil and Boyd Rice came to your attention.*
A: Boyd wrote to me in 1986. He saw some of my literature. In 1987 I was contacted by Adam Parfrey. Some of my stuff wound up in *Apocalypse Culture* and *EXIT*.

Q: *How would you describe those people?*
A: Freethinkers.

Q: *What did you think about Anton LaVey?*
A: I admired LaVey. I learned a lot from him.

Q: *Tell us about Charles Manson.*
A: It was a weird thing with me. Just as it was with Hitler, it was with Manson. It was something that began to come over me. There was a pizza parlor with a jukebox that had The Beatles' "Helter Skelter" on it. I hate Rock, but whenever I went to that place I had to play "Helter Skelter." I became aware of Manson the way everybody else did, through the news. I saw the same negativity attached to him that was attached to Hitler. My instincts were able to see through that. I went for Hitler in '66 as much out of anger as anything, as the threshold of anger. When I went for Manson in '77, it was as the threshold of alienation and a symbol of radicalism beyond the most radical extreme. I didn't pursue contact with him until 1980 when I contacted the girls—Lynette Fromme and Sandra Goode—and they said, "We only represent the moon. We only reflect the sun's light. You must go directly to the sun." So I contacted Manson in '81 and stayed in close touch for the next ten years.

Q: *He was a source of inspiration for you.*
A: I learned a lot. He broadened my horizons. Manson said, "The truth is one." The truth floats around as an element of the universe. Now and then it will land. Two thousand years ago it might have been Jesus Christ, sixty years ago it was Adolph Hitler—different names, different symbols, but it's still the truth. It comes and goes.

Above: Eva Hoehler, Peter Sotos, Mason, 1993
Below: Printing press and paper cutter, American Nazi Party headquarters, late Seventies. "I ran an offset press, a Davidson Duo-Lith. The guy who taught me how to use it said, 'This turns it off and on, and here's the manual—you might want to read it. I'll see you later.' I slept on the floor next to the press."
Collection of James Mason

"Whilst we ..... the conventional ..... were wasting our time on education, agitation and organization, some independent genius has taken the matter in hand........"

George Bernard Shaw

Post Office Box 42
Chillicothe, Ohio 45601

Flyer for National Socialist Liberation Front, graphics by James Mason, 1985
"Manson is really the leader because without his example—
made known to the rest of us only at the cost of the sacrifice he continues to make—
we'd be a lot further away from the truth than we presently are."
Collection of the author

"The most revolutionary thing one can do is to drop out of the System. It starts in the mind and it ends physically. Anybody aspiring to a revolutionary position has got to expect to be in prison sooner or later."

Q: *Tell us about Eva Hoehler.*
A: In 1977 Alan Vincent, who formed a San Francisco group, National Socialist White Workers Party, came to visit me in Ohio. He was accompanied by Carl Hoehler. That was the year Eva was born. Well, in 1993 I was living in Colorado. I had just split from my ex-old lady, JoDean. I had seen pictures of Eva, who had been engaged to Boyd Rice. I sent a message to her through Michael Moynihan and soon I got a letter from her with her phone number. I called her and asked her to visit me. She said, "When do you want me there?" So, she came out after Christmas. What a beautiful girl! God almighty—every young guy's dream, much less every old guy's dream.

Q: *How old was she?*
A: She was fifteen, which was just barely legal in Colorado. It wasn't legal to photograph somebody that age in the nude. You can screw them but you can't photograph them. Some law!

Q: *Tell us about Carl Hoehler.*
A: Carl was a sincere guy, very dedicated, but wow! The way he raised that girl—god almighty! I think she raised herself. Eva was totally insane, totally unruly; she couldn't wash a dish, she couldn't empty a cup. I was shocked and horrified. Within a couple of days, it was, "This person has to go!" There are far worse things than being alone. She was one of them. All the good looks and all the sex wasn't worth it.

Q: *So y'all became an item—*
A: We were an item immediately. I was kinda shocked.

Q: *What did her dad have to say?*
A: He was glad to have her out of his hair. He gave her money every month. She was very violent. I was exhausted most of the time just defending myself from her. She pulled knives on me, she pulled a gun on me, and she tried

Groovy gathering, Denver 1993
Shane Lassen, Michael Moynihan, Thomas Thorn, Boyd Rice, Giddle Partridge, Shaun Partridge, James Mason. Giddle: "The short-haired girl was some German girlfriend of Moynihan's. The girl I'm next to was my brother's bitch at the time, doesn't deserve a name."
Collection of James Mason

Flyer for National Socialist Liberation Front, James Mason, 1985
"I literally grew up with Adolf Hitler as my god. When I talk to god, I'm talking to Hitler. That will never change. Nor should it—it fits and it's right. As I've grown older, however, I've learned—just as Manson pointed out—that the Truth is One, and that Hitler was but the most recent living manifestation of that."
Collection of the author

Convicted Nazi wants nude photos back

By LOU MOLITERNO
Gazette Staff Writer

A Chillicothe Municipal Court judge is expected to decide April 4 whether a self-professed Nazi will get back nude photographs of two teen-age girls for which he spent 30 days in jail in 1989.

James Mason, 38, of Ault Road, said Ross County Sheriff's deputies searched his home in mid-1988. They 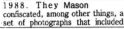 confiscated, among other things, a set of photographs that included nude photos of two Chillicothe sisters, ages 15 and 17.

Now, Mason wants his pictures back.

But Prosecutor Rich Ward said the law clearly states that it is illegal to possess nude photos of children and that if Mason were to possess them again, he be breaking the law again.

Mason, however, says the photos are "art."

A grand jury indicted Mason on five counts including one count of gross sexual imposition, three counts of child pornography and one count of possession of child pornographic material after the photos were confiscated, Mason said.

"I guess they thought they had something," Mason said, adding that he could have spent up to 10 years in prison if convicted of all five counts.

Mason said he pleaded guilty to the possession charge in exchange for the other four counts being dropped in January 1989. He was sentenced to serve 30 days in the Ross County Jail.

He has filed a suit in Chillicothe Municipal Court asking the court to order Sheriff Thomas Hamman to return the material.

The pictures are listed in the suit as being worth about $25.

Mason said he was targeted by sheriff's deputies because he is a Nazi. He has been since 1966.

"They weren't just after a case," Mason said. "They wanted to put a political opponent out of business."

When the prosecution was unable to gain more than a 30-day sentence, law officers held the material out of frustration, Mason said.

"I say they are holding on to the album out of pure meanness, pure spite," Mason said. "I'm an amateur photographer and I'm very proud of the work that's in there."

To which Ward said: "I would say a Nazi would know meanness when he sees it — or he should know."

Article from Chillicothe (Ohio) *Gazette*, 1991
Collection of James Mason

to shoot me but she didn't know how to use an automatic. I wanted to love her but you couldn't. She was a violent individual. She kept me emotionally off-guard at all times.

Q: *Did she go to school?*

A: No. I tried to get her to get a GED, and I taught her to drive, but then the shit hit the fan.

Q: *Tell us about that.*

A: Well, unfortunately I got hung up on another fifteen-year-old, Crystal Martin, in the town of Los Animas, and I had occasion to shoot a series of nude pictures of her, in a town of twenty-five hundred people where everybody knows everybody else. Her father was a drinking buddy of mine. Unbeknownst to me she was trying to put the make on a city cop, Robert Keenan, who at the time would have sold his soul to the devil to get some goodies on me in order to help his career. Out of that came the arrest.

Q: *What were the charges?*

A: Exploitation of a minor. It stemmed from the photography. She was trying to impress this married cop who was seeing her on the side. She asked him, "Would you like to see some dirty pictures of me?" and he said, "I'd love to. Where did you get them?" "Oh, James took them. This won't get him in any trouble, will it?" "Oh no, no—" It was like that.

Q: *What was the sentence?*

A: I served all over the place. I started out in then I bonded out, then finally I went to the state pen. I started out in minimum security and wound up in maximum security. I did my time and was on the street for three weeks when I got busted on a bogus series of parole violations like pornography and association with extremist groups. I went back in for four months and got back out on the street. I was out for eight months and I got popped again so I went back into medium security. Basically I had a good time because the Colorado prison system is one of the most advanced in the country. I met quite a few interesting people. There's anything you want in prison. The guards bring it in. Prison is no worse than anything on the street.

Q: *How long were you in?*

A: My sentence was three years. They could have given me thirty years. I did less than three with good time. Then I was on parole, and I went back in for a year. As a prisoner you had no rights, but as a parolee you had even fewer rights. I was free as of August 25, 1999—the anniversary of Rockwell's assassination.

Q: *Bravo on your thing for young chicks!*

A: Anybody who tells you they don't have a thing for young girls is either a queer or a liar. But I paid a heavy price. The men were pissed off at me because they weren't doing it, and the women were pissed off because nobody was doing it to them.

(These are 2 poems that Richard Ramirez (the night stalker) wrote for me. The first poetry he's ever written. I think he did a pretty good job.)

"Agony." By Richard Ramirez
Years fly by,
Night calls to me.
Unable to spread my wings
To hear the scream of things
To awake from sleep
To wish it was always so deep
The eyes that see all and wonder
Sounds of clap and thunder.

"Eva". By Richard Ramirez
With Raven hair
A mystery behind her smile.
She is one for whom I do care.
Distance and solitude separate us
And to think of what it could of been
Time and space will bring together
"The love we lust."

Poems by Richard Ramirez,
Transcribed from phone conversations
by Eva Hoehler, 1994
Collection of the author

**Example of James Mason's photography: Eva Hoehler, circa 1994
Collection of Michael Andros**

CASE NO. 95/96AS09

COLORADO DEPARTMENT OF CORRECTIONS
CLASSIFICATION SUMMARY–ADMINISTRATIVE SEGREGATION REVIEW
COLORADO STATE PENITENTIARY

INMATE NAME	MASON, JAMES	DOC NUMBER	86520
CURRENT SECURITY DESIGNATION	Ad. Seg.	CURRENT PAROLE ELIGIBILITY	Past

REASON(s) for initiating placement in Administrative Segregation:
- **X** Conduct poses serious threat to security of a facility;
- ___ To prevent imminent injury to an inmate(s) or to an employee;
- ___ To contain or prevent or quell a riot;
- ___ To prevent serious property damage;
- ___ To prevent escape; and/or,
- **X** Other, Specify: DISRUPTIVE INFLUENCES C.R.S.17-1-109

WITNESSES:

EVIDENCE RELIED UPON:
Books and Pamphlets Mason has received from disruptive groups advocating violence, correspondence/association by MASON with disruptive groups, Working File and Pod Staff.

Subjects S code was changed from 1 to 4.

FINDING OF FACT:
No negative behavior has been reported and Mason continues to demonstrate behavior favorable of Level III Quality of Life; However, Mason continues to associate and correspond with disruptive organizations. Due to this association/affiliation with disruptive groups, Colorado Revised Statute, 17-1-109, authorizes placement in Administrative Segregation.
Continued placement in Admin. Seg. is fully warranted.
Recommend Retain at CSP, pending further evaluation and behavior.

DECISION:
Retain in Administrative Segregation at CSP: ___ No **X** Yes
Variance Required ___ No ___ Yes; If yes, attach Variance Request

REASON(s): Continued assessment

S/ [signature] Chairperson   8-14-97 Date

DATE OF HEARING	8-18-97	TIME OF HEARING	1:30 pm	LOCATION OF HEARING	CSP

COMMITTEE MEMBERS PRESENT: Carlton Reid Riddle

SUPERINTENDENT/DIRECTOR REVIEW:
✓ AFFIRM ___ MODIFY ___ REVERSE
COMMENTS:

S/ Donice Neal Administrative Head   SEP 02 1997 Date

Administrative Segregation Review of James Mason, 1997
"If I have to be in, I'd rather be in on the charge I'm here for, having already confronted what we call racial treason. I think I have a few more credentials now."
Collection of James Mason

Above: Strand Theatre, San Francisco, August 8, 1988
Below: Participants in the 8/8/88 show, including Bob Heick, Zeena LaVey, Boyd Rice, Evil Wilhelm, Felina, Nikolas Schreck, Wendy Van Deusen
Photos by Nick Bougas

JOHN AES-NIHIL: "The 8-8-88 show in San Francisco was the culmination of the deliberate will to evil in action."

BOYD RICE: "It was my show—it was a NON concert. I was the headliner. NON that night was myself with Adam Parfrey, Zeena LaVey, Nikolas Schreck and the drummer from Radio Werewolf, Evil Wilhelm." *An all-star band!* "Yeah. [laughs] Zeena read a passage from *The Satanic Bible*. Adam played the oboe. The theme of The Secret Chiefs' concert was the Zodiac Killer.

"The line went all the way around the block. Geraldo Rivera sent a film crew. Malcolm Barber, a creator of *COPS,* interviewed us. What ended up on *The Geraldo Show* was twenty seconds of me appearing to exhort the audience to murder, saying, 'Murder is the predator's prerogative,' and, 'There is no Earth without blood.' They took the most outlandish moment and put it on TV.

"We showed a film called *The Other Side of Madness,* about Manson. When it came out, Roman Polanski and Warren Beatty bought up all available copies. There was one copy left, and we showed it. It was the first and last public showing.

"One guy said he was going to come onstage during the show and inject me with AIDS-tainted blood, because he thought I was homophobic. I found out who it was, called him up and straightened everything out." *Who was it?* "He was a weird guy who had been a secretary at *ReSearch*. His name was Mark. He'd heard I was a member of a militant Gay-bashing group. He had a crush on me, and was devastated that I might not like homosexuals.

"We were supposed to do a destruction ritual that Anton LaVey had done on the nights of the Tate-LaBianca murders. 8-8 was the aniversary of the LaBianca murders." *Did it happen?* "Not really—I think Nikolas Schreck read it on stage. It was exactly the time the murders had happened—just before midnight. Strangely enough, there was a race riot going on over on Market Street just as the show ended."

ADAM PARFREY: "8-8-88 was a show Boyd did at the Strand Theater. 88 was the way Neo-Nazis would say 'Heil Hitler.' So he thought he would use that as a way of making people anxious and putting across his own love of the man. He asked me to be involved with it. I did agree, and I played *Valley of the Dolls* theme music on the oboe. He had Zeena LaVey speak. He had Nikolas Schreck play organ. Schreck made sure to call up the Geraldo Rivera show, who were doing a special on Satanism. He got them to come and film 8-8-88. So it was part of that highest-rated ever prime-time documentary on Satanism."

JOHN AES-NIHIL: "It was the last time those deviant personalities all worked together, and it set the stage for the mutual hatred to come. After that, they all despised each other."

Ticket to 8-8-88
Come to a Satanic rally mocking Sharon Tate!
Collection of Nick Bougas

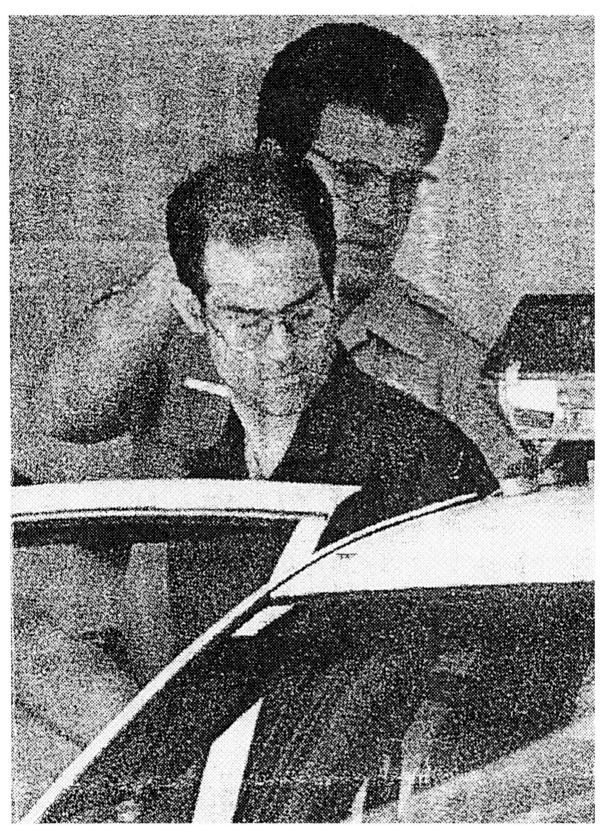

Jonathan Haynes after his arrest for murder, Wilmette, Illinois, August 8, 1993
Enlargement from photo by Jim Robinson, *Chicago Tribune*
Collection of Michael Andros

JONATHAN HAYNES: *"I'm not sorry at all. I have nothing to lose. I have no friends, no lovers, no emotional attachments. So it was a dream come true. I finally got up the courage to do something. I fantasized for a long time about it. And it finally came true. So I'm a happy man."*

HAYNES: "In many ways my early life was like that of my hero, Osama bin Laden. My family was not nearly as wealthy as his, yet we both had the benefits of an upper-middle-class life: good neighborhoods, good schools, good books. And yet, driven by fiery fanaticism, we both forsook our comfortable backgrounds. Osama left his Saudi home to sleep in cold, drafty caves in Afghanistan. I left a safe berth with the Federal Government to live the rest of my life in a 6x9 cell in a mental hospital.

"I was what psychiatrists would call 'passive aggressive.' FBI profilers would say I have a 'going postal' personality—shy, timid and quiet on the outside, yet filled with burning rage on the inside."

What trouble did your art cause?
"When I joined the ATF I was subjected to a pretty thorough security screening going back ten years. Over that time I sent out some violent terrorist signals through letters to Jews and Nazis: confessions of murder, offers to commit political assassinations, threats of nuclear annihilation, and, of course, my Nazi collages to Aryan POWs. But the background check failed to unearth any of these, any one of which would have disqualified me for ATF employment. So maybe ZOG is not so all-seeing and all-knowing as we paranoid anti-Semites like to think."

I. Pre-Murder
  A. Prison rape law
  B. AIDS blood test
II. Wilmette County Jail
  A. Written confession
  B. "I don't have AIDS—if raped, sue!"
  C. Interrogation
    1. Looked like a kid
    2. Gave me orange & vitamin C
    3. Confessed to Sullivan & Ringi killings
    4. Two ADL men sat in (who were they?)
    5. Didn't tell them where I lived
    6. Withdrew favors
    7. Miranda over and over
  D. Finally said I didn't want to talk
  E. How much time?
  F. Court appearance
III. Cook County Jail—Psych Unit
  A. Arrived 11 P.M.
  B. Noise: TV on, people talking loud
  C. Met Clark Mortell of CASH
    1. Arrested for spray-painting synagogue
    2. Tried to remove tattoo from forehead
    3. Machiavelli's *The Prince*
    4. Hate crime—nine year sentence
  D. Seventeen grandchildren
  E. "You a mass murderer"
  F. Death threats—private rooms
  G. One week

Collage of Göring photos by Jonathan Haynes, 1988
This appeared in *EXIT #4*
Collection of the author

Hakenkreuz:

A Kaleidoscopic Vision of the Third Reich

Collages by Jonathan Haynes

Copyright 1991 by 3R Productions

Thanks to John Heartfield and David Irving

$10.00 per copy from

    Jonathan Haynes
    1827 Haight St. #210
    San Francisco, CA 94117

Permission to reproduce is hereby given, with the proviso that appropriate credit is given.

Title page from *Hakenkreuz* ("Swastika"), self-published by Jonathan Haynes, 1991
"Yeah, that was called *Hakenkreuz,* and I mainly circulated it to very young POWs in prison, former members of the Order—also called the Silent Brotherhood—who were responsible collectively and convicted for the murder of Abe Berg, the Jewish talk show host."
Collection of the author

> "I favor violence, the elimination of the weak,
> the cleansing of the earth of excess population.
> Since I myself am weak, I think along the lines of the Golden Rule."

IV. Cook County Residential Treatment Unit
   A. Later learned that everyone knew me from TV
   B. No one let on
   C. Settled into a dull routine
   D. Beaten at chess by Blacks
   E. "He thinks we're dumb!"
   F. Death threats in yard
      1. Sitting on bench
      2. Suicide attempt
      3. About to get beaten up
      4. Prison guard wades in

V. Death Row—Pontiac, Illinois
   A. Twenty-two hours in a 6x9 cell
   B. Suicide attempt
   C. One year
   D. Extradition to San Francisco

VI. San Francisco County Jail
   A. In solitary for six years
   B. Hands & feet shackled to go to the shower
   C. Demonic possession
   D. Made noose but didn't use it
   E. "Not Guilty by Reason of Insanity" plea accepted

VII. Hospital for the Criminally Insane
   A. January 2001
   B. How I spend my time:
      1. Work out three hours per day
      2. Study math three hours per day
         a. Differential equations
         b. Multivariate calculus
         c. Linear algebra
         d. Abstract algebra
      3. Read physics
         a. Schrödinger biography
         b. Heisenberg biography
         c. Popular works by:
            I. Ledermann
            II. Pagels
            III. Pais
            IV. Weiskopf
      4. Read general interest
         a. Bible
         b. Koran
         c. Bhagavad-Gita
   C. Just getting along with:
      1. Satanists
      2. Jews
      3. Rapists
      4. Wife-beaters
      5. Blacks
      6. Gays
      7. Jehovah's Witnesses
      8. Hare Krishnas
      9. Forcible oral copulators
      10. In general, very angry people

"I did the collages in my bedroom in my spare time while studying. My tools were simple and cheap: scissors, X-acto blade, glue-stick and a black marker. What planted the original seed was a collage printed in *ReSearch #3*, along with my dystopian techno-Fascist prophecy, 'Needles In The Mind's Eye.' I also read the collected manifestos of Marinetti's Futurist art movement. Other influences include German collage artist Herzfeld-turned-English-Heartfield. Who changes nations so easily?"

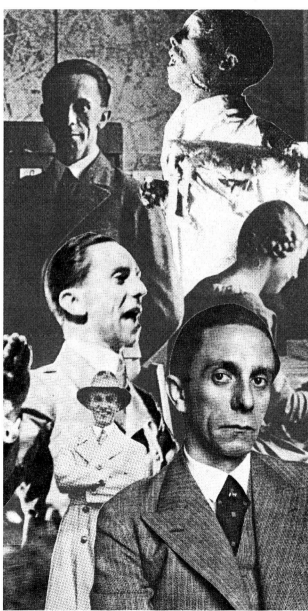

Collage of Goebbels photos by Jonathan Haynes, 1989
This appeared in *EXIT #4*
Collection of the author

Birch society, threatening to expose the financial backers if they didn't repudiate the society's anti semitism.

The Jews have that talent, bred over two thousand years of city living.

As we seem to be striking up a business relationship, let me lay my cards on the table. In some ways I'm really psychologically twisted: I've committed murder, its been 8 years since I've had sex, I'm still taking money from my folks at the advanced age of 30.

I'm kind of proud of the first two, not at all proud of the last. The thing is, <u>I hate people</u>, I have a gut level revulsion of disgust for my fellow man. When I'm cooped up in a room with ~~anyone~~ over an extended period I start wanting to blow their brains out. So I'd sell my soul to Satan to be alone all my ~~life~~ never have to chatter + make small talk.

<u>I hate humans</u>, and the good possibility of a rapid and massive depopulation of the planet is a constant source of inspiration.

Another good possibility is that life's pressures will force me to commit another racial/political murder within the next few... (months? years?) and <u>this</u> time I'd get caught.

    Be forewarned,

    Jonathan Haynes

Page from a letter from Jonathan Haynes to the author, April 1988
Collection of the author

3-5-'94

Neo-Nazi found sane, fit to stand trial
Murder defendant Haynes dismisses his attorneys

By Terry Wilson
and Jon Hilkevitch
TRIBUNE STAFF WRITERS

A Cook County Circuit Court judge Friday ruled neo-Nazi Jonathan Haynes legally sane and fit to stand trial in connection with the slaying of a Wilmette plastic surgeon.

Immediately after Judge Earl Strayhorn announced his ruling, Haynes dismissed two assistant public defenders who had been working for him and repeated his intention to defend himself.

Haynes, 34, a former chemist, sat quietly through the hearing as public defenders Crystal Marchigiani and Bernie Sarley called psychologists to counter prosecution psychiatrists who had testified that Haynes was sane.

He is charged with killing Dr. Martin Sullivan on Aug. 6 in Sullivan's North Shore office because he believed Sullivan was giving "real human beauty to non-Aryans."

Determinations of legal sanity rest solely on whether Haynes understood the nature of the charges against him and on whether he was mentally able to cooperate with his defense attorneys.

Marchigiani and Sarley had presented Paul Fauteck, a clinical psychologist who administered several tests on Haynes and who had spoken with Haynes several times. He testified that Haynes is paranoid schizophrenic and was unfit to stand trial.

Fauteck testified that although Haynes understands the nature of the charges, he is unable to make rational decisions about his defense.

Fauteck pinned such beliefs on Haynes' belief that he was the sole defender of Aryan beauty from the alleged threat that plastic surgery, hair color and tinted contact lenses posed to Aryan beauty.

"He does not want to be seen as mentally ill," Fauteck testified. "He wants to be seen as a rational person who has discovered some major secret the rest of us need to be aware of."

Prosecutors Scott Nelson and Bruce Paynter called psychiatrist Dr. Mathew Markos, who ruled that Haynes showed no signs of a major psychotic illness, was in "good touch with reality" and was willing to die for his cause.

"The fact that he can cooperate with his defense attorneys is firmly established here," Paynter argued at the close of the hearing. "The fact that he does not wish to is also firmly established."

Paynter reminded Strayhorn that delusions are different from firmly held, albeit unacceptable beliefs. Medications for mental illnesses will not cure beliefs, Paynter said.

Strayhorn agreed that strong beliefs do not render a defendant unable to assist his attorneys with his defense and ordered Haynes to be ready for trial on April 25.

Strayhorn appointed Haynes' public defenders to be stand-by counsel for Haynes at trial. Strayhorn said all the experts who had testified before him over the last three days had believed Haynes to be very intelligent.

Article from *Chicago Tribune,* March 5, 1994
Collection of the author

Excerpts from People's Response in Opposition to Petition for Executive Clemency, by Richard Devine, State's Attorney of Cook County

Introduction

Defendant, Jonathan Haynes, is a Nazi. Acting on his Nazi philosophy, he plotted to kill people whom he viewed as threatening the purity of the "Aryan" race. The people defendant targeted were chosen because their professions, in defendant's view, all involved them taking actions by which persons who did not look "Aryan" could alter their appearance so that they could look "Aryan." In furtherance of his ideology, defendant first murdered a San Francisco hairdresser.

Eventually, defendant came to the Chicago area pursuant to this plot, and began to conduct surveillance of another one of the people he had identified as a threat, a man named Charles Stroupe of Lake Forest. Defendant developed an elaborate plot for the murder of Mr. Stroupe and his getaway, but was unable to find a suitable opportunity to kill Mr. Stroupe despite several tries.

Defendant then changed his target to Dr. Martin Sullivan, a plastic surgeon in Wilmette. Defendant devised and carried out a plan to kill Dr. Sullivan by making an appointment, pretending to be a patient, then, when alone in the examining room with the doctor, emptying his gun into Dr. Sullivan's body and making his getaway. He was, however, caught two days later and charged with the murder.

Facts of the Case

Dr. Martin Sullivan was a 68-year-old plastic and reconstructive surgeon who, together with Dr. John Smith, ran the Center for Plastic Surgery in Wilmette, Illinois. On Friday, August 6, 1993, Dr. Sullivan arrived in the office in the late morning. Several patients were scheduled for afternoon consultations, including a new patient by the name of John Rothman who stated that he had seen Dr. Sullivan's ad in the yellow pages. Mr. Rothman's appointment was scheduled for 2:15 P.M.

Around 2:45, the nurse went to the waiting area and called out the name of John Rothman,

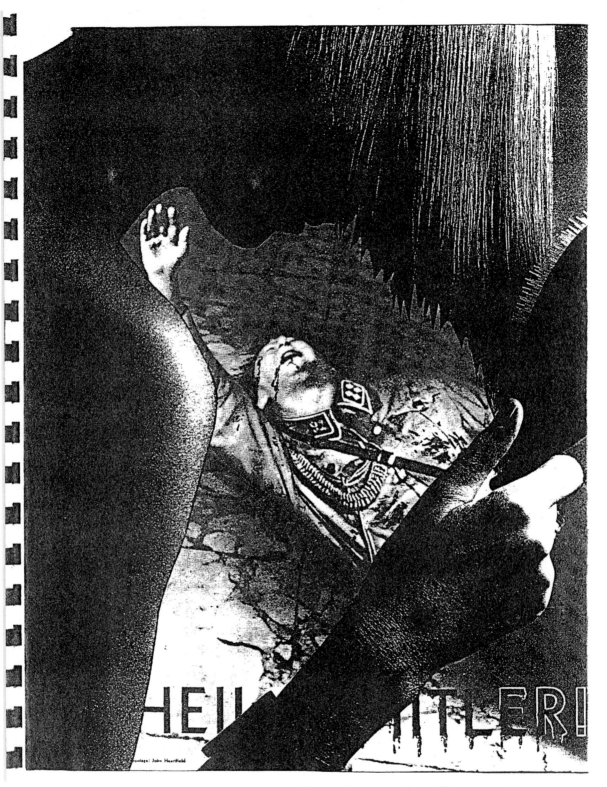

Collage from *Hakenkreuz*, self-published by Jonathan Haynes, 1991
"Did you like *Propaganda* magazine?" *Of course.* "Actually I sent them my collages before I sent them to you. And I got an insulting response from them: 'It must have taken a long time to slop all that together. Very creative.' That's insulting."
Collection of the author

"I smoked a joint on Death Row and it was the worst Marijuana experience I ever had. I shudder to think what an Acid trip would have been like."

at which a man got up from the couch and approached her. She brought Rothman alone into Exam Room #1, and put his forms in the outside slot on the door. Several minutes later, the office workers heard pounding on the walls, glass shattering, and popping noises coming from Exam Room #1. The door to the room opened and the nurse saw John Rothman run out of the room. He said nothing and looked very frightened. At this point, Dr. Sullivan stumbled out of the room and, leaning against the wall with blood on his tie, said, "Call an ambulance."

The name "John Rothman," a description of his vehicle, and a sketch of the suspect were distributed to local police agencies. A Skokie police officer was on patrol in the early morning hours of August 8th, when he saw a car matching the description of the wanted vehicle being driven by a male, white driver. The officer called for backup, and curbed the Volkswagen in a driveway. The driver exited and the officer told him to put his hands on the car, which he did. The officer asked the driver his name, and he said Jonathan Haynes. Defendant was then taken to the Wilmette Police station.

As defendant was being led into the station, he asked if the car was the reason the police had found him. The police did not answer the question, but read defendant his Miranda warnings. They also gave him a Miranda waiver form which he signed after orally waiving his rights. Defendant requested something to eat and drink and this was provided for him. He also requested that he be given a pen and some paper so he could write out a statement. These items were provided for him and he was taken to a cell where he spent about fifty minutes writing out a statement.

In his statement, defendant began, "I, Jonathan Haynes, confess to the murders of Frank Ringi, San Francisco, in May of 1987, and Mr. Sullivan in August of 1993, and to the attempted murder of Mr. Charles Stroupe, also in August of 1993. My motivations for these murders are as follows."

He then explained that because of his fundamental sympathy with the neo-Nazi movement and the fact that he fell in love with the Hitler Youth movement when he was young, he had to set himself up against "fake Aryan cosmetics" which make "vain attempts" to achieve Aryan beauty. He explained that certain practices were allowing people to appear more Aryan. As examples, he listed plastic surgery, the bleaching of hair to blonde, and the manufacture of blue-tinted contact lenses. To stop fake blondes, he killed hair colorist Frank Ringi in San Francisco. To stop the sale of blue-tinted lenses, he tried, but failed, to kill Charles Stroupe, president of a manufacturer of such lenses. After this failure, he set his sights on Dr. Sullivan, a plastic surgeon "guilty of the criminal practice of altering facial structures to appear more Aryan."

Jonathan Haynes, 2001
He resides in a California hospital for the criminally insane, awaiting the day he's judged "sane" and can be put to sleep. Two states sentenced him to death.
Photo by anonymous prison employee
Collection of the author

"If they decide to put me to death, I'm going to tell them to forget the last meal. When I shuffle off this mortal coil, I want a tab of Acid and Joy Division blasting from my Walkman at maximum volume. What a *bon voyage* that would be!"

205

Douglas P., Death In June, Pyramid Club, NYC, 2001
Camouflage chic. No, it's not a floor mop; it's a German sniper's mask.
Photo by Herbert List

DOUGLAS PEARCE: "We're in that empty void again with people being artificially enthusiastic about nothing."

SECONDS (MICHAEL MOYNIHAN): *What attracted you to Punk?*
DOUGLAS P.: I was twenty years old, White, working class, lost, frustrated, alienated and generally hating life. Suddenly, I belonged and life made sense! You could be all those things, and more, and you fitted in, perfectly. For once, you felt you had the upper hand.

People forget how truly horrible the Seventies were until Punk swept all that mediocrity away. Abba were always the worst of the worst—never let anyone con you into thinking any different. It was all vacuous rubbish, and the fetishistic approach to re-evaluate them now just shows how similar 1995 is to 1975. We're in that empty void again with people being artificially enthusiastic about nothing. Boyd Rice is naturally excluded from this generalization, as his standpoint of appreciation of anything has always been so totally different from anybody else, that his attraction to Abba is sickly acceptable.

SECONDS: *Death In June employs symbols of politics and history which left deep scars in the Western psyche. Have you been misinterpreted as a result?*
DOUGLAS P.: Any misinterpretation, or interpretation, of the work of Death In June is valid because it all contributes towards the lifeforce of Death In June.

SECONDS: *Do you even concern yourself with the ways in which DIJ is labeled by others as to its beliefs and ideology?*
DOUGLAS P.: I care nothing for the anonymous opinion. Who are these people who feel I should take notice of them? Egotistical nobodies falling, slowly but surely, into the black hole of life. Goodbye to you—

SECONDS: *Have the political systems of this century really meant anything to you?*
DOUGLAS P.: Perhaps parts of one and bits of another, but that really is irrelevant because it's the now we are concerned with.

SECONDS: *Could there ever be a political system you'd feel compelled to identify with in practice?*
DOUGLAS P.: A meritocracy with a sword of fire, a pure heart, and a soul the size of the universe. Now that would be a propitious start! Love comes to your town and its running partners are hate and impatience.

Examples of Death In June album cover art
The *Not Guilty But Proud* picture disc displays an illustration of a wistful Waffen SS soldier, copied from an actual photograph of a Norwegian volunteer en route to the Russian front, 1942.
The *Sun Dogs* album cover is just another challenge thrown down to DIJ detractors.
True to the Samurai code, Douglas wholeheartedly believes "many enemies bring much honor."
Collection of Fred Berger

Example of Death In June's pervasive influence on fashion, 1989
Unidentified girl sporting DIJ logos on a black leather jacket. For all its heroic homoeroticism and militarism, DIJ attracted an audience of morbid Goth girls smitten by the band's deathly iconography and world-weary romanticism.
Photo by Fred Berger

> *"I listen. I hear. I obey, because I think Death In June is so instinctive — the strength of the life force itself. The utmost law that governs that expression is the purity of intent. Everything else is secondary."*

FRED BERGER: "The SS death's-head emblem has been synonymous with this legendary Dark Folk group since its inception in 1981. Although frontman Douglas Pearce remains taciturn with regard to the origin of this infamous insignia, as well as all the other Third Reich-era items the band employs for dramatic effect (camouflage uniforms, daggers, belt buckles, et cetera), anyone interested in the Second World War could tell you that the references are as plain as Hitler's moustache.

"So, the question which arises—regrettably, given his indisputable artistic prowess and sincerity—is, 'Is he a Nazi?' Never mind that Douglas is a big old cock-crazy nancy-boy and that much of his lyricism is laced with romantic disappointment and man-hungry desire, and that by virtue of this morose yearning it is the sentimental Goth girl who best fits the profile of the typical DIJ fan—not the head-stomping skinhead. It is a question which will not go away.

"Of course there are several songs that have perpetuated the myth of the Hitlerist Douglas P., most notably 'Rose Clouds of Holocaust,' 'Lullaby to a Ghetto' and 'Heaven Street' (Nazi slang for the ramp leading to the gas chambers), but there are many more which show him to be the maudlin poet and toilet-boy he really is—songs such as 'The Golden Wedding of Sorrow' (a reference to jailhouse sex from Jean Genet's queer prison novel *Miracle of the Rose*), 'Hollows of Devotion' (a song inspired by Douglas' men's room tryst with a Catholic priest), and 'Death Is the Martyr of Beauty' (with its reference to giving head ['...drunk with the nectar of submission...']). However, despite Nazism's Gay-bashing tendencies, Fascism and homosexuality are not mutually exclusive, and one can make the case that Douglas represents a synthesis of the two, a synthesis found throughout the ranks of Hitler's Brown Shirts—particularly its leader Ernst Roehm and his lieutenants, who were liquidated by the SS in the Night of the Long Knives on June 30, 1934 (hence the band's name, 'Death In June'). In fact, the title of the DIJ album *Operation Hummingbird* is taken from the code name for this operation which established the ultra-racist and bloodthirsty SS as the most powerful organization in Nazi Germany.

"Regarded as leftists and faggots by National Socialist purists, the Brown Shirts as a whole did not share in the Führer's dreams of world conquest and racial extermination, and it was this disloyalty which marked their leaders for death. And if Douglas, who frequently brandishes an SA ceremonial dagger in publicity photos, and who has flirted with British Red Front and National Front politics (as well as with their respective bully boys), is the true heir to the Roehm legacy, then in fact he stands in opposition to the Hitler cult, which puts the aforementioned 'Holocaust' songs in an entirely different light—especially in view of the fact that homosexuals and Reds were viciously persecuted under the Hitler regime.

Douglas Pearce, unmasked
Angel Orensanz Foundation, NYC, 1997
Photo by Fred Berger

"But why the obsession with Nazi uniforms? Well, to be fair, Douglas confines his stage attire to German camouflage wear of the period, which, compared to a black SS uniform with flaming swastika armband, is relatively innocuous, although it still possesses that rugged-yet-aesthetic 'superman' allure which was unique to Third Reich-era military fashion. And since most Gay men are inclined toward fetishism anyway, in this case uniform fetishism, why shouldn't our pansy division commander treat himself to the best, courtesy of Hugo Boss and other top German designers of the Thirties and Forties? So, when Douglas P. puts on his trademark dot-pattern camo outfit he becomes more than just a performer, he becomes a romantic warrior and sex god. However, when his sartorial brethren and occasional partners-in-crime Boyd Rice of NON and Michael Moynihan of Blood Axis (both breeders in good standing) do the same, they come off merely as war movie extras or poseurs, and when they add their Nietzschean psycho-babble to the mix, they elevate themselves to the status of self-parodies at best and, at worst, hate-mongers. Even so, the company a man keeps is insufficient reason to convict. Therefore, in the interest of artistic license and fair-mindedness, the defendant is hereby found not guilty of crimes against humanity, waging aggressive war, and poor taste.

"But for all you hardheads who reject this verdict, and who can not accept that artists are by nature more passionate and irrational than the artless masses, and therefore beyond pedestrian notions of right and wrong, consider the words of Douglas Pearce himself: 'It is all instinctive; there is no why. It just is—nature needs no justification.'"

Michael Moynihan, 1995
Photo by Stephen Hamilton

MICHAEL MOYNIHAN: *"I don't know anybody who comes from the Faustian European civilization who wouldn't want to step onto a starship if they had the opportunity. The dismantling of the Space Program is certainly one of the more unfortunate signs of the decline of the West."*

MOYNIHAN: "A lot of Industrial Music is as psychedelic as quote-unquote 'Psychedelic Music.' I don't think it's all about being peaceful and flowery—one-half of Psychedelia is a bad trip." *Did you have a bad trip?* "No, but the black side is a part of it."

Tell us about Psychedelia's black side. "At the center you have the status quo, and as you go all the way out to the edges, and off the edges, and 360 degrees around that, you get to a point of perspective where you can look at everything and not be disturbed by it; in a certain way it becomes psychedelic when your perception isn't clouded by taking sides, or by the middle."

Did you want to hurt your audience? "There was an element of that. At an early show I presented really loud music, which tortured the audience. It was me with a barrage of tapes and a PA system and a synthesizer. I was screaming at the top of my lungs, mixing it all live, setting things on fire. I made flyers that were designed to make people feel unsafe and threatened, and to have second thoughts about everything they believed in.

"I've gotten a few death threats because of that stuff. You become more aware."

Instead of four guys with long hair and guitars, it was just you making noise. Was that new? "I suppose you were seeing something that hadn't been seen before. There was no pretentious Rock Star stuff. There's no bar, no pick-up scene. It was very intense and visceral, in close quarters."

"I felt more of an attraction to Europe than America." *Why?* "It seemed like home. There was nothing of interest in American culture. Most of the people I was in contact with were European. The things I was interested in came from Europe and not from America." *Is that a revolt against popular culture?* "Maybe. But I've never had that much interest in popular culture.

"There were exceptions in California. Monte Cazazza, Factrix, Boyd, Deviation Social from L.A. Everything else was from Europe."

"Films by Richard Kern and Nick Zedd were entertaining and they were sort of invigorating. It was no frills, no budget—they did it all by themselves, it was in your face—that was good.

"Those films would be shown at hole-in-the-wall places in South Boston, empty rooms and storefronts, and there'd be twenty-five people drinking beer out of paper bags. Sometimes people smoked Pot there. Those films definitely contributed to the look of the Industrial scene."

"If you remember how P.C. everything was, it's perfectly reasonable to try and redress the imbalance." *Is that an exercise in futility?* "Yeah, on some levels. But things do swing back around. Ideas that are trendy and fashionable today soon will be on their way out."

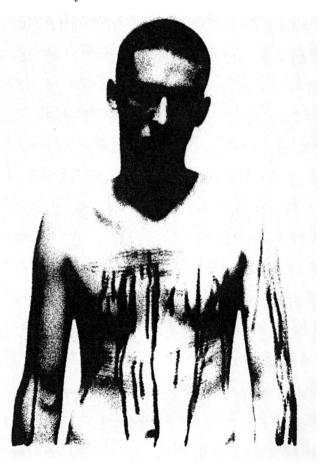

Moynihan, Bar Europa festival, Amsterdam, 1987
The Southern Poverty Law Center called him "a major purveyor of neo-Nazism, occult Fascism and international Industrial and Black Metal music." Wow!
Photographer unknown

Poster for show by Moynihan's first band, Coup De Grace, Boston, 1985
"I recorded cassettes and sent them out like mail art. That's how I got stuff to Monte Cazazza."
Thomas Thorn: "Coup De Grace was not a band or music group as I had anticipated, but some sort of cross between a think tank, a secret society, and a terrorist organization."
Collection of Michael Moynihan

> "The number of six million is just arbitrary and inaccurate. If I were given the opportunity to start up the next Holocaust, I would definitely have more lenient entry requirements than the Nazis."

Tell us about the Abraxas Foundation. "Boyd started calling and we talked constantly. He wrote to the effect, 'I knew there were people like you out there—' He was excited that someone was on the same wavelength. He wasn't finding common ground with people in San Francisco—just with Adam Parfrey and Schreck, and Monte. Anyway, we discussed music, and there was a good chemistry brewing. Boyd wanted to get away from pure noise music. I wanted to use concert instruments that were more bombastic, and he said that's what he was thinking, too. We were on the same line. He invited me to perform in Japan. We met in San Francisco and flew to Japan.

"Boyd wanted to move out of San Francisco. He was invited to do a show in Denver. We met there again, did the show and hung around for a week. The city had just underwent an oil bust, so it seemed really empty and down-and-out. We found a place, went and got our stuff, and moved in." *How long did you live together?* "From 1990 to the end of '92."

What sort of stuff were y'all doing? "You could do a tour where you set up shows across the country and then inform the local Communists that you were going to play. You let the Communists shut down the show, and you keep the deposits and guarantees. The Cancellation Tour!"

How did y'all get along? "I thought it was a good relationship for a while. It allowed bigger and better things to happen." *How did it end?* "It's the age-old thing of being in too close of quarters, getting sick of the other person, and going your separate ways." *It's a famous feud.* "In retrospect it's not very exciting. It's just fodder for gossip.

"There's people who assume that I hold all the same ideas as Boyd, since we did so much stuff together. We did try to project this coherent thing—we were dressed in black uniforms, so on some level I can understand people assuming it was some sort of monolithic doctrine." *Was the relationship a career builder for you?* "I think that everything that happens is good and leads to where you are now. I don't have any regrets." *Was Schreck part of the equation?* "He was on his way out. I talked to him on the phone a few times—Boyd told him he should talk to me." *Did you like Radio Werewolf?* "No, I thought they were terrible, but I never liked Goth music. Schreck had this different aura. He says all this extreme and disturbing stuff, yet he's wearing white pancake makeup and looks like an extra from *The Munsters*. I thought that if you looked serious, it would be far more effective and frightening to the average person."

SECONDS: *On* The Gospel of Inhumanity, *there's a sample of Ezra Pound.*
MOYNIHAN: Ezra Pound is probably the greatest American poet of the Twentieth Century.
SECONDS: *One could be branded Fascist for liking him.*
MOYNIHAN: Ezra Pound got into a little bit of trouble with the authorities in the Thirties. He had radical opinions about economics and was adamantly opposed to usury. Pound was one of a number of Avant-garde artists who supported what is now classified as Fascist ideology. He was living in Italy because he appreciated Italian culture and was inspired by the way of life. When the war broke out, he made propaganda broadcasts from Italy to the United States. He was speaking to his fellow American citizens and instructing them not to enter the Second World War—saying that if they did, they would be on the wrong side of it, fighting for interests that were not their own. After the war, he was caught, and the U.S. government was in a real predicament. It was obviously treason and governments usually try to make a strong point when they prosecute people for treason—traitors are traditionally hung. Guys like William Joyce a.k.a. Lord Ha-Ha, who went to Germany and broadcast back to England and America with pro-German sentiments, were hung after the war.

***Lords of Chaos*, Feral House, 1998**
Lords of Chaos won a Firecracker Alternative Press Award. Other Firecracker honorees include leftist historian Howard Zinn and Zapatista leader Subcommandante Marcos.
Collection of the author

"If they can't put you in jail, they'll find some other way to handle you."

SECONDS: *Tell us about Absinthe.*
MOYNIHAN: I first heard about Absinthe when I was fifteen years old. A friend of mine, a woman who was a botanist and horticulturist and very knowledgeable in the psychotropic effects of different plants, grew Wormwood and the other herbal ingredients of Absinthe. I knew from reading decadent literature that it had been an influence on people. I'd never met anybody who knew what it was, except this woman who was making it, and she started sending me bottles.

SECONDS: *What is it?*
MOYNIHAN: Absinthe is a liquor distilled from Wormwood, the Latin name of which is *Artemisia absinthium*. The distillation process extracts alkaloids from the Wormwood plant. There's a number of other herbs that are part of it, too—Melissa, Angelica, a slew of them.

SECONDS: *Are they essential to its intoxicating properties?*
MOYNIHAN: No one knows what causes its intoxicating properties exactly. There's different theories. Some people argue that it's just the incredibly high alcohol content, but that's not true from my experience.

It certainly has a psychotropic effect. Having drank enough of it, I can understand why it was a "favorite drink of writers and artists."

SECONDS: *Why?*
MOYNIHAN: Because it creates a state of mind which allows you to focus intensely on one specific thing. You can zoom into one thing and look at it with luminescent clarity as everything around it turns into a blur. It has tricky effects. Sometimes it has the feeling of an LSD flashback coming on. It disrupts your sense of time and brings out a lot of intensities in your vision—how visual information is filtered through your brain. It's optical and mental. A poet searching for a specific word to use in a poem where every word counts would find Absinthe appealing.

I put the seeds back out into the mind of the public, and that grew into the Absinthe revival, which interestingly enough led to its re-legalization in Europe. Now you can buy Absinthe legally and the old distilleries are making it—the same ones who made it a hundred years ago.

I read an article where they talked to a customs guy and asked him if he'd found anybody trying to import Absinthe lately and he said no, but admitted he didn't know what it looked like. He said, "Whatever it is, we don't want it in the country."

Above: Cover of *The Gospel of Inhumanity,* Storm, 1995
Painting by Franz von Stuck
"We were drinking a lot of liquors and intoxicants, specifically Absinthe, when we recorded *The Gospel of Inhumanity,* and in fact we recorded an ode to the drink."
Below: Moynihan, Rice, Douglas P., Denver, 1990
Photo by Casa Bonita

TAKE A STAND, BAY AREA!
Neo-Nazi Bonehead Band To Play This Monday

This fascist group was already shut down in Seattle. They THINK they're playing at the Paradise Lounge on October 5th...

BAY AREA WORKERS AND YOUTH:

UNITED WE STAND, DIVIDED WE FALL! AN INJURY TO ONE IS AN INJURY TO ALL!

Let The Nazis Know They'll Always Be Denied Recruiting Space In Our Clubs and In Our City! Smash "White Power" Music!

CHECK OUT THESE QUOTES FROM BLOOD AXIS' LEAD SINGER, MICHAEL MOYNIHAN...

The "Blood Axis Cross." Taken from the band's webpage....

ABOUT YOU:
Q: If you were given the opportunity to gas blacks, Jews, whomever, would you do it?
MM: *If I were given the opportunity to start up the next holocaust I would definitely have far more lenient entrance requirements than the Nazis did.*

ABOUT RACIAL SEPARATION:
Q: Are whites-only total environments a possibility, or will such be desirable in a "Satanic" future?
MM: *I would hope so. I'd love to see the re-creation of lost Euro-centric environments as we speak.*

ABOUT THE HOLOCAUST:
...My main problem with the [neo-Nazi holocaust] revisionists is that they start with the assumption that killing millions of innocent people is inherently "bad." I'm inclined more and more to the opposite conclusion. It's not as if I'd be upset to find out that the Nazis did commit every atrocity that's been ascribed to them—I'd prefer if it were true.

ABOUT HIMSELF:
Q: Are you yourself a "fascist," "white supremacist," "neo-Nazi" or "National Socialist"?
MM: *All the labels you mention seem a bit archaic and limiting to me. So, no, I wouldn't consider myself any of them. Of course, I'm interested in a lot of those ideas, but with the modern world as complicated as it is, one needs to go even further beyond the ideologies of the past. I would take issue with the term 'white supremist' or 'white supremacist' as these are just stupid labels—they're meaningless. 'Supremist' isn't even a word, although I've heard talk show hosts say it repeatedly. And they call racialists ignorant!*

FUCK YOU, MOYNIHAN. You don't fool us with the whining you did on your website interview. You're a double-talking racist piece of shit. Get ready for another Seattle. We'll crush you and all your pathetic Nazi shithead friends like bugs! Go back to wherever you hide and tremble—your miserable "artistic" career is over!

Flyer by anonymous anti-Nazi vigilante group, 1998
This was distributed outside a Blood Axis show in Portland.
Collection of Phil Luciani

> "*Apocalypse Culture* inspired me when it came out. The ideas in there hadn't really been documented, and when that came along, you could tell that things were changing."

SECONDS: *Would you go on a UFO?*
MOYNIHAN: Sure. In a second.
SECONDS: *Where would you want to go first?*
MOYNIHAN: The dark side of the Moon. I don't know anybody who comes from the Faustian European civilization who wouldn't want to step onto a starship if they had the opportunity. The dismantling of the Space Program is certainly one of the more unfortunate signs of the decline of the West.
SECONDS: *What do you see in the future scientifically?*
MOYNIHAN: I see the continuing proliferation of computer technology allowing ever more volumes of trivial information to be transmitted at faster and faster speeds to more and more places and inundating more and more people with useless data. That will continue exponentially and people will have a continued illusion that it's going to lead to some leap in consciousness. Anybody who's looked at the Internet will see the fallacy of that.
SECONDS: *That leap of consciousness happened with television, actually — it was a leap backwards.*
MOYNIHAN: And the Internet makes television look like nothing.
SECONDS: *And in agreeing on this we're not Luddites, right?*
MOYNIHAN: Most of what's on the Internet seems useless. It's turned into a giant shopping mall.
SECONDS: *And a chatroom for liars.*
MOYNIHAN: Losers, liars—it's the ultimate expression of democracy where everybody in the peanut gallery has a voice and everybody can blow their uninformed opinions before the world.
SECONDS: *What's the social history of the future?*
MOYNIHAN: I think the days of conquest and glory and proudly elevating civilization are over. Everything is lowered down to where you're going to have masses and masses of people that subsist at a menial level and consume entertainment.
SECONDS: *Is the demise of the Space Program an indication of where we're headed?*
MOYNIHAN: It's a barometer of losing the will to explore, which was always intrinsically a part of the West. That "fearlessly stepping into the unknown" is absolutely gone at this point. Now the goal is to make everybody happy and take away their problems — and those were never considerations before. You just marched on whether your feet were blistered and bleeding or not. Now you have a nation of whiners.
SECONDS: *Can the process of degeneration be stopped or reversed?*
MOYNIHAN: No.

Michael Moynihan, Annabel Lee
Garden of Franz von Stuck, Munich, 1996
NYC Violinist Lee joined Blood Axis
and wound up marrying the frontman.
She'd previously modeled for Richard Kern.
Photo by Torsten Cornils

SOUNDTRACK TO 1994

First Blood Axis concert, Denver, Halloween, 1992

Photo by David L. Thomas

NON live, Club Z, Orlando, 1997

Photo by Fred Berger

Laibach, Limelight, NYC, 1992

Photo by Fred Berger

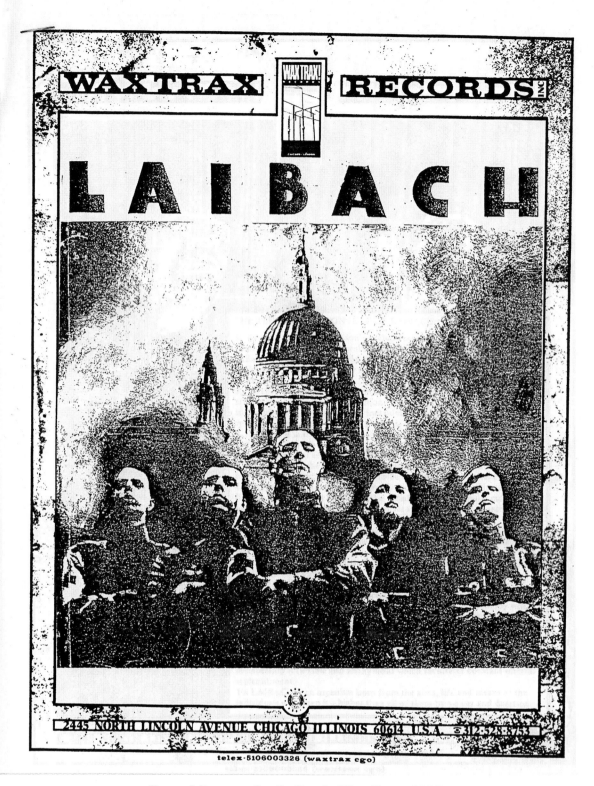

Press kit cover for Laibach, Wax Trax, 1986
Fred Berger: "With grim faces, SS haircuts, and the fashion sense of Stalinist commissars, these five Yugoslavs look like the Thought Police of *1984*. They are a gray, unemotional propaganda poster trumpeting the virtues of dictatorship and the inevitable demise of individualism. The individual is an enemy of the common good, a fiction created by capitalists."
Collection of Fred Berger

The collective voice of LAIBACH: "Everything should be presented. In an ideal system, anything could be presented in the market and people would decide for themselves what is good for them."

*I interviewed one of the guitarists. When I asked to whom I should ascribe the answers, he replied, "Just **LAIBACH**."*

SECONDS: *Did you have any problems with the government about your music?*
LAIBACH: It was part of the game. We did provoke strong reactions. For us, it was a choice between the rules and breaking the rules, between the law and breaking the law. Because we do understand that law has to exist to be broken.

SECONDS: *What do you think about the dismantling of Communism?*
LAIBACH: You have to understand that basically Communism was a utopian system, and as a utopian ideological system it could not allow itself to develop a strong economy. The West developed an effective, pragmatic economy, and the two systems were not able to compete for long. People's wishes are always on the side of material goods. Utopian systems can easily vanish. That's actually what has happened with most Eastern European Communist countries. Communism has ended as an economic system as well as a utopian system. But there is a reverse of that process. Capitalism is ending as well. That's obvious.

SECONDS: *What's with the political thing?*
LAIBACH: Decodification of symbols is always very important, but whenever you decodify a certain symbol it translates into another one. We are using certain universal symbols because we do believe that the ritual onstage represents a political meeting as well.

SECONDS: *Have you had problems with that?*
LAIBACH: We always incorporate problems into the expression. Problems are part of the work the same way as mistakes are a part of the process. You cannot avoid those misunderstandings.

Publicity photo, Mute Records, 1994
Collection of Fred Berger

Genitorturers: David Vincent, Gen, Chains, Knitting Factory, NYC, 2000

Photo by Fred Berger

Flyers for Genitorturers shows, Tampa. Above: 1999, below: 1997

Gen: "I'm someone who knows what they want so I'm dominant in that sense. I possess a lot of leadership skills. When something needs to be done, I get the forces together and move forward. That extends into my sexuality, but as for spirituality there are elements of dominance and submission, male and female, in all of us. I understand the need for balance."

Collection of Fred Berger

GEN of GENITORTURERS: "Our performance consists of the things people can only dare to think about in private. Through us, they can witness those things, and become a part of it all."

SECONDS (MICHAEL ANDROS): *So, what draws people to the S&M lifestyle?*
DAVID VINCENT: All the things that have disappeared from society—honesty, trust and discipline—what better way to do them than in a sex fantasy?
SECONDS: *So many things are banned—*
DAVID VINCENT: That's good for business. There's all kinds of trouble. Gen's had a lot of problems with feminist groups. Bob Larson, a radio preacher from Denver, has been to our shows, to "gather information"—but I think he's in the back room jacking off.
GEN: He paid to get in, so I don't care. In Canada, we have a member of the Canadian Parliament who comes out. He wears a mask onstage but we know who he is. We also have a judge and a state representative.
SECONDS: *Are there things that aren't allowed?*
GEN: There's so many odd laws in America, not one law across the board. A lot of things are meant to be gray areas. If they have gray areas, they can arrest you for anything they want. A lot of times they say you can't do something "lewd and lascivious." Obviously, that's subjective. We consult with the clubowner and the promoter. We don't want to close down clubs and put promoters in jail. We find out what type of show they're interested in—is it more of a fetish club or a Rock club? It boils down to the relationship the clubowner has with the local police. There's clubs in Miami where we do our X-rated shows—and next weekend the cops are driving around on new jet skis. We did an X-rated show where they even parked a police car outside—that was to keep the other cops from coming! It's crazy, but we've got a lot of cop fans.

CHAINS: "We were doing our standard U.S. run. This psycho bitch came along as a stage performer and vomit glorifier! So we're somewhere in Pennsylvania—after the show the clubowner decided to invite us for a sort of after hours open bar play time. Soon into some shots, this public pee queen started invading people, with some volatility. Our drummer was punching her in the face repeatedly to try and knock her out. He tried choking her out but was taking a bit of a beating himself and couldn't do it! Mildly entertaining—pour another drink!"

Publicity photos, Gen of Genitorturers, IRS Records, 1993
"There is duality in that as a sadist, I can become a facilitator of the desires of the masochist. Or I can be a facilitator of my own desires. Everything's circular when it comes to S&M."
From the *Seconds* archive

Cop Shoot Cop: Jack Natz, Tod Ashley, Phil Puleo, Jim Coleman, 1992
Tod and Natz stole the flag from a construction site.
**Photo by Michael Lavine
Collection of Jack Natz**

TOD ASHLEY of COP SHOOT COP: "We invented the concept of god to explain everything about the universe that we were too stupid to understand."

What was COP SHOOT COP? PHIL PULEO: "A Rock Band in the Nineties. Two bass guitars, samples and a stand-up drummer who not only banged on drums but also on found metal objects.

"We were detained by the police during the Rodney King riots in L.A. because we looked dangerous and suspicious—and our label never did anything to publicize it!"

JIM COLEMAN: "There was a scene of sorts, or perhaps it was just a good number of New York bands making really intense music at the time. Cop played regularly with The Unsane, Helmet, Foetus, Surgery, Motherhead Bug—to name a few. We shared a rehearsal space with The Unsane and Pussy Galore in a roach-infested basement on Avenue B and Houston, conveniently located next to any number of drug spots. Thirlwell was a mentor of sorts. He was definitely a big supporter from the get-go, and mixed a few songs on *Ask Questions Later.*

"Cop's early shows were hit-or-miss. We could never know for certain if we would ever finish a set, as there was always some sort of outbreak of violence either within the audience or between the audience and the band. Both Natz and Tod definitely had a way of goading the audience on."

JACK NATZ: "My first show with the band was in New Brunswick. Tod, Phil, Dave Ouimet and I hadn't quite worked out enough of a set-list—we padded it out with a long version of Suicide's 'Rocket USA.' On either side of the stage was a TV set plugged in and set to white noise and static, the words 'smash' and 'retro' stenciled across the screens. The show ended with the TVs being hurled into the crowd and smashed to bits along with a good deal of our equipment. We weren't asked back."

SECONDS: *Can you relate to your average fan jockeying backstage to give you a blow-job after a show?*
NATZ: Ha! Gone are those days. Who wants to approach a bunch of thirty-year-old sleazebags from New York for a blow-job backstage?
ASHLEY: I can't get a picture of our average fan, if there is such a thing. I guess there are people who buy our records, because we've sold some, but it's hard to get a typecast of what they're like.
PUELO: They seem pretty excited.
ASHLEY: And that's because you're so cynical.
PUELO: Kind of bouncy and alive.
ASHLEY: Because we're so dead and stagnant, like scum on a pond.

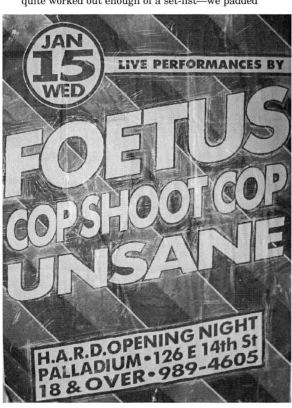

Posters for Cop Shoot Cop shows, Left: NYC, 1992; Right: Chicago, circa 1993
Graphics by Tod Ashley
Left: Collection of Daniel Langdon Jones; Right: Collection of Phil Puleo

Marilyn Manson, Hammerstein Ballroom, NYC, 2001

Photo by Fred Berger

Peter H. Gilmore, 2001
Photo by Peggy Nadramia

PETER H. GILMORE: *"The true Satanist will rise above the socio-political context in which he finds himself and will achieve his own ends, using whatever labels work to his best advantage."*

PETER H. GILMORE: "It was a time when a few of us felt that what was readily available from common sources—whether it was music, art or literature—was all rather mediocre and tepid. The dominant artistic ideology fostered by galleries and museums promoted leftist agendas, and eschewed the need for mastery of technique in whatever was being passed off as 'art.' Thus, the pabulum coming from commercial venues was dull, and the so-called 'cutting edge' was producing amateurish dreck that extolled victimhood. So, a number of folks, many of whom found the philosophy of Anton LaVey to be a focal point, decided quite independently to produce works that championed identification with leadership instead of with the downtrodden, and of technical mastery as a required criterion for being a valid creator.

"Through Dr. LaVey and the Church connection, Peggy and I got to know Boyd Rice, Nick Bougas, Adam Parfrey, Michael Moynihan, Larry Wessel, Rex Church and Steven Johnson Leyba, among others. Since the Satanic Panic was in full swing, a number of us were busy with presenting the truth about Satanism to the media."

PEGGY NADRAMIA: "Dr. LaVey was excited and impressed to see what this new generation of Satanists was up to—and he liked exposing us to each other's projects when he could. When we started publishing *The Black Flame*, we were able to promote the stuff other Church of Satan members were doing, and it led to a lot of cross-pollination. And it shocked some people—especially those who associated Satanism with the usual Heavy Metal culture. Satanists liked Elevator Music? What was that about?"

PETER H. GILMORE: "In 1989 we launched *The Black Flame* as we thought that it was time for there to be a Satanic Forum that appeared on newsstands, that was not just an internal publication read only by Church of Satan members. We had come to know a number of members who had fine writing skills and excellent ideas regarding the application of Satanism to the real world, and we had garnered experience with production and distribution of our horror magazine, *GRUE*—and so that particular fire was lit. *The Black Flame* was an excellent platform to inform folks about what was really happening with contemporary Satanism, and was truly opening a door onto something that had hitherto remained the province of rumor."

Above: Peggy Nadramia, photo by Peter H. Gilmore
Below: James Mason, Nadramia, Eva Hoehler, Gilmore, 1992. "Satanists learn from the Nazis' techniques—they were skilled at manipulating the masses and redirecting the culture."

Volume 1, Number 1 *A Quarterly Forum for Satanic Thought* **Vernal Equinox XXIV A.S.**

HAVE YOUR CAKE AND EAT IT TOO!

This publication is a forum for discussing issues of interest to contemporary Satanists. For those encountering this philosophy for the first time, I point you to Anton Szandor LaVey's *The Satanic Bible*. This volume will give you a working knowledge of Satanism as it was embodied for the first time in 1966 C.E. with the founding of the **Church of Satan**, thus beginning the year I of the Age of Satan. Since then, a full-fledged movement has begun, embracing individuals from all walks of life who hold in common their refusal to be part of the herd of humanity.

Satanists hold themselves as their own highest value, seeing themselves as their own God. Satanists reject the concept of an external, supernatural parent figure and take the responsibility for their own lives into their own hands, whether they succeed or fail in their endeavors.

The watchword of Satanism is **Indulgence**. We assert that life is to be lived for one's own pleasure. Ah, but pleasure, as well as pain, is in the eye of the experiencer. Satanists practice our Indulgence in accordance with the laws of society (the "Rules of the House") and firmly believe that we should not infringe on anyone else's right to his own Indulgence, a "live-and-let-live" attitude. Satanists have no desire to convert anyone, as we see all people as individuals who have every right to believe whatever they wish, so long as they also do not try to force *their* beliefs and values on Satanists.

We also view the facts of nature and acknowledge that people are not all equal. We see the populace as stratified, with a small percentage of Creators at the top, who are highly valued, a larger percentage of Producers beneath them, who are also cherished, and a very large percentage of Believers beneath them, who are tolerated as the major masses of our species.

Most Satanists come from the two highest levels of this pyramid of human stratification. They are individuals filled with talents that they hone to perfection, mastering the material world which they embrace fully. We are not waiting for some fabled afterlife but live to enjoy the here and now to the fullest!

As Satanists, we love life and are motivated by a burning drive to advance ourselves, mastering our various talents with our own judgement as the standard of our success. That burning drive which reveals our cherished individuality, and fuels us to soar to heights of achievement is **The Black Flame**.

This forum will present the thoughts of many contemporary Satanists, which may not all be in agreement. If you find some of the contents to be different from your way of thinking, please form your thoughts into a rational and cogent article or essay and send it to me. I look forward to your responses to each issue but will not present a letter column; I'd prefer that you take the time to formally organize your thoughts into a well-reasoned form worth presenting to our readers.

Let's see the breadth and depth of contemporary Satanism, the maturity of a philosophical movement that is now in its 24th year. And, of course, let's have fun doing it! May you all have had a Wicked Walpurgisnacht! **Indulge!**

Peter H. Gilmore, ye Editor.

Any and all articles, letters, essays or commentary submitted to this publication yet demonstrating an ignorance of the principles and ideas in *The Satanic Bible* by Anton Szandor LaVey (Avon Books) will be ignored.

The Black Flame #1, **1989**
Peter H. Gilmore: "I had a magic circle of particularly talented Satanists with ideas that I felt would enrich other Satanists. I thought that having an open forum would be a great place to allow differing applications of the basic philosophy made clear in Dr. LaVey's writings to find an arena. Needless to say, it worked."
Collection of the Church of Satan

Dysgenics, Peter H. Gilmore, 1991
Collection of Peter H. Gilmore

Thomas Thorn, 1998
From a Cleopatra press photo, photographer unknown, treatment by Eric Hammer
From the *Seconds* archive

THOMAS THORN: *"We all know violence is golden. But as far as The Electric Hellfire Club 'advocating' it, it's like advocating breathing. It's such a fundamental part of human existence—why deny it?"*

You have a reputation as a scrappy fucker.
THORN: "Yeah, I have a reputation as a brawler. I've been arrested for battery so many times, the list would probably be as long as I am tall." *Do you like to hurt people?* "That's definitely been part of my persona. I'm getting a little older and a little wiser now. And I've had my ass kicked enough times to know what it feels like. I think I really enjoy getting in a fight. 'Saturday Night's Alright For Fighting' used to be one of my favorite songs." *You fucked people up, too.* "Absolutely." *Can you give us one example?* "A lot of that stuff is wrapped up in alcohol and drug abuse, so it gets pretty blurry. I have the dubious honor of being arrested for public intoxication in New Orleans—a city where it is legal to drink in the street. Dude, I was insane."

Boyd Rice: "A riot broke out in Portland when I played with The Electric Hellfire Club. One of the security people was fucking with Thomas Thorn, and the guy says, 'Wanna take this outside?' Thomas smiled his evil smile, jumped offstage and started beating the hell out of the guy. Shaun Partridge started shouting, 'Altamont! Altamont!' A full-scale riot broke out against the club security. Thomas is pretty hot-tempered. He's not the kinda guy to whom you'd say, 'Wanna take this outside?' He's had his share of fights."

SECONDS: *Would you advocate church burnings?*
THORN: I wouldn't condemn them, I'll say that. Two kids were taken into custody in Jacksonville for spray-painting a church—and they cited a band called "The Electric Hellfire Club" and a song called "Book Of Lies" that says, "There's a church across the street, Let's spray-paint the walls." I'll say that brought a smile to my face. There's some people whose station in life is to do something stupid and rot in prison for it. Why not burn a church rather than shoot a convenience store clerk? That's my message to the youth of today.

Above: Cassette cover of Thorn's first band, Slave State, 1990
Thorn & Boris Dragos, who committed suicide a few years later.
Collection of Michael Moynihan
Below: The Electric Hellfire Club, 1995.
Thorn sports horns; Sabrina Satana pours; Shane Lassen stands tallest; Ricktor Ravensbruck drinks. **THORN:** "The Hellfire Club has never been a democracy; it's always been a dictatorship. The problem I've encountered is that I have a violent temper and am difficult to deal with. The thing is, it gets things done. Shane acted as a buffer between me and the rest of the band. The people that walked away didn't belong here anyway. The band is an extension of my personal war."
Cleopatra Records press photo
From the *Seconds* archive

**Untitled collage by Thomas Thorn, from the CD booklet of EHC's *Kiss The Goat*, 1995
Collection of the author**

> *"You don't fuck with me, I don't fuck with you. It's like I say to the people who give me shit while I'm doing a show: 'Hey man, I don't come to McDonald's and fuck with you while you're flipping burgers —'"*

Tell us about the kid who killed somebody. "We were playing in Philadelphia at The Asylum. This kid comes up to me and Shane. Kinda pudgy, flabby face, and he had scratches across his face and he just looked all disheveled and demented—and he's like, 'I wonder if you can help me.' Shane and I were just looking at each other and going, 'Maybe. What do you need help with?' He's like, 'I need help establishing a more personal relationship with Satan. I've tried *The Satanic Bible*. I've tried Satanic rituals. I've tried the Necronomicon—' And he's just rattling shit off. What he neglected to include in this list was the fact that he had mere hours before killed a mother and her child and raped their corpses, and then hidden the bodies before coming to our show. His name was Caleb Fairley. His parents owned a children's clothing store and he worked there. His last customer of the day—when it's closing time and somebody refuses to leave, sometimes you lock the door so that more people don't continue to come in. So he apparently locked this woman in and got an idea, decided to kill her. I think he strangled her and the little girl. I don't think he was demonically inspired—he was just kinda demented." *But he had been trying to get in touch with Satan nonetheless.* "Or so he told us. He wanted our help and we just said, 'Dude, I don't know what to tell you, I can't help you,' and he was like 'Oh, okay—' And he just kinda wandered off. That was all we saw of him. The next day he got arrested and he said that the scratches on his face were from the moshpit at our show." *That wasn't true.* "No, because he had the scratches before the show."

"I'm down with the trouble. In Portland we played a show. This girl stands up on stage and starts fucking with me. I picked her up and I threw her, and she hit this metal pole—and rang it like a bell. There's all sorts of shit going on. There's one bouncer and he's throwing our friends out. I stopped the show. I said, 'You know, I wish security would get their shit together!' And the bouncer says, 'Hey, you asshole, you and me, right here, right now!' The guy's about a full head taller than me. But he wasn't expecting I would walk off the stage and go at it with him. We exchanged a few blows and finally got into one of these bear hug things. Then I thought, 'What am I worried about?' I've got like a hundred skinheads in the audience. And within fifteen seconds I could feel all these guys just kicking the shit out of him. That guy got taken out in an ambulance. We played five songs in that show. All the skinheads were screaming, 'Fuck this place up!' I'm on the mic saying, 'Wait, wait, stop!" And I gave the owner of the club an opportunity to pay us. I said, 'You pay me right now and I will get all these guys out of here and nothing will happen to your club.' And he gave me all my money and I shooed everybody out the door. We moved the whole thing to the roof of a warehouse. So we were up there and next thing we know, there's some guy trying to break into our van. So we run down there and chase this guy back to his car. The guy gets in—Bob Hite's jumping up and down on the car, kicking the windshield in. Pretty soon there's like forty skinheads on top of the fuckin' car, kicking this guy's car in while he is trying to drive away. The last I heard, they said, 'Remember that guy who tried to break into the van? He's not living any more!'"

Thomas Thorn, 1998
"I swore to myself that if there was a cross on Shane's tombstone, I would go and chisel it off. His tombstone had a keyboard and an engraving of a picture of him. It's tasteful. I go there a lot and if I had to look at a cross, I'd blow it up."
Photographer unknown
From the *Seconds* archive

Shaun Partridge, Portland, 1997
Photo by Marmalade Partridge

SHAUN PARTRIDGE: "Here in the Partridge Family Temple, the television is our god. Our symbol is the eternal CBS Eye. Everyone worships TV. We're more real than Christianity. You can turn on your TV and see our religion—in color!"

Q: *Sock it to me.*
SHAUN PARTRIDGE: The Partridge Family Temple was founded in 1988 by me and Keith King Partridge. It's a religion based on absolute fun and full-blown magic. All the Partridge Family members represent ancient archetypes. The War God, Loki, is Danny Bonaduce; Shirley is the Mother Isis; Lori is the Whore of Babylon; and Bobby Sherman is also intertwined—he represents Saturn, Death, Time. It's a wonderful religion. It's based on reality and truth.

Q: *My spies tell me you guys have a violent side.*
A: People are uptight and they don't dig fun. They freak out on magic and full-blown homosexual reality. And because we spread the word in so many different forms and realities, people get bummed out. But keep in mind: There are many members in the Temple. Most of the bad press comes from me, the Partridge In The Pear Tree.

Q: *You're the bad apple?*
A: People say that. But I'm a good apple and a bad apple. Sometimes one gets in fights and arguments. The reason is because we worship the Partridge Family. And people are jealous that we have found truth. Here. Now. And we're wearing make-up and Glam clothes!

Q: *Why the get-up?*
A: Because that's the way you dress. When you truly love God and you truly understand the teachings of Ray Kroc, the philosopher of fire, you wear groovy clothes. And Glam-Rock psychedelic clothes are the best clothes ever invented on this planet. You must be a dandy. You must be a Glitter Rocker to really bang your gong and get it on.

Q: *Are you a bit of Alex in* A Clockwork Orange?
A: I think I was at one point. I am Peter Pan. Yet the dark side must be a part of me. So I let it out. Much like going to Burger King—because I always go to McDonald's. But I decided Burger King also exists; I'll go there. And so I let that shadow out. But eventually I had to rope that shadow back in, because it got out of control.

Q: *Did having it your way entail too much choice?*
A: Yes. Because when I let the shadow out, I thought I had discovered gold. But I had actually discovered fool's gold. Once you discover the magic of golden french fries or golden cheese enchiladas, everything is perfect.

Q: *You paint a rosy picture but you seem to associate with an unsavory crowd.*
A: That's because life is duality. There is good and evil in life. You need to be both. You eat of the tree—the apple-pie tree of good and evil. But the goal is to reel your shadow in. Integrate that shadow. And then become full-blown. And I'm a full-blown homosexual scientist.

Flyer for the Partridge Family Temple, 1988
Graphics by Shaun Partridge & Keith King Partridge
Collection of Giddle Partridge

Q: *Tell us about your sister.*
A: Giddle Partridge was born on the 3rd of September. That's when the magic of many things happened. She's the Queen of Hollywood.

Q: *I hear she gets some people's dander up.*
A: They're not having fun. It depends on the situation, because Giddle calls a lot of people on their bullshit. Sometimes assholes get their feelings hurt. That's why I'm the Maytag Man. I don't hang out with people. People are beyond tedious. They are simply depressing to me, so I have become a reclusive Maytag Man.

Q: *What do you say to those hurt by your art?*
A: They can fuck off! I'm offended by things every day. I hate whiners. Hurt by art—what does that mean anyway? What's the bumper sticker—"Art saves lives"?

Q: *Not around here it doesn't.*
A: Wasn't Hitler an artist? How many lives did that save?

Shaun & Giddle Partridge, 1993
Photo by Trixie Doll

Flyer for the Partridge Family Temple, Giddle & Shaun Partridge, 1989
Shaun: "The Partridge Family Temple is a religion based on fun, truth and reality. We believe in freedom, truth and enjoying life every day, because we all know we're going to die. Life is scary and miserable and we say, 'Come On, Get Happy!'"
Collection of Shaun Partridge

> *"I became fascinated with racism and sexism, and I jumped into the ocean of ugliness. It's fascinating stuff. People started saying foul things about me. And I was like, 'yeah, fuck you.'"*

Q: *Shaun, where were you born?*
A: I was born in the Land of Albuquerque. I grew up in my mother Shirley's soft, golden, honey vagina. I am a Caucasian that is transracial. Of course, my religion is the Partridge Family Temple.

Q: *What did your parents do?*
A: My mother is an obsessive-compulsive. My father is a well-adjusted Vietnam vet. Because of their merging, the Partridge In The Pear Tree and the Giddle Partridge were hatched.

Q: *Were you a violent person?*
A: I was never a violent person, but like any healthy pink boy, violence was my first love. In fact, it was also my first problem with school psychiatrists. If it was red, wet and spraying everywhere, my pink face was full of happy smile U.S.A.

Q: *Ever arrested?*
A: I was arrested for my spiritual beliefs at a David Cassidy and Danny Bonaduce concert. Crimes are illegal—and silence is golden as Shirley Partridge's hairdo.

Q: *Were you into pornography?*
A: I liked Sixties, Mod and hard-core, shit-eating, leather, AIDS, fag sex. As well as JonBenet Ramsey.

Q: *What drugs did you do?*
A: Let me say one thing: Psychedelic!

Q: *What were your sexual proclivities?*
A: Masturbating to *I Dream of Jeanie* and the *Mork & Mindy* episode with Raquel Welch—and drinking lemonade from little girls' lemonade stands.

Q: *Did you see the world in terms of good and evil?*
A: Well, Anne Frank lives in an attic and Hitler lives in a bunker. Anne Frank is a swinging, Sixties, Mod, go-go girl. Hitler is an uptight, classical artist who doesn't understand Anne Frank's happening scene.

Q: *What effect did you want your work to have on others?*
A: To make them cry—because they are wrong and I am right on! To show them the magic that is inside a Happy Meal. Hate Crime is my middle name.

Q: *When did you first realize that your work was having an impact?*
A: The cops were called on me and I had to flee a liberal, intellectual college—because my art was apparently a thought crime.

Q: *What put you on the map?*
A: Partridge Family Temple, working with AIDS patients, fingerfucking five-year-old Slopes, bringing Black money into the Black community, eating at McDonald's seven days a week, and loving God.

Q: *What themes recurred in your art?*
A: Anne Frank, Partridge Family, Ray Kroc, alchemy, JonBenet Ramsey, Larry David, Judy Blume, Psychedelia, Casa Bonita, Carl Jung, Glitter Rock, Feminism, leather fags and Op Art.

Q: *How do you describe the scene from which you came?*
A: The scene is not only flourishing, it is growing larger because all roads lead to fun, groovy, UNPOP, full-blown, homosexual magic lands of "Work Sets You Free"! Yeah!

'Keith's Sperm Is Milk'

The Partridges live on, as true idols

At least two of the Partridge Family's most passionate followers didn't get to see their heroes—no, make that their *gods*—when David Cassidy and Danny Bonaduce played Toad's Place last week. The Reverend Placenta Rising Partridge (commonly known as Reverend Dan) and his fellow disciple, named Partridge-in-a-Pear-Tree, say they were ejected by Toad's Place security staff "based on our appearance and religious beliefs."

The Reverend admits that "we were passing out some stickers that were kind of militant. They told us 'These stickers have words we don't want our patrons to see.'" Partridge-in-a-Pear-Tree was later arrested on the street by New Haven police and charged with breach of peace.

Reverend Dan also admits he is only 20, which makes him not only underaged, but a mere child of 3 when the Partridge Family show was canceled in 1974. He and a few of his Partridge flock arrived in Connecticut from Colorado about a month ago.

Because truth is often stranger than situation comedy, we offer Reverend Dan's description of his chosen religion without further comment.

"The church started in Denver, Colorado, and there are branches in New Orleans, San Francisco, and now Middletown, Connecticut. We worship the Partridge Family and believe that each member of the family has a religious counterpart. Shirley is the Goddess and Earth Mother; there is no Father. Laurie is the Whore of Babylon. Danny is Loki, the God of Mischief. Keith is the War God, the militant faction, the male creative force. Keith's sperm is milk and Laurie's juices are honey. The more you watch the show, the more you get out of it. The cancellation was like the crucifixion."

"People always ask us 'Why the Partridge Family? Why not the Brady Bunch?' Well, the Brady Bunch is more of a patriarchal family, with Mr. Brady as the fascist leader."

"We've collected the lunchboxes, the thermoses. There's also a series of paperback novels in which the Partridge Family basically fights evil—more evidence of their holiness." So what were the brethren attempting to accomplish at Toad's?

"At the very least, we just wanted to see the show. I couldn't believe what was happening. People are just silly."

And if they had been able to commune with the mortal forms of their saviors?

"We would have kissed their feet and said 'I think I love you.'"

Interested converts, or people with too much time on their hands, can write to Reverend Dan and his Partridge clan care of: Partridge Family Church, P.O. Box 18877, Denver Colorado 80218.

— **Christopher Arnott**

Article from *New Haven Advocate*, September 11, 1991
Collection of Giddle Partridge

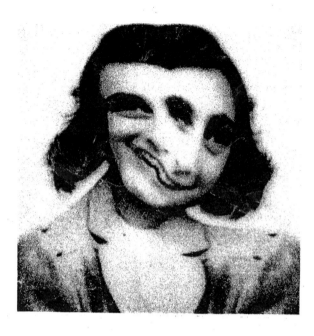

Missing Flyer for Anne Frank, Shaun Partridge, 1998
Collection of Shaun Partridge

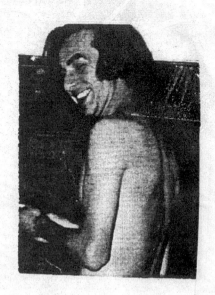

OUR DEAR FRIEND **RANDY GONZALES** WAS BRUTALLY STABBED TO DEATH FRIDAY NIGHT JANUARY 22ND. HIS BODY WAS FOUND BEHIND THE BUFFALO BILLS RESTAURANT AT 45 WEST 1ST AVE. (1/2 BLOCK WEST OF BROADWAY AT 1ST AVE.)

IF YOU SAW RANDY ON THIS NIGHT AT EITHER *CLUB 22* OR *THE COMPOUND*, PLEASE CALL US. WE NEED TO TALK TO YOU. IF YOU WERE IN THE AREA ON THE NIGHT OF JAN. 22, AND SAW A MAN COVERED WITH BLOOD, PLEASE COME FORWARD. YOUR INFORMATION COULD HELP US CAPTURE THE MURDERER.

SOMEONE IN THE DENVER AREA IS KILLING GAY MEN.

DO NOT GO OUTSIDE ANY OF THE CLUBS ALONE.
DO NOT LEAVE THE CLUBS WITH ANYONE YOU DON'T KNOW.

RANDY WAS THE KINDEST AND MOST GENTLE PERSON WE'VE EVER KNOWN.

PLEASE HELP US TO CATCH THIS KILLER
AND AT THE SAME TIME PROTECT YOURSELF.

DON'T BE THE NEXT VICTIM.
CALL ▬▬▬▬▬

Real-life flyer presented as art, Shaun Partridge, 1998
Collection of Shaun Partridge

Giddle Partridge, Hollywood, 1998
Photo by Dan Kapelovitz

GIDDLE PARTRIDGE: *"Nothing beats being a psychedelic glamour queen who's full of hate and who won't hesitate to retaliate against you. Who are the cops gonna believe — a doll-like go-go girl like me, or you?"*

Q: *GIDDLE, how did you find out about this stuff?*
A: Well, my brother Shaun introduced me to Boyd Rice when I was prepubescent. I later met James Mason—who is a fucking nutcase, I might add—and Michael Moynihan. Michael introduced me to Thomas Thorn, which later lead to me joining The Electric Hellfire Club in which I go-go danced and did some backing vocals. Sadly our keyboardist Shane Lasson died in a car accident, so after recording the album which, in my own opinion, is the last good EHC album—*Calling Dr. Luv*—I took over for him on keyboards. I quit the band soon after. I think Thomas should have bowed out gracefully then as well.

Q: *How would you describe that scene?*
A: I hate the term "scene"—but the people with whom I surrounded myself were the elite. There were always deadbeats trying to latch on to us, but I'm never fooled by squares.

Q: *What drugs did you do?*
A: I've tried everything except for Quaaludes, because they were before my time, unfortunately. I myself prefer smoking a little Weed and drinking red wine. Unless, of course, someone offers me Blow. Two weeks before Rick James died, he offered me a huge Pixie Stix full of it. But I love drugs! And just as I have always done drugs, so too have I always done art. In fact I consider myself a living, breathing piece of fine art.

Q: *What did you collect?*
A: I collect groovy dolls and Sixties Pop Art. And I have a huge Partridge Family collection, as you might have guessed.

"I'm either your best friend or your worst enemy—and there is no in-between. I don't allow people to fuck with good friends of mine, either. I do have an awful temper, but luckily can control it a lot better these days."

"My dad is a train engineer and possibly the most sadistic person I know. He is one of the only people to say that he wanted to go back to the Vietnam War because he had a blast! My mom and dad split when I was six years old. Therefore my brother—who is eight years older than me—filled my need for a father figure. I get along very well with my parents, and get stoned with my dad every time I see him. My mom is a little hard to deal with, though. But I really have no complaints and think they raised me in the best way possible. I could do anything I wanted, stay out all night and dye my hair any groovy color I wanted—which for me started in the sixth grade."

Above: Giddle, Shaun, Twiggy, Pogo & Marilyn making the official Partridge Family Temple hand sign, Denver, 1994
Photo by "some groupie"
Below: From Scramblehead CD, Scorpion Records, 1996
"Before I joined The Electric Hellfire Club, I was in Scramblehead, a groovy Manson Family cover band."
Photo by Andrew Novick
Collection of Giddle Partridge

rise   war
valentine

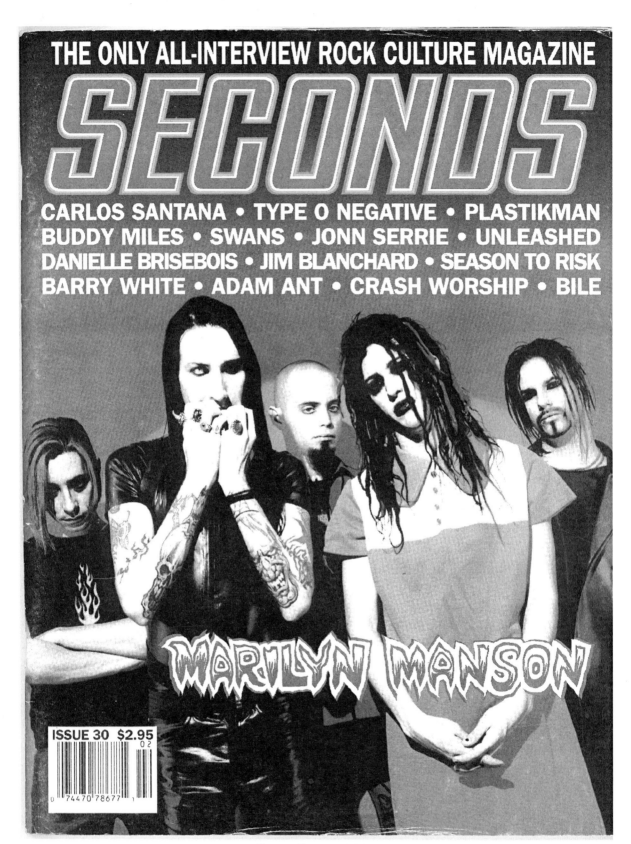

Seconds #30, 1995
Cover photo by Michael Lavine
Manson's first national cover story, arranged through his first publicist, Sioux Z. of Formula.
Collection of the author

> **STEVEN BLUSH re: SECONDS:** *"When I launched a mag that asked musicians — be they Punk, Rap, or Metal — gnarly questions about sex and drugs and extremist politics, there was zero demand for such a product."*

STEVEN BLUSH: "Mid-80s America was very different from the present. Cultural cross-pollination was nonexistent. Sonic segregation was the order of the day. HC bands lost their audiences overnight for 'going Metal,' Heavy Metal poodleheads avoided all 'nigger shit,' while gold-chained rappers didn't know a moshpit from a love-in. The music critics who propped up the biz were junket-fed hacks spinning kiss-ass pabulum. So when I launched a mag that asked musicians—be they Punk, Rap or Metal—gnarly questions about sex and drugs and extremist politics, there was zero demand for such a product.

"Along the way, *Seconds* accidentally developed a new lexicon of Rock Criticism. The editorial struck a perfect balance — the artists were the stars because they spoke freely, the writers were the stars because they presided over the madness. Some have said *Seconds* was the final frontier of gonzo journalism—the last spasms of that vaunted Jack Kerouac-Hunter Thompson trip, before all forms of rebellion were stomped out by the corporate powers that be. Who knows?

"There were two distinct currents to *Seconds*: my Punk/Metal bombast chock fulla HC bravado and Spinal Tap-isms; and the 1992 arrival of editor George Petros, with his psycho-intellectual world of astronauts, scientists, Serial Killers and hookers. GP was the most decadent fucker I'd ever met.

"The Blush/Petros era of *Seconds* warrants a book onto itself. Call it Woodward and Bernstein meets Cheech & Chong. High-octane hooch truly propelled the project. Effects of heavy usage include paranoia and delusions of grandeur—we thought everyone hated us, and knew that we were the shit."—Introduction #1 to *.45 Dangerous Minds*.

GEORGE PETROS: "In the *Seconds* universe, vice sat alongside virtue; good and evil coexisted. We helped major labels break bands while milking them for advertising revenue. We told people we liked their stuff even if we'd never heard it. We ran free ads for PETA and other animal rights organizations alongside interviews with Serial Killers. We burned printers. We were flown around the country, put up in luxury hotels, fed dinners at overpriced restaurants on unlimited expense accounts. We hung out into the wee hours with Coked-out publicists; we had breakfast with beautiful radio astronomers. Music's biggest stars took time out of their busy schedules to schmooze us. But most of all we got lavished with respect and accolades because our interviews were the best. We set the standard for Rock Journalism. We got interviews with elusive and reclusive characters. We got our subjects to tell the truth."—Introduction #2 to *.45 Dangerous Minds*.

Above: *Seconds* staff: Blush standing, managing editor Adam Stern (left), yours truly, circa 1996
Photo by Thomas Colbath
From the *Seconds* archive
Right: Ad from program guide to Expo Of The Extreme
A gathering of degenerates in Chicago, 1998
Collection of Shane Bugbee

***Answer Me! #1*, 1991**
Goad: "I'm not going to fucking be a sanctimonious draper of the First Amendment.
I'm of the libertarian tint: we give the government rights, not vice-versa.
It's ludicrous that they should even meddle."
Collection of Nick Bougas

JIM GOAD: *"The prosecutor intended to use passages from ANSWER ME! against me at trial. He even blew up the layout of 'Let's Hear It For Violence Against Women!' onto giant posterboard for maximum shock value."*

GOAD: Events in my personal life over the past five years:
- an obscenity trial;
- a man shoots at the White House and quotes my writing;
- a trio of British kids kill themselves, one of whom sends me her life's savings;
- Debbie's cancer and our divorce;
- a year of live-action topless comic terror with Ann Ryan;
- and now prison.

SECONDS (ADAM PARFREY): *How'd you wind up in the joint?*
GOAD: We pull up to her building. The whole way from my apartment to hers, I've been insulting her and tell her it's over. I throw the car in park and say, "I'm going to get a girlfriend who isn't so fucking crazy—so just go." Instead of leaving, she screams "No!" and lunges at my face, scratching my cheek. As I restrain her arms, she tries kicking me with her shoes. "You're never gonna get rid of me!" she howls, her eyes wide and foam flying from her mouth. "I'm gonna write tons of shit about you! People'll be laughing at you—it'll be like *Carrie!*" We both notice a Black gentleman approaching the car. She ceases trying to hit me, and I let go of her arms. The Black man asks us if everything is okay. We both say yes. I watch him enter the apartment building. As I'm turning my head back to face her, she clocks me in the nose with her fist. I again grab her arms, and as we're rocking back and forth, I catch a glimpse of myself in the rear-view mirror. There's a scratch on my cheek and blood dripping from my nose.

At the sight of my own blood, something primeval erupts from within me. I pull away from her building and smash her ugly fucking skull in. She had threatened to kill me so many times, I decided to show her the difference between a wannabe terrorist and a real one. She initially had two chances to leave the car. Instead of leaving, she hit me both times. Ten minutes later and five miles away, she was glad to leave the car. Believe that.

SECONDS: *How has life changed for you?*
GOAD: I don't miss my whiny ex-wife or my psychotic ex-girlfriend. I don't miss working a full-time job. I don't miss having to cook meals or pay rent.

There's more good than bad in all this. I feel as if I'm entering my life's most interesting phase. I'm in superb physical shape and am mentally stronger than ever. I now have a ferocious will to live, and anything that had previously been weak or half-assed about my personality has been burned to a crisp. For the first time in my life, I really like myself. Surviving prison will give me a stamp of legitimacy I couldn't have otherwise acquired. Considering the sort of literary turf I plow, going to prison is a solid career move.

Above: Jim Goad, circa 1999
Photographer unknown; from the *Seconds* archive
"Lower your expectations; trust your instincts. Shit can be used as fertilizer."
Below: Back cover of *Answer Me! #2*, 1993
Illustration by Nick Bougas

We're BACK. Are you going to KILL yourself, or do we have to do it for you?

***The Fifth Path* #1, 1990**
Ward: "My obsession is with true modern tribalism, not the pathetic new urban-boredom shock-tactic fashion-victim stupidity that passes itself off as culture in this big mess we live in."
Collection of Fred Berger

ROBERT WARD re: THE FIFTH PATH: *"It's been called Gothic, Occult, Satanic, Fascist, neo-Nazi, evil et cetera. I didn't force you to buy it. If you don't like it, shut the magazine and your mouth."*

WARD: "Being White and proud of my ancestors and our culture, I of course cover a lot of Indo-European tribal issues, more often than issues of other cultures. I don't see why this is so shocking to so many people. Come on now, admit it: Vineland, i.e. North America, is mostly White, and the people who listen to so-called Industrial and Gothic music are mostly White, too. It really boggles my mind that I am accused of racism for talking to Boyd Rice and talking about skinheads without making value judgments. I thought the underground didn't like to be told what to think—perhaps I am wrong? Maybe there are people out there who aren't smart enough to watch television, or to read. To all you media-corporate church puppets: Things are seldom as simple as your masters have bred you into believing. For those of you out there who are ashamed of your own culture, and who try to imitate the culture of a people whom you are not, there are terms for your kind in those other races—Zebra, Uncle Tom, Aunt Jemima, Apple et cetera. So, if *The Fifth Path* is supposed to be so racist, I would like to know exactly where the derogatory racial epithets are, and I would also like to know why there are articles on the Japanese and Native Americans in *The Fifth Path*.

"I have little patience for mainstream or alternative media, be it left or right. They all pass off opinions as facts. I'm tired of the way they define themselves by what they dislike and claim to be against. I think this magazine has escaped that trap, or at least tried to."
—From an interview in ***Ohm Clock #1***

Left: *The Fifth Path #3*, 1992; Right: Robert Ward, photographer unknown, circa 1992
Collection of Michael Moynihan

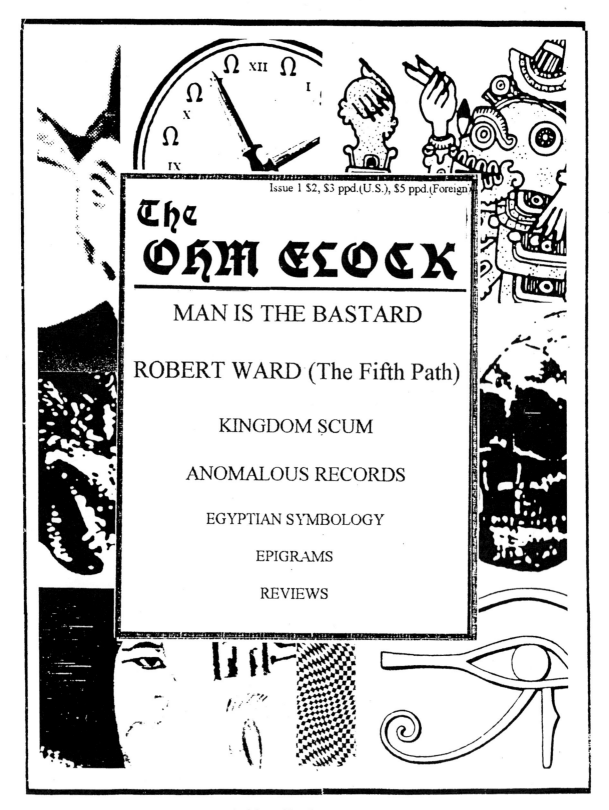

***Ohm Clock #1*, 1993**
Garland: "One hundred copies were pressed. Highlight: Interview with Robert Ward. Other contents: Interviews with Man Is The Bastard, Kingdom Scum, Anomalous Records, article on Wagner, music reviews. Technical info: A cut-and-paste job. A friend did the typesetting on his PC for first two issues before I finally bought a Mac."
Collection of Aaron Garland

AARON GARLAND: "I published OHM CLOCK as an open forum of political incorrectness, and based it on the premise that true awareness and discernment often come from the most reviled, misunderstood and unpopular sources."

GARLAND: "The magazine delved into the Far Right, the Occult, and fringe culture. My only prerequisite for this kind of subject matter was that it be presented in an intelligent, articulate and well-informed manner.

"Much of the material was, and perhaps still is, intense and extreme to many folks, but I was never interested in these attributes for their own sake. That's why Charlie Manson was discussed in an early issue, and GG Allin wasn't."

What sort of trouble did you want to cause? "To give so-called open-minded freethinkers a run for their money—liberal or otherwise. Or, as one reviewer put it, 'to ruffle a few feathers if it gets into the wrong hands.' The underground in Las Vegas consisted either of lame alternative weeklies or Christian Identity skinheads—neither of which I could stomach. I'll admit that publishing *Ohm Clock* in the beginning was a sanctuary from my surroundings in Vegas—a city which I hated at the time and lost interest in. Looking back, it wasn't all that hard to stick out like a sore thumb. That was the early Nineties.

"Initial influences: *The Fifth Path #3, Answer Me! #2, Apocalypse Culture, Exit #3, Lamp Of The Invisible Light* (compilation CD released in 1992 by Cthulhu Records), and my hatred of Las Vegas, where I grew up and was living at the time. I started corresponding with Michael Moynihan around this time. He encouraged me to publish the first issue.

"Moynihan invited me to play bass as a member of Blood Axis on a tour of Europe. I obliged and spent the next few months rehearsing with him, Annabel Lee and Markus Wolff. I even sold copies of the final issue of *Ohm Clock* at some of our shows over there."

Ohm Clock logo, 1992
"Some prisoner in Arizona maximum security did the artwork—no name, unfortunately. I pasted the *Ohm Clock* logo over it."

Ohm Clock #2, 1994
"To sum up *Ohm Clock*: 'I basically managed to avoid fanzine culture, never joined any organizations—political or otherwise—and got a free trip to Europe.'"
Collection of Aaron Garland

James Mason (left) and Aaron Garland read *Screw,* 1994
Photo by Michael Moynihan
Garland: "There may be more trouble on the horizon—trouble for me of a more personal nature once this goes to press."
Collection of Aaron Garland

PROPAGANDA

The Book of the Dead
Issue Number 15

Fall 1990
$3.50

The Mission · Peter Murphy · 9" Nails

***Propaganda* #15, 1990**
Propaganda, vehicle of choice for Fred Berger's sex-and-death trip, began innocently enough as a masturbatory, quasi-fascistic adolescent fantasy rag. It eventually took that final fatal plunge into the abyss of homoerotic, transgender and sadomasochistic excess.
Collection of Fred Berger

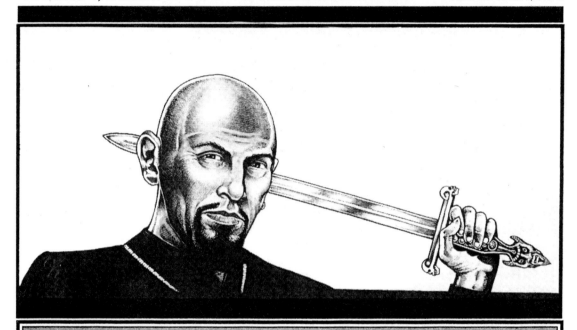

The Black Flame Volume 4, #1 & #2, XXVII (1992)
Illustration by Nick Bougas
The Church of Satan produced this mag, along with *The Cloven Hoof*. Both featured LaVey's continued philosophical ponderings. Peter H. Gilmore and Peggy Nadramia, now High Priest and Priestess, served as editors. It eventually evolved into a slick organ.
Collection of the Church of Satan

Shane Bugbee, 1996
He's stabbing Mike Diana comics, which he published, and a Bible.
Adam Parfrey: "I mailed him a check for $500 to get him off Feral House's back.
Sondra London was not happy and was anxious to get the police involved."
Photo by Lloyd Degrane

SHANE BUGBEE: *"Think you're thick-skinned? Think you've seen it all? Well, think again. I have a magazine, a fanzine, a CD, a video, a book, a postcard or a sticker that will evoke anger, fear and disgust in even the most jaded of you."*

BUGBEE: "Hurt the audience? Yeah, hurt 'em by ripping their fucking eyes open to the real. You can only hurt the lame and stupid, anyway. I want to expose hypocrisy; I actually believe in the revolution, so I hope to stoke the fires of hatred of the system.

"Crime—are you fucking kidding me? Criminals make the fucking laws! I know I have the right to express myself—so fuck those motherfuckers!!!"

"Dude, I'm livin' in my fuckin' car and surfing couches and shit, so I saw the world as hopeless, scary and way wrong—all I could see was constant contradiction. Religion—right! I absolutely was attracted to anything anti-religious. My religion was Heavy Metal! I saw the baphomet as a rebellious symbol, not a religious symbol.

"I was political. I don't like the word 'Art'; it's a bullshit label to try and make someone who's not special, special. I'm a creator; I create, I express, and I think that's an essential part of the animal that is the human. As essential as eating, sleeping and fucking—it's the thing they beat out of us when they tame our animal nature. So, I wasn't so much spontaneous as I was evolving. I eventually obtained the skills to pay the bills, so I guess it's a bit of both.

"Everything excites me sexually. That being said, and knowing what I think of 'art,' creating is like sneezing for me, it just happens.

"What's on my mind when I work? Shit, bro', that's a day-to-day thing. First thing to come to my mind today was pussy, death, pain, censor-shit, constant contradiction, hypocrisy."

"It was *Naked Aggression,* man. I was doing that zine outta my car. I was all over the western suburbs of Chicago. I dropped out of school at sixteen and started living in my car. It was a little gray Chevette. Imagine loading it with five thousand zines fresh from the printer. I'd take it to local bars and stuff, just trying to make money, trying to sell ads. I don't know. I was just following the lead of the things that were out—the magazines, the free weeklies and stuff. I said, 'I can do that.'"

"I published the worst of the worst. There are no books that are worse than the stuff I have put on the Earth. Let's give credit where credit's due. We get all these brand names—fuckers like Peter Sotos or Jim Goad. Creation and Feral House would never put out the shit I put out. I started putting this stuff out because nobody else would. I don't care about the message. I like a brick to the head. It's all about hate."

"Zines: There was my *Naked Aggression,* with GG Allin's last interview. Comix: I was Mike Diana's publisher. True Crime: I was first to sell Gacy paintings. Metal: I'm co-creator of the Milwaukee Metal Fest. And, I staged two Expo Of The Extreme festivals."

Naked Aggression #1, 1991, published by Shane Bugbee "I couldn't get the first issue printed because the cover said, 'Censor This Asshole.' It was all about the PMRC. Nobody would print it because of the word 'asshole.'" Collection of Shane Bugbee

The Trench Coat Diaries, published by Shane Bugbee, 1999
Bugbee: "I do the best I can to make statements, not publish books. Book publishers are all full of shit—they'll kill trees and put out a bunch of crap just to make their distributor happy. And they wonder why nobody buys books anymore."
Collection of Michael Andros

"I do the best I can to make statements, not publish books. Book publishers are all full of shit."

"As far as me starting to publish other people's hard art—well, that shit started with Mike Diana. When they started to fuck with him, I called him—he told me he'd stop publishing until after the trial, and maybe forever. I told him, 'Fuck that—they can't stop us together, you dig?' I told Mike I'd put his shit out, and when they arrest me, someone else will pick up the ball and run with it. They only make it bigger the more they try to stop it.

"But I was angry at you for not being there, George. I was angry at every artist that didn't show for Mike until after the fact. I was mad at everyone who turned their back on him when he needed them. When he didn't need it anymore, everyone was there for him.

"The only motherfucker who ever responded in a positive way was Joe motherfucking Coleman. He gave me his home number, let me call. 'Anything I can do for Mike, you got it.' He was the only guy.

"You asked about Jim Goad. I got to know the guy. He's just a fuckin' educated guy who goes out there and hangs around truck drivers and writes about it for other college folks that would never dare sit next to a truck driver. But it ain't the real, man."

"The curse of Shane Bugbee: I had the honor of doing GG Allin's final interview. I signed Sverre Kristensen to do his comic *Bad Pills* two months before leukemia killed him. I had the honor of doing Anton LaVey's final interview. Rozz Williams' final performance was at my Expo Of The Extreme.

"The Goth/Metal band Morgion signed on to the second Expo; their keyboard player died the next day. Dana Plato fell victim to the curse while on the phone with me. Literally her last breath was to me. She was gonna MC the second Expo."

Left: Mike Diana and Bugbee outside Pinellas County Courthouse during Mike's art obscenity trial, 1994, Photo by Amy Stocky; Inset: Note from Diana, 1994
Right: Cover of CD box, *Dana Plato's Last Breath*, 2000
The TV strumpet-turned-Crack Whore died while on the phone with Bugbee; he recorded it.
Collection of Shane Bugbee

Flyer for Expo Of The Extreme, presented by Shane Bugbee, 1997

Bugbee: "Boyd didn't perform. He said, 'My machine doesn't work.' I think he didn't want to go in front of Hardcore Metalheads who will kill. On the day of the show, the money fucked up. The venue couldn't open unless I hired off-duty cops for security. I couldn't open, couldn't get money. I was gonna rob a drug dealer but then I had a nervous breakdown. I shook down store owners who owed me small amounts of money."

Collection of Shane Bugbee

Flyer for *Angry White Male* tour, presented by Shane Bugbee, 2001
Bugbee: "The *Angry White Male* tour came about because the books I put out are so hard-core that distributors won't touch them. My only choice is to go direct to the folks who want it."
Collection of Shane Bugbee

Mike Diana, 1996
Photographer unknown, from an unpublished feature for *Paper* magazine.
Collection of Mike Diana

MIKE DIANA: *"I felt like a witch in a witch hunt. They had to make an example out of me and win their case. So I showed up for court and there were protesters there—women opposing pornography, women holding signs saying, 'Down With Diana.'"*

```
          IN THE COUNTY COURT FOR THE SIXTH JUDICIAL CIRCUIT
                   IN AND FOR PINELLAS COUNTY, FLORIDA

   STATE OF FLORIDA         :
                            :
   vs.                      :
                            :     Case No. CTC 9307226MMANO
   Michael Diana,           :
              Defendant     :
```

DIANA: "The Gainesville murders were happening. I heard the news, and I was very excited by that." *What do you mean by excited?* "Everything was so boring in Florida. I hated the people. I often thought to myself that it would be fun to be a Serial Killer or Mass Murderer, and kill a lot of people, and get a good slot in history. I know I would have gotten caught eventually. I was drawing a lot during that time. It was crazy." *Was it a sexual thing?* "I guess it was more like I was angry and I thought that someone should be killing the people around here—people who commit suicide should take some people out with them. It was exciting because it was something new. I got to read about it in the paper, see it on the news.

"I did some art inspired by the murders—a portrait of me with an erection, and I was cutting a dead girl open and pulling a fetus out, and it said, 'I love engaging in anti-social behavior.'"

"Two detectives—a male and a female—were waiting for me outside my mother's house. They opened a briefcase that had *Boiled Angel #6* in there. They said I was being charged as a suspect in the Gainesville student murders. It was exciting, but I was also worried. They pulled #6 out of that briefcase and said, 'Because of this, you're a suspect.'

"I had to get a DNA blood test. It was at the Florida Department of Law Enforcement office in Largo. They took blood, and asked me about the address list in *Boiled Angel*. I didn't answer. I was very angry—I felt like they were stealing my blood.

"There were eventually ten thousand suspects in the case. They used it as an excuse to build a DNA database." *With all that scrutiny, how would you commit a sex crime?* "I'd have to be very careful. I'd cover my whole apartment in plastic. I'd get rid of any evidence. I'd have to figure out how to get rid of the body. It wouldn't be worth the stress."

Is your art about anger or sex? "It's combined. I thought about girls I knew, and what it would be like to rape them, murder them—

Dahmer Rulez, Mike Diana, 1992
"Some people are just scared because they're not used to seeing that stuff in regular comic form."
Collection of Mike Diana

"My artwork was a way of dealing with feelings of wanting to be violent.

"In my early comics, I drew weird sexual stuff—sexual creatures, big dicks, lotsa breasts." *Was it exciting to draw it?* "Yeah. I drew things I wouldn't show other people. I felt they were unacceptable. I felt turned on." *Do you still feel that way when you draw?* "Sometimes afterwards.

"Around '92, I would actually get erect when I was drawing the sexual scenes. Sometimes I'd have to stop and masturbate. I put a little drop of semen on some pages—a DNA marker."

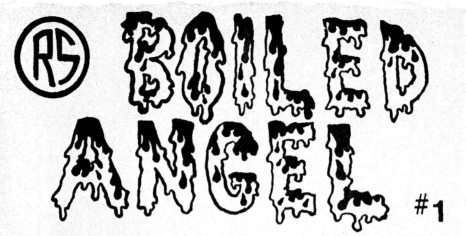

Boiled Angel #1, 1989
Mike, did you get laid because of your court case? "Yeah, I think so.
I had long blond Florida hair. I'd go to the beach, get a suntan."
Collection of Mike Diana

> "The judge gave the probation office and police permission to conduct warrantless searches of my apartment for any signs of me creating artwork that might be considered obscene."

"I was printing *Boiled Angel* at work, at the Pinellas County School Board in Largo, Florida. I left a drawing in a Xerox machine. My aunt was a teacher at an elementary school. A cop went to the teachers' lounge and showed her a copy of what I drew.

"This cop was keeping tabs on me. I started printing at Staples at the Sunshine Mall in Clearwater. I'd rip them off; it was the honor system as to how many copies you made. Then I got a letter from a Mike Flore, saying he just moved to Largo and heard about my books. He sent me ten letters, one of which said, 'I'm not a police officer.' So, I sent him my books. He also ordered a horror video I made called *Second Cumming*. This was 1992. I didn't know he was a cop until late '93 when I got the summons.

"He had put *Boiled Angel* on file in the state's attorney office. Stewart Baggish, the prosecutor, came across it and was personally offended. They came after me two years after I mailed that cop the books.

"When the cop testified, they couldn't film his face because he was in the middle of an undercover operation. He infiltrated a gang of Nazi skinheads. He could get lynched.

"Stewart Baggish was saying things like, 'This is how people become Serial Killers. First they watch the movies, then they read the books, then they read *Boiled Angel,* and the next thing they know, they're actually killing.' That had no scientific value—it was just scaring the jury. Right before my case, the Gainesville thing happened. Danny Rolling was caught and pled guilty, so at least they knew I wasn't that killer. But TV reports started by saying, 'The one-time suspect in the Gainesville student murders went to court today...' There was footage of the bodies being brought out of the dorms, footage of the victims. People came up to me and said, 'I thought you killed those people!' They kept saying in court that I was once a suspect in the Gainesville murders, and that my art is supposed to cause people to kill—
'It's dangerous material that cannot be protected as freedom of speech!'—so they had to prove that it was not art, because if it has literary, artistic, scientific or political value, then it's protected by the First Amendment."

section B
MONDAY, APRIL 19, 1993

Magazine boils down to smut, state says

■ Michael Christopher Diana calls his magazine *Boiled Angel.* The state calls it obscene. Prosecutors say he deserves jail for publishing stories of sadism, sodomy and serial murder.

By LAURA GRIFFIN
Times Staff Writer

In the case of a magazine called *Boiled Angel,* the pictures speak louder than words. And the words scream.

There are graphically illustrated comics and stories of sadism, sodomy and serial murder, including drawings illustrating child molestation and satanism. There are news items about priests and boys, and obituaries of young men who have committed suicide.

The state has charged *Boiled Angel*'s creator, Michael Christopher Diana, with three misdemeanor counts of publishing and advertising lewd and obscene material. He is scheduled to be arraigned in Pinellas County Court today.

Diana, a self-described artist and onetime suspect in the Gainesville student murders, is proud of his work and sees this case as a clear First Amendment issue — similar to "the whole 2 Live Crew thing."

After seeing two editions of *Boiled Angel,* Assistant State Attorney Stuart Baggish scoffs at the idea that the magazine merits constitutional protection.

"The First Amendment was framed and built for the benefit of society," he said. "It was never contemplated for the protection of obscene material, the contents of which weaken the moral fiber of society."

The homemade magazine, filed in court records, includes articles by convicted murderers under the headline "Killer Fiction."

The magazine claims that the stories, written

Please see **MAGAZINE** 4B

Above: Mike Diana on TV, Tampa, 1993
Right: Article from St. Petersburg Times, April 19, 1993
Collection of Mike Diana

The Cycle Of Life, Mike Diana, 1991
"I imagined what it would be like to go on a killing spree. Then two kids went on a killing spree at Pinellas Park High School. They killed five teachers. I wanted to do it myself. I was angry. I'd read Serial Killer books. I put a lot of the blame on Florida, for being harassed all the time by the police." *Why?* "For having long hair."
Collection of Mike Diana

"After sentencing I went and had sex and smoked Pot."

"The art expert was kinda funny because he was like the Nutty Professor—a weird guy. He had enlargements of panels from my *Baby Fuck Dog Food*, from a true case about a couple who killed a baby and fed it to the dogs. The story's about turning babies into dog food. He made huge posters and brought them into court. He had to prove that it was not art. He was an artist and art teacher. But he drifted off from what he was scripted to say—'Oh, I love the way he drew this, with the lines of energy, you can see the power—.' It was complimentary, and it was backfiring on the prosecution. The prosecutor would say, 'But it is not art, right?' and the professor would say, 'Oh yes, it's not art, this cannot be called art.' He told a story of his own art being rejected by a Christian newspaper. He said it was too graphic—a guy sitting at the table with a knife and fork, eating a dead man, and the caption was, 'It's all a matter of taste.' At one point it was just too much, and I blurted out, like I was laughing, and the jury members all gave me mean looks—'This is not a laughing matter'—it was a very strange situation. Then I got up on the stand for about four hours. They were reading interviews with Ottis Toole and Schaefer, asking me why I did what I did. The thing they disliked the most was the Serial Killer stuff.

"The jury deliberated for forty minutes—not very long. They came back with a guilty verdict on all three counts." *Were you shocked?* "I was very shocked. They put the cuffs on me and took me out to Pinellas County Jail. That was a Thursday. Sentencing was the following Monday. The four days in jail was interesting. I wasn't allowed to have pencils or paper. I was very angry. People recognized me. I was in maximum security—there was a fluorescent light on twenty-four hours, people constantly going in and out, getting a baloney sandwich through a slit under the door, and unsugared Kool-Aid. People recognized me from TV. There was a TV and bunk beds and people were in there for repeat DUIs and not paying child support." *Did they cheer when your story came on TV?* "Yeah."

"After sentencing I went and had sex and smoked Pot." *With who?* "This girl Suzy, who I shared an apartment with. During the lunch breaks of my trial we would go and have sex.

"Suzy Smith was a stripper and lap dancer at Mons Venus in Tampa. She had a cable public-access show called *Morbid Underground*. She ran footage of GG Allin takin' a shit on stage, and they arrested her for it. We had the same lawyer, Luke Lerot, who also defended Joe Reddner, owner of Mons Venus. She made over a thousand dollars a night.

"She got off on her charges because defecation was not covered under the obscenity laws. They immediately wrote it in.

"She invited me to her house in Lutz. Her mother was a dancer and her father was a biker. They thought she was just a go-go dancer, not a nude lap dancer. We started going out. I'd go with her to Mons Venus. She liked making money. She was into music. We did nice things together."

St. Petersburg Times

14A TIMES ■ TUESDAY, MARCH 29, 1994

EDITORIALS

'Boiled Angel' case is troubling

Whether they truly believed the material in question fits the legal definition of obscenity or they allowed themselves to be misled by an overzealous prosecutor with a penchant for absurd comparisons, six jurors concluded last week the cartoons created by Michael Diana make the 24-year-old convenience store clerk a genuine criminal. Diana was convicted of publishing, distributing and advertising obscene material in a comic book called *Boiled Angel*.

There is nothing funny about the material in *Boiled Angel*. Diana's cartoons and stories portray rape, murder, drug use, dismemberment, satanic ritual and child abuse. The depictions are bizarre and disgusting. But legally obscene? That's a much harder case to make given the standards set by the U.S. Supreme Court.

The requirements for a judgment of obscenity are that a work have a dominant theme appealing to prurient interests, that it be patently offensive because it goes beyond contemporary community standards *and* that it be utterly without redeeming social value. In order to be declared legally obscene, material must meet all three tests. If it doesn't, no matter how disgusting, it is protected by the First Amendment. Diana argues his work mirrors society and its problems. If higher courts buy that argument, the obscenity judgment will not and should not stand.

There are other things troubling about this case. Assistant State Attorney Stuart Baggish told the jury: "This is how Danny Rolling (the confessed Gainesville serial killer) got started. Step one, you start with the drawings. Step two, you go on to the pictures. Step three is the movies. And step number four, you're into reality. You're creating these scenes in reality." That simply isn't true. There isn't a shred of evidence to link Rolling with material some might judge pornographic or obscene. Since when are prosecutors allowed to win convictions by fabricating stories to appeal to jurors' emotions?

And what possessed Pinellas Judge Walter Fullerton to order Diana to jail over the weekend? Diana's not a threat to society. He didn't try to flee during all the months leading up to his trial; there's no reason to expect him to flee now. He had a right to bail pending his sentencing Monday to three years' probation, 1,248 hours of community service, a psychiatric evaluation and a journalism ethics course.

This is a trial that shouldn't have happened in the first place. It created an audience *Boiled Angel* might not have had but for the publicity. The best thing to do with warped imaginations is to ignore them. In a vacuum of inattention, they usually dry up and blow away.

Article from *St. Petersburg Times*, March 29, 1994
Collection of Mike Diana

```
                CERTIFIED MAIL - RETURN RECEIPT REQUESTED
                    COUNTY COURT, PINELLAS COUNTY, FLORIDA
                              MISDEMEANOR DIVISION

       CASE NO: CTC9307226MMANO    DIVISION: L              SPN: 00774744


       STATE OF FLORIDA

              VS

       MICHAEL CHRISTOPHE DIANA
       519 CLEVELAND AVE S.W.
       LARGO        FL 34640



                                    SUMMONS
                       ***** PLEASE BRING THIS SUMMONS WITH YOU *****

       YOU ARE COMMANDED TO BE AND APPEAR BEFORE THE JUDGE OF THE ABOVE COURT AT
       01:30PM AT COURTROOM L  MISDEMEANOR COURTHOUSE, 14255 49TH ST N, CLEARWATER
       ON THE 19 DAY OF    APRIL   1993, TO ANSWER A COMPLAINT FILED AND NOW
       PENDING IN SAID COURT, FOR SAID COUNTY, FOR ARRAIGNMENT ON THE CHARGE(S) OF
       (3CT) PUBLICATION OF LEWD AND/OR OBSCENE MATERIAL, ADV. FOR SALE,
       PUB. AND/OR DIST. OF LEWD AND/OR OBSCENE MATERIAL
              IF YOU FAIL TO APPEAR A WARRANT WILL BE ISSUED FOR YOUR ARREST


                                            KARLEEN F. DE BLAKER
                                            CLERK OF THE CIRCUIT COURT


                                       BY: Julie D. Meade
                                            DEPUTY CLERK


       COPY OF SUMMONS MAILED TO DEFENDANT A, MICHAEL CHRISTOPHE DIANA
       519 CLEVELAND AVE S.W. ON THE 31 DAY OF   MARCH   1993, AT
       LARGO       , FL 34640
       BY CERTIFIED MAIL, CERTIFICATE NO. 13209, RETURN RECEIPT REQUESTED.

       IF PARKING IS NOT AVAILABLE AT THIS    KARLEEN F. DE BLAKER
       LOCATION, YOU MAY CROSS 49TH STREET    CLERK OF THE CIRCUIT COURT
       AND PARK AT THE FELONY COURTHOUSE
       LOCATION. A SHUTTLE BUS RUNS EVERY
       15 MINUTES BETWEEN THE TWO LOCATIONS.
                                            BY: Julie D. Meade
                                                DEPUTY CLERK
```

Summons from the State of Florida to Mike Diana, 1993

"I got a certified letter from the State. It demanded that I appear in court and plead to three charges of obscenity. The case made the newspapers. My dad said, 'This is not good. They're gonna do to you what you draw in your comics.' In the newspapers it said I was facing three years in prison and a three-thousand-dollar fine."

Collection of Mike Diana

NOTES RE: MICHAEL DIANA

REFERRED BY: Stuart H. Baggish, Assistant State Attorney
Pasco and Pinellas Counties

It is this examiner's opinion the material reviewed in Exhibit I and Exhibit II, reportedly developed by Michael Diana, represents obscene material within the Statutes, as I understand them to be, with regard to obscenity.

Taken as a whole, it is my opinion this material appeals to the prurient interest in sex, and portrays sexual conduct in a patently offensive manner, and which taken as a whole, has no serious literary, artistic, political, or scientific value.

Mr. Diana's work describes sexual conduct which, in my opinion, is obscene. Applying contemporary community standards, in this examiner's opinion, I would consider the material obscene. The materiels depict or describe patently offensive "hard core" sexual conduct. The material is designed for and primarily disseminated to clearly defined deviant sexual groups, to that segment of society generally which finds perverted sexuality to be stimulating and appealing. More specifically, the material appears specifically directed to that disturbed or marginally stable proportion of persons who may have a genuine or sincere hurt or animosity toward the Church, particularly the Catholic Church.

The artist, Mr. Diana, appears bright and quite capable of justifying, rationalizing, and projecting. He is not only provocative, but is also a conscious provocateur, dispensing bizarre and warped concepts of sexuality to that deviant segment of society who would identify with Mr. Diana's depicted perversions.

Some persons could become so desensitized to exposure to over powering sexualized psychopathic stimuli, so that only increasing amounts of gore, terror, sadistic hostility, and severely distorted sexual behavior, moves them to further arousal. Then, those persons will seek even higher levels of gore, etc. since prior desensitization had already taken place.

The warped, unusual, and bizarre sexual imagery appears designed to act as a significant aphrodisiac.

Page from a court-ordered psychological evaluation of Mike Diana, 1993
"My lawyer told Stewart Baggish that the State of Florida was doing me a favor because I was famous in New York, and I was selling prints of my work for a thousand dollars—which was totally true. At my sentencing, Baggish told the judge, 'The State of Florida has made him rich, so there's no real punishment unless he spends time in jail.' I got three years probation, a three-thousand-dollar fine, three years of community service, had to maintain a full-time job, stay at least ten feet away from anyone under eighteen years old, get a psychiatric evaluation at my own expense; the police were allowed to make surprise, warrantless searches of my apartment to look for signs of artwork."
Collection of Mike Diana

**Sondra London, on set for an interview for the German TV news show *Taff*,
Jacksonville, Florida, 1997
Photo vy Uri Shwartz
Collection of Sondra London**

SONDRA LONDON: "We like to focus on the impulse to kill. We say, 'Serial Killers want to kill and that's what makes them different'. But that is not true, because lots of people have that same impulse."

FIENDISH MURDERER WAS MY TEEN LOVER

Headline from *National Examiner* article, 1991

Why did you and Schaefer break up?
LONDON: "He started talking about wanting to kill. He told me there was this woman on his street. He had planned to kill her. All right. And in the course of telling me that, he would say stuff that was pretty creepy, like, 'Oh, she was an occasion of sin,' and 'No body, no crime,' and 'She'd be gator meat by morning.' And he would write stories. So between one thing and another, I moved on.

"So then I came back into the picture in 1989 and said, 'Do you still write those stories?' and he said 'Boy howdy, do I!'—and although he had been sitting in prison for sixteen years, he hadn't written anything. When I came along and put my voodoo on him it produced a new volume of writing which is part of *Killer Fiction*. So in *Killer Fiction* you have some of those old texts he had written as a police officer and that were found and used against him. Then you have some of the things he wrote for me. He did a lot of things as an author that shocked and horrified and disgusted me. It took a lot of soul-searching for me to develop a respect for the material itself, in that it has a dignity. Because it is real. I would be performing a gross injustice to interject an editorial niceness into it, to prettify it or soften it in any way, or to stand apart from it and look down upon it. I developed my aesthetic as an editor going through that—the best approach I could take would be to provoke the production of as much material as I could, to be faithful to the totality of what was in the material, and not to edit it in service to some preconceived program or in an attempt to simplify something that at times is intolerably contradictory."

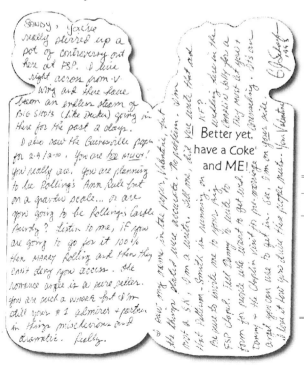

Left: Letter from imprisoned cop-turned-Serial Killer Gerald Schaefer to Sondra London, 1993
London dated Schaefer in high school. Years later, she read about him in the paper, got back in touch, teased him and got an incredible book, *Killer Fiction,* out of him.
Above: Schaefer & London, Florida State Prison, 1991
Photo: "Prison pic some anon prisoner"
Collection of Sondra London

MEDIA QUEEN PUBLICATIONS 1992

WARNING: EXXXPLICIT SEX & VIOLENCE

BEYOND KILLER FICTION
In Zine Format $10 US

KILLER FICTION
3rd Ltd. Ed. $18 US

Time Magazine: "Incredible... real or imagined acts of murder, necrophilia, dismemberment and burial."
Inside Detective: "Lurid & violent sex stories."
Mike Gunderloy: "Most revolting book I've reviewed... the real thing."
Joe Bob Briggs: "One of the strangest books we've ever found. His style has a raw energy that shocks you -- not so much because the subject matter is disgusting, but because it has the ring of truth."
Dom Salemi: "Brutal fantasies from the heart of death's dream kingdom."
Fla. Bar: "Inappropriate in the hands of a prisoner."
DA Robt Stone: "He's a madman... he's dangerous. If he gets out it's like signing people's death warrants."
Fla. Dept. of Corr: "Graphic presentation of sexual behavior & graphic violence in violation of state law."
Amok Books: "One of the most amazing books I've ever read... quite intense... eye-popping... such a *crazed* book."
Mike Newton: "Grabs the reader in a stranglehold & never lets go... smacks of a collaboration between Elmore Leonard & Jack the Ripper... an extended walk on the dark side with no holds barred. Required reading for students of serial murder."

Stories & Drawings That Convicted The Author of MURDER!
Tales of Sex, MURDER & Execution Written in Prison & Confiscated by Officials!

True Detective: "Depraved fantasizing from a horrendously vivid & morbid imagination."

Writings Tell of Fighting Off Craving To Kill Women

Fatal Visions: "Schaefer deserves the electric chair or the Pulitzer prize – probably both!"

People (Australia): "The sickest writer in America today. His so-called fiction is rocking America with its sadism, violence & sexual perversion. Realistic ripper tales."

The Palm Beach Post: "It's sleazy sex & gruesome murder... terribly repulsive, but you can't take your eyes off it!."

Cover of Media Queen Publications catalog, 1992
"There is one group of people who will be shocked and disgusted by what you put out there, and another group who will be turned on by it."
Collection of Michael Andros

> "Some readers are going to be insane and some are going to be serious researchers and some are going to know more than I do. Some are going to be actual practitioners of what I write about."

I'M IN LOVE WITH ACCUSED SERIAL KILLER

Headline from *National Examiner* article, 1993

I'm wondering if at a certain point there isn't an attachment you develop with your subjects. "Well, I had a relationship with Danny Rolling. It was pretty intense. It lasted about four years. That developed because, well, I judge a person on how they are with me. It may be true that you may have committed terrible crimes, but that is not my problem. My problem is, are you going to tell me the truth? Are you going to allow me to be your exclusive source and not talk to anyone else? Are you going to put up with my bullshit? Are you going to respect me? Are you going to avoid conning me or bullying me or threatening me or talking ugly to me or being indecent with me in any way? All right, if that's the case, then we're good to go. And from there I will continue to judge you by how you are with me. Danny Rolling was perfectly well-behaved with me, throughout, beginning to end."

Did you ever have sex with him? "No. I only met him once, behind bars. It was tense. It was manipulated by the state. It was part of getting him confessed and convicted." *So they used you.* "Yes indeed they did." *Were you aware you were being used?* "The awareness came on in time. At first I thought that *x* and *y* was going on, and later on I realized what was really going on—I was being really, really, really fucked. Looking back, I could say I made a mistake doing this or that, but it was like I was in a chess game. If I would have made another move, they would have had another trick up their sleeve. They had a trick up their sleeves for everything and they still would have had the trick even if things went differently. They were out to get me, no doubt about it. And they did get me and they did hurt me bad. At one point my attorney said, 'Don't underestimate the situation you're in. If they could, they would take you out on a dark night and blow your brains out. But because they can't do that, they're going to do everything but. And you can count on that'."

An amazing story of romance behind bars
By SONDRA LONDON

Sondra & Danny, Danny Rolling, 1995
Collection of Sondra London

"I had an injunction filed against me by the State of Florida as a form of prior restraint, informing me that the State would hold a lien 'superior in dignity over all others' against any proceeds I might collect for publishing accounts of crime in the case of Florida versus Danny Rolling. Rolling stood accused of five murders but had not been tried, nor had any such accounts of crime been written or sold."

In what capacity were you present at the trial? "I was there in the press, representing *The Globe*. I was threatened to be killed in open court. That was witnessed by dozens, all of whom refused to be named as witnesses— even though they were right there in open court when I was threatened to be killed by brothers of victims of Danny Rolling." *Why did they threaten you?* "I believe the State manipulated their sentiments in that direction." *Why were they angry at you?* "Because he loved me." *And everyone knew it.* "Yes, and I allowed that I loved him." *Do you still love him?* "No."

IN THE CIRCUIT COURT OF FLORIDA, EIGHTH JUDICIAL CIRCUIT,
IN AND FOR ALACHUA COUNTY, FLORIDA.

Indictment filed

SUBPOENA DUCES TECUM

STATE OF FLORIDA,
      Plaintiff,

CASE NO.: 91-3832-CF

vs.

DANNY HAROLD ROLLING,
      Defendant.

IN THE NAME OF THIS STATE OF FLORIDA, TO ALL AND SINGULAR THE SHERIFFS OF SAID STATE:

    You are hereby commanded to subpoena **Sondra London, Post Office Box 43608, Jacksonville, FL 32203** if found in your County, to be and appear before the **STATE ATTORNEY, 120 WEST UNIVERSITY AVE., GAINESVILLE, FLORIDA ON THURSDAY, SEPTEMBER 23, 1993 AT 1:30 P.M.** to testify and the truth to speak in behalf of the State of Florida in a certain matter before said Court pending and undetermined, wherein State of Florida is Plaintiff and **DANNY HAROLD ROLLING** is Defendant.

    And the said **Sondra London** is hereby commanded to bring into the Court with **her** the following described records, to-wit:

    Any and all correspondence, memoranda and other documents, including but not limited to electronic documents, videos and transcripts of taped interviews from May 22, 1992 to the present pertaining to :

1. Danny Rolling
2. Russell Binstead
3. Bobby Lewis
4. Danny Reichert
5. Department of Corrections employees at Florida State Prison and/or administrators located in Tallahassee, Florida

And this you shall in no wise omit.

Witness: J.K. "BUDDY" IRBY
Clerk of our said court and the seal of said Court at the Courthouse at Gainesville, Alachua County, Florida, aforesaid, this _17_ day of September, A.D., _1993_.
J.K. "BUDDY" IRBY
    Clerk,

ROD SMITH
State Attorney

James P. Nilon
Assistant State Attorney,
#904/374-3670

By: _Shirley F. Geiger_
    DEPUTY CLERK

Original   Praecipe   Witness Copy   File Copy

Court Order to subpoena Sondra London re: profits from writings, 1993
Danny Rolling: "There have been times while writing about the horrible suffering of those fine people murdered in Gainesville that I just want to break down and cry. It is a very painful thing to relive, but my writing has returned to the place of blood and bone, screams in the hollowed night—and tears of shame."
Collection of Sondra London

> *"As for victims of Serial Killers, it doesn't matter who they are, because that is not why they are killed. There's no point in going on and on and on about what put them at that intersection of fate. They became involved in something that had nothing to do with them personally."*

Who brought you to court? "The State of Florida." *What was the charge?* "Publishing Danny Rolling's confessions and selling his artwork and autographs." *What year was that?* "1992. It's a horrible situation because of the Son of Sam law, which was declared unconstitutional in 1991. I felt very confident that I was supported by the Constitution.

"The original agreement was that his brother and I would split the profits from any accounts of Danny's crimes, fifty-fifty. The State said they had a claim to my money under the Son of Sam law. To my money—not his money, my money. And then when Danny saw what they were doing to me, he filed a paper withdrawing his claim for the fifty percent, and stating that any money made should go to me, and that he would take nothing." *That wasn't enough, huh?* "They managed to conveniently ignore that document, and proceed as if it did not exist.

"They declared this thing a unique and special relationship, inventing that term and a new legal principle in order to use it against me—to enforce a law intended to apply to convicted felons. This was done as prior restraint against me when I had no story, there was no confession, there was no conviction. They found me liable for all the money I'd received—not only for the accounts of crime, but for selling artwork and autographs, which has nothing to do with 'accounts of crime.' So we have an unconstitutional law, prior restraint, doesn't apply to me—and yet they won."

Do you feel like anything you have ever written has inspired anyone to commit a crime? "No, but it could, I guess. If you are really insane and you want to commit a crime, a doorknob can inspire you. It doesn't take anything in particular to fit into your mental justification and work you up to commit a crime. So people who are prone toward committing crimes are not short of inspiration. I'm not going to allow that sector to keep me from presenting the material for others who have need of it, such as those like myself who say, know your enemy, know him damn fucking well, know how he really, really thinks. Don't fool yourself, girl. Don't fool yourself that there is something you can do. If one of these fuckers wants you, they will get you."

Is there a fetish behind all this? "Oh no. The fetish is just to be a writer. After I started working with Schaefer, it just so happened that Danny Rolling was a sex criminal. I didn't go out looking for anyone like that at all." *But were you turned on?* "No. It's very sad. When you get down to what is done at crime scenes, my overall feeling is one of deep sadness."

The Gainesville Sun Saturday, September 17, 1994

Judge stops Rolling's tabloid profits

■ Judge Stan Morris orders him and Sondra London to give any money from The Globe series to a court registry.

By MARY SHEDDEN
Sun staff writer

The $20,000 a supermarket tabloid paid for Danny Rolling's tales of rape and murder was placed under a temporary injunction late Friday by Circuit Judge Stan Morris.

The injunction orders Rolling and his fiancee, true-crime writer Sondra London, to place money received from The Globe magazine into the Bradford County Court Registry. State Attorney Rod Smith said London planned to receive more than $15,000 for a three-part series Rolling wrote on the Gainesville student murders.

The money will be held until the state and attorneys for Rolling and London can argue in court about the state's "Son of Sam" statute, which forbids felons from profiting off tales of their crimes. Morris, who sentenced Rolling to Death Row in April, will decide what to do with the money.

Smith said a New York based writer's clearinghouse, The Literary Group, and a California agent helped set up the deal between the Boca Raton tabloid and London. Assistant State Attorneys Don Royston and Amy Burch traced the money from South Florida to California to New York before a check reached London, who lives in Georgia.

Danny Rolling is not going to get this money. Sondra London is not going to get this money unless some other court tells me otherwise," Smith said. He said prosecutors have spoken with The Literary Group, which may be willing to send the money intended for London to the court.

London, who had been unaware of the injunction, said Smith is lying. She said Rolling never has been the intended recipient of money from the Globe — an amount she said even she doesn't know. She said her First Amendment rights have been violated.

"They know damn well Danny is not getting anything. I am a journalist. I get paid for my work," she said. "Danny Rolling does not get paid anything. I have never sent Danny Rolling any money, and I never will."

The three stories being published by The Globe are excerpts from a completed but still unpublished book written by Rolling and edited by London. Each story describes in gruesome detail each of the three crime scenes, something Smith claims is in direct violation of the so-called "Son of Sam" statute.

"It's unlike a product by a journalist or other third person. This is where the criminal or someone on their behalf is trying to gain a profit," Smith said. "...These are expressed descriptions — and marketed as such — of what he did to these victims."

Smith said if the money is seized, 25 percent will go to Rolling's daughter; another 25 percent to the five victims' families; and 50 percent to offset costs of the prosecution. Dave Remer, victim advocate for the State Attorney's Office, said the families do not want Rolling's money.

"The issue for them is not money, it's about Sondra and Danny," Remer said. "They're upset about it all ... it's about their children."

London said Smith is using this issue as a political ploy.

"The State Attorney's Office in Gainesville has characterized this whole vendetta as a victory for victims' rights ... It has nothing to do with that. It has to do with First Amendment rights," London said.

Article from *The Gainesville Sun*, September 17, 1994

"The press announced that I was engaged to marry Danny. One item that keeps that alive is the video of him in shackles, belting out a love song to me in court. This footage is always included in TV shows about Serial Killers. I just stood there trying to keep a straight face. But it sure does make me look silly forever."
Collection of Sondra London

279

Hello Princess... 5-30-93

I miss my baby badly. Yeah I do... I'm thinking of you, my Love... Faithful & True. As WAlly KENNEdy so poeticly put it... "So woody Allen SAys, the heart wANts what it wANts, ANd you SAy... woody"? That was one Super Duper INterview with W. KeNNedy ...LizAbeth StAr... and you!

Sondra honey... I rededicate my Love to you, as though it were FRESH from my heart-N-soul. I Love you darling... I will always Love my Media Queen, SONdrA LONdON ...Forever and a day!

So... WAlly said, "The pAth to true Love never runs smooth". Very profound... you and I have become the Romeo & Juliet of Crime. you, the beautiful, talented, intellegent, author & editor

"I THE HuNchbAck of Norter DAme."

What a pair we make? Well... to tell you the truth Princess... I dont give a rAt's ASS what people think? I Love you..... I will always Love you.....

Letter from Danny Rolling to Sondra London, 1993

London: "There has been a concerted campaign to characterize me in as unflattering a way as possible. The very least of it is the widely-disseminated description of me as a 'prison groupie.' This marginalizes me and denigrates me as a reliable source of information. At one point I thought that meant my career as a writer was over, but I find there is life after disinfo."

Collection of Sondra London

> *"The only reason they pick up a pen and draw is because they are locked up. So it's an artifact of the lifestyle. It has nothing to do with gifts or talent."*

"There's a distinction between prison art and Killer Art. Prison art is just any art done by a prisoner. Killer Art has a component of fame and collectibility to it. The status of the Killer Art depends upon the name-brand 'Killer' attached to it. Its value would be as a collectable. In prison art, the prisoner is unknown and the art stands or falls on its artistic merit. In Killer Art, an item is an autograph with a drawing attached. It's not so much the crime as it is the fame. The fame of a criminal, unfortunately, is considered the same as the fame of a Prime Minister or a Rock Star. The very idea that someone's name is in a headline or their face is on the TV—that's what it's about, it's not about crime."

So people are attracted to the celebrity more than the crime. "The fame. Because the name is in the paper and the face is on TV." *Do these artifacts make the collector feel as if they're plugged into some sort of evil aura?* "They might. Some people buy it and use it to channel evil. Some may touch it and get a thrill—'Oh, so-and-so touched this.' So, yeah, I guess the collectors feel plugged in, but that doesn't mean everyone does."

What about these people who collect, for example, Gacy's art? "I hate them. I scorn them. They are amoral, immoral. They do a lot of forgeries. The whole field has been taken over by awful people who are just looking for something to exploit. So you'll see a smart-ass attitude about everything, including the killers they are collecting as well as their customers who they treat with equal disdain and should harbor no expectation of fair dealings or plain old-fashioned good manners.

"I am the one who coined the term 'Killer Art' because I had Media Queen and I published *Killer Fiction*. I also coined that phrase. Then Schaefer introduced me to Toole, and Toole was illiterate. I was not going to get any intelligent letters from him, so I asked him to draw. In order to add that Toole artwork to the Media Queen catalog, I put out a little brochure called *Killer Art*. I used the same logo as I did for *Killer Fiction*, the same word 'Killer' so you could tell it was another product in a line Media Queen was doing. It would cue you to that graphically. So that was the first time the word was used.

"I knew the people who collected Killer Art back when it was done by gentlemen. I would say Rick Staten and Nick Bougas would be the two premier collectors of Killer Art who do not come under my scorn and disdain. Old-school.

"I'm interested to see what someone draws in the same way one analyzes handwriting and signatures. I don't think you produce anything that will not portray who you are. So if you make a drawing there is information in there. You can't lie. The hands can't lie."

Left: Suzy Smith, Mike Diana, London, Tampa 1993   Right: w/ Diana & his art, Largo 1994
Photographers unknown
Collection of Sondra London

Example of Creation's output: *The Satanic Screen* by Nikolas Schreck, 2000
Among the stable of writers: Peter Sotos, Jack Sargeant, Stephen Barber, Gerard Malanga
Collection of the author

JAMES WILLIAMSON re: CREATION BOOKS: "I had no knowledge of publishing, and just did it Punk Rock style. It was a narcissistic scene of drinking, drugs, world tours and Japanese groupies."

What was on your mind as you formulated publishing projects?
WILLIAMSON: "Propagating a manifesto of Punk Rock, Surrealism, Satanism, sex and violence through an ongoing art-piece called Creation Books." *Did you want to hurt others with your books?* "Not to hurt, but to educate or alienate—depending on the reader—with some clarity and forcefulness. Not as a crime, but an act of severe provocation." *What put you on the map?* "Probably *Killing For Culture* was the first book which gained some attention, due to its then-shocking subject matter. I describe our books as 'popular books for popular people.'"

Williamson, circa 1992
Creation Creator
Photo: Anita Pallenberg

Excerpt from Lydia Lunch's 1997 Creation classic, *Paradoxia, A Predator's Diary:* "Obliterate the safety net that separates the spectator from the exhibitionist. The doctor from the patient. Play wet nurse to nightsickness. Detail every form of madness, hysteria, torture, obsession. An unholy vortex of verbal abuse. A hideous din. Around which forms a cult of negation. The figurehead, a fallen Goddess, whose cruelty and hatred would be embraced. Revered. Reviled. Feared. A classic nihilist's philosophy the only dogma: 'That which does not kill me, makes me stronger.'"

Above: Creation's first offering, *Raism* by James Havoc, 1989
Collection of James Williamson
Right: Jack Stevenson's epic *Addicted: The Myth and Menace of Drugs In Film*, 1999
Collection of the author

EVERYTHING YOU KNOW IS WRONG

THE DISINFORMATION GUIDE TO SECRETS AND LIES

NAOMI KLEIN • HOWARD BLOOM • HOWARD ZINN • PAUL KRASSNER • WILLIAM BLUM • ARIANNA HUFFINGTON • NOREENA HERTZ • THOMAS SZASZ • GREG PALAST • JAMES RIDGEWAY • WENDY McELROY • KALLE LASN • RICHARD METZGER • TRISTAN TAORMINO • JONATHAN VANKIN • PETER BREGGIN, M.D. • LUCY KOMISAR • MIKE MALES • JOHN TAYLOR GATTO • EDITED BY RUSS KICK

Everything You Know Is Wrong, 2001
Published by The Disinformation Company Ltd., co-owned by Metzger
"We do DVDs. We publish books. We do live events and produce TV shows. Stuff like that. Things that are edgy, somehow forbidden. In counterculture literature, dangerousness is relative. We live in a Burroughsian world now. Magic run amok, science gone insane, consumer addictions, bizarre media, programming and deprogramming—Burroughs prophesized Snitch Culture."
Collection of the author

RICHARD METZGER re: DISINFORMATION: "We want to get people thinking, get them questioning everything they see in newspapers, on TV, in advertising or on the Internet. We want to promote the idea that media is a mixture of truth and lies."

METZGER: "I've always thought the most subversive thing to be is popular."

What's the deal with Disinformation? "We were at one time affiliated with Razorfish. We're dotcom survivors—one of the very few. When the stock market imploded, the dotcom boom became a dotcom bust. We were profitable because we were making books that were selling. Instead of being a pure internet company we became a publisher. Became successful. Almost a fluke, but that's what happened.

"Using electronic media in pursuit of witchcraft and magic became my. I have a certain demeanor and a slickness that allows me to get on TV.

"I'm not a conspiracy theorist, although I do play one on TV. Are we talking about criminal conspiracies that can be proven in a court of law? Or are we talking about UFOs and other bullshit?"

Tell us about the Disinfo Conference. "We had this dotcom money, so we decided to do something that would get a lot of press and help brand us in the public's eye. To go offline. To do something outside of cyberspace. Do something real. And also something that we could use as content for my show. It was cost-effective in a way, too—to repurpose some of that material. Okay, let's do this Rave-type magical day of mindfuck and transgression. It was at the Hammerstein Ballroom in New York. Genesis said the reason the people showed up was to hear the people onstage say things that people aren't supposed to say. Joe Coleman, Paul Lafelly, Marilyn Manson live via satellite from L.A., Kenneth Anger—Robert Anton Wilson was the headliner. Adam did a great speech. Douglass Rushkoff did the keynote. Kembra Pfahler did the Wall Of Vagina. February 19, 2000. There was a Dream Machine tent. There was an Absinthe bar. There were a lot of drugs going around that day. My god!"

Tell us about GG Allin. "GG did a gig at the Cat Club. Thurston Moore and Gerard Cosloy were in the backup band. They were all backstage tuning up and GG comes in with two big plastic jugs of whiskey and two boxes of chocolate Ex-Lax, which he proceeds to eat. That was the night he was shitting into his hands and jacking off—and a chick gave him a blow-job. The Cat Club's bouncers took a piece of carpeting and cornered him. He was totally nude. He was covered in his own feces. They wrapped him up and took him outside. And they kicked him unconscious."

Metzger, L.A., 1991
Photo by Sean Fernald

"We were talking dangerous ideas espoused by William Burroughs—about bending reality and using a very technological form of witchcraft. It's extraordinary that a man whose writing was that obscene and that abhorrent would be on a mainstream TV show like *Saturday Night Live.*"

You're the Rod Serling of the modern age. "There's a conscious effort in what I did on the TV show and what I do as a persona, where I consciously ape Rod Serling—it's showbiz. People think I'm some kind of malevolent dark character. I'm not; I'm a total sweetheart."

DVD cover, *The Disinformation Series*, 2000
Cover photo by Alice Arnold

***Torso I*, Stephen Kasner, 1993**
"Rarely would I do something thought-out or planned. Images stem from just starting to draw. If I latch onto something that becomes an icon, it comes about truly accidentally."
Collection of Stephen Kasner

STEPHEN KASNER: *"I've experienced these images in a dream state. Some doctor telling me I haven't really experienced them is bullshit. Life is so dreamlike — it doesn't seem real. Many might associate those feelings with psychosis, but who knows who's right?"*

How do you describe the scene from which you came?
KASNER: "Explosive, detached and alive. I think the time period of the Nineties, with all its false wisdom and self-deprecation, produced a healthy group of artists and musicians who managed to climb through the hideousness of Pop Art. It encouraged the growth of many who were innate survivors of the pre-apocalyptic. Those who knew the score, knew we were all doomed, and began to create the characters of the language in which humanity's suicide note will be written."

What effect did you want your work to have? "At first, I had no particular intention of what effect, if any, I wanted my work to have. It all came about so spontaneously and curiously—it took me a good deal of time to begin to understand how it even impacted me, or if it could continue to grow on its own.

"If everything's working properly, I describe my work as a linear, continuous stream of unconscious thought that filters—as spontaneously as possible—from one canvas to another. Each a small part of a greater whole. That which I continuously know nothing of the outcome."

STANTON LaVEY: *Let's talk about Serial Killers.*
KASNER: "My interest started around 1992, when I heard that some movie star purchased a painting by John Wayne Gacy. I thought, 'Wait, John Wayne Gacy paints? Pictures? How do I get one?' A friend connected me; I bought my first piece, 'Christ Head,' directly from Gacy, and I was immediately hooked. I developed a serious interest in these murderous types who were painting and drawing, and for what reasons. In a matter of months I must have acquired almost a hundred pieces, as well as curious friendships with the likes of Gacy, Elmer Wayne Henley, Ottis Toole, Henry Lee Lucas, Kenneth Bianchi, Herbert Mullin and Richard Ramirez. Some of them are serious about their work. It was quite impressive how close these men allowed me to get to them psychologically.

"Gacy continually tried to convince me to visit him. He would coax me by telling me that in the visitors' area—which were several separate rooms monitored by cameras—he had knowledge of a particular room where the camera in the closet was broken. He told me that, because of his stature in prison, he could convince the guards to allow he and I to use that room, in particular the closet, to 'talk.' I would always repeat the phrase, 'Uh, John, I'm not Gay,' and every time he would laugh coldly and say, 'Yeah, right.'"

"They seemed to trust me completely based on this mutual, deep interest in exploring visual elements of oneself. Of course, the same thing can't be said for the true con men, out to make some quick bucks. I can't fault those guys for that either, though."

Above: Anton LaVey & Stephen Kasner, 1994
Photo by Blanche Barton
"In The Satanic Bible, I had finally, beyond time and space, been welcomed home."
Below: Letter to Kasner from Ottis Toole, 1994
Collection of Stephen Kasner

Marilyn Manson, NYC, 1996
Richard Kern: "It was pretty apparent when I worked with Manson that he was extremely talented and intelligent and knew exactly what he was doing."
Photo by Richard Kern

MARILYN MANSON: "Great art is born in great pain. Art is a combination of pain, craziness, confusion, drugs and sex."

SECONDS (DAVID AARON CLARK): *What are you going to do when you get bored with Rock? Does Marilyn Manson have planned obsolescence built in?*
MANSON: My big plan—it's supposed to be a secret, but I'll tell you anyway—would be to become a born-again Christian and then a TV evangelist, so I could collect money to help stop people like Marilyn Manson. But, secretly, I'll be taking that money and funding new Marilyn Mansons all over the place.
SECONDS: *The Rock & Roll machine is designed to drain off discontent and revolutionary thought more than fuel it.*
MANSON: You can't be idealistic, and think you can change the world. I don't want to change the world. America's fucked up and I like it that way. I'm not complaining about it. I'm just acknowledging it. If there weren't places like Salt Lake City, I wouldn't exist. It's that whole balance—you can't really have one without the other. I can appreciate the other side and respect it, but at the same time, I'm opposing it.

SECONDS: *Serial Killers have become folk heroes for young, dissatisfied people. Now, the kids have grown into a viable demographic and the entertainment establishment caters to that interest.*
MANSON: What I'm trying to say is that "Marilyn" and "Manson" are two words that in America are very powerful. America, technically, should be very proud of Marilyn Manson, because it's very responsible for us. But they're going to be ashamed of it, point it out as a problem, when it's a symptom of something that they've created. Only in America would a phenomenon like Serial Killers really exist. If people realize they can become famous by killing as much as they can by being in a Rock Band, then that's the message that America has given out to people. The classic American family raises children in such a masochistic way, makes them feel guilty for thinking differently, makes them feel ashamed for not being like their parents. Then you get the kids growing up—"Well, someday, I'll show you"—and that's where your Serial Killer and your teen suicide mentality come from. It's never about Heavy Metal music, or whatever they want to blame it on. They want to shuffle the blame off because they don't want to be responsible for the way they raised their kids. What I'm saying to them a lot of times is, look, you better raise your kids better, or I will.

SECONDS: *Do you get male and female groupies?*
MANSON: Both, usually.
SECONDS: *So do the guys or girls give better head?*
MANSON: Fourteen-year-olds. I think girls give better head. However, I did suck some guy's dick on stage in Miami, in front of my parents.
SECONDS: *Was that liberating for you?*
MANSON: Not really. It was just a strange thing.

Flyer, graphics by Manson, Boca Raton, 1990
Senator Joseph Lieberman called the band "…perhaps the sickest group ever promoted by a mainstream record company."
Collection of Gidget Gein

I was just caught up in the moment. We were on stage and apparently there's some sort of warrant out for my arrest in Miami. I don't ever try and put a label on anything. But I technically felt that, since I didn't have a hard-on, that it only made him Gay, my sucking his dick. Yeah, we try and justify things.
SECONDS: *And when we're talking about whether it's male or female, it's just really an esthetic thing, you know.*
MANSON: When we see people, all across the country—if you see a guy that's more attractive than a girl in a feminine way, what would really make that different than being with a girl? I haven't always set out to be completely androgynous, but sometimes I've been mistaken for a girl, until people see my tattoos or five o'clock shadow. I think not having those boundaries is definitely part of what I've always been about. That's really what Marilyn Manson has always been about — transcending the borders of morality and sexuality. Deciding that what works, works. Don't try and justify it, or label it.

Flyer, graphics by Manson, Miami Beach, 1991
Manson, Gidget Gein, Daisy Berkowitz, Sara Lee Lucas, Madonna Wayne Gacy
"Marilyn Manson is not just an image we put on for the stage.
The music and our show go hand-in-hand. Marilyn is real."
Collection of Gidget Gein

"The media held me responsible for every act of violence that happens in America, no matter what. So what should I do? Stand there and let them fuck me over, or turn around and smash their teeth in?"

SECONDS (BOYD RICE): *So, you always knew you'd be famous?*
MANSON: I've always been the type of person that doesn't accept failure. When I do something, I set my mind to it and take it as far as it can go. I don't know if being famous is my ultimate goal.
SECONDS: *When I first met you, you hadn't been signed and were home watching daytime talk shows. Yet, you had a plan to do exactly what you're doing now.*
MANSON: I think that's the key to succeeding with anything—never doubting it, never looking back. The analogy I've used before—if you buy into the mythology of The Bible—is looking back over your shoulder and turning into salt. Belief is ninety percent of success.
SECONDS: *You seem to be part of a guiltless new generation who not only embrace fame, but ride it for all its worth.*
MANSON: It's not that people who're famous and embrace being a star aren't sincere in what they do, it's just they're accepting it for what its worth and what it is. At the same time, I love the idea of every man and woman being a star and that's what I try to relate to our fans. If anything, they use me as an inspiration for their own success.
SECONDS: *I've never bought into that "every man is a star" thing. There's a few stars, a lot of planets, then some asteroids—*
MANSON: You're right about that. Every man and woman has the potential to be a star but very few realize it. Everyone wears a crown—but who will stand and be a king?

SECONDS: *You're a priest in the Church of Satan. How seriously do you take Satanic theology?*
MANSON: Most of my ideals are based around things LaVey and Crowley have written, and Nietzsche also. Recently, I've been reading other ideas just to broaden my knowledge—numerology and Hebrew Kabbalism. I always try my hardest to bring a better understanding of Satanism to America because I have a Pop status. If I explain Satanism to people in a way they can understand, it may open up their minds to it, more than if I was brandishing a pentagram. If the concern is to educate people, sometimes you have to change the way you present things—and that's what I've tried to do. A lot of times we're extremely Satanic in our nature and other times I present things in a less Satanic way. That in itself is overtly Satanic.

SECONDS: *So, have you come for the children?*
MANSON: I think the children have come for me. I still consider myself a kid no matter how old I get. I like kid's things. I like toys. Imagination is the key to everything—and children have such strong imaginations. You become an adult because of TV and your job and whatever bullshit is laid on you. Nobody cares about imagination, except when you're a kid. That's why I was so drawn to something like Dungeons And Dragons as a kid, because it was all about escapism and being whatever you wanted to be. That's what Marilyn Manson became to me—you know, being whatever you want to be.

SECONDS: *What's your favorite color and why?*
MANSON: I would normally say black, but I think I really like purple. It's very rich. It just seems very colorful to me, but at the same time it's not cheery—it's kind of royal. It's colorful without being happy.

SECONDS: *Florida seems like a weird kind of part of the United States.*
MANSON: I think it was kind of a necessary breeding ground for Marilyn Manson, because we provided a balance. We were the ugly underside of that. If Florida's about girls laying out in the sun at the beach, we were the yeast infection they got from not having a good bikini.

Manson's membership card, 1996
Collection of Marilyn Manson

Tony Ciulla
Ciulla Management
Los Angeles, CA 90068

July 14, 1998

VIA HAND DELIVERY

Timothy Michael Linton
p/k/a "Zim Zum"
s.
Los Angeles, California 90046

Re: Marilyn Manson Records, Inc., Jimmy's Touring, Inc., and Satan's Bake Sale, Inc. -w- Timothy Michael Linton ("Employment Agreement")
-- Termination of Employment Agreement

Dear Tim:

Please be advised that your employment by Marilyn Manson Records, Inc., Jimmy's Touring, Inc., and Satan's Bake Sale, Inc. (collectively, "Company") as a member of the musical group known as "Marilyn Manson" is hereby terminated "for cause," pursuant to paragraph 3.3 of the Employment Agreement. A detailed statement of Company's grounds for this "for cause" termination will be provided to you upon request.

However, as a personal consideration to you and without waiving any of Company's rights under the Employment Agreement or at law, Company is willing at this time to classify your termination as "without cause" solely for the purpose of calculating your post-term compensation.

Please refer to the Employment Agreement for an explanation of your rights and obligations upon termination. Specifically, you have certain rights under the Employment Agreement to receive a pro-rata share of future record royalties earned in respect of the exploitation of Marilyn Manson master recordings embodying your musical performances. In addition to the matters set forth in the Employment Agreement, you are also entitled to receive future publishing income, subject to the rights of Emerald Forest Entertainment, in accordance with your interests in Marilyn Manson compositions. The foregoing are in addition any monies that may be due you pursuant to the Employment Agreement in respect of income earned, but not yet received by Company, in respect of Marilyn Manson activities occurring prior to the date hereof.

As you know, you currently have an outstanding balance with Company, as a result of salary advances and other payments made by Company on your behalf. At your earliest convenience, I would like to discuss with you the open financial matters between you and Company, in order that we may prepare a document setting forth such matters in detail for future reference and the avoidance of confusion. Alternatively, please feel free to have your attorney call Company's counsel, David Codikow, Esq., to discuss these matters.

This letter is not, and is not intended to be, a full and complete statement of all of the facts and circumstances concerning the termination of your employment by Company. Nothing contained herein shall be deemed an admission of any fact, or constitute a waiver or relinquishment of any of Company's legal rights and remedies with respect to the subject matter hereof, all of which are expressly reserved.

Despite the events and circumstances which have brought us to this conclusion, please know that I and everyone else associated with Marilyn Manson wish you the best of luck in your future endeavors.

Very truly yours,

Tony Ciulla

cc: Brian Warner
    , Esq.

Letter from Manson's manager Tony Ciulla to former guitarist Zim Zum, 1998
An example of the litigious nature of the Rock business.
Manson: "Those who try to change the world end up being changed by the world."
Collection of Marilyn Manson

"America's fucked up and I like it that way."

"Marilyn Monroe wasn't her real name, Charles Manson isn't his real name. So what's real? You can't find the truth; you just pick the lie you like the best. As long as you know everything's a lie, you can't hurt yourself."

"People like to pass me off as a devil worshipper. I think that could only be true if I considered myself to be the Devil, because I tend to be narcissistic and believe in my own strength and my own identity. I find god to be what exists in what you create. I make music."

"We did a protest benefit—the only benefit I've ever done or ever will—for this small comic book store that was doing a Serial Killer art exhibit. And the police were told to shut it down, so we played out in front of it. That's how I obtained seven Gacy paintings. Now I think I have just four. I've given them as gifts. I had two of his Elvis paintings—and one I gave to Anton LaVey. He said it had collector's value because it had my signature, it was given to him, it was painted by Gacy, and it was also an Elvis." *I wonder where that painting is today.* "I do too. I've seen the ones I have, and some that other people have—and they look almost identical. I'm assuming they were paint by numbers."

My favorite is of the Seven Dwarves in the mine. "That's not the one I have. The one I have is the Seven Dwarves sitting around a campfire. I know the one you're talking about. Because the victims were found beneath the house, that sort of has a sick tie-in.

"I've always thought that real criminals, particularly Serial Killers, take their work as seriously as artists do, so there's a fine line between how you find your expression. Luckily for me, I've found it outside of prison."

Q: *What do you think of Manson as a visual artist?*
NICK ZEDD: "You mean his image? Well, I saw him on some awards show. I thought it was pretty amusing when he came out and did that speech denouncing organized religion. I thought that was pretty good, with the marching band and all, because it didn't seem to have anything to do with the music. The music is worthless anyway, so at least he got some kind of message out there. That whole thing seemed like something I would do if I was in his position. Marilyn Manson seems to have gotten the message of the Cinema of Transgression."

Above: Manson noted the number of times certain words are heard on his 2000 album *Holy Wood*
Collection of Marilyn Manson
Left: Flyer by Mike Diana, Metro, Chicago, 1995
Collection of Mike Diana

Photo by Richard Kern

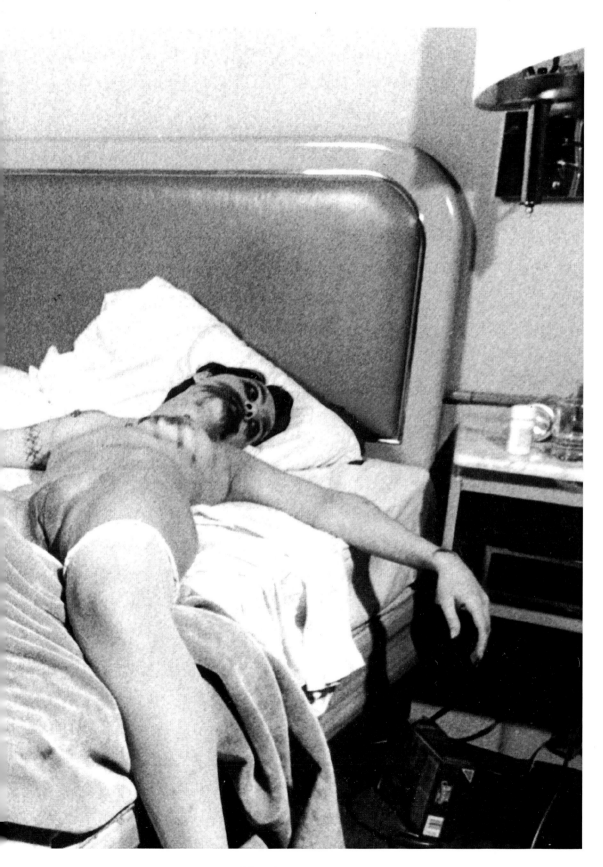

Marilyn Manson, 1996
Model: Tristan Taormino

Stanton LaVey, 2001
Photo by Cyndee Arroyo

"I am STANTON ZAHAROFF LaVEY, only grandchild of Anton LaVey and the first person ever born into the Church of Satan."

STANTON LaVEY: "I was baptized by my mother, Zeena. She and my grandparents raised me in a Satanic environment. I was being groomed for something big.

"When I was very young, my grandfather Anton and I spent so many private moments together, during which he taught me the most amazing things in the world.

"Anton LaVey is the greatest man I will ever know! He is my all-time hero! Hail Satan! Hail Anton Szandor LaVey! Regie Satanas!"

"People never step to me. There are times when I feel like fighting, but nobody ever steps to me. I'm six-foot-four and I scare the shit out of everybody. You've got to be a real big guy to be bigger than me. If you're bigger than me then you're a big motherfucker."

"I couldn't take it anymore so I came to L.A. and opened my bookstore, Odium. I am Stanton LaVey, and I didn't make my name up or ask for this existence and I, unlike my idiotic mother Zeena, am proud of my namesake and bloodline! Should I deny who I am to prove myself a rebel? Or should I rebel against those that diminish the value of my family heritage? I hope my choice is obvious now."

"I've robbed so many houses I don't even remember half of 'em." *Did you draw when you were committing crimes?* "Yes. But I was just so out there, man. When I was committing crimes, that was my sex. My life was an orgasm. I was on Speed all the time, robbing the world—and I had the biggest entitlement chip on my shoulder. I was gruesome. I was the epitome of evil, man. The lifestyle I have led is the lifestyle that inspired my grandfather to look into the dark side of life. The life of crime I have led, and the dramatic emotional and psychological sweeps and tornados that have run like a current through my existence so far are exactly what my grandfather saw outside of his world as a child—because he had a fairly standard family life when he was a little boy. He was not abandoned or fucked over or done wrong or abused or mistreated whatsoever when he was a child."

Tell us about your artistic life as it intersects with your life of crime. "Well, I'm a lifestyle artist. I look at the world as a canvas. I like to head-fuck people all the time. I love giving people false vibes and tweaking with people's minds. People are simple and pathetic. They're all generally the same unless they're superior, and superior people are few and far between, and those ones I leave alone. And everybody else—open season, man, I don't give a fuck. Fuck everybody. Nobody else gives a fuck, why should I? Fuck 'em. That's been my attitude and my motto for ever and ever, and I am still saying it today. Our time here is so stupid and meaningless—it doesn't matter what we do with it. Art is all about what you make out of anything."

"I'm an honorary member of Partridge Family Temple and proud the heck of it—because it's the grooviest place on Earth. When I'm there, everything is out of sight and totally McDonald's! When I die I will go to Albuquerque!"

Anton holding grandson Stanton, 1979
Photo by Diane LaVey
From the *Seconds* archive

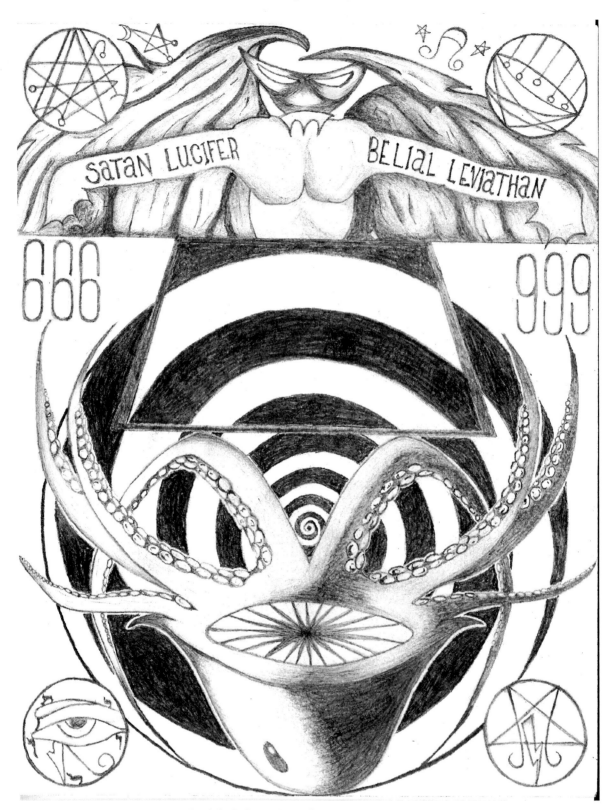

Untitled drawing, Stanton LaVey, 2001
"My grandfather taught me to draw. He showed me how to pee, for Christ's sake! He gave me my first shot of his favorite drink, Campari. He taught me my first songs, jokes and tricks. He was the first man to treat me with respect. He taught me a valuable lesson: Provide zero respect to those who show none for me."
Collection of Michael Andros

"Everyone should hate me. The more people hate each other, the sooner this stupid fuckin' species can get booted off this beautiful planet of ours."

"Satanism was created by my grandfather to provide outcasts of society with a strong identity and social sphere within which to find acceptance. Before Dr. LaVey, a loner was a loser—now loners are rebels! Back to the drawing board. Losers are losers, and they are easy to spot! In fact, they rise to the surface to be scraped off like fat or dirt in a cauldron."

"Satanism is not meant to be a religion owned and administered by mindless clones! It is the ultimate way of existence! Satanism is for Armies of One! True Leaders! Men and women of power and diversity! Take a look in the mirror. If you are wearing a Boyd Rice-style hat—yeah, the leather military one—or you have a shaved head and a goatee, and you raise your eyebrow in that impish, faux-Mephesthelean smirkish way, you make me sick. You know what type really gets my goat—the guy with the horns in his head, tail in his ass, and chiseled-down teeth, who compulsively holds his hands in the sign of the horns! My god man, what do you say at the supermarket when old ladies faint in horror thinking that *Lord of the Rings* isn't fantasy? And the Cro-Magnon type of modern CoS-ist cracks me up, too! The guys that have wizard beards, a contrived biker grimace, and hokey names that sound like they come from role-playing games like Dungeons And Dragons.

"I know that certain people will take offense to what they are reading here, and that is unfortunate and pathetic. The Satanic Few that exist as self-assured individuals independent from the Black Bible Thumpers will surely be able to appreciate a little LaVeyan honesty."

"Zeena hooked up with literally everyone in the super hip, totally under-the-radar 'Counter-Culture', including Adam Parfrey, Boyd Rice and King Diamond—and then finally Nikolas Schreck!"

Left: Zeena & Stanton, 1990
Photo by Nick Bougas
Above: Karla, Stanton, Anton, Xerxes, 1996

Stanton: "I lived with him until Zeena denounced him as being her unfather or whatever. I saw him again when I was 18. It was a great foggy night in San Francisco. I pull up in my '81 Buick Regal, wearing a leather coat. I've got my hair slicked back. I look like a modern transformation of him when he was 18. I was heavily into drugs, and each time I went to see him I detoxed for three days first, so that I was as clear as I could be for him, out of respect. The moment I laid eyes on him he smiled. I had to choke back a yelp of laughter—it was just too funny. My grandfather had a great sense of humor. He had his little ego quirks, like we all do."

Collection of Stanton LaVey

Szandora & Stanton LaVey, 2001
Stanton: "We're the first family of Satanism. We're taking over."
Photo by Cyndee Arroyo

"I am SZANDORA, the wickedest woman alive. My fascination with Satanism and the occult grew out of my mother overexposing me to Horror films and Serial Killer bios, basically from birth."

What is this new generation of Satanism?
SZANDORA: "Well, I see there being two kinds of Satanists these days: the Bible-thumpin' Anton LaVey-clone types who view Satanism as a dogma or formal religion that has strict rules based almost entirely on the personal preferences of one person or another.

"Then there is the other kind. My kind. The Modern Satanist. I call it Modern with a capital 'M' because it really is a separate movement altogether. Anton LaVey talked about Modern Satanism and how his religion was an evolving one.

"There are also many role-players, gamers, dorky coven groups havin' witchy meetings—they're typically depressed, and they read *The Satanic Bible* way too much, so much that it becomes a rule book."

"I'm a stay-at-home mother to my son and lover Stanton by day, and a Hula-Hoopin' Devil Girl by night! I pride myself in my abilities as a homemaker actually—especially my cooking, which is very well-received by the Prince of Darkness. Sometimes I'll whip up a long-pig, marinated in Absinthe and pineapple liquor, with roasted water bugs and lard soup—but usually I stick to my specialties: southern chicken 'n' dumplin', cheesecake and iced coffee drinks, to name a few. I listen to a lot of music and play with my animals. Most of my time is spent accommodating Stanton. He's had it pretty rough, and I like to think I'm making up for a lot of lost times with him. I love my life. I don't want to ever die!

"I predict a very sexy, stimulating and sinful future for Satanism!"

Left: *Death Is Glamorus*, Szandora, 1997, Collection of Stanton LaVey
Right: Szandora, 2001, photo by Cyndee Arroyo

Photo by Andrea Cardona

From '84 through '94 I put out *EXIT*.
From '90 through '00 I edited and art-directed *Seconds*. From '00 through '05 I was a contributing editor of *Juxtapoz* and the senior editor of *Propaganda*. My work appeared on DEVO album covers and in *Thrasher*, *Paper*, *Screw*, *Apocalypse Culture 2*, and *Needles Ink*.
I edited Blush's *American Hardcore*.
I compiled and produced Cleopatra Records' Tampa Goth/Industrial comp *Black Sunshine*.
My other books are:
Exploding Hearts, Exploding Stars
The EXIT Collection
.45 Dangerous Minds (with Steven Blush).

www.georgepetros.com

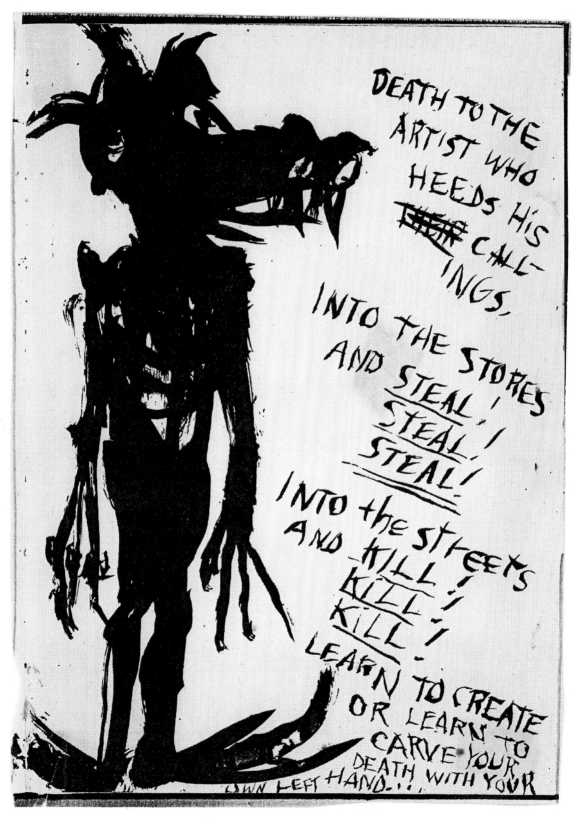

Example of the mood of the times:
Untitled illustration by Lung Leg, circa 1986
Collection of the author

www.creationbooks.com